She didn't believe in ghosts . . .

What was she doing? This was ridiculous. It was crazy. But so what? There was nobody around to see her make a fool of herself. "It's time you took off," she said. "Not that I believe in ghosts, you understand. But everybody else here does so I'm just going with the flow. There's the door. Come down, walk out, and don't come back."

Nothing stirred. Nothing spoke. Kathryn waited a moment longer, then expelled her breath in a long, explosive sigh. It was silly, she knew, but now that it was over, she was shak—

"Hello, Kathryn."

The voice behind her was deep, masculine, and frighteningly familiar.

Slowly, slowly, she turned around.

He was tall and golden-haired; he was handsome enough to steal her breath away. And she could see the stairs straight through him, see the pattern on the Persian runner.

"Must I introduce myself?" He paused on the bottom step, his tone cool, but his green eyes hot on her face. "Surely you have not forgotten my name?"

"Certainly not," Kathryn said, in a voice that was very calm and clear. "You're Matthew McDowell."

Her eyes rolled up into her head and she tumbled to the floor in a dead faint.

. . . until she met Matthew McDowell!

'TIL TOMORROW

SANDRA MARTON

PINNACLE BOOKS
KENSINGTON PUBLISHING CORP.

PINNACLE BOOKS are published by

Kensington Publishing Corp.
850 Third Avenue
New York, NY 10022

Pinnacle and the P logo Reg. U.S. & TM Off.

First Pinnacle Books Printing: February, 1996

Printed in the United States of America
10 9 8 7 6 5 4 3 2 1

For My Husband,
With Love For All Our Yesterdays and All Our Tomorrows.
Oh yes, definitely an 'E' ticket!

One

It was very early on a cold January morning, a day for burrowing deeper into down quilts, and that seemed to be what everyone in Greenwich Village was doing. The narrow streets were silent and deserted, except for the dog walkers and joggers.

In her brownstone apartment five stories above a tiny, winter-killed garden, Kathryn Russell was debating whether or not to do some burrowing of her own. Her single, dark braid was dangling over her shoulder, as she scrunched herself up on her elbows, yawned, blinked the sleep from her eyes, and looked at the face of the old-fashioned alarm clock on her night table.

Kathryn groaned, fell back onto the pillows, and flung her arm across her eyes.

6:05. Fifteen minutes until the alarm went off, but what good were fifteen minutes when she felt as if she hadn't slept a wink?

What a night! First she'd been wide-eyed, trying desperately to fall asleep but stopped every time by the realization that she'd finally agreed to marry Jason. Not that she wasn't happy about it. Jason was perfect for her, she'd known that for weeks.

It was just that she'd surprised herself with that sudden yes almost as much as she'd surprised him.

Then, after she'd finally managed to drift off to sleep there'd been those dreams about her father and how things had been years ago, before her parents' divorce, and then about Charon's Crossing, the house in the middle of nowhere that he'd left her—the house that was sure to be just another infuriating reminder of the way her father had spent his life, tilting at windmills.

Sighing, Kathryn snuggled deeper into the blankets. Maybe Jason was right. Maybe she should have waited until summer, when he could take some time off and go to Charon's Crossing with her. Maybe . . .

No. There was no point in waiting. The time to sell the house was now, during the height of tourist season. It was just that her father's attorney insisted it needed repairs before it could go on the market.

"If you wish, I can authorize them for you," Amos Carter had said, his accent crisp and very properly British.

Kathryn didn't doubt the man's honesty but only a fool would agree to an unnamed expenditure of funds without seeing first-hand what needed to be done. She wasn't about to drop dollar after dollar into a bottomless well.

She yawned again and her eyelids drooped. I might as well get up, she thought, very clearly.

And then her lashes fluttered to her cheeks and she tumbled into darkness.

She is standing on a verdant green plateau, overlooking a crescent of white sand. Beyond, a huge sun floats on the breast of a sapphire sea. There are rocks below. She cannot see them, but she can hear the beat of the surf as it hurls itself against the shore.

The scene shifts, kaleidoscoping around her with dizzying swiftness. The sun has finished bleeding into the sea. It is late and very dark; the only illumination is from a sickle moon that rides high overhead. Kathryn is standing before an arched white trellis. It is overgrown with roses: she cannot see them, in the darkness, but their perfume surrounds her. Ahead, she sees a delicately curved wrought-iron gate. It is closed but she knows instinctively that it leads deeper into the garden. She is barefoot, and the grass is soft and damp to her toes.

She turns in a tight circle and tries to see beyond the narrow perimeter of pale moonlight that surrounds her, but she can't. She feels uneasy, as if she is not alone, as if there is someone else here, someone standing just off in the darkness . . .

"Kat."

The voice is a whisper, deeper than the night that surrounds her, yet it seems to resonate through her body. She whirls around, her hand to her breast. The wrought-iron gate has opened and a man is coming slowly towards her. She cannot see his face—the moon has fled behind a lacy froth of cloud— but his presence is imposing.

He is tall and broad-shouldered. His hips are narrow, his legs long and muscular. His stride is slow, almost lazy, yet there is something of the predator in it.

Her heart trips crazily, then begins beating wildly in her breast.

She wills herself to take deep, calming breaths.

I am dreaming, Kathryn thinks very clearly. I am not here at all, I am at home, safe in my bed.

"Kat," he says again.

She steps back quickly but there's something behind her. A bench. Her legs feel boneless. Wake up, Kathryn tells herself fiercely, come on, come on, wake up!

He is standing inches from her now. He reaches out, touches his hand lightly to her cheek, sliding his fingers along her skin, and she flinches back.

"Who are you?" she says sharply.

He smiles; she can see the flash of his teeth in the darkness. "No games, Kat," he murmurs. "Not after we've found each other again."

His hand slides along her throat. His fingers curl around the nape of her neck, his thumb settles against her racing pulsebeat. He exerts the lightest of pressure, yet she has no choice but to move forward, closer to him.

"Sweet Jesus," he says, "how I've missed you."

She wants to speak, to tell him she has never seen him before, *but she cannot. She is becoming entangled in the misty reaches of the dream. His hand continues its journey, slipping to her shoulder, then down the length of her arm. He catches hold of her wrist, lifts her hand, brings her fingers to his mouth.*

"I've been waiting such a long time, Kat."

His arms encircle her and he gathers her close. Kathryn catches her breath at the feel of him against her. He is all heat and hard muscle, and a wild excitement begins to course through her blood.

This is crazy. Crazy! The part of her mind that is dancing on the knife edge of reality, the part that knows she is dreaming, races furiously in an attempt to regain control. She must open her eyes and wake up!

But when he clasps her face between his palms and sweeps his thumbs across her cheekbones, she trembles.

"You are so beautiful," he whispers.

His hands are in her hair, undoing the neat braid that hangs down her back, letting the dark strands cascade to her shoulders like ebony silk. He catches the hair in one hand, wraps it around his fist so that she has no choice but to tilt her head back, exposing the long line of her throat to him.

He bends to her, feathers kisses along her temple, along her jaw.

"Kat," he groans, and finally—finally—his mouth slants down over hers.

Heat, swift and dangerous as summer lightning, arcs through her blood.

His hands go to the row of tiny buttons that adorn her nightgown from throat to breast. Kathryn reaches up to stop him; her hands clasp his wrists but his fingers are swift and nimble and, in truth, she doesn't want to stop him, not really. She wants this to happen, wants the buttons to fall open, exposing her flesh to the warm night air.

And to his mouth.

Oh, his mouth! He kisses his way the length of her throat

and she burns everywhere he touches. When, at last, he presses his lips to the high, curved slope of one breast, she cries out.

"Yes," he growls, "yes," and with a soft moan, she loops her arms about his neck and lifts herself to him, rising on tiptoe, pressing her body to his.

She is on fire for him, she wants him with a passion that obliterates everything else. She moans and digs her fingers into the thick, silky hair that covers the nape of his neck. She brings his mouth down to hers. The kiss is deep, passionate, and when it ends, he makes a sound of his own, one that is part male triumph, part elemental desire.

"Tell me that you never stopped thinking of me," he says in a fierce whisper. He lifts her into his arms. "Tell me that you want me now, deep and hard inside you."

She is beyond speech, beyond everything but sensation. The answer he seeks is in the way she clings to him, in the way she moves against him. He bends her back over his arm, kissing her again and again, his tongue thrusting into her mouth, and she feels the flooding warmth of her desire building between her thighs.

Is she dreaming, or is what is happening real? A whisper of fear dances along her skin.

"No," she says, but it's too late. His mouth is on hers, he is drawing her down, down into the softness of the grass, into darkness and desire to the sound of thunder, rumbling far out over the sea . . .

"No!"

Kathryn sprang up in her bed, the cry bursting from her throat. Her heart was racing, trying to leap from her chest.

"No," she said again, but this time the word was only a hoarse whisper.

The dream was already fading, collapsing in on itself like a dying star in the blackness of space, snatching her from the imagined heat of a tropical night and casting her into the frigid gloom of a winter morning and, in the process, turning the swell of thunder back into the persistent growl of her old-fashioned alarm clock.

She silenced the clock with a quick swat, gave a shaky laugh, and fell back against the pillows.

"Wow," she said softly.

For someone whose dreams usually had all the symbolism of a Walt Disney movie, this one had been a winner. An X-rated, adults-only winner.

After a minute she sat up and stretched her arms high over her head. So much for eating *moo goo gai pan* late at night, she thought with a rueful smile. The smile became a grin. Poor Jason. If only he'd tried a little harder, maybe she wouldn't have insisted on going home last night after all.

Kathryn stuffed her feet into her slippers, grabbed her robe from the foot of the bed, and pulled it on. Maybe someday, after she and Jason were old and grey, she'd tell him what had happened.

"Remember the night you proposed to me" she'd say, "and you wanted to make love, but I couldn't keep my mind on anything but the trip I was leaving on the next day?"

Well, no. She wouldn't do that, either. The details of the dream were fading now but one thing was certain.

Jason hadn't starred in it.

She made a face as she headed down the narrow hall to the bathroom. No doubt about it, the sooner she got this trip out of the way, the better. There was a limit as to how much stress you could handle, and she seemed to have reached hers. It was a relief to think she'd have this whole mess settled by this time next month.

The bathroom was cold enough to make her gasp.

"Welcome to Iceberg City," she muttered, dancing her fingers across the undersized radiator tucked beneath the window. As usual, the damned thing was sending up the barest minimum of heat. It always did, unless it was midsummer and then you could almost count on the heating system to go crazy and do its damnedest to cook you right out of your socks.

Well, she thought as she drew back the shower curtain, you won some and you lost some. There were lots of things to love about this apartment. The private little garden in the rear courtyard, for one, where you could sit in the shade of a leafy plane tree on a spring evening, tilt your head and watch the moon rise over the city.

And the apartment's location was wonderful, just a twenty-minute bus ride from work and maybe ten minutes more than that from everything Kathryn loved about New York. The theaters, Lincoln Center, the museums, all the stuff she'd grown up with and couldn't imagine living without.

She made a face as she turned on the hot water. You just had to take the good with the bad, that was all. Like the cramped size of the rooms.

"It's a good thing you're not claustrophobic," her mother had said drily, the first time she'd seen the place.

And like the shower being better suited to polar bears than people. The water was finally reaching tepid. Another couple of minutes and she'd grit her teeth, pull off her robe and night-gown, and go for it.

At least it would be warm, where she was going. Charon's Crossing was in the Caribbean on some island Kathryn had never heard of. Her mother had seen the place once. Or she might not have. She wasn't sure.

"I think I was there years ago, after your father and I first got married," Beverly had told her. "You won't like it much, Kathryn. If I'm right, it was this gorgeous, romantic old white elephant of a house. Not the kind of thing that would appeal to you at all."

Romantic, hell. It was probably a disaster. Only Trevor Russell, who'd prided himself on what he'd called his artist's eye, would have been fool enough to have hung onto it.

The truth, as her mother so often said, was simply that he

was blind to reality. Wasn't that why Beverly had finally divorced him?

Kathryn spread a white ribbon of Colgate on her toothbrush. The divorce, and the separation from his wife and daughter, hadn't seemed to bother Trevor very much. Except for an occasional postcard from places she couldn't even find on the map, Kathryn had never seen her father again.

And then, a few months ago, word had come of his death, followed by the news about Charon's Crossing.

Well, in just a few hours, she'd see the place for herself. Right now, it was time to be brave and deal with the shower. Kathryn took off her robe, hung it behind the door. Slippers next, then the braid . . .

But the braid was already undone. How . . . ?

The dream. Of course. That silly dream. A soft flush rose in her cheeks.

"Audience participation, Kathryn," she whispered.

Well, that was a first. She had never . . .

. . . *his fingers, tunneling through her hair until it falls loose* . . .

Kathryn went very still. Images were surfacing, rising from her subconscious mind as if through layers of dark, still water. A tropical sun, setting on the sea. A garden, lit by moonlight. A man stepping out of the shadows, a man with a voice that whispered of desire and hands that brushed her with flame.

She stared into the mirror. Wisps of steam had risen past the shower curtain. They eddied in the air around her, curled lightly over the silvery surface of the glass so that it seemed as if she were standing in some faraway place of distant enchantment.

Her hand rose, crept to the high, frilled collar of her nightgown and to the row of opened buttons that marched from the hollow of her throat to the rounded curve of her breasts, and she swayed a little.

His hands at the buttons of the gown, opening them one by

*one, baring her throat to his mouth, baring the swell of her
breasts, her head falling back, her lips parting . . .*

Five stories below, Jason Carr stepped out of a taxi, a bag
from Mister Donut in his hand and a clutch of hopeful expectations in his heart.

He tugged at the waistband of his grey sweatpants and ran
a hand through his dark hair.

Hell, Jason, are you sure this is really such a great idea?

He'd asked himself the question at least six times in the past
half hour. The answer this time was the same as it had been
before. Of course it was a good idea. What woman wouldn't be
thrilled to have her new fiancé drop in for breakfast?

Jason opened the door and started up the stairs. Besides,
he'd resorted to a little spontaneity last night and look where
it had gotten him. A grin spread over his face. Engaged, that
was where, and by God, he still couldn't believe his luck.

He'd never know what had made him pop the question again
last night. Heaven knew Kathryn had turned him down enough
times over the past months. But he had, somewhere between
the take-out *moo goo gai pan* and the fried dumplings. And
Kathryn had looked up, chopsticks poised, smiled and said
yes. He'd been so surprised he'd damned near knocked over
the coffee table in his rush to leap up, take her in his arms
and kiss her.

But when he'd followed that wonderful, extraordinary moment with the suggestion that she spend the night with him,
she'd gone back to being the Kathryn he knew, not only the
most gorgeous lady computer analyst he'd ever laid eyes on
but also the most sensible.

"It's a lovely thought," she'd said, smiling just enough to
take the edge off his disappointment, "but it's late and I have
a long day ahead of me tomorrow. It's just not practical."

Jason paused on the third floor landing and let an old lady

and a tiny white poodle dressed in look-alike Black Watch plaid maneuver past him.

She'd said the same thing when he'd wanted to drive her home instead of letting her take a taxi, and then again when he'd offered to take her to the airport this morning. She'd even turned down the idea of having breakfast together.

"I won't have time," she'd said.

And he'd accepted that—until half an hour ago, when he was in the middle of his morning run through Central Park. He'd stopped dead in his tracks and said, to the astonishment of a drunk sleeping it off near the statue of Alice in Wonderland, "To hell with being practical!"

Jason took a deep breath. So now here he was, standing at Kathryn's door, as nervous as a kid on his first date.

Would she be happy to see him, or wouldn't she?

He glanced at the paper sack he was holding. Two large coffees, black. Two whole-wheat donuts. Two buttered bagels, and a handful of Sweet and Low packets. He began to smile.

It might not be sensible, but it was breakfast.

Even Kathryn would have to agree to that.

The shrill sound of the doorbell pierced the tattoo of the shower like the wail of a wounded animal. Kathryn spun away from the mirror and stared out the bathroom door. The hallway seemed to stretch into a shadowed infinity.

But the bell bleated again and the hallway was exactly what it had always been, a short, narrow corridor in desperate need of new carpeting.

Kathryn blew out her breath, snatched her robe from the door, and thrust her arms into the sleeves.

"May all the calories in the fried dumplings go straight to my hips if I ever eat Chinese food after nine o'clock again," she muttered as she flew down the hall.

"You're early," she said through the door in a no-nonsense tone, before the cabbie could lean on the bell again. "I'm sorry, but you'll have to wait downstairs. I told the dispatcher to send a cab at eight-thirty, and—"

"Would you really send a poor man back out into the cold, lady, when he's here to deliver breakfast for two?"

Kathryn blinked in surprise.

"Jason?"

"Yup—unless that cab company offers room service."

She smiled as she undid the locks and bolts that were the price of living in a big city.

"Jason, what on earth are you doing here?" she said as she flung the door open.

"I decided nobody should have to depend on an airline for breakfast." He held out the Mister Donut bag as he stepped into the entry hall. "So I stopped at one of New York's most elegant *pâtisseries,* picked up some *croissants* and *café* for two, grabbed a taxi, and—"

Kathryn snatched the bag out of his hands, tossed it on a table, and threw her arms around him.

"Oh," she said happily, "what a nice surprise!"

Jason stood there for a moment, his expression a combination of delight and astonishment, and then his arms closed around her.

Oh yes, he thought, it certainly was a nice surprise. In his heart, he'd half expected she might open the door, see him standing there with a silly grin and the even sillier Mister Donut bag, and blurt out that agreeing to marry him last night had all been a huge mistake.

Now, with her warm and soft in his arms, he felt his doubts fall away.

Kathryn was really happy to see him this morning. And she was different somehow, not just in looks, although that was part of it. She was wearing a flannel robe, her bare toes were peeping out from under the hem, and her hair was hanging loose and shiny down her back. It was all a far cry from her usual, businesslike self.

But for all her sexy, sweet dishevelment, it was her vulnerability that was making his head spin. She needed him, he thought in amazement. Kathryn needed him. She was clinging to him, and that was something she had never done before.

It was something he'd dreamed of, but the reality of it was a little frightening.

"Hey." He drew back a step and looked into her eyes. "Are you okay?"

Kathryn thought of the dream, of its intensity, of how even the hallway had looked so frightening just as the doorbell rang. She laughed, shut her eyes and leaned her forehead against Jason's chin.

"I'm fine. But I've decided I'm never going to eat Chinese food again."

He laughed, too. "I knew it," he said lightly. "Now the woman's going to claim she was under the influence of foreign agents when she agreed to marry me."

She smiled. "I really did do that, didn't I?"

"Yup, you did." His voice took on a good-humored gruffness. "And I'm telling you right now, lady, it's too late to change your mind."

Kathryn drew back and looked at him, taking in the handsome, almost boyish face with its open, pleasant expression. She gave a little shake of her head and sighed.

"I really am glad you came by this morning. Just seeing you makes me feel better. I had such an awful night. One bad dream after another."

His arms tightened around her. "It's this rotten trip. I wish you'd put it off and wait until I can go to Elizabeth Island with you."

Kathryn burrowed closer to him. He smelled of cold air, of New York traffic, even faintly of male sweat, but she didn't mind. They were good smells, down to earth and real, and reality was what she needed right now.

"We've been all through this," she said gently. "I have to go now. You understand."

"Yeah." He puffed out his breath and rested his chin on the

top of Kathryn's head. "Well," he said with a little laugh, "I guess there's something to be said for marrying a woman whose father leaves her a Caribbean estate."

Kathryn leaned back in his arms. "We'd better hope it's an estate and not a shanty on the beach or it'll cost me more to get rid of it than it's worth."

"He must have been quite a character, your old man. I mean, who leaves anybody an estate?"

"Don't exaggerate," she said with a teasing grin. "It's only a mansion, remember?"

"Inherited from the British side of the family."

"Veddy, veddy British."

Jason laughed. "Think how much easier it would be if he'd left you a string of pearls."

They smiled at each other.

"I really wish I could go with you," Jason said softly.

"I know. But I'll be back before you know it."

He sighed. "Yeah."

"I'm so glad you decided to come by this morning. This really was such a nice surprise."

"I thought so, too," he said smugly. "Do I get a kiss as a reward?"

"Well, I don't know. A gold star, maybe . . ."

Smiling, he lifted her face to his. "A kiss," he whispered, and his mouth closed on hers.

His kiss was warm and tender. Kathryn sighed and her arms crept around his neck. It was nice to be kissed this way. No, it was better than nice. It was sweet. It was gentle . . .

It was nothing like the way the man in the dream had kissed her. His kisses had demanded surrender. Give yourself to me, they'd said. And she'd wanted to, oh yes, she'd wanted to . . .

Kathryn twisted her face away from Jason's.

"Kathryn?" He clasped her chin in his hand, gently urged her to look at him. His brown eyes were dark with concern. "There's something wrong, isn't there?"

Tell him, she thought. Tell him about the dream. Bring it

out of the darkness and into the open so you can laugh about it together.

Laugh? How could they laugh at something that would embarrass them both? How could she ever tell him that a man in a dream had turned her on more than the man in her arms ever had?

The thought was so shabby, so disloyal, that she hated herself for even thinking it. She reached up, clasped Jason's face between her palms, and dragged his mouth to hers for another kiss. Then she slid her hands down his shoulders to his forearms.

"It's the shower. I just remembered that I left it running all this time."

"The shower!" Jason burst out laughing. "I'm kissing you, and you're thinking of the shower?"

"I dare you to say something like that next summer, when the city's in the middle of a drought," she said, smiling as she stepped out of his embrace. "Look, why don't you heat up our gourmet breakfast while I shower and dress?"

Jason touched his finger to the tip of her nose. "I could do that. Or I could help you scrub your back."

Kathryn grinned. "Not in that shower, you couldn't." She kissed him lightly on the mouth. "I'll only be a minute."

Jason watched as she hurried down the hall. Then he sighed, picked up the paper sack and headed for the kitchen. He took the two coffee containers from the bag, popped off the lids and put the containers into the microwave. Then he dumped the bagels and donuts on a plate, put that into the oven, too, and punched in the right settings.

The oven began to hum and he leaned back against the counter.

Kathryn was right. She'd be back from the Caribbean before he knew it and they could begin planning their future.

Then, why did he have this feeling of unease?

Two

Amos Carter was not a vain man but he was definitely an honest one.

That was why he couldn't pretend that talent and ability were the reasons he was Elizabeth Island's busiest attorney.

The facts were simple. Amos had the island's most active law practice because he had its only law practice.

If a storm wrecked your fishing boat and the insurance company gave you a hard time collecting your money, if you quarreled with your neighbor over whose land his pigs were destroying, you either went to Amos or you went to another island. And that wasn't easy, considering that Elizabeth Island was tucked away from the tourist track, many miles to the west of Martinique, St. Lucia, and the other Windward Islands of the Caribbean.

Amos had come here a dozen years ago, ready for peaceful retirement after forty years of practicing law in the Caymans. He bought a house in the dunes above a beach, and a thirty foot gaff-rigged catboat to play around in, and he spurned all efforts at hospitality.

When the first neighbor had appeared at his door in search of legal advice, Amos had not been subtle.

"I am no longer prostituting myself in the name of justice," he'd said, his voice plummy with the upper-class elegance of his British public school training.

But the man persisted. The case had a flavor and nuance

that piqued Amos's curiosity. He became interested. A few days later, he'd found himself once again practicing law.

Now, as he paced impatiently alongside the narrow strip of crushed pink shell that was Elizabeth Island's pitiful excuse for an airport, he berated himself for having let that neighbor in the door ten years before.

If he hadn't, he'd be out in his sailboat right now, sipping a cold lager, his well-thumbed copy of Cicero in his lap, the prospect of a dinner of freshly caught flying fish looming pleasantly ahead.

Instead, he was sweating out here in the hot sun, impatiently awaiting the arrival of the twice-weekly plane from Grenada which was already almost an hour late.

Amos scowled, slipped off his wide-brimmed Panama hat and used it to fan his glistening black face. Not that that was unusual. The plane was always late. In truth, it was the fact that he was here at all that had him so irritated.

He was waiting for a woman named Kathryn Russell. He'd never set eyes on her, never had more than a few telephone conversations with her, but he knew, without question, that she was going to be one monumental pain in the ass for the next seven days.

Amos's scowl deepened as he snapped a spotless white linen handkerchief from the breast pocket of his white linen suit and mopped it across his bald head.

It was bad enough he'd gone back to the profession that had sent him scurrying from the distasteful company of humans in the first place. That he'd taken on a client as eccentric as Trevor Russell was even worse, but Russell had come to him with what had seemed the simplest of requests.

"I'm at that age where I suppose I should have a will, Mr. Carter," he'd said.

Amos, taking a look at the face made ruddy by too much sun, whiskey and women, had silently agreed.

He hadn't liked Russell very much. The man's cavalier, devil-may-care attitude had been almost personally offensive to someone who believed in responsibility, hard work and commitment.

A month after Amos had drawn up the will, Russell had died in a spectacular car crash in Lisbon. Amos figured it had probably been more in keeping with the sort of life the man had led than beachcombing on an all but forgotten Caribbean island.

It had fallen to Amos, as executor, to convey the news of Trevor Russell's bequest to his sole heir, his daughter, Kathryn.

It had been his experience that talk of wills and inheritances following the death of a loved one was usually greeted with choked sobs. Amos was not a sentimental man himself but that was not to say he didn't understand emotion. Anticipating the shock and grief the loss of her father would bring, he'd telephoned the girl, prepared to offer soothing words of condolence and assistance.

But Kathryn Russell hadn't wanted either. She'd wanted answers about the property she'd inherited. What was it worth? And how quickly could she sell it?

Amos had tried to be diplomatic. Elizabeth Island was not what one would call a tourist mecca. It was too far off the holiday path. And, though its beauty was spectacular, its amenities were few.

As for Charon's Crossing itself—the kindest way to describe the house was to say it needed work.

Amos hemmed and hedged and finally said that the house's value was dependent on a variety of factors, beginning with its condition.

"I am afraid, Miss Russell," he'd said politely, "that Charon's Crossing requires repairs before we can assess its worth."

"I see," she'd said, but he felt certain she didn't.

With that in mind, Amos had offered to determine the cost of making necessary repairs to the house. Russell's daughter had responded in a way that still had him bristling.

"Thank you, Mr. Carter," she'd said, "but I prefer to do that myself."

What she'd really meant was that she could not entrust

something so important to a stranger but Amos did not consider himself a stranger. He was her father's executor.

The only thing that offended him more than dealing with a client who did not trust his honesty or his competency was dealing with a woman.

The world had changed. It was filled, he knew, with women who insisted on being treated like men, but Amos was of the old school. Attorneys advised the female of the species, they did not take orders from them.

Kathryn Russell, as subsequent phone conversations had proved, was superb at giving orders.

He was to draw up a list of local contractors.

He was to draw up a list of local real estate agents.

He was to arrange to have the house cleaned in anticipation of her arrival.

He was to arrange for her to have use of a rental car.

He was to have a taxi meet her plane.

And he was to understand that she had only a week to spare.

Amos scowled, pulled out his handkerchief, and mopped his head again.

Kathryn Russell was as ignorant as she was presumptuous.

Contractors? There was a man in town who had a truck, a few pieces of equipment, and a brother-in-law who was his sometime crew. Realtors? There was even one of those, too. Olive Potter had been selling houses on Elizabeth Island for more years than anyone could remember.

One house a year, at least. That was about the market turnover.

A taxi, to meet her? The only taxi on the island was sitting where it had been sitting for as long as he could remember, down on a little back road near the beach and slowly turning to rust.

As for the Russell woman's assumption that you could get anything done in seven days in this part of the world . . . that was almost enough to make him laugh.

Amos had thought of telling her so. He also thought of

telling her other things, that there were disquieting stories of some dark force that roamed the huge, empty rooms of the house she'd inherited.

But each talk with Trevor Russell's daughter only went further to convince him that she would take nothing he said at face value.

And so he had told her nothing. Let her learn the truth for herself, that the island was a sleepy backwater, that Charon's Crossing was a gloomy ruin, and that she'd be lucky if she could sell it for a fraction of what she obviously thought it was worth.

His duty was to implement the terms of Trevor Russell's will, nothing more.

And if, in the process, there was a certain pleasure in watching the imperious Miss Russell brought to heel, well, so be it.

Childish squeals interrupted Amos's thoughts. He looked around and saw a rag-tag band of children racing towards him in hot pursuit of a pair of wild-eyed goats.

Amos danced back sharply but not quickly enough to keep one of the goats from brushing his leg as it bounded past. He glared at the fleeing animal and at the shrieking children, who looked almost as untamed and unkempt as their prey.

Angrily, he whisked his hand across the impeccable crease in his white trousers, brushing away goat hair and something he hoped was only dust.

"Miserable little creatures," he muttered. And, just at that moment, he heard the approaching drone of an airplane.

Amos looked up. Finally, there it was, the ancient red and white Cessna 402 that was Elizabeth Island's solitary acceptance of the fast pace of the modern world.

The plane dipped woozily towards the pink airstrip, the wings waggling as it zoomed over the heads of the children and the goats.

The children laughed and Amos could only assume the pilot was laughing, too. As far as he could tell after ten years here, only crazies flew this run.

Amos looked at the plane as it wobbled to a stop.

Welcome to Elizabeth Island, Miss Russell, he thought.

For the first time all day, he smiled.

Kathryn peered out the window, saw the ground whooshing towards her, saw a blur of waving children and frantic animals coming closer, and decided her life was about to end.

She shrank back in her seat, shut her eyes, and did what she'd done most of the trip from Grenada.

She prayed.

The flight had been a horror from the minute she'd transferred planes, leaving behind the air-conditioned terminal to search for something called the Out-Island Shuttle.

She had expected to find something like the efficient commuter craft that flew between New York and Boston. What she'd found instead was a plane that looked as if it should have flown by rubber-band power.

The pilot, in oil-stained khakis, had taken her luggage and tossed it into the rear of the tiny aircraft. Then he'd told her to find a seat and put on her seat belt.

After an hour of roasting in the sun, the plane had lurched into the sky, carrying Kathryn, three passengers who chattered to each other in something that was not quite Spanish, and a piglet and a crate of live chickens.

The flight had been terrifying. The plane had dipped low over the water, lurching upwards unsteadily whenever an island loomed ahead. The piglet had squealed, the chickens had squawked, and the passengers had muttered under their breaths while they'd crossed themselves.

That they'd survived the trip was almost impossible to believe. That they were to land on what looked like a pale pink ribbon stretched between scrub-covered hills that began at the edge of a cliff was even harder to accept, especially since it seemed they were going to make mincemeat out of a bunch of children and a couple of goats in the process.

Kathryn could see the children laughing as the plane skimmed past. The animals' eyes rolled with fear.

I'm with you, she thought grimly.

But somehow, the plane's wheels touched down safely. The engines made a slow, groaning sound and then, mercifully, the Cessna shuddered to a stop.

"That's it, folks," the pilot said as he turned towards them. "Welcome to Elizabeth Island."

Kathryn's fellow passengers were already rushing for the exit. She'd have rushed, too, if her knees hadn't felt like rubber.

The pilot was just tossing her suitcase out onto the runway when she got to the door. She opened her mouth to protest, then shut it again. What was the sense? It was too late to do anything but grit her teeth and get on with what she'd come here to do.

Stepping out of the plane was like stepping into a furnace.

The heat seemed to lick up from her toes and coil its way around her like a living thing. The air was flame, searing her lungs as she breathed it in. The crisp linen of her pale yellow suit was surely wilting.

She glanced at her suitcase, still lying on the runway, then shaded her eyes with her hand and looked around her. There was nothing out there but blue sky and green grass. If the taxi she'd requested was anywhere within hailing distance, she certainly couldn't see it.

"Miss Russell?"

Kathryn swung around. A small man in a white suit was striding towards her. The wide brim of a Panama hat shaded his eyes but she could see the glint of perspiration on his fine-boned, ebony face.

"Good," she said. "I'd begun to think Mr. Carter had forgotten to send a taxi to meet me."

"Miss Russell, I am Amos Carter."

Kathryn's brows lifted. She had formed an image of the man from his voice. Amos Carter should have been tall, slender, and young. This man was slender but he was also short and he had left youth behind decades before. And he was looking at her with something that could only be described as polite hostility. That didn't surprise her. He'd done everything during their phone conversations but tell her, flat out, that her arrival on Elizabeth Island was going to be one huge imposition.

Kathryn smiled politely and held out her hand.

"Mr. Carter. How kind of you to meet me."

Carter's hand clasped hers. His fingers were bony but his grasp was surprisingly strong.

"A matter of simple expediency, Miss Russell." He dropped her hand and reached for her suitcase. "This is yours, I take it?"

"Yes, but I can manage it myself."

"Nonsense." Carter gave her another thin-lipped smile. "You will find we are somewhat old-fashioned, here in the islands. Men believe in being courteous even if women do not wish it."

It was Kathryn's turn to smile thinly. The putdown was subtle but it was a putdown nevertheless. Terrific, she thought, as Carter set off along a rutted track that led through the scrub. That was just what she needed, an attorney who was an aging male chauvinist. Well, at least now she knew why he'd seemed hostile over the telephone.

She thought of a couple of sharp-tongued rejoinders, then decided against them. She would only be here a week and she needed this man's help. There were negative vibrations in the air already. Why make things worse?

Carter led her to a dusty Land Rover. He put her suitcase in the rear, then opened the passenger door and motioned her inside. When he was settled behind the wheel, Kathryn cleared her throat.

"It really was very kind of you to meet me yourself," she said.

Carter swung the wheel sharply to the right, swerving around the goats that were once again fleeing their pursuers. The Rover shuddered as its tires hit a bumpy dirt track that Kathryn assumed was the road.

"I told you, Miss Russell, it was a matter of expediency." He shot her a faintly amused smile. "I know you expected a taxi to meet you, but I am afraid we have none here on the island."

Kathryn looked at him. "No taxis? On the entire island?"

"I am afraid we lack many amenities."

He didn't sound "afraid" at all, Kathryn thought, her eyes narrowing. What he sounded was damned well smug.

"That's quite all right," she said politely. "I haven't come here for a vacation."

"No. You've come to sell Charon's Crossing. I understand that." Carter glanced over at her. "But I would hope you will understand that your expectations for the house may not quite be in accord with reality."

Kathryn had already been thinking the same thing.

She had never been in the Caribbean before but, like almost everyone else, she'd come here with an image in mind.

Islands in the sun were supposed to be dazzlingly beautiful, with lots of lush, green vegetation, tall palm trees and bright flowers. The sky was supposed to be fairy-tale blue, the clouds puffs of white cotton, the sea emerald green and the sand anything from bone white to flamingo pink to lava black.

When it came to those things, Elizabeth Island delivered on all counts. The scenery, so far, anyway, was spectacular.

But where were the hotels? The charming villas that should have dotted the gently sloping hillside they were climbing? Above all else, where were the people?

Not that there weren't people. There were, and lots of them, but even Kathryn could tell they were islanders, not American and European tourists.

Her heart sank, but she clung to hope.

Amos Carter had described Charon's Crossing as a mansion. Surely, no one would have built a mansion on an island that didn't get its fair share of tourists?

"The house your father left you was built over two hundred years ago," Carter said, as if she'd spoken aloud. "At that time, the island was an important link in the British Empire."

"And now?"

The Rover was flying along at high speed and the wind was playing havoc with her hair, trying to tug it from the confinement of its usual French braid. She put her hand up to her head and pushed the errant dark strands back from her forehead.

"And now," Carter replied with a shrug of his narrow shoulders, "the Empire is no more."

"I know that," Kathryn said, trying not to sound impatient. "I meant—"

"I know what you meant. What of the island? Have tourists discovered it? Do they flock to its beaches? Do they befoul its waters with diesel fuel, do hotels threaten our limited supply of water?"

Kathryn looked at him. "Why do I get the feeling I know the answers to those questions, Mr. Carter?"

"We who live here are blessed, Miss Russell. We lead an idyllic, almost forgotten, existence."

Kathryn scarcely missed a beat. "Well, then, that's what the realtor's ads for the house must emphasize, that this is a perfect place to get away from it all and enjoy blissful peace and quiet."

Amos laughed. He had to admit, this young woman was not one to be put off easily.

"Perhaps you ought to offer to write the ad for Olive yourself," he said.

"Olive?"

"Olive Potter. She's the local realtor. I told her you'd want to see her."

"*The* local realtor," Kathryn said.

Amos heard the question in the words and nodded.

"That is correct. I told you, we are—"

"A backwater. Yes. I know." She sighed. "Is there anything else you should tell me before . . ."

Kathryn broke off in midsentence. There was a house in the distance, standing alone on a cliff that overlooked the sea. Its multipaned windows caught the sunlight and reflected it back to the waves beating against the shore. Made of white stone, with a slate grey tile roof, the house seemed enormous even from here.

"Charon's Crossing," Amos Carter said.

Kathryn nodded. She had known that instinctively. The house was an impressive sight. And yet, there was something about it she didn't like. Despite the hot glare of the sun and the sharpness of the bright blue sky, there was a sense of brooding darkness here, something that sent a chill up her spine.

The engine of the Land Rover protested as Amos jammed down on the gears.

"Steep incline," he muttered.

Kathryn nodded again, but without really hearing his words. She edged forward on her seat as they started up a twisting dirt road, heavily overgrown with shrubbery and palm trees. Branches beat against the sides of the Rover as they climbed; leafy fronds sighed as they tapped the window glass.

The house was out of sight now but Kathryn still felt uneasy. It was as if she'd been here before, which was ridiculous. She'd never been to this island, never been in this part of the world.

But she knew that the road ahead would suddenly take a sharp turn to the left, that it would then angle back towards a cascade of bright red and pink flowers that tumbled in almost obscene profusion down a high stone wall.

"Kathryn."

Kathryn's heart thumped. She swung towards Amos Carter.

"Did you hear that?"

"Hear what, Miss Russell?"

"A voice," she said, fighting to keep her tone calm. "A man's voice."

"You must have heard the wind. It plays tricks, up here on the cliffs."

The wind. Of course, that was what it had been, the wind, sighing as it swept through the palm fronds. Or the sea, perhaps, whispering as it brushed the white sand below.

Kathryn sat back again. She was edgy, but who wouldn't

be? Once they reached Charon's Crossing and she saw exactly
what kind of albatross she'd inherited, she'd feel better. And
there was always the hope that she'd judged it wrong. Now
that she'd seen its size, the way it stood on the cliff, looking
out over the sea . . .

The Rover came to a shuddering halt. Kathryn looked up.
Tall, rusty iron gates loomed ahead.

"Number one on your repair list," the attorney said wryly
as he opened his door. "The entry gates need to be sanded,
primed and painted. They've almost rusted shut." Carter
dropped stiffly to the ground. "I'll only be a moment."

Kathryn stared at the house through the gates. A structure
like this would have seemed more at home on an English moor
or lost in the mists of a Scottish highland.

"Might as well leave the gates open," Carter said as he
climbed back inside the Land Rover. "Is that all right with
you?"

"Yes, that's fine." Kathryn cleared her throat. "Charon's
Crossing doesn't suit the landscape very well, does it?"

For the first time, Amos wondered if there might not be
hope for his new client.

"That's true. But the people who built it weren't interested
in adapting to these islands. They were English, and they
wanted to remain that way."

Kathryn smiled. "Some things never change, I guess."

Amos permitted himself a faint smile. "We'll be at the house
in a moment. I'm sure you'll be glad to get out of the heat."

"Yes. And I'm really curious to see the place. It's looks very
impressive."

The old man's smile faded. From the outside, perhaps. But
he suspected she would not be quite so pleased with her in-
heritance, once she'd gotten a closer look at it.

The house was impressive, all right. Kathryn blew out her
breath as the front door shut behind them.

Martha Stewart probably would have loved it.

But she wasn't Martha Stewart. She didn't have unlimited resources and endless time to turn a sow's ear back into the silk purse it must have been a long, long time ago.

Drafty, antiquated, falling-down-around-your-ears New York apartments were bad enough. Drafty, antiquated, tumbledown houses built on sand spits in the middle of nowhere were impossible.

She put her hands on her hips and turned in a slow circle, taking in what must once have been an elegant octagonal foyer. Now, if you wanted to be charitable, you could best call it a disaster.

Doorways sagged, window frames tilted. The floor was encrusted with filth. The walls sprouted irregular splotches of damp rot. The woodwork, ornate where it still existed, had been mostly reduced to splinters.

"Termites," Carter said, when Kathryn bent down to take a closer look.

"Termites?" She snatched back her hand. "In a stone house?"

"The house is stone but the trim is wood." Carter strolled the perimeter of the room, running his hand lightly over what was left of the wainscoting. "Termites dine where they can, Miss Russell. Fortunately, they seem to have spared most of the furniture."

Kathryn looked at the lumpy, sheet-draped shapes that had been shoved against the stained walls.

"What an oversight," she said dryly.

Carter's narrow shoulders rose and fell in an eloquent shrug.

"Charon's Crossing needs repair. I told you that when first we spoke."

Repair? What it needed was a miracle or a bottomless bank account, and Kathryn didn't have either.

She peered into a huge room that opened onto the foyer.

"The ballroom," Amos Carter said.

She nodded and looked up at the chandelier that hung in

the center of the ceiling. The crystals were grimy and the whole thing looked as if a strong breeze might send it crashing to the floor. She was no fan of antiques but even she could see that it was beautiful. She supposed there were some who'd say that of the entire building.

Well, perhaps there was hope. The house stood in an absolutely magnificent location. The view from the foyer alone was impressive. And the old man was right about the furniture. Kathryn pulled the sheet from the nearest piece, revealing a small, delicately inlaid table. Some of it, perhaps most of it, might be pretty good.

Charon's Crossing had possibilities. It needed scrubbing from top to bottom, the furniture needed polishing, and she supposed it would be wise to make some basic repairs. Rehang the doors, maybe, and replace the missing woodwork.

And then she'd put the house on the market. There had to be a buyer somewhere who'd want it. An eccentric millionaire, maybe, seeking privacy. Or one of those spas that were cropping up in the most unexpected corners of the globe and catered to the rich . . .

"I am sorry that you are disappointed, Miss Russell."

Kathryn turned around. Amos Carter had spoken politely, but she knew his words were empty of meaning.

"Disappointed?" Kathryn's smile was as polite as his tone. "Don't be silly, Mr. Carter. The house is pretty much what I expected. You said it needed work, and it does." She unbuttoned the jacket of her yellow linen suit. "Now it's time to do something about it. You've arranged for me to meet with some contractors, I hope?"

"We have only one, Miss Russell. I told him you'd be flying down and asked him to get in touch, yes."

"That's fine. And the realtor . . . What did you say her name was?"

"Olive Potter. Yes, she will contact you, too." Amos hesitated. "I hope you're aware that it may not be easy to find a buyer for a house such as this. Elizabeth Island is not a name on everyone's lips."

"And you like it that way, Mr. Carter. Yes, I understand." Kathryn smiled. "Well, maybe that's for the best. Any investor with enough money to buy this property would want privacy."

Amos smiled. That was twice this young woman had surprised him.

"That's true enough."

"We'll just have to make the most of Charon Crossing's strong points." Kathryn scuffed her toe across the floor. A swath of flecked white appeared in the dirt. "Marble?" she asked.

Carter nodded. "I should think so."

"And the upstairs? What's it like?"

"No better and no worse than what you see here."

Kathryn walked to the foot of the wide staircase that rose towards the second floor. The banisters and newel posts were handsome. Mahogany, she thought, and reached out to touch the old wood . . .

Cold. Cold so deep that it was almost painful, played across her fingers.

Kathryn snatched back her hand. "Is there an open window upstairs?"

"I don't know, Miss Russell. I didn't notice any, from outside."

"Neither did I, but there must be. Don't you feel that chill?"

Amos's brows lifted. "Chill?"

"Yes. And—"

Kathryn.

"Did you hear that?"

"Did I hear what?"

That voice, she almost said. But that would have been silly. It was the wind, just as the attorney had said, rustling through the palms and blowing in through an open window somewhere in the house.

"Never mind," she said briskly. "Let's see the rest of the downstairs, shall we? Does the electricity work?"

"I assume so." Amos touched the light switch. A pair of wall sconces near the front door flickered, then blazed to life. "Yes, Miss Russell. It works."

"The heating?"

"I assume that works, as well."

"And the plumbing?"

"I assume—"

"Are we playing some sort of game here, Mr. Carter?"

"No game, Miss Russell. I offered to find out what needed doing at Charon's Crossing but you said you would see to it all yourself." He smiled coolly. "And so you shall."

Kathryn sighed. Enough was enough. "Mr. Carter," she said, "why don't you tell me the problem?"

"I beg your pardon?"

"Come on, don't be coy. You don't like me and I'd like to know the reason."

Amos looked her straight in the eye. "I see no need for me to like you or for you to like me."

"You're right. But I'd still appreciate an answer."

"Very well, if you insist. I am accustomed to holding the trust of my clients."

"I've no idea what my father thought of you, one way or the other."

"I am not referring to him. I resent the way you reacted when I offered to determine the need for repairs here."

A lawyer with a tender ego. Just her luck.

"Fair enough. Is there anything else?"

Amos shrugged his shoulders. "I am not accustomed to taking orders from females."

Kathryn nodded. Somehow, that revelation came as no great surprise but that didn't make it any the less infuriating.

"Well, prepare yourself for more orders, Amos." Kathryn folded her arms. "I asked you to have this place cleaned in anticipation of my arrival but I don't see that it was done."

"On the contrary. One of the local women came in. She tidied up the kitchen and the West Wing. You'll find them acceptable, if not luxurious. Since there are numerous other rooms, and since you made it clear you wished to personally approve whatever was done in this house . . ."

"Touché." Kathryn smiled coolly. "One point for your side."

"Is there anything else before I go, Miss Russell?"

"Do I have a telephone?"

"You do."

"I suppose you assume it works?"

"On the contrary. I know that it does not. Telephone service is erratic at best on Elizabeth Island. I tried to tell you, Miss Russell, we have limited—"

"Amenities. Yes, I know." Kathryn sighed. "All right, Amos. It would seem the contractor—Hiram, was it? It would seem his work's cut out for him. Please phone him and tell him to be sure and come by tomorrow."

Amos nodded stiffly. "Very well."

"And the realtor. Olive. Was that her name? I'd like to see her, too."

"I can only convey your message, Miss Russell. I cannot guarantee—"

"Tomorrow," Kathryn said firmly. "I have only seven days to spend here and I want everything settled before I leave. Please keep that in mind."

What he was keeping in mind, Amos thought sourly, was that this arrogant, contentious female couldn't leave Elizabeth Island quickly enough to suit him.

Addressing him as Amos, indeed! And handing out orders . . .

Who did she think she was?

"I shall do my best," he said coldly.

Kathryn's chin lifted. How was it possible to dislike somebody you hardly knew? Amos Carter was the most pompous, insufferable man she'd ever had the misfortune to meet.

"I hope so," she said, every bit as coldly. "Now, if that's all, I'd like to unpack my things."

She was dismissing him, was she? Back straight, Amos marched to the door. At the last second, he turned and smiled pleasantly.

"There are a few things I should tell you," he said. "The woman who cleaned the house stocked a few foodstuffs in the refrigerator."

"Thank you."

"I've made arrangements for a car to be delivered to you in the morning, as you requested."

Kathryn folded her arms. Impatience was etched into every line of her body.

"Good."

Amos opened the door. The heat and the scent of the tropics swept in on a breath of salt-tinged air.

"There is one last item . . ."

She sighed, and he knew she was doing her best not to let him see that she could hardly wait for him to shut up and leave. It made his parting shot all the sweeter.

"And what would that be, Amos?"

"I don't suppose you've ever heard of jumbies or duppies, have you?"

Kathryn looked at him as if he'd spoken in tongues.

"Jumbies? Duppies? What are you talking about?"

"Spirits, Miss Russell. Ghosts. Do you believe in them?"

"No. Of course I don't."

Amos smiled. "Good. In that case, it won't concern you that the locals claim that Charon's Crossing is haunted."

He put on his Panama hat, tipped the brim, and shut the door after him.

Three

Catherine was here.

And she was alone.

Matthew had watched from the attic window as the old man who'd brought her to Charon's Crossing left the house. The old man had not returned, and now the day had drawn to a close.

It was time to stop savoring the anticipation of revenge and take it.

He could have settled the score many times already. While she'd strolled through the house. While she'd unpacked her luggage or when she'd dawdled among the books in the library, or made herself dinner in the kitchen. He could have simply reached out, put his hands around her slender throat, and ended it all with one quick twist.

But there was such sweetness in the imagining.

He had waited for this moment. He could wait a bit longer. There was no rush.

Time had no meaning for him; the sun rose and set and he saw it do both but it was as if he watched a painter making brush strokes upon a canvas. What were the meanings of sunrise and sunset to a man who was dead?

But Catherine was not dead. She was very much alive. How many times had he wished that she would return to this house? Wished? That was far too simple a word. He had yearned for her return, prayed for it . . .

And his prayers had been answered. How she had come to be here was beyond his comprehension, but then, nothing that had happened to him since that last terrible night in the garden made any sense.

Besides, what did it matter? She had come back, come to him and to Charon's Crossing. He could do with her as he pleased. And what he pleased, he thought with a cold smile, was to destroy her as she had once destroyed him.

His life had been ended by Lord Waring's blade that warm June evening in 1812.

But it was Catherine who had truly killed him.

He knew just what would happen when he revealed himself to her. How her eyes would widen with terror. How she would try and deny his existence.

Eventually, she would have to accept the truth.

Oh, then she would plead for mercy! She would weep and beg to be saved from the damnation that had been his lot since she had betrayed him. She would promise him the moon and the stars, just as she had before. And they would be promises she never meant to keep and that would be as it had been before, too.

Matthew smiled thinly. He would relish all of it. Her fear, her pleas. He would let her sob while he laughed and told her that there was no logic in asking compassion of one to whom she had showed such cruel duplicity.

He would put his hands around her neck and press his thumbs into her flesh and squeeze and squeeze until her eyes, those beautiful, lying eyes, turned opaque and filled with death.

Then, at last, he would be free.

And that was why it was a moment worthy of delay. The slow anticipation was half the pleasure.

That was why he'd been content to observe her as she walked through the house and familiarized herself with the things that had once been hers, though watching had given him a moment's pause.

Time had lost all meaning for him so that he had not thought overly much about the condition of the mansion. But seeing

Catherine's reactions to the dirt and the ruin, it struck him that many, many years must have gone by.

How could that be, when she was still so young? Her hair was as he remembered it, black as midnight and shiny as silk. Her eyes were as blue and as unchanged as the sea. Everything about her was still beautiful.

He puzzled over it, but not for long. One did not dwell on things for which there were no answers, for in that direction lay insanity. He had learned that the hard way, after he had fallen, dying, at Lord Waring's booted feet.

After that, there had been only . . . Only what? How did a man identify something that was beyond definition? How could he describe the nothingness in which he'd found himself? The Sunday preachers of his childhood had warned of the afterlife that awaited sinners. Now he knew they'd been wrong. Yet, the fires of hell could have been no worse.

It was safer for his own sanity to remember only that he had eventually awakened and found himself adrift in a place where there was only darkness. There'd been no dimensions. No walls or windows, floors or ceilings.

No escape.

There was only blackness. Blackness—and, at length, his awareness that he was not completely alone.

There was Something Else out there. He sensed a presence of some sort, not inside the blackness with him but just beyond it. It was not there all the time but when it was, he could hear the sounds it made. He could smell the stink of its evil and he knew instinctively that it searched for him.

The Thing terrified him. Whenever he sensed its nearness, he curled up within himself, holding his breath until it was gone.

But that reaction hadn't lasted long.

Captain Matthew McDowell was a man who had never run away from anything while he was alive. Why should that change now?

So he began to taunt the Thing, to tease it through the curtain of darkness that separated them. Luring it closer and closer became a game. A dangerous one, perhaps. But it was far better than hiding from it.

He could sense the creature's growing frustration and it pleased him enormously. One day, or whatever passed for a day in this place, he laughed out loud at its rage.

It roared. The air had begun to shimmer and a smell of decay and putrefaction rushed towards him.

"I am done for," Matthew had thought, not just with calm but almost with satisfaction.

Surely, there was another place to move on to, where one could spend eternity in peace?

He had shut his eyes, in preparation for whatever lay ahead . . .

When he'd opened them again, the darkness was gone. In its place was a white, curling mist.

He found himself in a room, a very ordinary one filled with bits and pieces of what looked to be old furniture.

"What is this place?" he whispered.

There was an oval mirror on the wall. He went to it and stared at his reflection, then raised a trembling hand to his face. His features were the same as they had always been: the sun-shot chestnut hair drawn back in a queue from a high-cheekboned face, the fierce green eyes, the straight nose, cleft chin and firm mouth . . . it was all familiar, yet at the same time, alien.

He turned from the mirror and went to the window. He took a deep breath, then pulled open the shutters.

At first, the rush of fresh, sweet air and glimpse of bright blue sky brought a faint smile to his lips. But then he looked down, and his heart leaped into his throat.

Below, just beyond a brick terrace, he could see a wrought-iron gate and a curved trellis, overgrown with lush pink roses.

Bloody hell!

He was in the attic of the house called Charon's Crossing.

It was in the garden of Charon's Crossing that he had been killed.

He sprang to the door and wrestled the knob, but it would

not turn. He raised his fists and beat them against the wood panels until his knuckles were raw and bleeding, but the door would not give.

"Let me out," he roared . . .

And just that easily, he found himself on the door's far side. He lifted his hand, lay it against the door, and watched in horror as his fingers passed through the surface as if it were not there.

God, oh God!

He was a spirit. A ghost. A thing, doomed forever to walk the dark halls and gardens of the place that had been the scene of his betrayal and death but never to leave it, for he quickly found that the boundaries of Charon's Crossing were his boundaries, too.

His anguish took the form of rage. People moved into Charon's Crossing, then moved out. No one appreciated the nighttime rattles or moans, though they were not always his.

Sometimes, they were the sounds of the Thing on the other side of the darkness. It had apparently passed into this new dimension with him, though it could not penetrate whatever curtain it was that still separated them.

The attic became Matthew's special place. There, among the spiderwebs and discards, no one disturbed him. He was able to find at least a modicum of peace.

He could shut his eyes and let his mind float into something that, for want of a better name, he called sleep.

At first, his sleep was peaceful. But then he began to dream, and the dreams changed everything.

He dreamed of an island, lush and green beneath a hot tropical sun.

He dreamed of Charon's Crossing, and of Catherine, smiling as he held her in his arms.

He dreamed of a tall-masted ship upon an azure sea. He could read her name, Atropos, *and he smiled, for she was his ship.*

But then his smile vanished, for the ship became a battered hulk sinking slowly into a dark sea, with her crew dead and dying on her shattered deck. He heard them crying out for him to help them but he could not, God, he could not!

He sprang awake racked with anguish.

"Why?" he whispered, and then his voice rose to a roar. "Why?" he shouted at his reflection in the oval mirror, and he pounded his fists against the glass.

The glass shattered, the shards falling to the attic floor in a hundred bright, shiny pieces.

Catherine had done this. She had destroyed him and everything he'd ever believed in.

There was a roaring in his ears. The pieces of glass flew into the air like arrows and into the frame that had contained them.

The mirror was whole again, and Matthew stared into it.

"When will I be free?" he whispered.

The mirror imploded and sucked him into a spinning vortex of light.

He'd cried out, certain he was being swept away to some plane even more awful than the one in which he'd so long languished.

Instead, he'd found himself in the rose garden, behind Charon's Crossing.

Catherine was there, too. And even after everything, the sight of her made the breath catch in his throat.

Like a starving man brought before a laden banquet table, he feasted on the sight of her. The soft, lush curves of her body were hidden beneath a demure cotton gown that buttoned to the neck. Her hair was plaited, giving her a look that was, he knew, falsely demure.

The memory of how it felt to hold her in his arms had raced through his blood. Despite himself, he'd whispered her name and when she turned towards him he'd gone to her, taken her into his embrace and kissed that luscious, lying mouth until her protests had become sighs of pleasure.

Matthew buried his head in his hands as he remembered that moment.

If only he'd killed her then. Christ, why hadn't he? It would have been so simple.

It was his disgrace that he had not done so. He'd been too caught up in tasting her, touching her. By the time he'd begun to regain his reason, a white mist had surrounded him. When it had cleared, he'd found himself back in the dreary attic, alone.

Enraged, despising himself for his senseless stupidity, he'd pounded his fists against the unyielding walls.

"Enough," he'd bellowed. "Damn you, let me out!"

But, of course, no one had come.

There was no jailer to hold him captive at Charon's Crossing. It was he and he alone who had sentenced himself to this eternal captivity just as it was he and he alone who could set himself free.

In Catherine's death, he would find peace.

Now, at last, the waiting was over. Catherine had come, and he would kill her.

His torment would end at last.

Matthew rose from the chair in which he'd been sitting. He walked slowly to the window and looked out. The sky was already beginning to lighten. It would be dawn soon.

He closed his eyes and grasped the sill with both hands, drawing in great breaths of air, savoring the scents of far-off places lying far beyond this prison. Then he turned and made his way to the door.

He slipped through it, a dark shade blending into the greater darkness of the silent house, and made his way down the narrow attic steps to the second floor. There would be no dramatic moans and rattles on this night.

He had no wish to warn Cat that he was on his way.

At the doorway to her bedroom, he paused. The door was shut, and he thought of slipping through it without bothering to open it. But it somehow seemed important to come to her as if he were still of her world on this night. Slowly, he put his hand on the knob, and turned it.

The door swung open on darkness. She must have drawn the

velvet drapes that covered the windows. Had she thought to protect herself from the night? he wondered with a twisting smile.

Darkness meant nothing to him. Still, he went to the windows, drew back the draperies, knowing in his heart that he was prolonging the moment until he would go to her.

At last, he turned around.

The cobwebs that had clung to the corners were gone, swept away by an old woman who had spent half her time cleaning the room and half of it making the sign of the cross.

Matthew had found it amusing, though he had not done anything to frighten her. The house's reputation, and the icy draft that swept down the stairs from the attic, had done that all by themselves.

But there was nothing frightening in this room.

There was only Catherine, asleep in the big, four-poster bed.

She lay on her back, with a pale pink blanket drawn to her chin. One hand lay palm up over the blanket's binding. The other was flung above her head, the fingers slender and lightly tanned against the white pillowcase.

Her guilt should have made her repulsive but it didn't. Her beauty still made his throat constrict.

He moved towards her slowly, his gaze sweeping over her. He felt a sudden painful hunger for the feel of her in his arms.

He hated himself for it but he understood. Hell, he thought with grim humor, what man wouldn't be stirred by the sight of a beautiful woman after he'd been locked up alone for so long?

He paused beside the bed and looked at her. His memory had played tricks on him, he could see that now. Catherine was even lovelier than he'd remembered. Her hair was more lustrous, her cheekbones more finely sculpted.

And her mouth, that beautiful, lying mouth. He had told her once that her lips were like the petals of the pink roses that grew at Charon's Crossing and that within them lay the nectar of the gods.

Now he knew that to compare her lips to rose petals was

to be overly generous to the flower, for surely none had ever been so perfect.

His gaze drifted slowly downward. What of the rest of her? His body stirred. Was her form more, or less, than he remembered?

A rush of blood sizzled through his veins and pooled in his groin.

"Are you some untried stripling? Think with your brain, man," he murmured through his teeth, "not with your rod."

But how could he not look at her? After all this time, he had to see her. Just this once. What harm could there be in it?

He bent towards her, took hold of the blanket's edge. Catherine stirred in her sleep and he froze, not wanting to awaken her until he was ready. She sighed, turned her face a little on the pillow, and then her breathing steadied.

Matthew's did, too. Slowly, carefully, he drew down the blanket.

One quick look, that was all. Just one . . .

His heart stood still.

Sweet Mother of God, what was she wearing?

It surely was not a nightgown.

He had never quite understood the need of women to undress at night only to dress themselves again, to put on garments that covered them from throat to toe.

Catherine had slept in such a gown. Not just in the dream. No, he'd seen her dressed for bed once; she had passed before the lit lamp in her bedroom window as he made his way along the path that led to the house. She had paused in the window, almost as if she'd known he was there. Her nightgown, white and full with long, frilled sleeves and a high neck, had revealed nothing except the faintest outline of her body, silhouetted by the oil lamp.

Not all women slept that way, of course. He was thirty-three years old now; he had been at sea more than half his life and he was not exactly of the face and build that frightened women off. He had tumbled his fair share—well, more than his fair share, perhaps—of ladies into their beds.

But he had never seen one dressed in anything even halfway resembling this.

He swallowed hard, trying to ease the tightness in his throat. The tightness in his groin was another matter.

What in hell was she wearing?

It seemed to be two bits of embroidered white cotton. One was a narrow-strapped, sleeveless cotton shirt. The other was—well, he didn't know what it was. Not underpants, surely. No one, not even a Liverpool strumpet, would call that tiny swathe of white cotton an undergarment.

The shirt exposed her shoulders and arms, and the fabric was so thin and fine that it seemed to cup her breasts. He could even see the faint outlines of her nipples just beneath.

And the underpants, if that was what they were, rode so high on her long legs that they exposed most of her gently rounded hips, covering only that sweet feminine delta she had never let him see nor touch.

Matthew groaned. Christ! His body was hard for her, hard and hot and aching with need. He longed to strip off those bits of cotton and bury himself in her. To watch her face as her eyes flew open and she realized what was happening . . .

"No!"

The cry rasped from his throat and he stumbled back from the bed, his chest heaving with the harsh labor of his breath.

Catherine had made a fool of him. She had ruined his name, turned him into a traitor. She had been the very instrument of his death.

But he would not let her turn him into a beast.

He would take his vengeance but he would do it honorably, as he had planned. Not like this.

Never like this.

He drew a shaky breath as he looked down at her again. And yet—and yet, the need to touch her was overpowering.

Moments slipped by. Then, slowly, he reached out his hand and stroked it over the black silk of her hair.

It felt so good to touch her.

He dropped to his knees beside the bed and held his breath as he let his fingers drift the length of her throat. Her skin was warm and firm to the touch; the scent of soap and roses and woman floated to his nostrils and he drew it deep into his lungs.

Catherine sighed. Two vertical lines appeared between her dark, winged brows but they vanished almost immediately.

"Cat," he heard himself whisper. "Cat . . ."

His touch grew bolder. His hand moved lightly over her breast, feeling the weight of it, and the roundness. His thumb moved across the rise of her nipple. She stirred in her sleep; her flesh surged and hardened and pressed against his palm.

He clenched his teeth and groaned.

Both his hands were on her now, cupping her breasts, shaping them to his touch.

"Catherine," he said thickly.

A whimper caught in her throat. Her lips parted on the softest of sighs.

His hands went to her hips, stroked gently down her thighs. He knew what she was, a liar and a Jezebel, but what had that to do with desire?

"Cat," he said, and he lowered his head to hers. His mouth settled lightly against hers in the softest of kisses.

She was sweet. So sweet. Could he have forgotten the taste of her? He must have, for surely he could not recall her tasting like this. Her lips reminded him of summer rain and spring breezes, of the first cool touch of snow.

Her arms rose, twined around his neck. Her lips parted more fully under the hardening pressure of his. She whispered something in her sleep.

Yes, she was saying, oh yes . . .

Matthew shot to his feet.

What was he doing?

She was a lying, scheming bitch. Was she a sorceress, as well? Was she trying to cast a spell on him, even now?

His face took on the coldness of stone as he marched to the doorway. Hell, he thought, and he turned and looked at the sleeping woman in the bed.

"Catherine," he said, his voice as chill as the air that suddenly surrounded him. "Catherine, look at me."

"Mmm," Catherine said, and rolled onto her belly.

"Damn you, Cat. Open your eyes!"

The voice was coming from a long way off.

It was harsh and angry, and the last thing Kathryn wanted to do was respond to it. But it persisted, and at last her eyes flickered open.

"Kathryn," the voice said . . .

"Ohmygod!"

Kathryn shot up in bed, clutching the blanket to her throat.

She had gone to sleep in a bedroom that looked like the overblown set of an old Dracula movie. The velvet draperies had hung from the windows in tatters and the room had been bare, except for this bed and a rickety armoire. And the only thing on the walls, aside from patches of damp, had been the faded rectangles and ovals that showed where paintings had once hung.

Now, a soft spill of moonlight illuminated a room that was as elegant as it must have been when Charon's Crossing was new.

A pair of slipper chairs were angled towards a small settee; an elegant armoire graced one wall. Opposite it, a milk-glass kerosene lamp stood on a small round table.

Crimson draperies framed the windows, the sheer curtains beneath billowing softly in the night breeze from the sea. A painting of what looked like an English village hung on one wall; smaller landscapes and a pair of oval-framed portraits were arranged on the wall across from the bed.

Kathryn swallowed dryly.

This is just a dream, she told herself. *It's a dream.*

Her heart gave an uneasy thud. Was it? If you *thought* you were dreaming, then you *couldn't* be dreaming.

Could you?

She took a deep breath. Of course you could. That was the thing about dreams. Anything was possible, when you were—

"Good evening, Cat."

Kathryn shrieked.

A man had stepped from the shadows. He was tall, with broad shoulders, narrow hips and long, muscular legs. His clothing was old-fashioned: a frilled white shirt, opened almost to the waist; black, skin-tight trousers and high leather boots . . .

She knew him. *She knew him!* He was the man she had dreamed about yesterday morning.

"I'm dreaming," she said in a shaky voice.

Of course she was. She had to be. That was why the room looked so different, why the man walking slowly towards her was the man from her dream.

But if she was dreaming, why could she smell the flower-scented night air? Why could she feel the faint abrasiveness of the blanket she clutched in her trembling hands?

He paused beside the bed and looked at her. She stared back, the sound of her own frantic heartbeat pounding in her ears. It took all her energy and willpower just to keep her teeth from chattering.

"You aren't real," she said.

He laughed. "I am real enough."

"You aren't. This is just a dream."

His smile turned silky. "Shall I prove that it isn't?"

She thought of what had happened the last time she'd dreamed of him, and she shrank back against the pillows.

"Don't you touch me! If you do—if you do . . ."

"Empty threats, Cat. There is no fool to do your bidding this time."

"I'll scream! I swear, I'll scream until everybody on this island hears me and comes running . . ." Kathryn blinked.

What in hell was she doing? She was talking to a man who wasn't here.

"You aren't here," she said calmly.

"Of course I'm here. Dammit, Cat . . ."

She ignored him, scooted down under the blanket and screwed her eyes shut.

"This dream is over."

Her voice was firm, except for a barely discernible tremor. She had courage, he had to give her that much, but then, he had not expected her to accept his appearance easily.

"You disappoint me," he said softly. "Is this the greeting I get after we have been apart for so long?"

Kathryn's eyes flew open.

"It hasn't been so long. Just since yesterday morning."

Dammit, that had been a stupid thing to say. Not that it mattered. In a dream as wacky as this one, you could say anything you liked.

Besides, her remark didn't seem to have struck him as being stupid. It hadn't even made him twitch a muscle. He was still looming over the bed, his arms akimbo and his hands splayed on his hips, looking down at her in a way that made her feel about two feet tall.

It would have been lots better to stand up and confront him, toe to toe, instead of having him tower over her. But she'd have to get out of bed to do that and all she had on under this blanket was her underwear.

"Oh hell," she said weakly.

She really was nuts. None of this was real. What did it matter if she was wearing her underwear or not?

She swept the blanket from the bed in one deft motion, wrapped it around herself with whatever finesse she could muster, and shot to her feet.

"Listen, mister—"

"Such formality, Cat." He smiled coolly. "I would much rather hear you say my name as you used to."

"I don't know your name. And even if I did—"

"Is your memory so short, then?" His smile tilted. "Say my name, Cat."

"I told you, I don't . . ."

She gasped as he reached out and clamped his hands around her shoulders.

"Say it, damn you," he growled. "Say, Matthew."

Kathryn swallowed dryly. Dream or not, she knew better than to argue with a lunatic.

"Matthew."

"You say it as if it were new to you, as if you have never before heard the name Matthew McDowell." His mouth twisted. "And that is what you will wish before I am done with you, Catherine. I promise you that."

Matthew McDowell, Kathryn thought wildly, a dream image who introduced himself to you.

Maybe she wasn't dreaming after all. Maybe she was simply stark, raving crazy.

But if she was, if she'd conjured up this visitor, she'd certainly done one hell of a job. Lord, but he was gorgeous!

She had never seen eyes that color. They were like the sea, green and dark and stormy. And his hair. What color was it? Not brown. Not blond. It was gold. Burnished gold, and so thick and silken-looking she longed to reach up and touch it.

The rest of him suited that hair and those eyes. Her gaze skimmed over his face, taking in the straight, proud nose, the square, cleft jaw, the firm but sensual mouth. There was a little scar angling just above his right eyebrow. It suited him, as did the theatrical outfit. Not that it looked theatrical. It just made him look incredibly masculine. And just a little dangerous.

What was that poem she'd read, years and years ago? Something about a highwayman riding a ribbon of moonlight through the darkness . . .

"Are you done examining me, Cat?"

His voice was cold and harsh but there was something more in it. Pain? Could that be what she heard?

His hands tightened on her shoulders. "Did you expect to see the visible wounds of your betrayal? They are healed, at least to the naked eye."

"I don't know what you're—"

"Don't lie to me, damn you! It's too late for that."

Kathryn licked her lips. "Look, I don't know what's going on here. And I definitely don't know you. Maybe . . ." She bit back the rush of hysterical laughter rising in her throat. "Maybe you're in the wrong dream." She yelped as his hands tightened on her. "Hey! You're hurting me!"

"I want answers, Catherine, and I want them now."

"And I," she said, wrenching out of his grasp, "want you out of here!"

Matthew gave a bark of harsh laughter.

"Aye, indeed you must. But you cannot get rid of me so easily. Not this time."

"And you can't bully me," she snapped, her chin rising in defiance. "Not even in a dream."

"I can do with you as I damn well please."

"Listen, mister, either you get out of here this minute or I'll—I'll—"

"You'll what?" He caught hold of her again, his hands sweeping into the dark spill of her hair. "What can you possibly do to me that you haven't already done?"

Kathryn's heart began to race as she stared up into that hard, handsome face.

He isn't real, she told herself frantically. The feel of his hands on her might seem real. His fury might seem real, too. But she had made him up . . . and she could just as easily unmake him.

"Go away," she said, fighting to keep her voice steady.

Matthew laughed. "I will, when it suits me."

"You will go when it suits *me*. I made you up. You're . . . you're a creature out of my imagination."

"A creature, am I?" His eyes darkened. "Is that how you think of me?"

"Yes. No. Dammit, you're twisting my words! All I'm saying is that you aren't really here."

His smile made her breath catch.

"Aren't I?" he said, and before she could struggle or stop him, he bent his head and kissed her.

It was a kiss that branded her with fire; she could feel it sweep like molten lava from his lips to hers.

Kathryn's hands lifted. She balled them into fists but he caught her wrists in one hand and held them against his chest while he drew her closer into his arms. Her head tilted back as his lips moved over hers, urging her to surrender.

She would never do that . . .

Her fingers went slack as they pressed against the hard wall of his chest.

"Please," she whispered against his mouth.

Please, what? What did she want? Not this. Not the heat of him, and the hardness. Not his kiss, tasting of desire and of hate . . .

She made a sound, a soft, keening sigh that she barely recognized as coming from her own throat, and he answered by sweeping one hand down her back to the base of her spine.

"Catherine," he whispered, the word lost against her lips. "Catherine, sweet Catherine."

He felt her lips tremble and open to his even as he felt the sudden hot dampness of her tears and tasted their salt upon his tongue. Her fingers were curling into his shirt. She was his now. He had only to draw her down to the bed . . .

Christ, what was he doing? This wasn't vengeance, it was seduction. And Cat was doing the seducing! She was working her wiles on him as she had done in the past.

Had he learned nothing in the infinite darkness of his eternal prison?

Matthew cursed and flung her from him. She stumbled and fell back onto the bed.

"Bitch," he said. "Whore!"

Kathryn stared up into his fierce, angry face. Then she screwed her eyes shut.

"This is a dream," she chanted in a frantic whisper, "a dream, a dream, a dream . . .

Somewhere in the distance, a bell began to toll.

Four

Somewhere in the distance, a bell began to toll.

Kathryn sighed in her sleep and burrowed deeper into the blankets.

The bell pealed again, and she frowned.

"Mmm," she murmured . . .

She came awake all at once, heart pounding and eyes wide. In one swift motion, she rolled to the side of the bed, reached down and snatched her shoe from the floor, and brandished it wildly as she shot up against the pillows.

"Okay," she said, "okay, I've had it! You get out of here right now or . . . or . . ."

The room was empty. It looked exactly as it had when she'd gone to sleep last night. The drapes were shabby and old, the furniture was almost nonexistent, and the only things decorating the walls were patches of faded paint and splotches of dampness.

Kathryn let out her breath and slumped back against the pillows.

There were dreams. And then there were nightmares. And there wasn't a question in the world about what she'd just experienced.

It had been a nightmare with a capital *N*, the kind that would have sent half the population of Manhattan galloping off to see their shrinks.

She couldn't even blame it on *moo goo gai pan*.

"Not this time," she muttered.

She sighed, dumped the shoe on the floor, sat up and tossed back the blanket.

Which only proved, she thought, scrubbing her hands over her face and yawning, that a supper of Campbell's tomato soup and half a packet of Ritz Crackers could do their own artful job of putting you on the road to Nightmare City if you were spending the night in a place that looked like a reject from a bad movie.

At least she hadn't conjured up Freddy Krueger, she thought with a shaky laugh. As made-to-order dream characters went, Matthew McDowell was at least a little more appealing.

It was just that dreaming up a gorgeous guy in a costume who couldn't seem to decide whether he wanted to make love to you or kill you was a bit unsettling.

Kathryn pushed the hair from her eyes and rose to her feet. Sunlight streamed past the tattered velvet drapes, bathing her in warmth.

"Just another day in paradise," she said, and smiled.

Blue sky. Golden sun. Puffy white clouds that might have been painted by Gauguin.

Oh yeah. It was going to be a great day. A busy one, too. The contractor was coming by. Somebody would bring over the rental car she'd requested. The realtor would be along, too. And she was going to make a start at cleaning up this house, just as soon as she got the door of the dilapidated old armoire unstuck so she could get dressed.

Kathryn rolled her eyes, banged on one door with the heel of her hand while she yanked hard with her other until both sprang open. Her old denim cut-offs and a ratty pink tank top would do. The shorts bore permanent smears of the yellow paint she'd used on the walls of her Greenwich Village kitchen and countless washings had rendered the top almost white, but they were perfect for how she intended to spend her morning.

When you were knee-deep in buckets of hot water laced with Mr. Clean, you didn't worry too much about your appearance. And if there was one thing she was sure of, it was that scrubbing away some of the accumulated grime that marred the house would go a long way towards reducing the spookiness quotient that had probably helped bring on that awful dr—

"Miss Russell?"

Kathryn gave a wild shriek. The shorts and tank top fell from her hands as she whirled around.

A woman was standing in the open bedroom doorway. She was small, slender, and her skin was the color of coffee that has been stirred with a light dollop of cream.

"Oh, I am so sorry," she said. "I didn't mean to—"

"Who in hell are you?"

"My name is Olive Potter. Amos Carter sent me."

"To do what?" Kathryn said furiously. Her hands were shaking as if she had a fever. She reached behind her, felt for the cotton robe she'd hung in the armoire, and pulled it on. "Scare me half to death?"

Olive Potter bit her lip. "Truly, I apologize. But I assumed you were expecting me and I rang and rang the doorbell, but—"

"You thought I was expecting you?"

"Yes." The woman made a face. "I'm making a mess of this, I'm afraid. I own Potter Realty, you see. In Hawkins Bay."

"Oh." Kathryn swallowed, then cleared her throat. "Oh. Of course."

The realtor made a helpless gesture. "I rang the bell at least half a dozen times but there was no answer. So I walked around back and checked to see if you might be in the garden, enjoyin' the sun."

Kathryn tied the belt of her robe. Her hands had stopped shaking but her heart still galloped at a hundred miles a minute.

"I should be, I suppose." She gave a little laugh and hoped it didn't sound like a squeak. "I mean, I've no idea what time it is but I'm sure it's terribly late."

"No, no, it's not late at all. It's just goin' on eight o'clock. I did try callin', to say I'd be comin' over, but your telephone doesn't seem to work."

"Among other things," Kathryn said dryly. She lifted her hands to her hair and smoothed it back from her face. "Well, Miss Potter, I do appreciate your stopping by so promptly."

"Amos said you wanted to get Charon's Crossin' on the market as soon as possible."

"Yes. I certainly do." Kathryn's brows lifted. "How did you get in, Miss Potter?"

"Well, the gates were open."

"Right. I forgot that."

"As for gettin' into the house . . . well, when you didn't answer, I, ah, I thought I'd best see if you were all right. As I say, I checked out back and then tried the rear door, the one that leads into the kitchen. It was unlocked, so in I came."

"Was it?" Kathryn frowned. "I could have sworn I'd made a point of locking all the doors before I went to bed last night."

"I don't think you need worry. Our little island may be short on—"

"Amenities," Kathryn said with a little smile. "Yes, so I've been told before."

"It's also wonderfully short on crime."

"Well, that's a relief to hear, considering that this house is stuck out on a cliff, smack in the middle of nowhere."

"Oh, greathouses always were put up on the highest, biggest piece of land. Folks back then were no different than they are now. If you were goin' to spend lots of money buildin' a home, you didn't want it surrounded by other houses not anywhere near so grand."

Kathryn nodded. "That makes sense." She hesitated. "But if it's so safe on Elizabeth Island, why were you worried when I didn't answer the door?"

Olive Potter's mouth opened, then shut. "Well," she said, "well . . . I wasn't 'worried.' Not exactly. I was, ah, concerned. Amos told me Charon's Crossin' was in need of lots of repairs. I suppose I envisioned you fallin' on a rotted step and sprainin' your ankle or somethin'." She grinned. "Not that Amos would ever permit such a thing to happen to a client of his, of course."

Kathryn laughed. She liked Olive Potter, with her lilting island accent and her easy smile. She had a down-to-earth air about her and that was definitely what she needed this morning.

"You're right," she said lightly. "I can't imagine Mr. Carter letting anything happen to a client that didn't meet with his absolute approval." She smiled. "Look, Miss Potter—"

"Please. Call me Olive."

"And you must call me Kathryn."

Olive smiled and held out her hand. "How do you do, Kathryn? It's a pleasure to meet you."

Kathryn smiled and clasped Olive's outstretched hand.

"It's a pleasure to meet you, too. And to have a visitor on a morning like this."

"Your first in Charon's Crossin'?"

"My first. And, I hope, my worst." Kathryn turned around and slammed shut the doors of the armoire, grunting a little as she forced the right-hand door into place.

"Yes. It can't have been pleasant, wakin' up in a room that looks as if it's fallin' down around your ears," Olive said sympathetically.

"That's true enough." Kathryn puffed out her breath as she swung towards Olive. "But I was talking about . . . well, I know it sounds silly but I had the most awful dream."

"Dream?"

"A nightmare, really." Kathryn walked to the bed, picked up the pillow and gave it a vigorous plumping before tossing it back onto the sheet. "Nothing worth talking about." She gave a laugh that sounded forced, even to her own ears. "Just a costume drama, brought on, I suppose, by this spooky old house."

She turned and smiled at Olive, but Olive didn't smile back.

"A costume drama, Kathryn?"

"Yeah. You know, opulent settings, a guy in a shirt open to his navel . . . Don't look so worried, Olive. It wasn't all that bad, now that I think about it."

"Kathryn, you know, I was tellin' Amos, I have a nice little house for rent right on the beach in town. It's clean and modern and you could stay in it while you are on the island."

"Thanks, but I'm fine out here."

"Are you sure? This house is so big. And it's such a . . . well, it isn't in the best shape."

"It's a mess," Kathryn said cheerfully. "And I do thank you for your suggestion but really, I'll manage. I'm only going to be here a week and I'll get lots more accomplished if I stay at Charon's Crossing." She wrinkled her nose. "Like scrubbing it out. I'm going to get a start on that this morning."

"And I've interrupted you."

"No, don't be silly. You're a very welcome sight, believe me. Look, why don't you give me a couple of minutes to put myself together? Then I'll make some tea—I'd offer you coffee, but I haven't got any. We can sit down and have a cup while we chat."

Olive nodded. "That sounds fine, Kathryn. How would it be if I took a quick look through the house while you're gettin' yourself dressed? That way, I'll have a bit of an idea what it might bring if we put it on the market."

"Not 'if,'" Kathryn said. "When. Sure. You do that. Take the fifty-cent tour and I'll be down in a couple of minutes."

Kathryn came trotting down the stairs fifteen minutes later, her hair loose and still wet from the shower. She was dressed in the denim cut-offs, the pink tank top, and a pair of sandals.

"Am I having another dream, or do I really smell coffee brewing?" she said as she entered the kitchen.

Olive, who'd been standing at the back door looking out over the terrace, turned around.

"It is. I thought I'd surprise you with a pot. I hope you don't mind."

"Mind?" Kathryn plucked two mugs from a shelf and filled them to the brim with the hot, fragrant brew. "I'd have sold my soul for a cup of coffee last night. I looked everywhere for a can or even a jar of instant. Where was it hiding?"

Olive smiled as she took the mug Kathryn handed her.

"It wasn't. I stopped at Whitbridge's before I drove over. It's a little shop on Front Street. Everybody shops there for their groceries." She lifted her mug in salute and tapped it lightly against Kathryn's. "Thought you might appreciate somethin' like this, considerin' what I know of Amos's idea of stockin' groceries. I suppose he saw to it that you have some tea, a box or two of crackers, and a wedge of cheese, hmm?"

Kathryn laughed. "Plus a few cans of evaporated milk and soup." She blew gently on her coffee, then took a sip. "Do you know him well? Amos, I mean?"

"About as well as anyone can. He's a fine lawyer, our Amos, but he's not much for socializin'."

"That's all right with me. I didn't come here to socialize, I came to sell this house." Kathryn's eyes flew to Olive's. "Oh, hey. I didn't mean that the way it sounded!"

"No problem, Kathryn." Olive smiled. "I understand."

"It's only that I've just got this week to take care of everything. And I've already got the feeling that—well, that things don't operate quite the same here as they do back home."

Olive chuckled. "Meanin', you've figured out that island time isn't the same as regular time, hmm? Well, you're right. People tend to take things more slowly in these parts. But I assure you, I'll get your house on the market just as soon as it's ready."

"Ready?" Kathryn's brows drew together. "What do you mean, ready?"

"I agree with Amos, Kathryn. You will get a much better price for Charon's Crossin' if you attend to some basic repairs."

Kathryn sighed. She picked up the coffee pot, refilled both their mugs, then gestured towards the door.

"I was afraid of that. Look, why don't we sit outside while we talk?" She smiled a little. "I might as well soak up all the sun I can while I'm down here."

Olive followed Kathryn out into the clear morning.

"Mmm," Kathryn said, tilting her face to the sun. "Oh, that feels wonderful. It must be seventy-five degrees out here."

"Eighty," Olive said modestly. "A typical Elizabeth Island midwinter temperature readin'."

The women strolled across the old brick terrace, down the wide, shallow steps that led into what remained of a garden.

Kathryn sighed as she looked around her.

"This must have been a beautiful place, once upon a time," she said softly.

"A showplace it was," Olive said, just as softly. "I never saw it myself, of course. By the time I was born, Charon's Crossin' was long past its prime but all the old stories say . . ."

Kathryn glanced at her when she fell silent. "What do they say?"

Olive shrugged. "Oh, you know. This and that. Mostly that the house was spectacular. The grounds, too." She jerked her head. "That garden, most especially."

Ahead, rising like a splendid ruin against the pale blue sky, pink roses climbed in rich, almost obscene profusion over an arched trellis. The trellis had probably once been painted white. Now, all that remained were patches of color clinging to the grey wood.

Beyond the arch, framed within it, was a curving wrought-iron gate.

Just like the dream.

The coffee mug trembled in Kathryn's hand.

"Kathryn?" Olive put her hand over Kathryn's. "What's the matter?"

"Nothing," Kathryn said quickly. "It's—it's nothing. I just— It must be the heat. I'm not used to it."

"Of course you aren't. How foolish of me, not to think of that." The realtor put her arm lightly around Kathryn's waist. "Let's go back inside, where it's cooler."

"No. No, really, I'm okay."

"Are you sure?"

"Positive. Look, why don't we sit on that bench? The one under that tree."

"Well . . ."

"There's plenty of shade there. Really, I'd rather sit out here than go inside the house."

Olive nodded. "Very well. But you tell me if you begin to feel ill, okay?" She smiled. "Amos would have me horse-whipped if I let his client faint right under my nose."

Kathryn laughed. "Amos might not feel quite so proprietorial if he knew that his client was letting her imagination run away with her."

Olive's brows lifted as the women settled themselves on the bench.

"What do you mean?"

"Oh, it's not worth going into, believe me. It's just . . . I don't know, exactly. I've had these ridiculous dreams lately about—about . . ."

"About Charon's Crossin'?"

Kathryn swung towards the other woman. Olive had put on a pair of big sunglasses she'd pulled from her shoulder bag. With them on, her face was unreadable.

"Why would you say that?" Kathryn asked sharply.

Olive shrugged. "Just a good guess. From what Amos says, I got the feelin' you've had Charon's Crossin' on your mind a bit. And now here you are, alone in this big, spooky house stuck away out in the middle of nowhere. I tell you, Kathryn, if it were me, I'd be havin' nightmares, not dreams!"

Kathryn stared at her and then she began to laugh.

"You'll never know how glad I am you came by this morning, Olive. You're like a breath of fresh air, whisking the cobwebs out of my very foggy brain!"

Olive grinned. "Not as many cobwebs as I saw inside the house, I'll wager. My goodness, whoever did Amos hire to clean it? She must have been sleepin' on the job."

"Amos." Kathryn made a face. "He may be a good lawyer but he certainly hasn't got any bedside manner."

"Well, he's not known for his diplomacy, no."

"That's putting it mildly. He and I didn't hit it off. But that's no excuse for the really cheap parting shot he got in when he left yesterday." Kathryn crossed her legs and wiggled her foot from side to side. "Not that I believe in such nonsense, of course, but I have to admit, it's not the kind of thing you want to hear before you spend the night in a house where the floors creak and the pipes gurgle and a draft that feels like it's blowing in straight from Alaska comes whistling down the stairs."

"What did that impossible old man tell you?"

"Oh, it was so silly I hate to even repeat it. He said Charon's Crossing was haunted."

She waited for Olive to laugh or at least to smile. Instead, the realtor's head jerked up as if she were a puppet on a string. She put down her empty coffee mug and laid her hand over Kathryn's.

"That foolish old man! Listen to me, Kathryn. Amos Carter will draw up all the legal papers you need, do 'em right, you can bet on that, give you good legal advice, too, if you ask. But anything else he tells you is claptrap. You understand?"

"Well, sure. I didn't think—"

"This house you've got here is old. It's going to need a lot of work. But that's all."

"I know that."

"You start talkin' about ghosts and spirits, you won't ever get a buyer."

"Olive, really, I don't believe in such things."

"Maybe not. But other folks do, especially in these parts. You hear me, girl?"

Kathryn nodded. She knew it was true. Even some of the most sophisticated of the Caribbean islands were home to sects that believed in exotic combinations of Christianity and far older, darker religions.

"I've no intention of going around saying anything about Charon's Crossing." Kathryn smiled. "Except that it's going to make some rich person very, very happy."

It took a second or two before Olive smiled in return.

"Good." She gave Kathryn's hand one last squeeze and then she let go and rose to her feet. "Suppose we go inside now, walk through the place together, and I'll tell you what I think needs doin'."

Kathryn sighed as she collected the mugs. "What doesn't need doing, you mean."

The house was cool, almost cold compared to the outside heat. "One of the nice things about these old houses," Olive said pleasantly. "They're comfortable even without air conditionin'."

"And a good thing," Kathryn said as she dumped the mugs into the sink. "I'll just bet the electrical system's too old to handle AC."

Olive smiled. "You're probably right. Most everythin's outdated here, I'm afraid."

"Which brings us to the bad news, I guess." Kathryn leaned back against the sink. "What do I have to spend to put the place into saleable condition?"

"Well, startin' right here, in the kitchen, you'll have to have the hot water system checked." Olive walked to the sink and turned on the tap. "Cold," she said, lifting her brows as she dangled her fingers beneath the flow. "Cold as can be, finally workin' up to lukewarm."

"Yeah." Kathryn sighed and folded her arms. "So I noticed. But it's no worse than what I live with, back in my New York apartment."

"Maybe. But lots of these old houses have problems with their heatin' systems. I'm not talkin' about the comfort of a warm bath, you see, I'm talkin' safety. Be sure and ask Hiram to check, okay?"

Kathryn blew out her breath. "I will."

"There's more, I'm afraid."

"I figured that. To tell you the truth, I had no idea the house would be quite this bad. I mean, Amos tried to warn me, but I never dreamed so much would need doing."

"Didn't your father tell you anythin' about Charon's Crossin'?" Olive asked curiously as they walked through the kitchen and into the hallway.

Kathryn tucked her hands into the rear pockets of her shorts.

"My parents were divorced years ago. I didn't have much contact with him after that."

"Ah." The realtor's eyes darkened with sympathy. "I'm sorry to hear it."

"No need to be. It's just a fact of life."

"A sad one, though."

"The house is what's sad. What else needs doing, do you think?" Kathryn reached out a hand and ran it lightly over a wall where what looked like blue silk hung in shreds. "I can't afford to have these walls redone. Considering the size of this place, I don't even know if I can afford to have them painted."

"No need. You want to present a buyer with a structurally sound house. Aesthetics are not the issue."

"I'm delighted to hear it."

Olive smiled. "Same goes for things like redoin' floors and windows and such." She paused and frowned at the foyer walls. "Of course, it doesn't make such a good first impression, seein' that moldin' lookin' as if the termites have been at it."

"Yes," Kathryn said, sighing as she kicked a piece of molding aside. "I figured that."

"Well, check with Hiram. Ask him what he can do that will make things look better without it costin' you an arm and a leg."

"Right."

"You should probably also ask him to see to any leaks in the roof. And to check the plumbin' and electrical systems."

"I will. The first time the pipes began rumbling, I almost jumped out of my skin. And the lights have a really wonderful way of flickering on and off. The ones that work at all, that is."

"Anythin' else you've noticed that I've overlooked?"

Kathryn shook her head. "I don't think so. If you'll put me in touch with somebody who'll pitch in and help me scrub things down, it will help. I'd like to get rid of most of the grime and the yuck. And the spiders." She shuddered. "New York roaches are one thing, but spiders that build trampolines instead of webs are another."

Olive chuckled. "Fine. Well, is that it, then?"

They had wandered to the foot of the great staircase. Kathryn paused and looked up, to where the sunlit dust motes disappeared in the darkness of the second floor.

"Just about, except for that miserable draft. Feel it?"

Olive's gaze followed Kathryn's. "No. No, I can't say that I do."

"Really?" Kathryn gave a dramatic shudder and wrapped her arms around herself. "Boy, I certainly do."

"Maybe there's a broken window somewhere."

"I told that to our friend Amos. He assured me there wasn't. And I checked, after he left. He was right. The windows are fine."

Olive's head tilted further back. "Maybe the draft's comin' from the attic."

"The attic? You might be right. I never thought of looking there."

"Well, don't." Kathryn's brows shot up at the other woman's emphatic statement and Olive laughed. "Attics are always full of mice. And in this house, the trampoline-buildin' spiders are probably havin' themselves a fine time up in the attic, as well. Let Hiram do the lookin' for you, when he comes. Now, what can we say about Charon's Crossin' that will make it appealin' to a buyer?"

" 'For sale,' " Kathryn said in a mincing tone as they made their way out to the terrace again. " 'Handyman's special. All you need is a fat checkbook, a little imagination and a couple of dozen years and you'll have the vacation hideaway of your dreams.' "

Olive laughed as they leaned back against the rusted wrought-iron railing that rimmed the terrace.

"You're supposed to be tellin' me what a wonderful buy this house is, Kathryn. Don't you know that?" She turned and gazed out over the garden. "We can start by emphasizin' the beauty of the surroundin's."

"I agree. And the privacy. Seriously, I've been thinking about it, the fact that the house is pretty much off the beaten track, and it seems to me that our best bet is to deal with that head-on, turn it into an asset."

Olive gave Kathryn a wry look. "You sure you're not lookin' to take my job?"

Kathryn smiled and leaned her arms on the railing.

"What we need is a buyer with lots of money who's looking for a very private getaway. Right?"

Olive nodded. "Right." *What an old fool you are, Amos, not to recognize how bright and quick this young woman is*. "We want a man of discerning tastes and great wealth."

"A man," Kathryn said, "or a woman."

The realtor laughed. "Oh, I can just see how you must have jolted poor Amos."

Kathryn reached out and plucked a flower from a vine that had twined itself around the railing.

"It really is lovely here," she said, twirling the flower in her fingers. "Is the weather always this perfect?"

"Not always. We get storms sometimes, blowin' in across the sea. In late summer, mostly, but sometimes in the winter, too."

Kathryn spread her fingers and let the breeze carry the flower to the grass.

"I'll have to phone my fiancé and torture him a little," she said, and smiled. "Give him a first-hand weather report, you know? I'd have done it last night, but the phone doesn't work."

Olive nodded. "It is a problem on the island. I will speak with Hiram, see if he can think of a way to improve things."

"Hiram certainly has his work cut out for him. When he comes by later . . . What's the matter?"

"I wouldn't count on seein' Hiram today, I'm afraid. It is Saturday, and the bonefish are runnin' just off Coronado Cay."

"Tomorrow, then."

"Tomorrow is Sunday. No one on Elizabeth Island works on Sunday."

"Then, he's got to stop by Monday morning, first thing." Kathryn's voice took on a pleasant but firm tone. "I only have a week to devote to getting things sorted out here. That isn't very long."

"Especially not on this island. As I said before, things move at a slower pace than you are accustomed to." Olive dug into her shoulder bag and took out a pen and a small notebook. "Let's write down what we've agreed needs checkin', yes? So far, we've got the plumbin'. The heatin'. The electricity. The roof, maybe. The moldin'. The phone . . ."

"I think there's probably some wainscoting needs doing, too. Oh, and we'll have to deal with whatever it is that's turning the place into Siberia." Kathryn sighed. "Sounds like a year's salary to me—in which case, I'm up the creek without a paddle."

"Sorry?"

She smiled. "Never mind." Kathryn hesitated. "Olive? Why would Amos have said what he did to me?"

"About what?" Olive said, capping her pen and tucking it away with the pad.

"About the house being haunted."

"Because he's an old fool, just as I told you."

"Yes, but he couldn't have just come up with something like that off the top of his head, could he? I mean, is there some sort of local folklore about Charon's Crossing?"

"Well," Olive said slowly, "I suppose there is. We islanders are a superstitious lot, and Charon's Crossin' is very old. No one has lived in it for a very long time."

"My father did."

"Not really. He had this old sailboat, used to come sailin' in here a couple of times a year, dock at Hawkins Bay harbor, and put in some work on the house—you didn't know that?"

"No. No, I didn't. Did he ever ask you to sell the place?"

"Never."

"Well," Kathryn said decisively, "I certainly want to. Do I need to sign a contract or something?"

"It's not necessary. Amos vouched for you and that's good enough for me."

"You trust his judgment, hmm?" Kathryn said, smiling.

Olive nodded. "I know he didn't make a good first impression, but you can trust him too, Kathryn. He really is a fine lawyer. As for me—I'm goin' to do my best to sell Charon's Crossin' for you. It may need some attention, but the house itself is still sturdy."

"We hope," Kathryn said without conviction.

"Oh, I'm sure it is. These old greathouses were built to last. The English had every intention of stayin' in these islands forever."

"Well, I suppose the house was great, at one time, but—"

"No, no." Olive smiled and patted Kathryn's arm. " 'Greathouse' is the name for houses such as this. But time has taken its toll."

"Time," Kathryn said wryly, "and neglect."

The other woman nodded. "Neglect is the worst enemy. It gives the natural world the chance to reclaim what was taken from it. It's a special shame in this case, considerin' that Charon's Crossin' has been in the same family . . ." She smiled. "Your family, Kathryn, for almost two hundred years."

Kathryn looked at Olive with interest. "Is it really that old?"

"Oh my, yes."

"And why was it named Charon's Crossing? Do you know?"

Olive's smile tilted. "I'm afraid I don't."

"Are you sure? I have this feeling I should know what the name means, but I just can't place it."

"Certainly, I'm sure."

Certainly, she wasn't. Kathryn knew she was getting the brush-off, but there wasn't much she could do about it.

"Now," Olive said briskly, "where was I? Oh yes. I was tellin' you the history of your house. Well, it was built in

1799 by Lord Arthur Russell." Olive smiled. "Your great-granddaddy, I suppose, several times removed."

"Why? I mean, what brought him all the way from England? Do you know?"

"George the Third sent him, to govern the island. And to make money growin' sugar and turnin' it into molasses and rum."

"You mean, Charon's Crossing was a distillery?"

Olive's laughter was soft and melodious. "It was a plantation, with its land planted in sugar cane." She walked to the other side of the terrace and pointed out over the deep green landscape. "You see there? Where those flamboyants are bloomin'? Well, back behind them, all grown over now, you can still find what's left of the kitchen and the bathrooms."

"But the house has a kitchen. And several bathrooms."

"Added on, all of them. The rest of the outbuildin's, what's left, anyway, are further back. The sugar mill, the stillhouse, the boilin' sheds, the slave quarters—"

"Slave quarters?"

"Sure. There was slavery everywhere in these islands."

Kathryn grimaced. "I'd forgotten that." She looked at Olive. "Was the island really important to the English?"

"Very, until they lost the War of 1812." A mischievous grin lit her face. "Well, they didn't really lose it but they surely stopped thinkin' of themselves as the sovereigns of the seas, and all thanks to you Americans."

Kathryn laughed. "I know that much, at least. Tell me more about this man who built Charon's Crossing."

"There's not much more to tell. Lord Russell was typical of his time, I suppose. Pompous, dictatorial . . ." Olive frowned. "You know," she said slowly, "I'd forgotten, but he had a daughter. Her name was Catherine, too. With a *C* instead of a *K*. Could it be you were named for her?"

"I guess. My name—spelled all different ways—has always been a family favorite."

Olive hesitated. "Do people refer to you as Kat, then?"

Kathryn felt a sudden tightness in her throat.

"No," she said, after a moment, "no, they don't. Why do you ask?"

"Well, I think that was what she was called, this Catherine. Cat, you know?"

"Are you sure? How can you know that?"

"Oh," Olive said with a wave of her hand, "it is how she is spoken of in all the . . ."

"In all the what?" Kathryn said, when the other woman suddenly fell silent.

A flush rose in Olive's dark cheeks. "It's just jumbie nonsense, Kathryn. Surely, you are not interested in—"

"But I am." Kathryn forced a smile to her lips. "After all, this girl is my ancestor. What were you going to say?"

"Only that there are stories, that's all. Tall tales. Island tales. There is nothing unusual in that. My people have always been great storytellers."

"Tales about Charon's Crossing?"

"About everything," Olive said with a quick smile.

"And what stories are there about Cat Russell?"

"Kathryn, really, I have no wish to bore you with—"

"I'm not bored, I'm fascinated." Kathryn smiled stiffly. "What do they say about her?"

"Only that she was very beautiful."

"And? Come on, Olive. What else?"

"Well, they say men flocked to her. Powerful men. Handsome ones, the ones other women wanted." Olive leaned closer. "It is even said she had two different lovers at the same time."

Kathryn's smile eased. "Really?"

"Oh, yes. One was an older man, with lands and estates in England. Lord Waring, his name was."

"And the other?" Kathryn was leaning back against the railing now, enjoying the story. Why on earth had she been so nervous about hearing it? It was just what Olive had said, island gossip. And, she had to admit, fun to listen to, even though it was a couple of hundred years old. She shot the other woman a conspiratorial grin. "Don't tell me," she said, her voice dropping to a whisper. "He was young. And gorgeous. And a rogue. Right?"

"Young, yes. He was an American, the captain of his own ship. And some did call him a rogue."

"Why? What did he do?"

"In 1811, his ship was commissioned to sail under the British flag as a privateer, seizin' ships and goods owned by the French. But they say he took to lootin' any ship he could catch, regardless of her nationality."

"A pirate," Kathryn said with delight.

"So some called him."

"Well, go on. You said he was Cat Russell's lover."

"Yes."

"And gorgeous?"

"So it is said." Olive was laughing. " 'Course, what else would they say? A rogue would never be described as anything but tall and handsome, with hair the color of burnished gold and emerald green eyes . . ."

Kathryn clutched the railing for support, her hands as white as her face.

"Kathryn? Kathryn, what is it? My Lord, girl, you look as if you're going to faint!"

Olive was right. She was going to pass out, right here on the terrace . . .

"Kathryn?"

Kathryn dragged a breath deep into her lungs.

"I'm—I'm all right," she whispered.

"You are not," Olive said in a no-nonsense tone. "I knew we should have stayed out of this sun! You need time to acclimate to—"

"Olive? This man. Do you know his name?"

"What man? Honestly, Kathryn . . ."

"Catherine Russell's handsome lover." Kathryn gripped the realtor's hand. "What was his name?"

Olive clucked her tongue. The girl needed a cold compress,

at the very least. Her face was not only pale, it was shiny with sweat, and her fingers felt icy. But it was obvious there would be no convincing her to go indoors until she'd had her foolish question answered.

"I can't see that it matters, Kathryn," she said with a touch of impatience, "but if you must know, his name was Matthew McDowell."

Five

Kathryn stood at the front door, waving and smiling cheerfully as Olive's red Ford Escort wobbled down the rutted drive. She held the smile until the little car swung around a narrow curve and vanished in a swirl of dust, and then she groaned, slammed the door closed, and slumped back against it.

At least she'd managed to pull that off, though when you came down to it, waving your hand and smiling like an idiot wasn't half as hard as not passing out when you learned that the man who'd paid you a midnight visit had been dead for almost two hundred years.

Of course, she'd come close, but then Olive had taken over and Kathryn had been happy to let her lay the blame on the sun. Otherwise, she might have blurted out the truth and then they could both have spent the rest of the day trying to figure out if she really was going crazy or if she had, in fact, spent the hours before dawn playing hostess to Cat Russell's lover.

Instead, she'd let Olive swoop an arm around her waist, march her inside the house, put her into a chair and bring her a cold compress. Then she'd endured a lecture on fair skins and ultraviolet rays and overheated brain cells which had ended only when Olive had finally run out of breath.

By then, Kathryn had recovered her equilibrium, if not her sanity, though it had taken time to convince Olive.

"I really don't want to leave you, Kathryn," she'd said. "Maybe you want to reconsider rentin' that little house in town for the rest of the week."

Maybe I want to reconsider heading straight back to New York, Kathryn had almost answered, but that would have been out of the question. She had things to accomplish here and she couldn't accomplish them by running away.

Besides, there was nothing to run from. By then, she'd calmed down enough to know that whatever was happening had a perfectly reasonable explanation.

All she had to do was find it.

So she'd smiled brightly and assured Olive that she was fine and that she wouldn't set foot out the door until late afternoon, when the heat lessened.

"It's my English ancestors who didn't know enough to keep out of the midday sun," she'd said, "remember? 'Mad dogs and Englishmen' . . . ?"

But coaxing a smile from Olive had been hard.

"Kathryn?" she'd said worriedly, "Is there somethin' troublin' you?"

For just an instant, Kathryn had come close to blurting it all out. But then she thought of what Olive had said about how unfortunate it would be if people started whispering about Charon's Crossing being haunted and about how superstitious islanders could be, and weren't there enough stories about this place already without adding one about a ghost?

So she'd swallowed hard, smiled, and said that the only thing troubling her was how much work the house was going to need.

Two glasses of iced water later, she'd finally managed to ease Olive out the door.

Now, Kathryn took a deep breath and closed every bolt the door possessed which was pretty stupid, all things considered.

What good were locks and bolts against a ghost?

A bubble of wild laughter rose in her throat and she clapped her hands over her mouth before it could escape.

There was nothing funny about any of this, dammit! No way.

There were no such things as ghosts. That was a given. And

she had never heard the story of Cat Russell and Matthew McDowell before. So how could he have come wandering into her dream?

It was a reasonable question. Unfortunately, she had no reasonable answer. Not yet, anyway, but she'd be damned if she wouldn't find one.

Kathryn checked the door one last time. She was an old hand at finding reason in the midst of chaos, thanks to her parents. Living with them had been like riding a roller coaster, all highs and lows with very little in between.

She had learned early to ignore the fireworks around her by concentrating on emotionless things. Things she could trust, like math and computers.

And mops and brooms and plain, unvarnished hard work.

It had amused her father and baffled her mother to emerge from the scene of their latest battle, where the plates and whatever else they'd both hurled at the walls still lay broken on the floor, and find their daughter busily cleaning her bedroom or reorganizing her closet.

"Honestly, Kathryn, what are you doing?" Beverly would say in the same tone she might have used if she'd discovered a spaceship on the lawn.

"Nothing," Kathryn would answer, and she'd go right on cleaning and scrubbing and rearranging.

Now, she didn't even hesitate. She headed straight for the kitchen, banged open half a dozen cabinet doors before she found what she wanted, and set to work.

The explanation for what had happened came to her out of the blue in midafternoon.

She was on her knees in the downstairs bathroom, busily scrubbing away at a marble floor that had lightened and brightened perceptibly with a little elbow grease and a lot of Mr. Clean, when the answer popped into her head.

"Of course," Kathryn cried, "of course!"

She dropped her scrub brush into the bucket of grungy water, sat back on her heels and pumped her fist in the air in triumph.

It was so simple. So wonderfully simple. She'd tried to make sense out of Matthew McDowell's dreamtime appearance, imagining everything from smoke and mirrors to a hidden movie projector, and all the time the truth had been just waiting for her to recognize it.

She was busy cleaning up the cobwebs and junk that had accumulated in the house. Well, her brain had done the same thing. Dreams were nothing but a way of processing the odds and ends that lay around in a person's subconscious.

She grinned, thumbed her hair behind her ears and got to her feet. The only surprise was that it had taken her so long to figure it out.

She'd told Olive she'd never heard so much as a word about Charon's Crossing until she'd inherited it, or about Lord Arthur Russell and his daughter until today.

Well, that was true.

It just wasn't accurate.

Kathryn plucked the scrub brush out of the bucket and up-ended the dirty water into the toilet. Then she dumped the brush back in, collected the bottle of Mr. Clean, and made her way to the kitchen.

Her father would have surely talked about Charon's Crossing and its occupants at some point during the years. Trevor would have reveled in all that history and romantic nonsense. A mansion set in the midst of a tropical paradise, built by an ancestor with a beautiful, passionate daughter caught up in what might have been a love triangle . . .

Hell. Trevor wouldn't have been able to resist.

Of course, he'd have talked about it. Kathryn had either been too young to care or she'd tuned him out, something she knew she'd done a lot once she'd figured out that her father was never going to settle down and be like everybody else's father. Either way, her trusty subconscious had obviously stored the

information neatly away until she'd gotten word that she'd inherited Charon's Crossing. The news had unlocked that long
forgotten mental file drawer, and she had dreamed. Of the
house, the garden . . . of Cat Russell's lover. And yes, the
dreams would have been rich in detail. Her father would have
described everything, thanks to his artist's perspective.

Kathryn put her cleaning tools back into their cabinet,
slammed the door with a flourish, and smiled.

"Sorry about that, Matthew," she said, "but that's the end
of the story."

Her smile wavered. Well, no. Not quite. The tales her father
had told her couldn't explain the sexiness of her dreams. Her
own imagination had taken over there.

So what? A little erotic fantasy might be good for the soul.
Good for her relationship with Jason, too, she thought as she
trotted up the stairs towards her bedroom for a quick shower.

It really would have been nice if he'd been able to fly down
with her. A little sun, a little R and R . . . who knew what
might have happened? Charon's Crossing, decrepit as it was,
might be just the aphrodisiac they needed . . .

"Damn!"

Kathryn paused midway up the steps, her hand on the banister and her face tilted up to the shadows that late afternoon
had brought to the second floor landing.

There it was again, that bone-chilling rush of cold air.

Could it be coming from the attic, as Olive had suggested?

It was the only place she hadn't checked. Well, she could
do that now, before she showered, and spiders and their webs
be damned.

The steps leading to the attic were at the farthest end of the
East Wing hallway. It was the wing that had not been cleaned,
the one Amos had said was in far worse shape than the rest
of the house.

She'd made a quick circuit of it yesterday afternoon, during
her search for the source of the draft. She hadn't lingered in
any of its rooms. There were no broken windows but they all

felt chilly and the lighting in them had seemed dimmer and even less dependable than in the rest of the house.

And the steps leading to the attic had seemed to rise up and up into the shadows, becoming distorted until they'd disappeared into the darkness . . .

Kathryn stopped and turned around. What she needed was a flashlight. Hadn't there been one tucked into one of the kitchen drawers?

She found the flashlight easily enough. A flick of the switch proved that it worked, even if the beam of light it cast wasn't as bright as it might have been. Then she made her way back to the second floor and the staircase that led to the attic.

It was really little more than a ladder, narrow, and steeply pitched with an insubstantial wooden railing. She clutched it firmly with one hand while the fingers of the other closed tightly around the flashlight.

The steps creaked and sagged beneath her feet. She took each one carefully; the wooden railing felt so shaky that she had no illusions about its ability to prevent an accident.

At the top of the stairs, she paused. The landing ahead of her was narrow and dark; the enclosed space, coupled with the shadowy darkness, gave the closed attic door a strange perspective, making it seem tilted and weirdly out of plumb.

Kathryn hesitated.

Maybe it made more sense to wait until Hiram came by. Or Amos. Or . . .

"Oh, stop it," she muttered. "Are you a woman or a wuss?"

It was only an attic. And yes, there had to be a broken window behind that door; she could see a space between the bottom of the door and the jamb and feel a cold breeze blowing across her feet.

The breath hissed between her teeth when she closed her fingers around the knob. It was almost shockingly cold to the touch. A chill danced along her spine; she almost snatched back her hand . . .

Instead, she turned the knob, half-hoping it would be locked.

With a creaking sound, like a fingernail scraping down a blackboard, the door swung open into blackness.

The cold was much more pronounced. Kathryn hesitated. Maybe she ought to go back and get a sweater . . .

"Maybe you ought to stop looking for excuses," she said, and she turned on the flashlight and stepped forward at the same instant.

For one terrible, gut-wrenching second, she thought she had stepped into space. She cried out . . .

And recovered her balance. One low step led down from the door into the attic itself, and she'd just missed it.

Great. Just great! If she wasn't careful, she was going to scare herself to death. Hiram-the-Invisible would finally put in an appearance and he'd find her up here, stiff as a board, the flashlight clutched in her fear-frozen hand.

Kathryn gave a nervous laugh. At least she'd be rid of Charon's Crossing!

Or maybe it would be rid of her.

But, in the light cast by her flashlight, she could see that the attic was just an attic. The walls were unpainted, the floor wide-planked. Boxes and barrels stood along the walls; bits and pieces of old furniture cluttered at least half the floor space.

The flashlight beam swept over the windows. Both were shuttered, making it impossible to tell if the glass was cracked or broken.

She made her way to them gingerly. The windows opened easily but the shutters protested. Finally, she got them open and she could see that the glass was intact.

How to explain the draft, then? Although, strangely enough, now that she was inside the attic itself, it didn't feel very cold.

It was probably some kind of physical anomaly. She swung the beam of the flashlight up, towards the rafters. Yes. That was probably it. Olive had suggested the roof might need fixing. Well, if there was a hole in the roof wouldn't the air get sucked down through it and get funneled through here? Something like that, anyway.

There was plenty of light up here now, too, with the shutters open. Kathryn switched off the flashlight and took a longer look around her.

Not bad. Not bad, at all. She ran a finger across the dust-coated surface of what looked like a walnut secretary.

"Nice," she said.

The piece alongside it was nice, too. It was a rocker, almost definitely hand-crafted.

And a trunk. The trunk was really beautiful.

Kathryn knelt beside it. "Wow," she breathed.

You could put what she knew about antiques into a thimble and have room left to spare but even she could tell that this was one very handsome piece of work. It was very old, she was certain, and made of wood and brass. Both had stood the test of time surprisingly well. The wood—cherry, maybe?— glowed. The brass bands around it were as bright as if they'd been polished yesterday. The lock was open, and hung lightly from the hasp.

Kathryn ran her hand over the rounded lid. It felt smooth and warm beneath her fingers. She hesitated, then reached for the lock, slipped it through the hasp and lifted the lid.

Well, that was disappointing. There was nothing inside. Nothing important, anyway. A fringed silk square, very old and very delicate. A froth of ivory muslin . . .

She set both aside when she saw the book.

It lay centered on a swath of black fabric, its leather binding seeming to glow in the ray of afternoon sunlight slanting through the window. There were words embossed across the leather face in time-dulled gold, but it was impossible to read them.

Kathryn felt an odd catch in her throat. Carefully, she lifted the book from where it lay. She rose to her feet, carried it closer to the window, and angled it into the sun.

In the blaze of sunlight, the embossed words seemed to leap with flame.

The Journal of Matthew McDowell.

She felt her knees turn to jelly. She reached back, grasped the rocker, and eased down into it.

"The Journal of Matthew McDowell"? She stared at the slim volume. What was it doing here, in the attic at Charon's Crossing? After a moment's hesitation, she opened the book and turned to the first page.

Time had tinted it a soft shade of ivory but the entry penned upon it was as dark and legible as if it had been freshly made.

"October the third, 1811," she read softly. "At last, we have arrived at our destination . . ."

"At last, we have arrived at our destination."
Matthew McDowell, Captain of the sloop o'war *Atropos,* paused with his quill in his hand. Then he dipped it into the ink and bent over his leather-bound journal again.
On this day, we lay to anchor in the harbor of Elizabeth Island. The men raised a cheer in which I could not help but join, for the sea has been untimely rough these past days. All that is behind us now, and Atropos *is none the worse for wear, as I had anticipated, for she is the finest and fastest ship it has ever been my pleasure to sail.*

Matthew paused again and reread his words. It was nothing less than the truth, he thought, smiling as he closed the journal and put aside his quill. *Atropos* was a ship to make any man proud. The finest shipyard in Baltimore had built her, and her wealthy Virginia backers had not stinted on her cost. She was a beauty, a clipper-rigged, two-masted sloop, and she would surely outrun the wind, if he asked it of her.

And he would, for he had every intention of succeeding beyond his backers' wildest dreams. He would seize more French ships and contraband cargo than any other captain in these waters. How could he not? He had the best ship and crew, men who had sailed under him before, on the *Corinthian.*

His backers would recover their investment many times over.

And Matthew, at thirty-three, would be wealthy beyond his wildest dreams.

He put the stopper in the inkwell, then laid away his quill and his journal in the drawer of his writing desk. You didn't spend more than twenty years of your life at sea without learning the value of neatness. You learned to duck your head when you stood up, too; he did it now automatically, for at six feet, two inches he was too tall for the cabin.

Still, his quarters were damned near luxurious compared to any he'd known before. In his cabin on the *Corinthian*, flexing his broad shoulders and stretching as he was now, meant he'd probably have ended up putting his fists through the bulkheads.

Matthew crossed the cabin to the washstand, unbuttoned his shirt and shrugged it off. He would always have fond memories of the *Corinthian*. A man didn't forget his first command any more than he forgot his first woman, but there was no comparison between the creaking old merchant ship and this one.

Robins, his steward, had dutifully filled a pitcher with hot water and left it on the washstand, together with some shaving gear. Matthew poured a stream of water into the blue china basin, worked a bit of lather out of the coarse soap that lay on the stand, and briskly began washing his face, chest and arms.

Corinthian had been built to ply the trade route between Boston and Plymouth. *Atropos* was not destined for such a plebian existence. She was to sail the warm waters of the Caribbean under a British flag so that her American captain and crew could stop and seize the French merchantmen that were foolish enough to venture here, for the English and the French were at war.

Some said that privateers like *Atropos* were nothing but pirate vessels cloaked in a veneer of wartime expediency, but Matthew had never given a damn for anyone's opinion but his own. A man could make his fortune here, if he had the guts for it. Hell, the risks inherent in hunting down and taking a rich prize were what made the game interesting.

He was too young to spend the rest of his life rotting on

the beach with the other victims of a president's foreign policy that kept New England seamen from trading with the French and the English.

As for the danger of his new command . . . there ought to be some danger in life. Some challenge, to keep a man's blood flowing hot.

He looked into the mirror above the washstand and spread a lather of foam over his face, then reached for his straight razor and stropped it to a keen edge.

That was what he was hoping to find tonight. A challenge, but of another sort. Smiling, he tilted up his face, positioned the thumb and forefinger of his left hand on his jaw, and drew the razor down his lightly stubbled cheek.

He had been invited to have dinner this evening at Charon's Crossing, the home of Lord Arthur Russell. Russell was the Crown's representative in these waters but, of far more importance to Matthew, he was also the agent of the cartel that had backed *Atropos*.

Matthew rinsed the blade in the basin, then brought it to his face again. Russell was to provide him with the letter of marque that would permit him to stop and seize French ships and take them, and their cargo, as prizes.

Matthew looked into the mirror again, his straight white teeth flashing in a quick grin.

He wanted that letter, certainly. But he was equally eager for a first-hand look at Russell's daughter, Catherine.

No sailor would ever admit it but seamen were a romantic lot, as given to boozy flights of fancy as any poet. Matthew had heard more than one man sigh into his bitters as he extolled the fairness of Lady Catherine Russell.

He wiped the last traces of lather from his face, reached for a fresh linen shirt, and pulled it on. He had a fast ship, a sapphire sea to sail her in, and the promise of riches beyond his dreams. Now, if the stories he'd heard turned out to be true and not the fanciful tales of men who'd been too long at sea, he would also have a playmate with whom he could pleasantly while away the hours whenever *Atropos* was in port.

Matthew grinned at his reflection. It was immodest, perhaps, but what was the sense in playing at being humble? Even if Catherine Russell turned out to be a rival for Venus herself, she would succumb to his charms. Matthew had not been lucky in the circumstances of his birth nor of his early years, and whatever he had today—his command, his knowledge of the sea and of ships—he had worked mightily to attain.

But when it came to women . . . ah, when it came to women, he was charmed. They had always flocked to him, as a boy to offer comfort and as a man . . . He grinned again. As a man, they offered everything they had, eagerly, willingly. Excitingly.

He had left half a dozen conquests behind, in Boston, in Plymouth, in Baltimore and in places far more exotic. Tavern wenches, duchesses, ladies of the manor and even a royal princess had wept copious tears at each departure. Matthew had tried to feel sorrowful as he'd held them in his arms and soothed them but in truth, he'd already been thinking ahead, to the next ship and the next woman.

Now, he had a new ship, the finest on the seas. Tonight, with luck, he would find the other. A man needed a diversion. And that was all a woman could ever be, a diversion. A woman could warm a man's bed. But a ship—ah, a ship could steal a man's heart.

Matthew gave himself one final glance in the mirror. His hair was its usual defiant self, the sun-lightened, softly curling strands struggling to break free of their ribbon. His razor had left his face smooth without imposing any nicks. And the royal blue dress jacket with its high collar and gold frogs, made to order in Baltimore at the expense of his backers, would surely not be out of place at Russell's fancy dinner table tonight, nor would his cream-colored trousers and well-polished, black, knee-high boots.

A knock sounded at the cabin door.

"Come," Matthew barked.

The door swung open and Robins stepped across the threshold and knuckled his forehead.

"Sir," he said. "The gig is at the mainchains."

Matthew nodded. The boy was barely eleven, a year older than he had been when he'd first gone to sea. Had his youth, hopes and dreams, been as clearly inscribed upon his face as they were on this boy's? God, he surely hoped not.

"Thank you, Robins." He strapped on his sabre, then swung towards the boy. "Well? What do you think, lad? Will His Lordship be properly impressed?"

Robins nodded stiffly. "Aye, sir."

"And Mistress Russell? Will I impress her, as well?"

The slightest possible smile twitched at the corners of the boy's lips.

"Indeed, sir. I am certain you will."

Matthew grinned. "Thank you, lad. Oh, and by the way, Robins . . . ?"

The boy's heels damn near clicked together. "Sir?"

"If you're going to sneak into the galley and raid Cookie's sweets, you must remember to wipe your mouth."

Never pausing, Matthew made his way up the ladder to the deck, and to what he hoped would be the first of many pleasant evenings. The carriage Lord Russell had sent for him was waiting at dockside. It was an elegant barouche, emblazoned with the Russell coat of arms and drawn by a pair of perfectly matched, high-stepping greys. It was also complete with a liveried coachman and footman. Both men were black. Were they free men, Matthew wondered, or slaves? Slavery was a fact of life in these islands, as it was in some of the American states, but that didn't change Matthew's dislike of the practice.

The coachman tipped his hat.

"Evenin', sir."

"Good evening," Matthew said, waving off the footman who was already scrambling down to help him into the carriage.

The whip cracked the air and they set off. Matthew looked about him with interest. *Atropos* had docked the day before, but save for a brief visit to the Customs Office, he had spent no time in Hawkins Bay.

Now, by the fading light of dusk, he saw that it was a larger settlement than he had thought. Front Street, which gave onto the docks, was a hodgepodge of customs houses and narrow wooden buildings that seemed to offer everything a seafarer could possibly want. Shipbuilders, suppliers of salt pork and hardtack, makers of hemp line and tar jockeyed for position. And interspersed among those establishments were the taverns, what looked to be nearly one for every ship that lay at anchor in the harbor. The tropical air was heavy with the scent of rum and cheap perfume that wafted out their doors along with the shriek of coarse female laughter.

More dignified commercial buildings lined the next street. Not that banks and trading corporations were all that dignified, Matthew thought with a little smile. His Virginia backers, for all their blueblood lineage, fine homes and fancy airs, had proven themselves as determined to wring every penny from a dollar as any ship's chandler.

The paved roadway ended and became packed dirt. They were in the residential section of town now, first passing what were surely rooming houses. Matthew had seen enough of them in enough ships' ports halfway around the globe to be able to pick them out even at a distance. Then, as the road began to climb, the houses grew bigger and stood further apart, the homes, no doubt, of Hawkins Bay's merchants and bankers.

Finally, there were no houses at all, only the now-narrow road, climbing into lush hills that looked as untouched as they must have been when Europeans had first come to these islands. Everywhere there were flowers, sending their sweet scent into the night. Birdsong had given way to the chirrups of a chorus of insect voices. It was fully dark now, save for an enormous, butter yellow moon rising into a sky bright with stars.

Matthew sat back in the leather seat. He folded his hands behind his head, stretched out his long legs, and crossed his ankles.

Surely Lord Russell's daughter would be beautiful. How could she be anything less, in such a paradise as this? Half an hour later, the slowing of the horses roused him from a light slumber.

Matthew leaned forward as the carriage drew to a halt. Years at sea had taught him the value of caution; he laid his hand lightly on the handle of his sabre.

"Driver? Why are we stopping?"

"We got to open the gates, sir."

"What gates?"

"Why, the gates to Charon's Crossin'."

Matthew stood in the carriage. Ahead, like black stripes painted against the charcoal of the night, loomed a high iron gate. As he watched, the footman undid the lock and leapt aside just as the coachman shouted to the horses, which lunged ahead and up a rise. The scent of night-blooming flowers was strong, interspersed with the ever-present salt tang of the sea.

A blaze of light filtered through the trees. Matthew whistled softly through his teeth.

"Is that the house?" he said, raising his voice over the sound of hooves pounding against gravel.

The coachman nodded. "Charon's Crossin', sir."

By the time the coach pulled up before the house, the blaze of light had sorted itself into easily a dozen candlelit windows, augmented by the flames rising from oil-burning torchères in the courtyard.

The front door swung open at his knock. Laughter, conversation, music and the smell of fine wines and expensive foods encompassed him.

"Sir?"

Matthew looked at the liveried butler standing squarely in the open doorway. His face was black, but his accent was straight from the rarefied reaches of upper London society. And if the look on his face meant anything, so was his attitude.

Matthew smiled pleasantly. "Good evening. Captain Matthew McDowell, of the *Atropos*, to see Lord Russell."

The butler's nose almost twitched. "The American vessel, sir?"

"Exactly," Matthew said, still pleasantly.

The butler nodded. "I shall see if his lordship is available."

"I am sure he is."

"If you will wait here, sir . . ."

The door began to shut. Matthew wedged his foot in it and smiled coldly.

"I don't wait on any man's doorstep. Either announce me, man, or I shall announce myself."

"Sir, I am afraid . . ."

"Indeed, you had better be. I have been at sea for weeks and I am in no mood to be—"

"Brutus?" The voice coming from behind the butler was soft and feminine and delicately English. "What is the problem?"

"There is no problem, Miss. It's just this . . . this gentleman wants to see your father, and I've explained to him that—"

"He has explained," Matthew said, pushing the door open and stepping inside the marble-floored entry foyer, "that American upstarts are, perhaps, not quite good enough to mingle in genteel English society. And I, in turn, was explaining to him that—that . . ."

His words trailed away. The girl was standing at the foot of a wide staircase. Her hair was the color of night, drawn back from her face and piled atop her head, though soft ringlets of it lay alluringly against her delicate cheeks and brow. Her eyes were as blue as the sky on a summer morning, her mouth was small and full and looked as if it had been stained with wild cherries. She was wearing a white gown that looked as if it were made of gossamer, and cut so that the neckline framed her perfect white shoulders and creamy bosom.

Matthew's heart turned over. He had heard Catherine Russell was beautiful but no one had prepared him for this. By God, she was the most exquisite creature he had ever seen.

"Lady Russell?" he said, when he could trust himself to speak. "Catherine Russell?"

"Sir." The butler's voice was chill with disapproval. "I ask you again to please wait until—"

The girl waved her hand in a gesture of dismissal. "That will be all, Brutus."

The butler's eyes narrowed but he bowed respectfully. "As you wish."

Catherine Russell waited until Brutus had disappeared. Then she came slowly forward, smiling as she advanced.

"You have the better of me, sir. You know my name, but I fear I do not know yours."

Matthew plucked off his tricorn hat and made her a low, sweeping bow.

"I am Matthew McDowell, ma'am, captain of the *Atropos*, and I am your servant."

"Indeed," she said softly. Matthew looked up. She was smiling at him in a way that made his head spin. There was an ivory fan in her right hand; she raised it and fluttered it lightly before her face. "My father has spoken of you, Captain. He said you were brave and courageous." Her eyes met his. "But he never mentioned that you were also handsome."

A slow smile angled across Matthew's mouth. "Then it is I who have the better of you," he said softly, as he covered the distance between them. He stopped inches away, so that Catherine had to tilt her head back to see his face. "For I knew, even before I laid eyes on you, that you were the most beautiful woman in all this hemisphere."

Catherine gave a low, breathless laugh. Life at Charon's Crossing and on this dreary bit of England in the New World was almost painfully dull. She had found the eligible males wanting in looks, the ineligible ones wanting in charm, and all of them wanting in wit. Her father, who had spoiled and coddled her all her life, urged her to maintain social relationships with the daughters of the bankers and rich merchants who populated Elizabeth Island, but Catherine had long ago found time spent with ambitionless members of her own sex boring.

"I wish I could do something to make you happier," her

father had said, just this evening, as she had lamented the awful sameness of another dinner party at which she had no wish to pretend to be the gracious hostess.

Now, it looked as if her father had fulfilled his own wish, albeit unknowingly, for she knew instantly that Matthew McDowell was going to make her happier. She knew of him, of course. He had come to sail these waters at the behest of her father and men like him, though she knew her father spoke of him with disdain.

"We need this man," she'd heard her father say, when she'd lingered outside his study as he'd discussed the war with the French with influential friends, "but we must not forget he is little more than a pirate, a hired ruffian to do our bidding."

Ruffian Matthew McDowell might be, but he was also stunningly handsome. Those shoulders. That chest, and those narrow hips and long, long legs. And oh, that hard, gorgeous face . . .

Oh yes. Clearly, things at Charon's Crossing were going to be much more interesting from now on.

"Ah, dear sir," Catherine said, fluttering her ivory fan with a practiced gesture, "I am disappointed, being told I am the most beautiful woman only in this hemisphere. I had hoped for more."

Matthew smiled into her eyes. "You misunderstood me, Miss Russell. The nations of the Old World have transplanted their fairest flowers here, to the New. And since you are, without doubt, the loveliest of them, so are you therefore the loveliest in all the world."

Catherine threw back her head and gave a peal of musical laughter.

"You are quick with words, Captain," she said, laying her hand lightly on his arm. "You must come and let me introduce you to my father. I am sure he will be delighted to make your acquaintance at long last."

* * *

"Delighted" was not the word Matthew would have used to describe Lord Russell's reaction to him.

Catherine's father was coldly polite but it was clear that he would never have invited a man like Matthew to dine at his table under more normal circumstances.

But these were not normal circumstances. The French ships that plied these waters were rich prizes but the Crown could not spare its own vessels to chase and capture them. British warships were busy blockading the French ports in the Bay of Biscay and in the Mediterranean, keeping imports from reaching Napoleon's armies on the Peninsula.

It was a situation that made for strange bedfellows. Or strange dining companions, Matthew thought, smiling to himself as he sipped an excellent glass of French wine and listened with half an ear to the breathy chatter of the woman seated to his right. She was a baroness, she was exceedingly beautiful and, as she'd made clear from the moment she'd laid eyes on Matthew, she was available.

But Matthew had eyes only for Catherine Russell. Every man at the crowded table did, for that matter. And she had eyes for all of them . . . but none for him.

What had happened to the promises he'd read in her eyes when they'd met in the entry foyer?

By the time dinner had ended and dancing had begun in the brightly lit ballroom, Matthew was half crazed with jealousy. Catherine laughed gaily at other men's jokes, she smiled at them and danced with them . . .

And ignored him completely. He waited until she was, for a brief instant, alone. Then he strode up to her and took her hands in his.

"You promised me this dance, Mistress Russell," he said.

Catherine looked surprised. "I believe you are wrong, Captain. I promised this dance to—"

Matthew had already swept her onto the dance floor.

"Do not argue with me," he warned, and when they danced past a pair of French doors, opened to let in the cool night breeze, he swept her through them and out into the darkness of the terrace. "Now, madam. Tell me why you have been deliberately ignoring me?"

"I shall tell you nothing, sir, for you are no gentleman to treat a lady thus."

"Nay." Matthew drew her deeper into the shadows. "I am no gentleman, Catherine. I am a man who takes what he wishes, and what I wish most is a kiss from your sweet lips."

Catherine laughed. "You must steal it then. But not tonight," she added quickly as he began to bend towards her. "I shall meet you tomorrow, in the rose garden."

Matthew nodded. He reached out and traced the outline of her mouth with his finger, gently parting it until he was stroking softly over the delicate, moist flesh inside her bottom lip.

"Tell me the hour, Catherine, and I will be there."

Oh, she thought, as he touched her, he was good at this game. She would not be able to toy with him as easily as she had toyed with so many others. That was good. The element of risk and of danger would add to her pleasure.

She looked into his eyes, smiled, and flicked the tip of her tongue against his fingertip. Matthew felt his body clench like a fist.

She was so beautiful. So seductive. And, by God, so innocent. It was a paradox but one he was sure he understood. She had felt the same lightning bolt as he; it was why she was almost swooning as she leaned towards him, why she sucked his finger into her mouth . . .

"Catherine?"

The harsh voice drove them apart. Catherine swung towards the doors that led back into the ballroom.

"Father!" Her smile lost its seductive tilt. She clasped Matthew's arm and drew him forward into the spill of light from the house. "How fortuitous! I was just about to go looking for you. Father, Captain McDowell is not feeling well."

Russell's close-set eyes narrowed. "Is that why you brought

my daughter out here, Captain? So that she might keep you company in your illness?"

Matthew started to answer but Catherine's hand squeezed a warning.

"It was my idea, Father. We were dancing and all at once, the captain turned pale, excused himself and bolted for the doors." Catherine let go of Matthew's arm and stepped closer to Russell. "I suppose I should have let him go, Father, but then I thought, how would it look if I shunned my duty as your hostess and permitted one of your guests to stagger off and collapse unnoticed?"

A muscle clenched in Russell's jaw.

"You could have sent one of the servants after him, Catherine."

Catherine sighed and laid her head against her father's shoulder.

"Of course. How I wish I'd been clever enough to have thought of that."

Russell's expression softened. "Go on inside, my dear, and tend to our other guests."

She smiled and kissed his cheek. "Yes, Father. Good night, Captain McDowell. I trust you'll remember what I told you? Some tea brewed from cinchona bark will have you feeling better in no time. Why, twelve hours from now, you'll be fit as a fiddle."

Twelve hours from now? Matthew's eyes shot to Catherine's and she gave him an almost imperceptible nod. That was when she would meet him, then, on the morrow.

The speed with which she'd woven a tale to deceive her father, coupled with the ease with which she'd given him the hour of tomorrow's assignation, was dazzling. Matthew revised his earlier estimate of Catherine. She was not only the most beautiful woman he'd ever met, she was also the brightest.

He smiled politely, took the hand she offered him, and bowed over it as he raised it to his lips.

"Thank you, Lady Catherine. You have been most kind and I am indebted to you."

She smiled brightly. "It was nothing, Captain. But if you truly wish, you may repay that debt by being our guest at Charon's Crossing again soon. You can tell me all the latest gossip from the colonies."

Matthew knew nothing of social gossip. And he had flattened more than one fool who still insisted on referring to the American states as "colonies." *But, at that moment, if Catherine Russell had told him the moon was made of green cheese, he would not have argued . . .*

A gust of wind, blowing in from across the sea, slammed one of the attic shutters against the wall of the house.

The book fell from Kathryn's hands. She jumped to her feet, almost totally disoriented. The shutter banged again, and she let out her breath.

Slowly, she bent down and picked up Matthew McDowell's journal. Landing face-down on the floor didn't seem to have harmed it any. She brushed it off carefully, shut it, and laid it on the rocker.

How long had she been reading, anyway? Long enough for the sun to have changed its angle in the sky. She had to lift her hand and tilt it towards the window in order to read her watch.

"Wow," she whispered.

What else could you say, when you found out four hours had passed in what felt like a minute?

The man wrote a heck of an interesting diary, she had to give him that much. Descriptive, too, she thought, and smiled.

Her smile faded. She remembered what he had written, that he had stroked his finger across Catherine Russell's mouth and she had parted her lips so she could taste his skin.

Kathryn felt the quickening beat of her heart. That was what had happened to her, last night. In her dream, Matthew had touched her mouth that same way. She could close her eyes now and still recall the eroticism of that moment, the heat of his fingertip moving across her lips, how she'd longed to do what the other Catherine had done, to draw his finger into her mouth and skim the tip of her tongue over it . . .

"Oh, for goodness' sakes!"

Enough already! The old book was fascinating. It was an interesting artifact and if she found the time, she'd probably pick it up again some afternoon. But that was all there was to it. The journal didn't have a damned thing to do with her or with her crazy dreams.

As for Matthew's grandiose description of himself as a lady-killer . . .

She laughed as she drew the shutters closed and locked them. Nothing much had changed, in two hundred years. Men still had mighty high opinions of themselves.

"You were probably a prissy old prude, Captain," she said.

She snatched up the flashlight and, without a backward glance, marched out the door and slammed it firmly behind her.

Silence filled the attic. Then a quicksilver light began to glimmer beside the rocker where the journal lay. The light moved swiftly towards the window and the shutters burst open, admitting fresh air and the natural light of the sun.

The light began to spin, slowly at first, then gathering speed until it became a whirlpool and the figure of a man appeared within its brilliant heart.

"A prude, was I, Catherine?" Matthew said.

He smiled tightly. The light began to shift and fade, as did he, until all that remained were dust motes, dancing in the fading rays of the sun.

Six

Kathryn was furious.

She'd been at Charon's Crossing for three days, and she had nothing to show for it.

No, she thought grimly, as she yanked a dustcloth and a spray-can of Pledge from under the kitchen sink, no, that wasn't true.

She had plenty to show for her stay. A clean kitchen, sanitized bathrooms, three broken fingernails and enough weird dreams to keep a New York shrink happy for the rest of his or her Freudian life.

"Damn," she muttered as she strode into the library.

This morning, she was going to dust the leather-bound books that lined the library shelves. Then she'd wax the furniture to within an inch of its life. And for an encore, she was going to drag all the Persian runners out to the terrace, spread them over the railing and beat the hell out of them with a broom.

Oh yeah. She was going to score a perfect 10 in housekeeping. Of course, that wouldn't change the fact that she'd scored a perfect zero when it came to doing what she'd set out to do when she'd taken a week out of her life and flown down here.

"Damn," she said again, and gave the closest books an angry swipe with the cleaning cloth. Dust erupted into the air. Kathryn jumped back but it was too late. Half a dozen explosive sneezes almost drove her back against the wall.

She flung the cloth to the floor, slapped her hands on her

hips, and eyed the library as if it had turned into her own personal Rubicon.

What in hell was she doing?

She hadn't come to the island to turn into a housekeeper, she'd come to ready this miserable house for sale and to manage that, she was going to need help from an attorney who didn't pull a vanishing act, a realtor who gave a damn, and a contractor who really existed.

And she couldn't even tell anybody that, dammit, because her rental car hadn't turned up and her telephone might as well have been used for a doorstop.

Kathryn dropped down into the sagging depths of a flowered settee. Dust rose into the air but she ignored it.

Now what?

She lifted one bare leg, crossed it over the other, pointed her toes towards the ceiling and swung her foot from side to side.

As far as she could see, she had two choices. She could sit here like a lump and wait until Olive or Amos or the Invisible Repairman decided to put in an appearance. Or she could take matters into her own hands. It was, what? Five miles to town? Make that more like fifteen, along a road that twisted like a snake.

Well, so what? Surely, she wouldn't have to walk the whole distance. Once she went out the gate and down to the road, somebody would stop and give her a lift.

Kathryn smiled. She hadn't smiled much, the past few days, and it was surprising how good it felt.

She uncrossed her legs, slapped her hands on her thighs, and got to her feet.

Her days of being a prisoner in paradise were about to come to an end.

Taking a shower in Charon's Crossing was almost a duplicate of taking one back home.

You got undressed, you put on your robe, you went into the bathroom, you turned on the hot water . . . and you waited.

And waited.

And waited some more.

Eventually, the water got warm enough and you stepped beneath the spray.

Then you shampooed and soaped and scrubbed and rinsed without wasting so much as a second because you knew the hot water wasn't going to last much longer.

Talk about destiny! Was she going to go through life plagued by heating systems that just plain didn't want to do what they were supposed to do?

Kathryn sighed, shut off the water, and shoved the shower curtain back just far enough so she could reach out and fumble for her bath towel. Even drying off wasn't easy. Whoever had mounted the towel bar had either never bothered measuring the distance from it to the tub or he'd had arms like a gorilla. The towels hung just two or three inches too far to be reached easi . . .

She froze.

The towel had just about leaped into her hand.

Either her arms had grown longer—or someone had handed the towel to her.

Goose bumps rose all along her skin.

"Don't be crazy," she whispered.

She was alone in the bathroom. And in the house. Every door was locked, even this one. She knew it was silly but ever since Olive had come into the house unannounced, she'd made it a point to lock doors. The front one. The rear ones. The one to her bedroom at night and to the bathroom, any time she was in it.

Okay. So there was a rational explanation for what had just happened.

She wrapped the towel around herself and held it together with one hand. Then she took a deep breath, pulled open the curtain . . .

. . . and burst into gales of relieved laughter.

She wasn't alone after all.

A tiny green chameleon, looking more like a lapel pin than a lizard, clung to the wall beside the sink. It was basking in the sun spilling through the open window along with a warm, lazy breeze—a breeze that, even as she watched, playfully lifted the edge of the remaining towel on the rack so that it flapped towards the shower.

So much for the Great Towel Mystery.

"You see?" Kathryn said to the chameleon. "There's always a rational explanation." She sighed. "I knew that, when I got off that plane the other day. My problem is that I've been trapped in this crazy house too long."

The tiny lizard fixed her with an unblinking stare and bobbed its head. Kathryn grinned.

"Thank you," she said, "I'm glad we agree."

Humming softly under her breath, she hurried down the hall to her bedroom to get dressed.

The shaft of sunlight that illuminated the bathroom blazed brighter and brighter, until it was a shimmering sweep of quicksilver.

The little green chameleon lifted its head, then scuttled away in terror as Matthew emerged from the light's pulsing heart.

"Hell," he growled.

What a damned fool game for a grown man to play. Well, maybe that was the wrong description, all things considered.

"Hell," he said again, shooting a hand through his hair.

Man or spirit, spying on Catherine had been stupid. It had been childish. It had even been dangerous. If Cat had somehow seen him, there was a damned good chance she'd have stumbled in fear, fallen down and, perhaps, snapped her pretty neck.

He was reserving that pleasure for himself. No slippery bathtub was going to cheat him out of his revenge!

A slow smile eased across his mouth. Still, it had been worth the risk. The sight of her, wearing nothing but that towel as she stepped from the tub . . . Her long legs, the thrust of her breasts, the water beading like tiny jewels on her creamy shoulders . . .

An all-too-familiar tightness curled through his loins.

"Hell," he said again, folding his arms over his chest and glowering.

Catherine wasn't the only one who'd been in this damned house too long!

He was behaving like a boy, and for what reason? That Catherine was beautiful had never been in dispute. That she could make a man want her in the same way he wanted to draw breath into his lungs was a given.

Delilah must have been beautiful, too, and desirable, to have talked Samson into that fatal haircut.

Beauty and desire weren't worth a damn when they were masks for that which was evil. And Catherine was evil; there was no doubt about that.

He took a deep breath, then another. He would have to be more careful from now on. He had been the soul of discretion since she had found his journal in the attic. It was important to him that she read the rest of it, before he put an end to the farce they'd been playing.

So he had kept his distance, watching and waiting . . .

But for what?

It was clear that she was in no rush to read the rest of his journal. His mouth twisted. Why should she, when she knew the ending?

Dammit, he wanted her to read it! Otherwise, how could he be certain she knew what it was that drove him? She had to understand that the memory of her treachery had not been dimmed by time.

Matthew frowned.

How much time, exactly? He had no way of telling. Had a year passed since his death? Two? More?

He was beginning to think it might be far more than he'd imagined.

There were changes in this house that baffled him.

There was no oil in the lamps, yet they blazed with light when night came.

There was no cooking fireplace in the room that was clearly the kitchen, but there was a white iron box on which Catherine cooked food. There was another box, too, one that kept things icy cold.

As for this room . . .

It was extraordinary. Water gushed from the tub and from a basin set in the washstand at the twist of a knob, and there was a porcelain chair whose function he thought he was beginning to comprehend even though logic told him such a thing could not exist.

Catherine's father was rich, but not even the King of England had such contraptions. Matthew thrust his fingers through his hair and paced the room. Some said George III was crazy, but he doubted if even a crazy man could imagine such wonders as these.

And that wasn't all of it.

The most astounding thing was the simplest.

Catherine had come here without servants.

There was no one to dress her, to brush her hair, to make her bed and cook her meals . . .

By God, there was no one to do the common cleaning. Coming upon her yesterday, on her hands and knees with a bucket of filthy water at her side and a scrub brush in her hands like any common housemaid, he'd been so stunned that he'd damn near materialized right in front of her.

Everything was different. Catherine, the house . . .

How much time had passed since his death?

He leaned back against the washstand, a muscle knotting and unknotting in his jaw.

Years. Far more than one or two. But not too many, for Catherine had not aged. Surely, she would not still be so young and beautiful if . . . if . . .

"I am not Catherine," she had said, that first time he had come to her in a dream.

But she was. Of course, she was. She was Catherine's image, she was in Catherine's house . . .

Matthew shut his eyes and took a deep, steadying breath. A second later, he slipped through her closed bedroom door. Catherine was standing before a cracked oval mirror, brushing out her hair. She was dressed in a white cotton skirt and a white top. Both exposed far too much flesh but compared to everything else she wore, he supposed you'd call them the height of modesty.

He leaned back against the door, arms folded, and watched her.

Last night, very late, he'd slipped through her closed bedroom, just as he had done a moment ago. The door had been locked, such a pitiful attempt to keep him out that he'd almost laughed. She had been asleep, lying curled on her side in the bed, her features a study in innocence. He had tried, and failed, to recall her ever looking that way in the past they had shared, but he could not.

The sight of her had made his breath quicken. The temptation to draw back the covers and look his fill had been almost overwhelming. Was she wearing that strange clothing in which she'd slept that first night?

He had gritted his teeth and slipped from the room without having satisfied his curiosity. What did it matter what she wore at night? In truth, almost everything she wore during the day had a potent effect on his pulse rate. She spent her days in smallclothes that left little to the imagination.

It angered him, that she would walk around thus. Didn't she give a damn that the sight of her dressed that way would make a man's blood run thick?

Matthew frowned. He was letting his imagination run away with him. Catherine did not think of him as a man. She didn't think of him as anything. Not yet. As far as she knew, he was still only a dream.

She was done brushing her hair. He watched as she gave herself a critical look in the mirror. Then she tossed the brush aside, picked up a purse with a long strap, and headed for the door—and for him.

He caught his breath as she approached. She could not see him. She would not see him, until he permitted it. He knew that. Still, it was folly to let her walk through him. She might sense something. A chill, perhaps; he didn't know . . .

She passed through him as lightly as a breeze would slip through a handful of flowers. He almost groaned as he savored the feel of her body melting through his. And oh, the scent of her . . .

He was wrong! She *had* sensed something. She must have. He saw her suddenly stiffen at the top of the staircase. She hesitated and he heard her breath make a catchy little sound in her throat.

"Oh," she whispered, and then she gave a soft, sweet laugh.

Matthew felt that laugh, right down to the marrow of his bones. God, he had to speak to her. To touch her . . .

"Catherine," he said.

But she was already flying down the steps, racing to the front door and flinging it open.

"Oh, this is terrific," he heard her say, her voice light with pleasure as it had once been only for him. "I thought I heard something coming up the driveway!"

Matthew came down the stairs after her and went through the closed door just as she slammed it.

What the hell was this?

Catherine was standing at the foot of the steps. There was a man at her side, and her laughing face was turned up to his.

And what a specimen the man was. Black hair hung to his shoulders in ringlets and a small golden hoop dangled from one ear. His red silk shirt was undone to the waist; his trousers were torn and ripped, and he wore thick leather sandals.

By God, the bastard was a pirate! Had Cat's passion for dallying with rogues sunk to a new level?

A carriage of some strange sort was drawn up in the drive-way. At least, Matthew assumed it was a carriage. It was the strangest-looking vehicle he had ever seen. It had wheels and doors but no horses to draw it.

"Cat," Matthew said sharply, "wait!"

The pirate opened one of the doors with a bow so deep it was ludicrous. Horrible shrieks rushed out, as if of creatures wailing in agony, but Cat ignored them. She slid gracefully onto the seat and the rogue shut the door after her, went around to the other side of the carriage and climbed inside.

A second later, the vehicle rocked with a small explosion. Black smoke rushed out from behind it and then it shot off down the drive.

Cursing, heart pounding, Matthew raced after it.

How could a carriage move so quickly? How could it move at all, without horses to draw it? There wasn't a chance in hell of his catching up.

The thing turned a corner, picked up speed, and rocketed through the gates that marked the eastern border of Charon's Crossing. Matthew charged after it, refusing to acknowledge what instinct warned him would happen.

The empty space between the gateposts might as well have been fashioned of brick. He hit full tilt, with main and stuns'les set. The force of the impact knocked him backwards and he fell, hard, into the dirt.

Slowly, he rose to his feet. He stared at the open gate, then walked towards it, put out his hand . . . and touched an invisible barrier.

Rage choked him. He drew back his fist, slammed it into the barrier he could not see. He whirled around, grabbed a coconut from where it lay under a palm, and hammered it against the invisible impediment.

It was useless.

The wall could not be seen and neither could it be destroyed.

Panting, he stared down the road. All that remained of the horseless carriage was a fading ribbon of yellow dust.

Matthew groaned, threw the coconut aside and fell back against the palm.

It had never occurred to him a ghost could be out of breath but hell, he certainly was.

And for what? Catherine wasn't worth saving. If she'd been lured away by a rogue, so what? Her welfare was no concern of his; it was only that he wanted to be the man who—the man who . . .

Matthew went very still. Then he turned and slammed his fist against the tree in a blind rage.

"Damn you, Catherine," he bellowed.

His image shimmered like waves of heat rising from a hot sand beach.

An instant later, he had vanished.

Seven

"I can't believe it," Kathryn said happily.

The old Volkswagen Beetle hit a crater-sized hole and the shocks, or what was left of them, groaned. "Here I thought I was going to have to walk to town and there you were, coming up the driveway!"

The boy behind the wheel of the VW looked at her and grinned.

"Cool timing, huh?"

Kathryn grinned back at him. "The coolest. I don't think I've ever been happier to see anybody in my whole life than I was to see you."

"I would have delivered the car yesterday but my father said to fix it up real good 'cause Mr. Amos told him to be sure and give you the very best car we got."

"And this is it," she said solemnly.

"Oh, yes, Miss Russell. You bet. She's as good as new."

The VW backfired, sending an enormous belch of black exhaust into the air, and Kathryn laughed. She felt almost giddy with freedom.

The boy reached out and lowered the volume on the radio. The rhythmic sounds of Bob Marley faded half a dozen decibels.

"So, miss, how do you like our island?"

Kathryn looked at the boy. He couldn't have been more than fourteen or fifteen, and he was dressed as stylishly as any kid back in New York. His hair was long and worn in dreadlocks, his gold earring discreet. His red shirt was casually unbuttoned to take full advantage of his hollow adolescent chest, his jeans were artfully torn, and his sandals were fashionably chunky.

"What's your name?" she asked.

"Efram."

"Well, Efram, your island is very beautiful."

"Is it more beautiful than New York City?"

Kathryn tucked her hair behind her ear and leaned her arm on the door.

"You know that's where I'm from, hmm?"

"Oh yes. You are the first visitor Charon's Crossin' has had in a long time, miss. People talk."

"Well, trust me, Efram. Elizabeth Island has it all over New York when it comes to beauty."

"Really?"

Kathryn smiled. "It was about twenty degrees when I left New York. The sky was grey and the weatherman was predicting snow."

Efram made a face. "Doesn't sound so good."

"Nope. Not if you like blue skies, warm breezes and bright sunshine." She cleared her throat. "So tell me, Efram. What do people say?"

"Ma'am?"

"About me. You said, people talk. I was wondering what it is they talked about."

"You know. That you are from New York, that you are thinkin' of fixin' up Charon's Crossin' . . ."

"I'm fixing it up so I can sell it," Kathryn said emphatically.

"So it is said." The boy shook his head. "Still, some folks are surprised."

"That I'd sell the place?"

Efram grinned. "That you'd stay in that old jumbie house all by your . . ." He shot Kathryn a guilty look. "I mean, that you'd be willin' to, ah, to deal with a job like that all by your-self, miss."

Kathryn scooted into the corner of her seat and looked at him.

"Is that what people call it? A jumbie house?"

Efram's Adam's apple bobbed as he swallowed.

"You know what that means?"

"A spook house, right?"

The boy nodded, his expression one of pure misery.

"Why do they call it that?"

"It is just silliness, miss. I did not mean—"

"I'm sure you didn't but now that you went this far, you might as well tell me the rest. Do people say Charon's Crossing is . . ." She hesitated. Just saying the word was ridiculous. ". . . is haunted?"

Efram hunched lower over the steering wheel. "They say all kinds of foolish things."

"I understand that, but I'm interested. Who haunts the house, do you know? I mean, who's supposed to haunt it?"

"Nobody."

The single word came out in such a rush that Kathryn knew it was untrue. She sighed and leaned her head back.

"Relax, Efram. I don't believe in ghosts."

"Oh, but . . ." The boy shot her another look. "I don't, either, miss."

"But if I did—if I believed in them, and if I thought there was one at Charon's Crossing, who would it be?"

"I don't understand, miss."

"I mean, what would the ghost look like?"

"I don't know."

"Efram, come on. You can tell me. Honestly, it won't bother me."

The boy shifted uneasily in his seat. "I really don't know, miss. I have only heard stories of—things."

"Things?"

"Noises. Moans." He swallowed. "Things."

"Have you heard these 'things,' Efram?"

"Oh never, miss. I would not go into that house . . . I mean, I prefer not to."

"And you've never seen anything?"

Efram looked at her. "Well . . . well once, I was with some kids. We meant no harm, of course."

Kathryn nodded. "Of course."

"We came through the garden, there at the back of the house. It was late at night, you see . . ."

"Go on."

"Well, we, ah, we saw someone."

"In the garden?"

"Yes."

"What did he look like?"

"I didn't get a good look, miss, except to see that he was tall and skinny. And he had long, funny hair."

Kathryn grinned. She leaned over and tugged lightly at one of his dreadlocks.

"Long and funny, huh?"

Efram was beyond seeing the joke.

"Not like mine. Tied back, you know, like in the old days. And he was carryin' somethin' in his hand."

"What?"

"I don't know."

He did; she could tell.

"Efram, come on. What was this—person—carrying?"

Efram shook his head. "I told you, I don't know."

"But you think he was a ghost?"

The boy's mouth tightened. "Don't know that either, miss."

"Well," Kathryn said carefully, "let's just assume for a minute that he was a ghost. Why would he be haunting my house, Efram?"

"I don't know."

Her patience snapped. "Will you stop saying that? Of course you know!"

"I don't."

"Efram . . ."

"Here we are," the boy said. The VW lurched violently as he swung it to the side of the road. Beyond it, a series of small cinderblock houses marched towards the harbor. Efram opened the car door and all but leaped out. "Good-bye, miss."

"Efram." Kathryn threw open the door and jumped out. "Hey, wait a minute . . ."

The boy waved his hand and took off.

Kathryn sighed. After a moment, she slammed the door, went around to the driver's side, and climbed into the car. She put one hand on the steering wheel and the other on the gearshift lever.

No matter what was going on at Charon's Crossing, there was a perfectly rational explanation for it. It was just infuriating to be the last to know what it was.

It would be even worse if it turned out she couldn't unload the damned place because of local stuff and nonsense.

Frowning, she put the car in gear. It was years since she'd driven a stick shift and the sound the VW made proved it. But the car finally shot backwards into the road and, after more horrible grinding noises, she coaxed it into first.

The Volkswagen bucked, then lurched forward.

"You'd better watch your backside, Amos," Kathryn muttered, "because ready or not, here I come."

Any other time, Hawkins Bay would have charmed her right out of her shoes.

Her father must have loved it on sight for it surely had to be an artist's idea of nirvana. Every street corner was worth sketching.

Even Kathryn, who was hardly in the mood for sightseeing, was impressed.

A sheltered, aquamarine harbor gave onto a wide pink sand beach bordered by a grove of palm trees. Beyond the palms were stuccoed, cinderblock houses which faced a narrow, cobblestone street.

Front Street, an old-fashioned street sign said, which made perfect sense considering that the only street that paralleled it was Back Street. The two thoroughfares were lined with modest buildings, each painted in one of the soft pastel colors of the Caribbean. Both streets were bisected by narrow alleys.

It was a charming scene. And a familiar one. Matthew's journal entry had described the town with accuracy and little seemed to have changed in the years since.

Well, Kathryn thought as a minivan shouldered past her, some things had changed. There'd been no cars or trucks lurching through these streets in his time. And no reggae music blaring from their radios. The music was loud, very different from the stately Bach fugues she preferred, but she found her shoulders swaying to the rhythmic beat.

A woman carrying a net shopping bag over one arm stepped down from the curb. Kathryn slowed the VW to a crawl. Nobody seemed to care very much if they walked on the sidewalk or in the road. People strolled as they liked; the cars, trucks and minivans drove the same way. If everybody did that in New York, there'd be bodies all over the place.

Kathryn smiled to herself. Maybe you caught on, if you lived here long enough.

She was more than happy to drive slowly. It gave her time to search for Amos's law office. She knew it was here, someplace on Front Street, but she couldn't remember the number. Not that it mattered. There didn't seem to be numbers on most of the buildings.

Eventually, she saw a discreetly lettered sign.

Amos Carter, Attorney at Law.

She pulled the car to the curb, edged it between a pink Studebaker that was older than she was and a spanking new Dodge minivan, and got out.

The door to Amos's office was locked. Kathryn jiggled the

knob, then peered in through the dust-smeared plate glass window. It seemed awfully early for him to be out to lunch . . .

"You lookin' for Mr. Carter?"

She turned around. A heavyset woman wearing a grey and white striped smock that stretched from her enormous bosom to her ankles had popped her head out of the shop next door and was examining her with friendly interest.

"Yes. Yes, I am. Do you know when he'll be back?"

"I'm Ada." The woman smiled and jerked her head towards the sign over the shop door. " 'Ada's Ladies and Gents Fine Apparel,' that's me."

Kathryn nodded politely and held out her hand. "I'm Kathryn Russell. I'm staying out at—"

"Charon's Crossin'. Yes, I know."

"I was looking for Mr. Carter. Do you know when he's expected to return?"

Ada shrugged. "Two, three weeks, maybe."

Kathryn's mouth fell open. "What?"

"He flew to England."

"To England? Are you sure?"

The woman nodded. "He has family there. Somethin' came up, he said, he had to go there to take care of it. He mentioned you might come by. Said to tell you he'd tried to let you know he'd be gone but your phone's not workin'."

"Do tell," Kathryn said with a tight smile. "Did he leave any other message?"

"He said you might want to go over to see Hiram Bonnyeman." The woman jerked her chin towards the opposite side of Front Street. "Walk up a bit, then cut down the next cross street. Hiram's house is blue and pink. You can't miss it."

"Thanks."

"Miss Russell?"

Kathryn swung around. "Yes?"

"How is it, livin' in that house?"

"It's fine," Kathryn said brightly. "Just fine."

"Glad to hear it. As for me, I don't think I could get a wink of sleep in a place like that."

"Listen," Kathryn said, grinding out the words through her teeth, "there's nothing wrong with that house that hard work won't cure."

"Oh, surely not," Ada said quickly. "I only meant that the stories about it . . . well, you know. And the name . . ."

"Charon's Crossing?"

"Well, it's peculiar, isn't it?" The woman's voice fell to a conspiratorial whisper and she leaned towards Kathryn. "Namin' a place for an old-time *loa,* I mean."

"A what?"

"A spirit, your people would call him. You know. The one used to sail dead folks over the sea to hell."

Kathryn's mouth dropped open. Ada wasn't talking about some voodoo spirit, she was talking about an ancient Greek god. Charon, whose job it had been to ferry the newly dead across the river Styx to the afterlife that awaited them.

How come she hadn't remembered that?

Her house, the house where she'd had such incredible dreams, where the cold came sweeping down the stairs, was a nineteenth-century metaphor for the river that separated the living from the dead?

The sun was high, the air hot. Despite that, a sudden chill swept the length of Kathryn's spine and she gave a little shudder. Ada, reading the swift play of emotions on her face, reached out a comforting hand but Kathryn forced a smile to her lips.

"Oh," she said, "of course. I should have realized."

She wanted to say more, something light and airy that would make it clear that she was above such nonsense, but she was too angry.

Damn her father for leaving her saddled with such a mess.

Damn Olive. And Amos, too, for not having told her about the house and whatever dark legends surrounded it, legends everyone but she seemed to know.

"Miss Russell? Are you okay?"

Kathryn smiled brightly. "I'm just fine," she said, and set off to find Hiram Bonnyeman.

It was easy, just as Ada had promised it would be.

The house was blue, its door and shutters pale pink. A sign hung out front, neatly lettered.

Hiram Bonnyeman, Plumbing, Heating, Electrical Work, Carpentry, and General Repairs.

It looked as if the era of specialization had not yet reached Elizabeth Island.

The door stood partly open. Kathryn knocked and waited.

"Yes, yes," a voice called. "Come in."

The interior of the shop was shadowy, almost dark compared to the brightness outside. She stood still, letting her eyes adjust, breathing in the pleasant mixture of smells that filled the air: new wood and wax, machine oil and something spicy. Cinnamon, perhaps, or nutmeg.

"Yes? May I help you?"

A man was coming towards her, stepping through a swaying curtain of small wooden beads. He was tall and wiry, with grizzled hair and ebony skin. A pair of wire-rimmed eyeglasses perched on the bridge of his aquiline nose, and was smiling so pleasantly that Kathryn immediately smiled back.

"I hope so. Would you be Hiram Bonnyeman, the building contractor?"

He smiled. "I would surely be Hiram Bonnyeman. And you would surely be Miss Kathryn Russell."

"Yes. Yes, I am, Mr. Bonnyeman. I've been hoping to make your acquaintance for some time."

The old man chuckled. "A polite way of askin' me where I've been keepin' myself, hmm?" He stepped forward, scooped a dozing ginger cat from a straight-backed wooden chair, and motioned Kathryn to sit. "Please, make yourself comfortable. I'll get us somethin' cool to drink."

"Oh, no. That's not necessary."

"It isn't. But it's what I'd like to do—unless you're in a hurry, Miss Russell?"

Kathryn sighed. "There's no sense in being in a hurry in these parts, Mr. Bonnyeman. I've learned that much already."

The old man grinned and ducked behind the curtain. Moments later, he reappeared bearing a round wooden tray on which he'd placed two tall glasses and a pitcher filled with a pale yellow liquid.

"Lemonade," he said, setting the tray down on a small table. "My wife makes it fresh, every mornin'. Best in town, if I do say so myself. She adds a touch of passion fruit. Give it a special sweetness."

Kathryn accepted the glass he held out to her.

"Thank you, Mr. Bonnyeman."

"Hiram."

She smiled. "And I'm Kathryn."

"How's the lemonade, Kathryn? Good?"

Kathryn sighed. When in Rome, she thought, and she took a sip.

"Delicious. Mr. Bonnyeman . . . Hiram. Look, I don't mean to seem rude, but—"

"But you want to know where I've been and why I haven't shown up and when I'm goin' to come by Charon's Crossin' and get to work. Am I right?"

Kathryn nodded. "I've only got a week, you see, well, not even that anymore. I'm flying back to New York Friday, and . . . what's the matter?"

"If you're flyin' home Friday, we have a problem."

"What do you mean, we have a problem?"

"I can't possibly get out to Charon's Crossin' until next week, the soonest."

Kathryn put down her glass. "I distinctly told Amos Carter I'd be here just for the week."

"Well, Amos never told me."

"I don't believe this! The whole reason for this visit was to find out what repairs the house needs and now—"

"I don't need to come by your house to tell you that."

Kathryn blinked. "You don't?"

"No. I don't."

"Olive spoke to you, then?"

"Your father spoke to me, before his death. He asked me to come over, check things, tell him what I thought." Hiram smiled. "He was a nice man, your father. And he had great plans for that house."

"Expensive plans, I'll bet. What did you tell him?"

"That it was sad, the condition of Charon's Crossin'. But that it was repairable, dependin' on what he wished to spend." He smiled gently. "Sad to say, he didn't have the money to do very much."

"A situation that runs in the family," Kathryn said crisply. "Not that I have any great plans for the place. I just want to do whatever needs doing so that Olive can sell it."

Hiram nodded. "Well, there's a long enough list of things to fix. The wallboard needs replacin' in some of the rooms. The wainscotin', too, in the entry and in the dinin' room, as well as the moldin'. Roof needs patchin' before the rains come. And it might be a good idea to shore up a couple of beams in the cellar. But the biggest problem is the hot-water heater."

Kathryn sighed. "Don't I know it. Well, the next owner can deal with that."

The old man shook his head."Maybe. And maybe not."

"Look, I know an outdated heater will take away from the value of the house, but—"

"I'm not talkin' value. I'm tellin' you that old heater is a cranky son of a gun and you'd best fix it, or . . ."

"Or what?"

"Who knows? The best that could happen would be for it to quit for good."

"And the worst?"

Hiram sighed. "Fire. Explosion. Anythin' is possible."

Kathryn felt like burying her head in her hands. She'd been wrong thinking of Charon's Crossing as an albatross. It was an anchor, and if she weren't careful, it would pull her down and drown her in debt.

"Look, Hiram," she said, "maybe I didn't make myself clear. I don't have any money to waste on Charon's Crossing."

"And I won't ask you to waste any. Once I do a thorough check of the heatin' system, I'll tell you what your choices are."

"Oh. I didn't . . . I thought you meant you were going to have to replace the entire system."

"Maybe. Maybe not. I cannot tell until I take a closer look, which I can do in a week's time." The old man smiled. "You can stand right by my side, sayin' 'yes, Hiram, do that' or 'no, Hiram, let that stay as it is.' How's that sound?"

"It sounds fine . . . except I won't be here in a week's time."

"Might be you could sign a paper, let Amos make those decisions for you."

"Might be—if he were on the island." Kathryn's nostrils flared. "But he isn't."

"Oh yes. Now that you mention it, seems to me I heard somethin' about that this mornin', at the market." The old man pushed back his chair and put his hands on his knees. "Well, I don't know what to suggest, Kathryn, except to tell you I wouldn't take the responsibility for makin' those decisions for you, even if you asked."

Kathryn stood up. "Wonderful," she said bitterly. "I don't seem to have much choice, do I? I'm going to have to waste another week!"

Hiram rose, too. "I am sorry. But I promise, I'll get to you as quickly as I can." He followed after her to the door. Just as she was about to open it, he put his hand lightly on her shoulder. "Kathryn? I never did ask. How are you doin' out at that house, all by yourself?"

Her eyes narrowed as she turned and faced him. "What do you mean?"

"Just what I said. The house is so big, and you're not used to it."

"To what? The rattles? The moans? The cries in the night?" Kathryn glared at him. "Isn't that what you're really asking, Hiram? How am I doing, all alone in a haunted house?"

He swallowed dryly. "Kathryn, I never meant—"

"Yes, you did. You and everybody else who wants to know how I'm doing. Well, I'll tell you how. There are ice cold drafts that come from nowhere, there's some guy popping in and out of my head, chains rattle, things go thump in the middle of the night and if skeletons start coming out of the walls I'll probably just stand there and say, 'Hi, how're you doing?' " Kathryn jabbed her index finger into her own chest. "I am angry as hell, Hiram! It turns out that the only person on this whole island who didn't know that Casper the Not-So-Friendly Ghost was living at Charon's Crossing was me!"

"Kathryn, please . . ."

"Is there a phone in this town?"

"A what?"

"A phone. One that works. Is there any such thing on all the island?"

"There is one on the next corner, near the Post Office. Kathryn, if you would just listen . . ."

"Good-bye, Mr. Bonnyeman. I'd appreciate it if you'd let me know exactly what day you'll be coming by. If my phone doesn't work, try sending a message by spook express!"

Eyes flashing, Kathryn stormed from the repair shop and headed for the Post Office. There was a phone, all right. Just one. Fortunately, it worked.

Jason answered on the first ring.

"It's me," she snapped. "Kathryn."

"Kathryn! Are you okay? I've been going crazy, waiting to hear from you. Your phone doesn't work, do you know that? I called information, got your number, but—"

"I know. Believe me, I know. Nothing works in this place."

"But you're okay? You sure? You don't sound it."

Kathryn sighed and sagged against the wall of the telephone booth.

"I am, really. It's just that . . . look, I can't go into details now. I just called to let you know I'm fine. And that I won't be home Friday after all. I'm going to have to hang in another week."

"Hell!"

"Yeah, I know."

"Why? What's the problem?"

"The guy who's going to give me a rundown on what needs to be done to the house can't get over to see me until next week."

"Well, get somebody else."

Kathryn shut her eyes wearily. "You don't understand. There isn't anybody else."

"You're right. I don't understand. You said you'd be gone a week."

Static crackled through the line. Kathryn shifted the telephone to her other ear.

"Jason, it's too complicated to explain right now. I'm standing in the middle of what passes for downtown, there are trucks and cars going by . . . Look, don't worry, okay? I know I'm losing a lot of time from work, but—"

"I don't care about work, Kathryn. I'm thinking of us being apart for another week."

Kathryn rubbed her forehead. "Of course," she said quickly. "I meant that, too."

"Look, I've got an idea. How'd you like me to fly down for the weekend?"

"It isn't necessary. Really."

"I know it isn't necessary. I just figured it was a nice idea but if you don't think so . . ."

"Of course it's a nice idea," she said quickly, hearing the hurt in his voice. "It's a wonderful idea. I just don't want you to go to all that trouble."

"It's no trouble, darling. I'll let you know when . . ."

The connection suddenly went dead.

"Jason? Jason, can you hear me?"

Kathryn hung the phone up with a bang.

Great. Just great. Jason was flying down; he was going to see for himself that Charon's Crossing was a mess, not a mansion. Not that she cared. It was just that . . .

"Kathryn? Oh, I'm so glad I caught you."

Kathryn looked around. Olive Potter was coming towards her. She hooked her arm though Kathryn's and drew her aside.

"Hiram came to tell me what happened," she said. "I'm so sorry there was this misunderstandin'."

"Well, I am, too. And I'm sorry I bit Hiram's head off. None of this is his fault. It's Amos's."

"Actually, that isn't what I wanted to discuss with you." The realtor hesitated. "Hiram said . . . well, he said you seemed upset about the doin's out at your place."

Kathryn drew her arm from Olive's. "What doings?"

"He said you spoke of things happenin'. Chains and drafts, noises and such."

"For heaven's sake, Olive. I was just being sarcastic."

"Kathryn, I think you should reconsider my suggestion that you stay someplace else for the rest of the time you are on the island."

Kathryn put her hands on her hips. "Why?"

"I've explained that. You told Hiram . . ."

"And I told you, I was being sarcastic."

"Nonetheless—"

"You lied to me, didn't you? I asked you if you knew anything about Charon's Crossing being haunted, and you said you didn't."

"I said there were stories, stuff and nonsense no sensible person would believe in."

"What stuff and nonsense?"

"Kathryn, please . . ."

"Dammit, I have a right to know!"

Olive knotted her hands together. "All right, I will tell you. But you must remember it is all—"

"Stuff and nonsense." A muscle twitched in Kathryn's jaw. "I know. But I want to hear it anyway."

Olive leaned closer.

"People claim they have seen things. Lights at night, flickerin' on and off."

"Kids," Kathryn said firmly, "or trespassers, fooling around."

"No one on this island would go into that house to play games, Kathryn, believe me."

"And that's it? That's what all the fuss is about?"

Olive looked even more unhappy.

"People say they've seen things in the garden," she said with obvious reluctance.

"What kinds of things?"

"Bad things. Evil things. A man with a drawn sword and blood drippin' from it."

Kathryn stared at Olive. Was that what Efram had seen? What he'd refused to tell her?

"And they say there's a cold spot on the staircase, and no way to account for it."

"I asked you about that, specifically." Kathryn tried to steady her voice. "I said, Do you feel this blast of cold air? And you said—"

"Never mind what I said, Kathryn. I'm tellin' you, now. And I'm not tryin' to convince you of anythin'. It was you who asked me to tell you what folks say, remember?"

This was insanity. It was out and out nonsense, and Kathryn wasn't going to let it carry her away. "Yes," she said, "I asked. And now you can tell them what I say. They're all nuts! Lights. Bloody swords." She gave a snort of disgust. "The only things living in that house are mice. And spiders. And maybe an occasional vagrant who's smart enough to know how to scare people off."

Olive held out an imploring hand but Kathryn swept past her. She ran to the VW, wrenched open the door, and stabbed the key into the ignition.

The gears shrieked as she shifted without regard for the clutch, and she sent the car into reverse.

"Olive," she barked.

The realtor sprinted to the curb.

"Yes?"

"Is there a doctor in this miserable town?"

"A doctor?"

"Yes. A medical doctor, not one who reads chicken entrails."

Olive swallowed dryly and pointed up the block. "Just before you reach the last house," she said. "You'll see his sign outside."

Kathryn nodded grimly and tromped down on the gas.

Malcolm Simpson, M.D., turned out to be a slight man. He was middle-aged, Harvard educated, and pleasant.

He was, he said, delighted to make her acquaintance.

"Frankly, Miss Russell, I've been curious about the American lady who's moved into Charon's Crossing."

"Well, I haven't moved in. I'm just here on a temporary visit, Doctor."

"And?"

Kathryn hesitated. "And," she said finally, "I haven't been sleeping well."

What else could she tell him? That she was afraid she had a brain tumor? That she feared she was going nuts? That she might be having hallucinations, brought on by a ghost-happy populace?

"I think it's the heat," she said, and smiled brightly. "But I figured I'd get checked over, just to be sure."

Dr. Simpson didn't bother pointing out that nights were cool this time of year, especially up on the cliffs where Charon's Crossing stood. He poked and prodded, tested and measured, and, at last, assured Kathryn that her health was excellent.

"I'm glad to hear it." She cleared her throat. "I wonder . . . I mean, as long as I'm here . . ."

Simpson waited with a patient, impersonal smile. Forty years practicing medicine had taught him that people rarely came straight out and told you what was really worrying them.

"I thought you might check my vision," Kathryn said casually.

"Have you been having vision problems, Miss Russell?"

Well, I've been seeing things . . .

"No," she said. "But, ah, I've had some headaches lately."

"Mmm. No spots? No blurry shapes?"

Just a man with a face like an angel and the disposition of a bobcat.

"Nope, not a one."

"Let's have a look, then, shall we?"

Dr. Simpson turned off the lights. He put on a gizmo that made him look like a miner and made Kathryn want to giggle. He peered deep into her eyes, pulled down an eye chart and made her read it. Then he peered into her eyes again.

"Twenty-twenty," he said, flicking on the lights.

Kathryn nodded. "I figured that."

"The headaches are probably from tension. Or they could be sinus-related." He smiled pleasantly. "I'm sure we've got more strange things growing here per square foot than you have in all of New York."

Kathryn smiled weakly. "I'll bet."

Simpson began scrawling on a prescription pad.

"I'll give you a couple of prescriptions, Miss Russell, something to help you sleep and a mild painkiller, but I think your best bet will be aspirin for your headaches, and brisk walks along the beach for that insomnia. Perhaps the mustiness of that old house is getting to you."

"Are you familiar with Charon's Crossing, Doctor?"

"Oh, quite." He ripped the prescriptions from the pad and chuckled as he handed them to her. "I take it you aren't bothered by tales of jumbies and haunts, hmm?"

Kathryn's lips felt as if they were sticking to her teeth as she smiled back at him.

"You've heard the stories, then?"

"Of course." He pushed back his chair and rose to his feet. "There was a time, a couple of decades ago, I thought about buying the house myself."

"But you didn't," Kathryn said, stuffing the prescriptions into her pocket.

Simpson took her arm and walked her slowly to the door. "No. I didn't."

"Do you mind telling me the reason?"

He laughed, and a light flush spread over his cheeks.

"It was my wife, actually. Sally said if I moved into Charon's Crossing, it would be by myself."

"But why?"

"I was born and raised in the States, Miss Russell. Sally . . . well, she's from Elizabeth Island."

"So?"

"So, she flatly refused to live in a house she said was haunted."

Kathryn swung towards him. "But you're a physician. Couldn't you convince her it wasn't true?"

Simpson paused, his hand on the doorknob, and gave her an embarrassed smile.

"Actually," he said, "I couldn't convince myself."

Was everybody on this island insane?

All the way back to Charon's Crossing, that was all she could think about.

Did they all believe there was a ghost in her house?

There wasn't. Hell, no. This was just a case of—of mass hysteria, like the Salem witch hunts or all those little kids in California who'd convinced themselves and everyone else that their teachers had dug secret tunnels under their classroom and spirited them off to heaven only knew where for God only knew what . . .

Ghosts.

"Ghosts," Kathryn snorted.

It would be a cold day in hell before she joined the ranks of those who thought she'd inherited not just a house but a spirit.

By the time she pulled up at the front door, she had gone from irritation to anger. She stormed out of the car, up the front steps, and threw open the door.

Legs slightly apart, hands on her hips, she glared at the wide staircase. The late afternoon light lent it an eerie look; the steps seemed to end in yawning blackness.

Kathryn hesitated for a moment. Maybe this wasn't so smart. Maybe . . .

Maybe, nothing!

"Okay," she said loudly, "Okay, here I am. And here's your chance. If there's anything or anybody here, come out and show yourself."

Silence filled the room.

"Come on, if you're up there. Listen, I'm from New York. I know all about street people. So if you moved in a while back, I won't be angry. Just come on down, walk out the door, and we'll forget this ever happened."

More silence. Kathryn took a deep breath.

"And—and if there's anything else up there . . ." What was she doing? This was ridiculous. It was crazy. But so what? There was nobody here to see her make an ass of herself. "If there's anything else hanging around," she said, her voice loud and clear, "it's time you took off, too." The wind had blown her hair around her face in wild, tumbling waves. She tossed her head and it fell back over her shoulders. "Not that I believe in ghosts, you understand. But everybody else here does, so I'm just going with the flow. There's the door. Come down, walk out, and don't come back."

Nothing stirred. Nothing spoke. Kathryn held her stance a minute longer. Then she let out her breath in a long, explosive sigh. Her hands fell from her hips. It was silly, she knew, but now that it was over, she was shak—

"Hello, Catherine."

The voice behind her was deep, masculine, and frighteningly familiar.

The hair rose on the nape of Kathryn's neck. Slowly, slowly, she turned around.

A shaft of late afternoon sunlight illuminated the staircase, falling like a spotlight on the man coming down the steps towards her.

He was tall and golden-haired; he was handsome enough to steal her breath away. He was wearing black tights and high black boots and a shirt with ruffles at the neck and at the cuffs . . .

And she could see the stairs right through him, see the pattern on the Persian runner . . .

"Must I introduce myself, m'lady?" He paused on the bottom step, his tone cool but his green eyes hot on her face. "Surely you have not forgotten my name."

"Certainly not," Kathryn said, in a voice that was very clear and calm. "You're Matthew McDowell."

Her eyes rolled up into her head and she tumbled to the floor in a dead faint.

Eight

Hell and damnation!

Matthew managed to catch Catherine in his arms just as she crumpled to the floor. She felt as boneless as a rag doll.

"Cat," he said urgently, "speak to me."

Was this what he had been reduced to, then, terrorizing women?

His heart hardened. And it was all her fault.

He carried her into the drawing room and deposited her none too gently on one of the settees. Then he rose to his feet and stared down at her, his arms folded and his legs apart.

"All right," he said coldly. "You've done your swooning act. Now open your eyes."

She didn't stir.

"Do you hear me, Cat? Stop this nonsense and look at me."

She lay there, as still as death.

Matthew frowned. There was no satisfaction in this. There was a vast difference between taking revenge and scaring a woman senseless.

A man could not be proud of that.

It was true, he had acted precipitously, coming down the stairs and revealing himself to her, but her taunting words had stung him.

She deserved retribution for that alone. As for the rest—what did it matter when he confronted her?

Except that there could be no confrontation, not when Catherine lay senseless on the settee.

His gaze flew to her face. She was so pale that her dark lashes seemed to cast purple shadows against her cheekbones.

"Cat?"

She didn't answer. She didn't so much as stir.

"Oh, for God's sake!"

He made a sound of disgust and knelt down beside her, but his frown had deepened.

Was it an act? Lord knew she was an expert in all the feminine wiles. Still, he suspected that not even Catherine could deliberately manage to make the blood drain from her face.

He reached for her hand and picked it up. It lay unmoving in his. He turned it over and placed his fingers lightly against her blue-veined wrist. The beat of her pulse was strong and steady.

Hell, he thought with a choked laugh, what did that mean? His pulse was strong and steady, too, and he was dead.

But she wasn't. He could see the color slowly coming back under her skin, flushing her cheeks the pale pink of morning. Her fingers stirred lightly against his, their touch as light as the brush of a butterfly's wings. Her lips parted, and a sighing whisper escaped from between them. Her breath was warm, and sweet . . .

Matthew dropped her hand and shot to his feet.

"Hell and damnation," he growled.

He strode across the room to the cabinet where he knew her father had kept his spirits. What she needed was something to get the blood flowing again.

What he needed was something to keep his from pooling in the part of his anatomy that had led him astray in the first place.

He opened the doors of the cabinet, his face grim. There was half a decanter of something dark on the bottom shelf; he unstoppered it, took a whiff, and nodded.

Rum. Good, West Indian rum. That would bring her around. He poured two fingers into a cut-glass tumbler, frowned, added another two fingers for good measure, then held the glass to the light.

It was a long time since he'd tasted rum. Now that he thought about it, it was a long time since he'd tasted anything.

Could he do such simple things? Could he eat and drink, if he wished to do so?

It was a good question. Thus far, little about his ghostly existence was predictable. Or known. He felt like an explorer in a distant land, learning the limits of his new world and adding to his store of knowledge hour by hour.

He could walk through walls but he couldn't pass through an open gate.

He could see his reflection in the mirror but there were occasions when he was transparent.

And right now, the smell of the rum was making his mouth water.

Matthew hesitated, then lifted the glass to his lips and took a small, questioning sip.

A beatific smile swept across his face.

The taste was heaven. The silken glide of the liquor across his tongue, the fiery kick of it as it slid down his throat . . . He had almost forgotten the pleasure of it.

He had the glass halfway to his lips again when Catherine spoke.

"You're supposed to give whiskey to the person who passes out, not drink it yourself."

He swung around. She was sitting up in a corner of the settee. Her face was still pale, though two patches of color had blossomed in her cheeks.

He felt a dark flush rise in his own face.

"It's rum, not whiskey. And I was simply testing it. Who knows how long it's been in that decanter? Its condition might be unsuitable for consumption."

Her dark eyebrows lifted a fractional inch.

"A taste test," she said. "How thoughtful."

Matthew cleared his throat. "It was nothing."

"Oh, on the contrary. An intruder with a sense of chivalry

is very definitely something. I think the police will find it a fascinating detail."

The threat wasn't worthy of a response, though he had to give her credit for courage. She was frightened; he could see it in the swiftness of her breathing, but her demeanor, and her tone, were cool.

Matthew dumped more rum into the glass and brought it to her. She shook her head.

"No, thank you," she said, and frowned.

No, thank you? Had she really said that?

He, on the other hand, obviously had no such constraints. He glared and shoved the glass at her.

"Drink it," he growled.

Kathryn drew back, wrinkling her nose at the smell.

"I don't want it."

"Dammit, Cat, this is not a tea party. Drink the rum."

Her chin lifted in defiance. "You're right. This isn't a tea party so I don't have to pretend to be a gracious guest. And for your information, my name is not Cat."

His mouth twisted. "Isn't it?"

"No."

"What is it, if not Cat?"

"It's Kathryn," she snapped.

"Forgive me, m'lady," he said, his voice tinged with sarcasm. "I had forgotten your preference for formality."

"I don't have a preference for anything, except for seeing your back as you go out the door!"

"Ah, Catherine, you cut me to the quick. To think you want only to wound me with words after being so long without me."

"Listen here, you . . ."

"Don't argue with me, dammit! Drink the rum and be quick about it."

Kathryn opened her mouth, then slammed it shut.

Maybe she was nuts! She had to be, to sit here and quarrel with a crazy man.

Maybe he was right. Maybe a stiff shot of something alcoholic was just what she needed to clear her head. At the very least, it might help her figure out what had happened to her.

All right, so it wasn't every day you strolled into your own house and found a man dressed like an extra from *Mutiny on the Bounty* coming down the steps.

But the rest of it . . .

Kathryn shot a quick look at his hand, curved around the glass.

Thank you, God.

It was a powerful hand, a very masculine one with long, blunt-nailed fingers. But it wasn't transparent. Given the choice, she'd much rather deal with a flesh-and-blood intruder than—than . . .

Oh boy!

Maybe a belt of rum wasn't such a bad idea.

"All right," she said, and rose to her feet.

His hand shot out and clamped around her wrist.

"Where do you think you're going?"

"I've reconsidered," she said with all the cool hauteur she could muster. "I think I'll have some of that stuff after all."

He shoved the glass at her; the rum sloshed from side to side. "Drink, then."

Kathryn looked disdainfully at his glass, then at him.

"I'd prefer a glass of my own, thank you very much."

Her eyes dared him to argue. Matthew gritted his teeth, then let go of her wrist.

"Of course. How foolish of me." He lifted what remained of the rum to his lips and downed it in one swallow. He shuddered, then wiped the back of his hand over his lips. "Perhaps if I wore a red shirt open to my navel and fashioned my hair into greasy ringlets, you might be less fussy."

Kathryn spun towards him, the decanter and a glass in her hands.

"What?"

"I would have hoped your taste in men would have improved

over the years, Cat. But it seems it has not. First Waring, then that—that disgusting excuse for a man this afternoon . . ."

"I don't know what you're talking about."

Hell, neither did he. Matthew's jaw tightened. What did it matter, her taste in men? She could be sleeping with the King's garrison and the Corporal of the Guard, for all he cared.

He shrugged and strolled towards her.

"Never mind," he said, slapping down his empty glass. "Your amusements are none of my concern."

"I'm glad we agree on something."

A corner of his mouth tilted up in a cool smile. He leaned back against the wall, folded his arms, and looked at her.

"I must say, you're taking this very calmly."

Calmly? God, if he only knew. If her heart raced any faster, it might burst from her chest and any second now, her teeth were threatening to chatter like castanets.

"Well, I'm trying to understand what, ah, what it is you're doing here," she said.

He laughed, as if she'd said something funny.

"Oh, I'm sure you'll come up with the answer."

There was an ominous undertone to his words. Kathryn licked her lips nervously.

"Were you—were you here, in the house, when I went out this morning?"

His smile was quick and condescending. "Of course."

She nodded, poured a dollop of rum into her glass, lifted it to her lips and swallowed it in one quick, throat-scalding gulp.

"Better?" he said, after a moment.

She nodded again, even though it was a lie. How could anything make her feel better? Here she was, talking with a man who'd somehow broken into Charon's Crossing, who traipsed around pretending to be someone who'd been dead almost two hundred years, right down to the costume and the old-fashioned speech.

He was clever. And dangerous. He was either a criminal or a lunatic . . .

Or both.

Kathryn put down the glass and the decanter. She shoved her hands deep into the pockets of her skirt to keep them from shaking.

It was not an encouraging situation.

"What's the matter, Cat?"

She looked up. The intruder was watching her, still with that little smile curled across his mouth.

"Why should anything be the matter?" she said quickly.

"You look as if . . ." He chuckled. ". . . as if you've seen a ghost."

Her heart rose to her throat. He was doing his best to terrify her. Well, he was succeeding. Her imagination had shifted into overdrive, racing for half a dozen different endings to this script.

The trouble was, not a one of them ended with her smiling in the winner's circle.

The second he knew that, it would be all over.

Life in New York had taught her that. You'd be walking down a street, minding your own business, and all of a sudden some fruitcake would pop out of a doorway, ranting about the end of the world.

You learned real fast that the only way to deal with things like that was to show as little reaction as possible. Besides, there was almost always someplace to pop into, a coffee shop or a drugstore and if you were really lucky, you might spot a police car cruising by.

On the other hand, this wasn't New York, it was Elizabeth Island. And *this* was Charon's Crossing. There were no shops, no people, no way to communicate with anybody.

If only the damned telephone worked. But it didn't; it just squatted on the console table, within reach but about as useful as feathers on a fish.

"Where did he take you?"

Kathryn's eyes flashed to his face. "Where did who take me?"

"Your pirate lover."

"My what?"

His eyes darkened. "Don't try my patience, Catherine. You know who I'm talking about. Where did your swashbuckler with the greasy curls take you for your little tête-à-tête?"

Kathryn's jaw dropped. Efram? He thought Efram, with his hollow chest and his acne, was her lover?

She almost laughed. Instead, she shrugged her shoulders.

"I don't think that's any of your business." Let him think she had a lover, someone who was liable to turn up at any minute.

"I'm making it my business," he said through his teeth. "Did he take you to his ship?"

"We went to town. We walked, looked at the shops . . . you know."

His mouth twisted. "Do you really expect me to believe you and your lover spent the afternoon shopping?"

Casually, she strolled past him, as if she were heading for the settee. He didn't try to stop her. Emboldened, she mentally measured the distance to the door. Ten feet, perhaps twelve. Yes, as far as she could see, that was her best bet. If she could just make it across the foyer to the library, she could slam the door in his face and jam it shut with a chair . . .

"Damn you, Cat! Answer my question!"

"He'll be back, if that's what you want to know." She turned and looked at him, forcing herself to speak calmly. "But—but I won't tell him about—about what's happened. I mean, we can just forget about your—your visit."

Matthew's eyes narrowed. "How generous you are, Catherine."

"I'm sure you had your reasons for break- . . . for coming to this house."

He smiled, his teeth very even and white against his tanned face.

"That's an interesting way of putting it."

Kathryn managed a smile. "Well, I'm trying to put this in the best possible light. For both our sakes."

"Really," he said, his voice almost a purr.

"Of course. There's no reason to end this on an unpleasant note."

His smile was cold and mirthless. It sent a whisper of fear feathering along her spine.

"Given the circumstances, I suspect I would make the same attempt to circumvent the inevitable." His smile fled. "But you must know that there's nothing you can say will accomplish that."

It was horrible, being toyed with like this, and Kathryn's composure slipped.

"Damn you," she cried. "Why are you doing this?"

"Why do you avoid using my name?"

"What?"

"Does it prick your conscience? Or did it mean so little to you that you truly have difficulty remembering it?"

"Please," she said, trying to keep her voice from trembling. "Please, don't you think this game's gone far enough?"

"On the contrary," he said softly. "It hasn't gone anywhere. Not yet."

There was no mistaking the threat. She took a deep breath and faced him.

"Let me offer you a choice . . . Matthew."

His eyes gave nothing away. "What choice?"

"If—if you leave Charon's Crossing now, I won't tell anyone you've been here."

A smile played across his lips. He walked slowly towards her and she forced herself to hold her ground, even though every nerve in her body was shrieking for her to run.

Half a dozen feet away, he stopped, sat on the arm of a chair, and folded his arms.

"It's a little late for that, don't you think?"

"It isn't," she said desperately, "it's not too late at all. We can still pretend none of this happened."

"None of what happened?"

"You know."

He shook his head. "I'd rather hear it from you."

This was touchy. Whatever she said next might be a mistake, depending on which he was, a nut who wandered into people's houses or a burglar with a taste for the dramatic who might resent being called a nut.

Although, she had to admit, he didn't seem to fit either category. Not a criminal. Not a lunatic . . .

"Why so quiet, Cat?"

"I—I'm thinking."

"What is there to think about?" His mouth thinned. "There's only one thing I want to hear you say and you know what it is."

Kathryn looked down and traced the seam of her skirt pocket with the tip of her finger.

"I won't tell anybody you've been here."

He laughed. "How generous."

Relief swept through her. "You'll leave, then?"

"I can't."

"You can! Just take my car."

"Car?"

"The VW outside. I know it isn't much, but—"

"I'd sooner ride a donkey without a saddle," he said, shuddering. He looked at her and his eyes darkened, so much so that for a moment he seemed to be in pain. "You don't understand. I can't leave, even if I wanted to."

"Don't be silly. Of course . . ."

She fell back as he rose and rushed towards her. His hands closed on her shoulders and he shook her roughly.

"Dammit," he snarled, "that's enough! I'm not going anywhere. And I'm weary of you playing the innocent."

"I'm not 'playing' at anything, Ma- . . . Matthew. I just—I don't understand what you want!"

"Answers, dammit. Answers!" His hands tightened on her. "Why did you do it, Catherine?"

"Do what?"

"I loved you. I worshiped you. And yet, you betrayed me, betrayed me with that pig!"

"I didn't," Kathryn said quickly. "Look, you've got this all wrong."

"Have I?"

"Yes. Yes, you have. I can explain—"

"Explain, then. Fool that I am, I'll listen."

"He was never my lover."

She cried out as Matthew shook her.

"Don't lie! That only makes it worse."

"I'm not lying. I know I let you think he was, but—"

"Think? Think?" He shoved her back against the wall, his eyes blazing with rage. "I *saw you with him,* damn you! You were in his arms, kissing him, telling him things you had once told me . . ."

"No! That's not true! I never kissed him. I was only with him once, how could I have kissed him? I don't know what you think you saw but—"

"What I *think* I saw?" His hand slid down to her wrist, his fingers clamping around it like steel, and he yanked her towards the French doors that led onto the terrace. "I was out there, in the garden, as were you." He spun her towards him, his eyes wild. "I saw everything, Cat, everything!"

"But you couldn't have," she said desperately. "Not from the garden."

Matthew flung her from him and she stumbled back, her eyes wide and terrified.

"Sweet Jesus, are you trying to drive me insane? I saw you with Waring! You know damned well that I did."

"Waring?" she repeated in an unsteady whisper. "Who's Waring? His name was Efram."

"Efram? Efram? Who the hell is Efram?"

"The boy you saw me with this afternoon, the one you thought was my lover. He's not. He couldn't be. He's just a child. A boy. He only came to deliver my car."

Matthew's bellow of rage filled the room.

"Are you telling me you've taken to consorting with children?"

"No. No, of course not. I only meant . . ." She held out her hand. "Please, calm down."

"I *am* calm," he shouted. "I am totally, completely . . . Damn!"

He whirled away from her and aimed a booted foot at a stupid little table against the wall. It made a satisfying crunch as it shattered and fell to the floor like so many matchsticks. Kathryn cried out and flew past him. She fell to her knees and began clawing through the pieces of wood.

"Hell and damnation," Matthew muttered. "It's only a table, just a stinking, miserable . . ."

"Look," she said, her voice filled with awe.

She was leaning back on her heels, clutching to her bosom two ugly black things.

"Look at what?"

"Oh, it works," she sobbed, her eyes glowing with happiness. "It works!"

Matthew stared at her. "What works?"

"The phone!"

"The fone?"

"Yes!" She jammed one of the black things against her ear. "My God, it really works. Didn't you hear the dial tone, when it fell?"

Matthew's brows knotted. "Catherine, I want you to calm down."

"I *am* calm," she said, scrambling to her feet. "I am completely calm." His gaze shot to her hands. She was holding the two black things as if they were precious jewels and backing slowly towards the door. "All right, Matthew. Last chance. Leave now, or I'll call the cops."

"The kopz?"

Catherine stamped her foot. "Will you stop that?"

"Stop what?"

"You know what! Repeating things as if I—as if you . . ."

Look, just go away. If you don't, I swear, I'll telephone the cops."

Telefone the kopz?

What the hell was she talking about?

Matthew had not been this confused since he'd been a cabin boy on a merchant ship bound from Boston to Dublin.

"You'll love the city, lad," the old Cookie had told him. "The beer is like nectar and the girls are beautiful, 'cept for them thinkin' it's English they speak."

It was how he felt now, listening to Catherine. She was speaking English but what was she saying?

Kopz? Fone?

If it was a threat, what did it mean?

His eyes narrowed as he watched her. She'd put the length of the room between them but even so, he could see that her cheeks were scarlet and her eyes far too bright.

Perhaps he hadn't caught her in time, when she'd swooned. Perhaps she'd bumped her head against the marble floor.

He'd seen that happen, on shipboard. A man would stumble in a heavy sea, bang his skull against something not hard enough to truly notice. He'd seem fine but then, a bit later, he'd suddenly turn shiny-eyed and puke up his lunch.

Not that he gave a damn if she'd bumped her head. Not that he gave a damn if she'd split it open . . .

"Hell and damnation," he snarled.

"Don't try and intimidate me," she said quickly. "I'm going to count to three, and then—"

"Cat," he said, his voice soft and easy, "does your head hurt?"

Kathryn blinked. "Does my head hurt?"

"Yes. Where you hit it."

"I didn't hit it."

"You did. You must have. Let me see."

"Stay where you are or I'll . . . I'll . . ." She'd what? Dial 911? For all she knew, dialing 911 didn't get you anything but a buzzing on the line. Besides, even if it connected you with the police, or what passed for the police, by the time they got all the way out here it would be too late.

"Catherine."

His tone was sweet reason itself, his smile kind and gentle. He was walking towards her slowly, as if there were no hurry about anything.

It was the performance of a lifetime. Or of a certifiable crazy.

Either way, it was time to act.

"Don't take another step," Kathryn commanded.

"Cat," he said, "I want you to take a deep breath. Now, put down that—whatever—and let me see your head."

He was still using that wheedling tone but it didn't match the glint of determination in his eyes.

"No," she shouted. In a burst of desperation she danced back, dropped the phone, made a rush at a mahogany secretary and then jammed her fist deep into her skirt pocket.

"Okay," she said breathlessly, "that's far enough. I've—I've got a gun!"

She might as well have said she had a sea lion for the look that came over his face.

"You've got a what?"

"A gun. I—I just took it from the secretary and now it's in my pocket." His eyes shot to her pocket and she stiffened her fingers behind the cotton fabric. "If you come any closer, I'll shoot."

"A pistol?" His eyes met hers and he smiled as if she were a naughty child. "Let me see it, then."

"No."

"Catherine, stop being silly. What would you be doing with a pistol? Come along, now. Let me help you to a chair and then I'll get you a nice, cold compress."

"I'm telling you, I have a gun! Must I prove it by killing you?"

He laughed, as if she'd made a wonderful joke. "You can't kill me."

He was still advancing on her, slowly but steadily. She risked a quick look over her shoulder. They were almost out in the foyer now. Could she make it out the door? Or would he rush her and call her bluff?

"Maybe I can't," she said, very calmly. "But are you really willing to take that chance?"

Matthew stopped in his tracks.

It was an excellent question. And it raised a lot of others.

Did Catherine really have a pistol? It wasn't likely. A flintlock pistol was much too big to fit in that small pocket. Maybe it was something new, like the fone, the kopz and the carriage that belched black smoke. It was possible.

And if she had a pistol, would she use it? She probably would. After all, she'd done her part in killing him one time already.

If she used it, what would happen? He was a ghost. Could a ghost be killed? It didn't seem likely but then, *nothing* that had happened to him seemed likely.

And if the answer were yes, would he awaken again to find himself trapped in that cold, terrible blackness?

A risk was one thing, but eternal damnation in that awful place he'd so recently escaped was another, especially if he awakened there without the comfort of knowing he had taken his revenge.

He shuddered. It was too ugly to think about.

"Well?" Kathryn said. "What's it going to be?"

Matthew's eyes met hers.

"It would seem you have won this time," he said coldly.

Kathryn bit her lip to keep from cheering. As it was, she could hardly stand. Her legs had gone from feeling boneless to feeling gelatinous. If she didn't lean on something or sit down soon, she was going to end up in a heap.

"Thank you," she said politely.

A corner of his mouth tilted up in a little smile. It softened his face, made him look less dangerous and reminded her of just how good-looking he was.

"But it's not done with, Cat. Remember that."

The hand in her pocket motioned towards the door.

"Go on, get out."

"I'm going."

"And don't come back, or—"

"Don't make threats you can't keep, Catherine."

"Don't you be stupid, Mis- . . . Matthew. I have this gun, remember? I'll use it next time, no questions asked."

His gaze dropped to her pocket again. His breath caught. Unless he'd missed his guess, she'd just made that defiant gesture with the wrong hand.

He jerked his head up, his eyes widening as he shot a look past her.

"Catherine, look out!"

It worked perfectly. She gasped, spun around . . .

He was on her in a heartbeat, his arms sweeping around her waist and hoisting her off the floor so that her back was pinned to the wall.

"Let me go," she panted, struggling against him, but he held her easily with one arm while he dug in first her left pocket, then her right, with his hand . . .

And came up empty.

She went still in his embrace as he lowered her to the floor.

"Ah, Catherine, Catherine." He cupped her face with one large hand, his fingers clasping her chin and tilting it up to his. "I know you have the morals of an alley cat and the conscience of a puff adder but really, I thought you were above petty lies."

"Damn you," she said, half-weeping with anger at having her bluff called, "damn you!"

"Saying you had a pistol when you did not . . . for shame, Cat. Have you no sense of honor?"

"Look, if you've come to steal—"

"Steal? From you?" He laughed. "What could you possibly have that I might still want?" His gaze dropped to her mouth. He thought of how warm she felt in his arms, of the press of her breasts against his chest and the racing beat of her heart. "On second thought," he whispered, his laughter gone, "there just might be something."

"No," she said, but it was useless.

His mouth dropped to hers, hard and hot. Kathryn tried to wrench her face from his but he was unrelenting, his arm tightening around her, his hand sweeping back from her face to twist in her hair.

"Bitch," he growled. "Heartless, scheming bitch . . ."

With a groan, he kissed her again. And again. His hands swept down her back and cupped her bottom. He lifted her onto her toes, urging her into the quick, hungry hardening of his body.

It had been so long, so long.

"Bitch," he said again, but it was a whisper this time and as he said it, his mouth softened against hers until he was rubbing his lips gently over hers, until his hands were slipping back up her spine and his arms were sweeping around her and he was kissing her passionately.

And she was responding.

Oh, she was responding. Seconds ago, she'd been fighting him in blind panic. Now, she was winding her arms around his neck, burying her hands in his thick, silken hair, and dragging his head down to hers.

The taste of his mouth was as she remembered it, from the dreams. The feel of him, hard and powerful, in her arms. The smell of him, and the heat of his body . . .

No. It wasn't like the dreams. This was reality, and it made the dreams pale by comparison.

"Cat," he said thickly.

His hands caught the hem of her skirt, fisted in the cotton fabric and swept it impatiently to her hips.

She made a sound in her throat.

"Cat," he said again, and all the urgency in the world was in that one word.

His fingers felt hot against her flesh as they hooked into

the elastic of her panties. His thumbs rasped against her skin as he began to draw the panties down . . .

Was she mad?

Kathryn jerked back. She jammed her elbows down and shoved both hands against his chest, hard enough so he stumbled back in surprise.

"Catherine," he said, his voice tinged with disbelief.

"Stop it," she hissed.

But he didn't stop. He reached for her instead and she lifted her knee and drove it straight into his groin, as hard and fast as she could.

For an instant, nothing happened. Then she heard the awful sound of the air rushing from his lungs, saw the color drain from his face. His lips formed her name but there was no sound.

Kathryn was shaking. She wrapped her arms around herself and stepped back.

"I told you to stop," she whispered. "Matthew . . . ?"

He made a horrible, gagging sound and then he doubled over, clutching his belly. Kathryn reached out her hand, then drew it back.

"If only you hadn't . . ." She thrust her hands into her hair and shoved it back from her face. "I'm sorry I had to hurt you, but . . ."

"Don't—be—sorry." He lifted his head and it seemed to her he smiled. "It—was—the—one—question—I—didn't—think—of," he gasped.

"What question?" she whispered, watching him in fascinated horror.

He gave a terrible little laugh that ended on a groan.

"Can—a—ghost—feel—pain?"

My God, he was fading! "Matthew," she said . . .

He was gone.

Kathryn reached out, carefully swung her hand through the air. Her fingers felt nothing, touched nothing.

The hair rose on the nape of her neck.

"Matthew?" she said in a tiny voice.

She swung around in a tight circle, staring into each bright, sunlit corner.

"Matthew, please, don't do this to me."

There was still no answer.

How could there be? There was no one in the room.

Kathryn's teeth began to chatter. "No," she whispered.

It was impossible.

It was absolutely impossible.

Things like this didn't happen in real life. People didn't just—they didn't just up and vanish into thin air . . .

Ghosts did.

A soft whimper burst from her throat.

Ghosts vanished. They came, they went. Poof, just like that. They did it all the time, in books, in movies, on TV.

But this wasn't a book or a movie or TV. It was the real world. And ghosts did not exist in the real world.

Kathryn tried to swallow but a lump seemed to have lodged in her throat. She worked at it for what seemed like a long time. Then she took a breath and walked to the telephone . . .

The what, Catherine?

She closed her eyes, took several short, shallow breaths. Finally, she picked up the phone, waited for a dial tone, and jabbed her finger into the hole on the dial that was marked O.

The phone was old-fashioned. And the static was awful. But things worked pretty much the way they did at home.

You dialed the operator, you reached one, you asked for information, you got it.

Hiram Bonnyeman answered on the first ring.

"Hello?" Kathryn said. She cleared her throat. "Hiram, this is . . . Yes. Yes, that's right. Well, I'm sorry, too. I, ah, I was . . . Look, I know you said you couldn't get here to do any work until next week but, uh, but I have a special favor to ask." Her legs wouldn't hold her up anymore. Slowly, like a deflating rubber doll, she sank to the floor. "Could you possibly find time to drop by and just check the door locks? No, no, nothing's happened. I just—I mean, I'm all alone out here, and . . . Tomorrow morning? Great. No, honestly. Everything is fine."

Kathryn hung up the phone and sat with it in her lap.

Why are you clutching that thing, Kathryn?

"Ohmygod," she whispered . . .

What would Hiram have said if she'd asked him what locks worked best against a ghost?

Nine

The phone call to Hiram was the easy part.

What had to be done next was a lot harder but Kathryn knew she could not spend the night in Charon's Crossing without checking it thoroughly from top to bottom.

If there were any more surprises here, she wanted to discover them now, while there was still some daylight left.

Armed with a flashlight, she made her way cautiously up the stairs, making sure she took a wide, wide detour around the cold spot.

Was it her imagination, or were the shadows deeper here on the second floor than they should have been this time of day?

The floorboards creaked as she made her way slowly along the East Wing corridor; she could hear the dull thump-thump of her heart beating in her ears. She put her hand on the door to the first bedroom and slowly, slowly eased it open.

The room was wrapped in muted shades of gloom . . . but at least it was empty. There was nothing under the bed but dust balls. That left only the closet to check. Kathryn took a deep breath, wrapped her hand around the doorknob, and pulled it open.

There was nothing in it but a couple of empty boxes.

Kathryn shut her eyes for a second, then opened them. Only another million rooms to go.

She bit back a choked laugh and set off down the hall.

Ten minutes later, she had finished checking the rooms on the second floor. Her knees wore badges of dirt from getting down and peering under all the high, old-fashioned beds and she'd had a shrieking run-in with an equally terrified mouse that had bolted for freedom when she'd opened one of the closets, but she was certain that nobody and nothing was hiding up here.

Reasonably certain, you mean.

Completely certain. There was nobody in the bedrooms and baths.

Nobody you can see, anyway.

Oh, for pity's sake!

What kind of nonsense was this? It was ridiculous to think that the intruder had been anything but a flesh and blood weirdo all gussied up for a late Halloween.

Sure. And he just happens to do a bit of hocus pocus on the side, as in escapes à la Houdini. Of course, Kathryn. That's perfectly reasonable.

Well, it was. Compared with thinking she'd been visited by a ghost, it was not just reasonable, it was right on the money.

All she had to do now was check the attic.

The thought made her shudder, which was silly. She'd been up there before. And it wasn't half as spooky as she'd imagined it would be . . .

Kathryn paused at the foot of the narrow attic staircase. She looked up.

Had the pitch of the steps always been this steep? Had the stairs and the landing beyond them been so terribly dark?

And the chill that poured down these steps . . . it made her skin crawl. She felt as if hundreds of tiny things were creeping over her flesh.

All you have to do is turn around and go downstairs, Kathryn.

Without knowing if anything . . . if anybody was hiding in the attic? No way.

Okay, then. Just go up there and lock the door. Don't open it. Don't even think about opening it.

And spend the rest of the night wondering if she'd locked somebody in the house with her? Uh uh.

She climbed the steps quickly. They really did seem steeper than before. It was just an illusion, of course. She knew that, just as she knew how stupid it was to let her imagination run away with her.

But she was trembling, and her breathing was shallow when she finally reached the landing.

She reached out for the doorknob. Once. Twice . . .

"Dammit, Kathryn," she said, and she switched on her flashlight, turned the knob, flung open the door.

Everything was exactly as she had left it. The lid of the old trunk was open, the rocking chair was tilted slightly towards the window, and Matthew's journal lay face down on the seat.

The shutters and the window were open, though. Had she left them that way? She couldn't really remember.

All in all, the scene was about as threatening as a photo layout in *Better Homes and Gardens*.

The breath spilled from her lungs in a long whoosh. She stepped into the center of the room and shined the flashlight beam into all the corners.

Except for some industrial-strength dust balls, they were empty.

Kathryn let out a relieved breath. Okay. She could chalk this room off the list, lock the door after her and leave.

Wait. The journal. Matthew's journal. She could take it with her, read it this evening. It might help make the time pass more quickly.

It might help her understand the crazy things that were going on in this house.

She walked quickly to the rocker and picked the book up. The old leather binding was warm to the touch, as if someone had just been holding it, but she knew it was only because the book had been lying in the late afternoon sunlight that was streaming in through the open window . . .

The window, and the shutters, slammed shut.

Kathryn whirled around, her heart pounding with fear.

"Who's there?" she demanded.

There was no answer.

"Dammit, is somebody here?"

She forced herself to step forward and swing the light around the room.

It was empty.

Take it easy, Kathryn. Be calm. Be logical. There's got to be a simple explanation.

The flashlight shook as she swung the beam over the room again. With the sunlight gone, everything was changed. The walls seemed to have grown closer and to rise at a strange angle. She flashed the light up over the rafters. They seemed to rise forever, with no end in sight.

And the corners . . .

She swung the light again.

Moments ago, the corners had been filled with nothing more ominous than dust balls. Now, they overflowed with shadows.

Shadows that moved.

Kathryn felt the hair rise on her arms. She wanted to scream, to run, to fling herself at the door.

But she didn't. Anything like that would be a mistake. The thing to do was to walk slowly but steadily from the room.

Pick up one foot. Now put it down. Pick up the other . . .

How long could it take to cover the twelve or fifteen feet to the door? An eternity, Kathryn thought, oh yes, an eternity. And every step of the way, she fought the terrible urge to take just one quick look behind her and see . . .

What?

Something, Kathryn. Something. Something that was, even now, reaching out to clasp her shoulder.

With a cry, she threw herself through the door and slammed it shut.

The bolt wouldn't catch.

"Come on," Kathryn whispered desperately, "come on, come on!"

The door turned icy cold under her hands.

Nausea rose within her.

"Close, damn you," she babbled, "close!"

The bolt snapped home.

A little sob of relief broke from her throat. She put her palm against her heart; it felt as if it were going to burst from her chest but she wasn't about to stand here, waiting for it to ease back to a gallop.

It wasn't until she was downstairs, safe in the relative brightness of the drawing room, that she figured out what had really happened in the attic.

The wind had played tricks.

It was playing them now, slamming shutters closed before she reached for them and rattling the loose windows in their frames.

A storm was sweeping in from over the sea. The warm afternoon breeze had become a gusty wind with the smell of rain on it. The changing weather, and her hyped-up imagination, had teamed up to scare her half out of her skin.

A storm wasn't anything to look forward to. Rain and wind, lightning and thunder, were stage effects she could have done without this night but it was lots better to know there was a rational explanation for the things that had gone on up in the attic than to think . . . well, not to think but to imagine she'd been the victim of something supernatural.

And the worst was over now. She'd checked all the rooms, peered in the corners, locked all the windows and doors. There was nobody in Charon's Crossing except for her . . .

. . . *and the man. The one who'd vanished in a puff of smoke.*

Kathryn straightened her shoulders. That kind of thinking would get her nowhere. The idea was to take a positive approach. Whoever he was . . .

. . . *whatever he was . . .*

He was gone. That was all that mattered. He was gone, the

house was secure, and by this time tomorrow, there'd be new locks on all the doors.

The wind was picking up. She could hear it rattling the palm fronds and tapping at the shutters. And the rain had started. She could hear it, too, pelting against the house.

But the house was brightly lit and as safe from intruders as she could make it. She'd change into something more comfortable and then she'd see to her supper—which would have to be soup and a sandwich again, since she'd never gotten around to doing any shopping in town.

And then she'd curl up on the settee and read Matthew McDowell's journal until she got sleepy because one thing was certain. She was not going to sleep upstairs. Not in that gloomy bedroom. She'd go up there just long enough to get what she needed.

"I'll be back," Kathryn said in her best Arnold Schwarzenegger voice.

She headed for the steps.

Okay. Now she was ready.

She dumped her pillow, sheet and blanket on the floor beside the settee and put her hands on her hips. Her supper was on a lamp table, the remains of the console table her visitor had smashed was kicked into the corner . . .

And the damned wind was still moaning, the shutters were rattling, but so what?

Kathryn picked up the sheet, flapped it in the air, then laid it over the settee cushions and tucked it in.

The room was pleasant. It must have been really lovely at one time. She smiled, thinking of how incongruous an addition she was, in her sweatshirt, sweatpants, heavy cotton socks and sneakers. But this was the perfect place to spend the night. The settee would make a comfortable bed, and never mind that her feet would probably dangle off the end.

Dangling feet were a small price to pay for a cheerful setting and a telephone.

A shower would have made things just about perfect but only a jackass would take a shower in this house tonight.

"Welcome to the Bates Motel," Kathryn muttered, and tried to laugh.

There. Her bed was all made up, ready and waiting.

She sat down, stretched out her legs and crossed her feet. She felt better than she had in hours. If only she had a roaring fire blazing in a fieldstone fireplace, things would be perfect. She remembered the house she and her parents had lived in when she was a child, the old Victorian back in San Francisco. The house itself had been close to falling down around their ears but there'd been a fireplace in almost every room.

She smiled a little, thinking of how she'd watched her father build a fire each night after dinner.

"Want to try it, Kath?" he'd finally asked.

Oh, the pride she'd felt when the first flames of that fire had licked at the logs.

Funny. She hadn't built a fire since that long-ago night. Would she remember all the little tricks that made for a good one? Could Jason build a fire? she wondered idly. He had a fireplace in his apartment but he never used it.

What was the point? he said. The radiators gave off plenty of heat. And it was true; she'd always agreed with him. It was impractical to build a fire when you didn't need one and Jason was always practical. That was one of the things she liked about him. Why, if he were here, he'd probably have figured out where this afternoon's intruder had really come from and what he really was . . .

Kathryn frowned. She didn't want to think about that now. And she certainly didn't want to doze off, not just yet, but she was getting drowsy. It was this sweatsuit. And these socks. The outfit was silly, far too heavy and warm for the tropics, but what choice did she have? She wasn't about to spend the night in her skivvies, not when there was the chance some guy might come popping out of the woodwork . . .

"Damn!"

She stood up and ran her fingers through her hair. She'd almost managed to forget the reason she'd spent the past couple of hours locking windows and doors and preparing to camp out in the drawing room. Now, reality hit like cold water pouring out of an upended bucket.

If her visitor, the man who claimed he was Matthew McDowell, was really an expert at the game of now-you-see-him, now-you-don't, all her preparations—the locked doors, the locked windows—were a joke.

It was dark in the room now, dark enough so that glancing back over her shoulder made her realize she should have turned on the lights a long time ago. She went quickly from lamp to lamp, switching them all on. There. That was better. Now she could see—

Bang!

Kathryn screamed and spun around in terror.

"Ba-bang. Ba-bang. Ba-bang."

The wind must have torn a shutter loose. It was flapping back and forth and sending up an ungodly racket.

For that matter, so was her heart. It was going ba-bang, ba-bang right along with the miserable shutter.

She opened the window and grabbed for the shutter but the wind had gotten stronger and it almost tore the shutter from her hand. She hung on to it, dragged it closed, and jammed the lock home. The wind came swooping down again, roaring like a freight train as it tore at the house.

The lights flickered, plunging the room into darkness.

No. No! The electricity couldn't fail. Not tonight. No electricity meant no lights. No telephone. No connection to the outside world.

The lights blinked, then came on. Even the telephone gave a quick, tinny shriek as if to prove it was still working.

But for how long?

Kathryn stared at the squat, old-fashioned instrument, the one Matthew had pretended not to recognize.

Maybe she ought to call somebody. The police. Or Olive. Or Jason.

No. Not Jason. He was half a world away. What could he do, except sit there in his apartment and worry and wonder if she'd lost her mind?

As for the police or Olive . . . what was the point? What could she possibly say?

"Hello, this is Kathryn Russell at Charon's Crossing, and I just saw a ghost?"

Oh yeah. She smiled tightly. Right.

Make that kind of call in New York, the odds were good nobody would give a damn. Make it here, the news would be all over the island by breakfast.

"Crazy American says Charon's Crossing is haunted."

What a great tag-line that would make for a real estate sign.

Besides, she was a long way from saying she'd seen a ghost. There was always a perfectly rational explanation for things like this.

What explanation, Kathryn?

Well . . . well, some kind of trick with mirrors. Magicians did stuff like that all the time. And they used hidden doors. Trap doors . . .

Kathryn sank down on the edge of the settee.

The last thing she wanted to think about right now was the possibility of hidden doors. Besides, she'd have known if he'd used one. Or if he'd used a mirror. After all, she'd been standing, what, six inches from Matthew when he'd disappeared.

But he couldn't have "disappeared." People couldn't do that any more than pigs could fly.

Another gust of wind tore at the house. The lights dimmed, blinked and went out. She held her breath until they flickered to wavering life.

That was twice. Three strikes, and you were out.

Kathryn sprang to her feet. There had to be candles in the kitchen.

There were. Three boxes of long, ivory tapers. She ripped every box open, stabbed the candles into anything she could find. Saucers. Cups. Jar lids. Then she set the candles on every flat surface in the drawing room and lit them all.

The room blazed with light. Kathryn stood back, arms folded, a look of defiance on her face.

Let the damned lights go out now!

She made a last quick trip through the house. She checked the front door. The back door. The French doors. Just for good measure, she checked the windows in the library and the dining room, the ballroom and the kitchen. Then, satisfied, she scooted back into the drawing room, shut the door after her, dragged a heavy wooden chair across the floor and jammed it under the knob.

"Ready or not," she said, and laughed. At least, she tried to laugh. The sound that escaped her throat seemed more like a croak.

Kathryn settled down on the settee with her sandwich and her tea. Her gaze fell on the splintered remnants of the console table. It really was too bad she didn't have a fireplace. At least, she could have given the antique a Viking funeral.

She smiled wryly. What a nasty display of temper *that* had been! Matthew hadn't thought twice, he'd just hauled back, given the table one good kick, and . . .

Kathryn blinked.

Matthew? Since when had she begun thinking of him like that? Just because he claimed he was Matthew McDowell didn't mean he was Matthew McDowell.

Because then, he'd be a ghost. And hadn't she just told herself she didn't believe in ghosts?

Okay. Okay, then maybe the whole thing had been a hallucination. Maybe she'd dreamed him up, complete with costume and . . .

"Hell."

The sandwich might as well have been rubber. Kathryn chewed and chewed before she could get the mouthful of bread and cheese down her throat.

You were in *big* trouble when you preferred thinking you'd had a hallucination to thinking you'd seen a ghost. Besides, her shoulders still ached, where his fingers had clasped them. She didn't know much about hallucinations but she doubted if they left bruises as calling cards.

So, what was she saying? That she'd changed her mind about ghosts?

Never. Never, in a thousand years.

So what if she could have read the *New York Times* through Matthew's hand, when she'd first seen him on the stairs?

So what if he could make the puff-of-smoke disappearances of a great illusionist like David Copperfield look pathetic?

So what if he stared at a telephone as if he'd just stepped off the shuttle from Mars and sounded like a refugee from a history book and wore an outfit that didn't look like a costume but looked real, and sexy, as hell?

"So what?" Kathryn said weakly, and she groaned and put her head in her hands.

All right. Just for the sake of argument, suppose . . . suppose she accepted the preposterous idea that Matthew was, in fact, a ghost?

Outside, the wind seemed to take a long, sighing breath, as if to say, Well! It's about time you came to your senses!

Kathryn rose impatiently to her feet. She stabbed her hands into the pockets of her sweatpants and paced back and forth.

It couldn't hurt to consider the possibility, could it? Of course it couldn't. There was nothing worse than a closed mind.

After all, once upon a time people had insisted the earth was flat. Where would the world be if nobody back then had ever said, Hey, wait a minute, let's try coming at this from another angle.

So, all right. She'd do just that, come at this from a different perspective. For the sake of argument, she'd assume that ghosts existed.

And that Matthew was one of them.

Why would he haunt Charon's Crossing? And what did he want from her?

The answers had to be in that journal. Where had she left it? Right there, on that table.

She plucked it up, then sank down on the settee and put her feet up. Where had she left off?

Here, a voice whispered, clear as a bell.

Kathryn looked up sharply, then stretched her lips in a humorless grin.

"No ad-libbing, please," she said in a giddy whisper.

She opened the journal, flicked the pages until she came to the next entry, and began to read.

October the twenty-first, 1811:
I have spent the last days preparing for our first foray in these waters. We have taken on every possible store, from ship's biscuit for the men to oil for the lamps . . .

Kathryn yawned. Boy, she was tired. It had been such a long day. She yawned again, blinked her eyes hard, and looked back at the page of the journal.

. . . oil for the lamps. Mr. Hauser, my first mate, has suggested we redistribute the shot for the Long Nines. I am not sure it is necessary, but have agreed to . . .

Kathryn stretched out on the chaise. Her eyes felt as if they were gritty with sand.

Maybe she'd just shut them for a couple of minutes. Not that she'd sleep. That was out of the question. Who could sleep in this crazy house?

But a minute's rest would be . . . would be . . .

The journal fell from her lap, and she was asleep.

* * *

The night grew darker.

The candles sputtered; burned down to stubs, then died.

The wind, moaning through the trees, snatched at the shutters.

And upstairs, high in the attic, something shifted and stirred in the darkness.

"Catherine," a voice whispers.

Kathryn's eyelids flutter. She doesn't recognize the voice. She doesn't want to hear it, or its summons.

But it is too late. She is already slipping into the dream.

She finds herself in a room. She can see little but she senses that the space is confining.

She is uneasy.

"Where am I?" she says.

A window flies open. Moonlight spills faintly across the floor. It paints an ivory swath across some old furniture, a rocking chair, and an open trunk.

Kathryn's breath hisses from her lungs. She knows where she is. She is in the attic at Charon's Crossing.

Her throat constricts. She doesn't like this place anymore. She wouldn't like it, even if she didn't remember what happened here earlier tonight. The air feels heavy and moist, almost like a weight against her skin. There is a smell in the air, too, one that is musty and unclean.

The faintest of whispers echoes from the puddle of darkness.

Kathryn's heartbeat quickens.

"Matthew?" she says.

Is he going to come to her?

After what happened today, she knows she should be frightened at the possibility. But she is not, even though she remembers everything of their encounter, his rage and his hard, crushing strength.

What she fears is something else, something she senses in the oppressive atmosphere of this attic.

The whispers fuse into sounds with more substance. Kathryn's hand flies to her throat. She can feel the swift race of her pulse under her fingers.

"Matthew?" she says again. "Please, if that's you, come out and show yourself."

There is no answer, but she hears the scuttle of tiny feet behind her. She swings around, heart clamoring, and sees something small dart into a corner. A spider? A mouse? She cannot tell but she has the feeling it is nothing so simple as a frightened fellow creature.

What is she doing here? Everything about this place unnerves her. The cobwebs. The sounds. The smells . . .

Kathryn shudders and suddenly, the moonlight is gone. She stands in total darkness.

The sound of her pulse drums in her ears. She takes a step back, feeling for the door she knows must be close by.

Something races across her bare toes. She cries out in horror and shudders. The feel of the thing was awful, it was feathery and altogether alien. She could hear it, too, making a high-pitched, chittering sound.

The smell in the air is stronger now. It is sweet, hideously so, and it makes her belly knot.

Kathryn starts to tremble. She can see nothing but she senses evil. Evil . . .

Something is here, moving in the blackness. Something terrible. And it is coming for her.

"No," Kathryn sobs, "please, no!"

She flings herself towards what must be the door but it isn't there. Her arms flail wildly, she runs her hands across a wall she cannot see . . .

There it is. She feels it. The door.

Her fingers close on the knob. She twists and twists . . .

It will not turn. The door is locked, and she is trapped.

Kathryn screams. She beats her fists against the wood.

"Matthew," she sobs, "Matthew, help me!"

"Catherine," a voice whispers, from behind her.

It is not Matthew's voice. It is a voice she has never heard before, and it strikes terror into her heart.

She bites down on her bottom lip. The coppery taste of blood fills her mouth.

"I'm dreaming," she babbles, "I'm dreaming, dreaming, dreaming . . ."

"Catherine."

She whirls around. The voice reminds her of leathery wings, flapping in dark caves. Of the papery whisper of thousands of insect feet sweeping across the dusty bones in a graveyard.

An eerie light is pooling in the far corner of the attic and, within the light, something is taking shape.

A moan bursts from Kathryn's throat.

It is a man, but it is not Matthew.

He is tall and thin. His hair is white, drawn tightly back from a face that is nothing but a skull over which skin has been drawn.

"Catherine," he says.

He smiles but it is like no smile she has ever seen, bloodless lips stretching evilly to become a terrifying display of sharp, white teeth. He steps slowly forward and raises a pallid arm. His hand is little more than bone and gristle and in it, he holds a sword that drips with scarlet blood.

Kathryn screams and screams, and suddenly the attic door crashes open. Matthew is on the landing just outside and she throws herself, sobbing, into his arms.

He holds her close, then shoves her behind him, towards the steps.

"Run, Cat," he says.

"Matthew," she cries, "don't go in there!"

Matthew's hand is in the small of her back, pushing her. She stumbles away from him.

"Did you hear me?" he roars. "Run, Catherine, and don't look back!"

The attic door slams, she hears the click of the bolt in the lock. Matthew has shut himself in with whatever is up there.

Kathryn flies down the stairs, all the way down until she is inside the drawing room. She slams the door, locks it and presses herself against it, arms outstretched, adding the weight of her body to the barrier.

"Matthew," she sobs.

She listens, but there is no sound beyond the rasp of her own breath. After a long, long time, she slumps to the floor and waits.

When she hears the sound of footsteps outside the door, she rises slowly, her body and hands pressed to the wood.

"Matthew?" she whispers.

"Cat. Open the door."

She knows his voice. She has known it, within her soul, from the day she was born. With a sob, she undoes the lock, flings the door open, and falls into his arms.

"It's all right," he says, and holds her close. "Cat, beloved, it's all right now."

"That—that thing . . ."

"Don't think about it, sweet."

She shudders and clings tightly to him, seeking solace in the warmth of his body, the security of his embrace.

"What was it?" she whispers.

Matthew strokes her hair, soothing her as if she were a kitten.

"It doesn't matter."

"How did you get away from it?" She presses her hands against his chest and leans back in his embrace. "I was afraid it would kill you!"

He smiles down at her.

"Were you?"

"Yes. Oh yes. It was so—so evil!"

"Catherine." He lifts her tenderly in his arms and carries her to the settee. He sits down, still holding her, and brings her head to his shoulder. "Close your eyes now, and sleep."

She gives a little hiccup of a laugh.

"But I am asleep," she says. "I'm dreaming, Matthew. I know that."

He nods and strokes her dark, silken hair back from her face.

"Then shut your eyes, Cat, and dream good dreams."

She shudders. Her arms tighten around his neck.

"I can't. I don't want to. If I shut my eyes, I might find myself back up there, with that—that thing."

"No. I promise, that won't happen."

"How can you be sure?"

Matthew leans back into the corner of the settee, taking Kathryn with him.

"Because I'll be with you," he says. "I'll stay right here, holding you and watching over you as you rest."

She gives a deep sigh.

"I can't rest," she whispers. "I can't . . ."

Seconds later, she is fast asleep.

Matthew looked down at her, lying in his arms. Christ, how beautiful she was, even now. Her face was ashen, the sweep of her lashes as dark as soot against her cheeks. Her hair was tumbled and wild; her eyes were still swollen with tears.

Gently, he reached out his hand and stroked the tendrils of hair back from her cheek.

What had happened tonight? Why did she go to the attic?

A muscle knotted in his jaw.

The Other must have drawn her there. No other explanation makes sense. But why?

At least, now, he knew the identity of the Thing that lived in the darkness. But why would it want to hurt Catherine?

Matthew looked down at her, lying soft and warm in his arms. What would have happened if he had not gotten there in time? The house had been lit up as brightly as if for a ball. He'd been walking in the garden, the wind and rain swirling around him, determined to avoid the house and Cat while he tried to work through his confused thoughts, when suddenly he'd felt the evil presence of the Other.

"Catherine?" he'd whispered.

He'd turned towards the house, his gaze going unbidden to the attic window. An eerie glow of light had been leaking through the shutters, and then he'd heard Catherine scream his name.

"Cat," he'd cried, and he'd raced into the house, up the stairs and to the attic . . .

And found her, found her just in time. His stomach had risen into his throat when he'd seen the Thing reaching out for her.

"Waring," he'd whispered, for that was who it was. What it was. What it had once been.

God, the ugliness of it. The vicious cruelty in its laugh, the inhuman fury in its burning eyes just before it had faded back into the darkness.

What if the Thing had caught Cat, wrapped her in its slimy embrace?

Matthew groaned. His arms tightened around Catherine; he bent his head and buried his face in her hair.

What in hell was happening to him? He could have killed her a dozen times over in the past few days but he hadn't. And all the reasons he'd given himself for waiting were not reasons but lies.

What he had wanted was to touch her. To kiss her and hold her, as he was holding her now.

He shut his eyes and drew the fragrance of her deep into his lungs.

His plans were collapsing like a house of cards. And Catherine . . . Catherine was not as he remembered her.

The woman he remembered had flirted and teased; she had worn costumes meant to make a man's heart beat faster. Everything about her had spoken of allurement and enticement.

The woman he held in his arms didn't know how to tease, or to flirt. She wore clothing that was a puzzlement. These things she had on tonight, for instance. A man's shirt and a man's trousers, so far as he could see, shapeless and over-sized . . . not that they truly hid her femininity.

Nothing could do that, not even the way she wore her hair. His Catherine had favored a style meant to look natural even though he had known it took a maid an hour to arrange it.

This Catherine wore her hair loose. Or pulled back at the neck, the way he wore his. She didn't bother staining her lips, either, or her cheeks.

She was different in other ways, too. She lacked a certain coyness, a feminine trait Matthew disliked but had come to accept as inescapable. But she possessed everything else in abundance. She had an independent spirit and a fiery temper. A smile twisted across his lips. By God, this afternoon she had kneed him, right in the balls! He could not imagine another woman doing such a thing.

Another woman? Hell. He could not imagine his Catherine doing such a thing . . .

What in hell was wrong with him? *His* Catherine? As opposed to what? The woman in his arms *was* his Catherine.

Who else could she possibly be?

"Matthew?"

The word was the softest of sighs in the deep silence.

He looked down. Catherine's eyes were open, and fixed on his. He could see a thousand questions reflected in their blue depths, and then their sudden widening as she remembered.

He drew her closer as she began to tremble.

"It's all right. I've got you."

"Oh God," she whispered. "What was it?"

"A dream," he said. "Only a dream."

"No. It was real. And it was—it was horrible. A creature. A hideous creature . . ."

He lay his finger gently over her mouth and stroked it over the silken curve of her lip.

"Hush. It's over now, Catherine. Close your eyes and rest."

She sighed, and her dark lashes feathered against her cheeks.

"Matthew." Her hand rose, lay light as the petal of a flower against his chest. "Don't leave me."

His heart constricted. He covered her hand with his. "I won't. Not as long as you need me."

Her eyes closed. She would be asleep soon. All at once, he knew that there was one question he had to ask.

"Tell me quickly," he said, his voice low and urgent, "what is your name?"

But he was too late. Her slow, steady breathing told him she was asleep.

The hours pass.
The storm subsides.
The candles sizzle and go out.
Night gives way to morning, and the shutters and windows open soundlessly, admitting a soft, fragrant dawn breeze.
Kathryn dreams again. She is within the circle of Matthew's arms. He has shifted them both on the narrow settee so that they lie full length, together. His body is hard and warm; it shields her from any harm.
She is safe, forever safe, in his embrace.

Ten

Hiram's red pickup truck came rattling up the drive promptly at seven.

Kathryn was waiting for him on the outside steps. She'd been half-convinced he wouldn't show up. Now, as he climbed down from the cab, it was all she could do to keep from racing up and throwing her arms around him.

" 'Morning, Kathryn. Isn't it a lovely day?"

Was it? She hadn't noticed. She'd been too caught up in trying to decide where last night's dreams of lying in Matthew's arms while he caressed her had ended and today's reality had begun.

She smiled brightly. "It is, now that you're here. Thanks for agreeing to stop by this morning. I know it was really short notice and you have lots to do."

"Well, you made this sound urgent."

"It is urgent." Kathryn tucked her hands into the back pockets of her jeans. "I, ah, I think there might be somebody sneaking around out here."

"A prowler, at Charon's Crossing?" Hiram smiled, as if she'd suggested an ocean liner had docked down in the cove. "What makes you think so?"

Careful how you phrase this, Kathryn.

"Well . . . well, I heard noises."

"Last night?"

"Yes."

The old man wiped his forehead with a red handkerchief,

tucked it into the back pocket of his denim overalls, and lifted a battered toolbox from the bed of the pickup.

"I'm not surprised."

"You're not?"

" 'Course not." He grunted as he set the toolbox on the verandah and knelt down in front of it. "Old house like this, get a bad rain storm, it's bound to rattle the doors and the windows."

Kathryn shook her head. "This had nothing to do with the storm."

"Wind slips under the shutters, sends them bangin' against the walls—"

"No. No, it wasn't the wind, Hiram. In fact, I phoned you before the storm hit, remember?"

"Mmm. So you did." The old man grimaced as he creaked to his feet. "Well, there's still lots of funny sounds in an old house, Kathryn." He looked at her and smiled. "The joints creak and groan, just like mine."

"Look, I know you think I'm crazy, but—"

"Not crazy. Just nervous, maybe, way out here all by yourself. I can understand that but truly, there isn't anything to worry about. There's no crime to speak of on this island." He chuckled. "Nobody's got anythin' worth stealin' and even if they did, who'd do it? Everybody knows everybody else. Why, if somebody showed up wearin' a watch wasn't his—"

"I'm not talking about a burglar," Kathryn said sharply. "I—I saw something, too."

She hadn't meant to let that bit of panic edge into her voice but now, at least, she had the old man's attention.

"Saw what?" he asked, turning towards her.

Matthew McDowell. And someone else. Or something else, something that still makes my blood run cold just to think about it . . .

"Kathryn? What did you see?"

Kathryn swallowed dryly. "A man," she said, after a moment.

"What man? What did he look like?"

Her eyes met Hiram's. He wasn't smiling anymore. In fact, he was looking at her with such intensity that a sense of foreboding swept over her.

"Well, he was tall. In his thirties, I'd guess."

"Was he white?"

"Yes."

Hiram's face was expressionless. "Anythin' else? Anythin' about him that was special, I mean?"

Oh yeah, Kathryn thought, yeah, there was something special about her visitor, all right. He dressed like a character in a late-night movie, he sounded like one, too, and sometimes when you looked at him, you could see right through him.

"Kathryn?"

Kathryn cleared her throat. "No," she said, "no, nothing special."

Hiram stared at her for a long moment and then he nodded.

"I'll do what I can to make you feel more secure here," he said. "You just tell me what you want done."

"Well, for starters, I'd like you to fix the shutters. Some of them won't stay closed."

"I can take care of that."

"Good."

"What else needs doin'?"

"I want the door locks changed."

"No problem."

"Be sure you change the one on the attic door, too." Hiram looked at her but if he thought the request strange, it didn't show on his face. "The lock that's on it now is old," she said, "and difficult to work."

He nodded. "Sure."

Kathryn hesitated. "There's one last thing."

"Yes?"

"I know it sounds weird, but . . . do you think there might be secret passages in the house?"

The look on the old man's face said that she'd gone too far.

"Secret passages?"

"Look, I admit I don't know much about Charon's Crossing. Or about this island, for that matter. But I do know that it wasn't uncommon for mansions of this period to have hidden doors and passages built into them. You can't tell me you never heard of such things!"

Hiram shrugged. "I've heard of them, I s'pose. But never with regard to Charon's Crossin'."

"Well, it won't hurt to check, will it?"

"No, I suppose not. I'm just not sure what you want me to do."

"Dammit," Kathryn snapped, "how should I know? You're the contractor, not me. Do whatever people do to find hollow places in the walls. Knock on them. Feel around the fireplace. Poke in the back of the closet . . ." She forced herself to smile. "Humor me, Hiram. Please?"

The old man nodded. "If that is what you wish, I will do it."

"Thank you. I'll be in the garden, if you need me."

She was heading towards the side of the house when Hiram's question stopped her dead in her tracks.

"Kathryn? Shall I change the lock on the cellar door, too?"

The cellar? Damn. Oh, damn. She'd been so busy worrying about the doors and the windows that she'd never even thought of the cellar. But she thought of it now, dank and damp and probably unlocked all the long hours since she'd first set foot in this house.

"Oh yes," she said, as if there weren't a sudden cold knot in her belly, "that's a good idea. Absolutely. Change the lock on the cellar door, too. That way, I'll be certain no one can get into the house."

"No one will," Hiram said, "unless, of course, it's haunts you're tryin' to keep out of Charon's Crossin'."

The old man's tone was so matter-of-fact, his expression so bland, that she thought she must have misunderstood him.

"Haunts?"

"Ghosts," he said calmly. "If that's what's payin' you visits, there's no lock in the world will keep it out."

She laughed. At least, she tried to laugh. But what came out sounded more like a croak.

"Why—why on earth would you say a thing like that?"

Hiram shrugged. "Well, considerin' the things you said yesterday, about chains draggin' and things moanin' in the night . . ."

"Come on, Hiram. I was joking!"

The old man was undeterred. "Folks say there's a spirit been trapped in this house for nigh onto two hundred years."

Kathryn felt as if a clammy hand had touched her.

"You didn't say that yesterday."

"You didn't ask."

"You're right. I didn't ask, because sensible people don't believe in such nonsense!"

Hiram shrugged his shoulders. "Sensible people admit that there are lots of things in this life that are beyond explanation."

"Yes, but a ghost . . ." Kathryn blew the hair back from her forehead. "Is that why you asked me if there was anything special about the man I saw? Because you think I saw this—this spirit?"

"They say his name is Matthew McDowell. And if you did see him, you'd be the first."

Kathryn stared at the old man. The sun was shining and the birds were singing. It was, she knew, a peaceful, even a beautiful, scene. But she felt as if she were standing in a dark cave with a chasm yawning at her feet.

She wanted to do something to defuse the moment. To laugh. To make a joke out of the whole thing. But the best she could manage was a wan smile.

"Let me get this straight," she said. "You're telling me there's a ghost in this house, that he's been here for two hundred years— and that I'm the first person unlucky enough to see him?"

"I'm only sayin' what I know," the old man replied.

"That's not only impossible, it's illogical. If no one's seen this ghost, how do you know who it is?"

The look Hiram gave her said that her question was patently foolish.

"Everybody knows who it is."

The wind, gusting in from the sea, sent a tremor across Kathryn's skin.

"Everybody but me," she said, trying for a light touch and failing miserably. "Well, that's what I said yesterday, isn't it? Here I am, the lucky owner of a house that comes complete with a built-in spook, and nobody tells me a thing." She cleared her throat, linked her hands loosely behind her, and rocked back and forth on the balls of her feet. "I, uh, I don't suppose you know why he'd be haunting this house, do you?"

Hiram took a hammer and screwdriver from his tool kit and tucked them into his back pocket.

"He died here."

The old man's matter-of-fact tone caught her off guard.

"Here?" she said, her voice rising to a squeak. "At Charon's Crossing? Was there an accident?"

"It was no accident. Matthew McDowell was killed here." Hiram jerked a box of nails from the tool chest and dumped it into a pocket. "Executed, for piracy, just through that old trellis, in the garden out back." He turned and looked at her. "But there are those who say it was more a murder than an execution."

Kathryn could no more have kept herself from spinning around and staring towards the rear of the house than she could have kept her heart from taking a leap into her throat.

"Man who killed him was a British officer. Some say he found out McDowell wasn't a privateer but a pirate, stealin' treasure meant for the English king and buryin' it on some spit o'land out in the middle of the sea for himself."

"But you don't believe that?"

Hiram shrugged. "McDowell fell in love with the governor's daughter."

"Cat Russell," Kathryn murmured.

He nodded. "She was high born, liked the good life. The rumor was McDowell wanted to make her his wife but she wasn't about to marry a rough-and-tumble American upstart who sailed under a flag some thought might as well bear the skull and crossbones."

"And? What happened?"

"All I know is what I've told you, Kathryn." Hiram let down the tailgate of his pickup truck and climbed up into the bed.

Kathryn gave a shaky laugh. "Let me get this straight," she said. "Does everybody on the island know that story?"

"Everybody." Hiram looked straight at her. "And not a one of 'em would think twice if you decided to move out of here and take a place in town."

So much for worrying about not spreading rumors about Charon's Crossing!

Kathryn looked at the house. She could feel nothing ominous here today. The only thing she could sense was a bittersweet sorrow. Besides, why would she lend substance to the fanciful tales of haunts and spirits?

She swung towards Hiram. "Thank you," she said, "but I think I'm going to stay right where I am."

"I had a feelin' you'd say that." The old man grinned. "Have the feelin' Elvira will like you just fine, too."

"Elvira?"

"My missus. She's as stubborn as a mule, same as you. You and she ought to get along real well."

For the first time in what felt like a long, long time, Kathryn really smiled.

An answering smile flickered across Hiram's mouth. "She said to tell you she'd be happy to come out here, give you a hand puttin' this place in shape. How's that sound?"

"It sounds terrific."

"Treat her right, might be she'll bake you some fresh cinnamon rolls while she's at it."

"If she'll make me some of that lemonade you served yesterday, it's a deal."

Hiram nodded. "She'll call you. Meantime, I'll fix your

shutters and your doors. Should take me a couple of hours, no more."

Kathryn tried not to heave a sigh of relief. "Good," she said. "And you'll check for secret passages?"

The old man chuckled. "It'll be the most fun I've had since I was a boy, playin' at pirates down on the beach."

She smiled back at him. "Can I do anything to help?"

"Not a thing. Go sit in the garden and get some sun. You don't want to go back to New York, lookin' pale as a gh- . . ."

He tried to bite back the word, but it was too late. Kathryn's eyes met his and they both began to laugh.

She had intended to see if she couldn't drag a settee onto the terrace, stretch out in the sun and read her way through Matthew's diary. But after her talk with Hiram, the terrace and the garden had lost their appeal.

Besides, she'd been here for days and she'd yet to walk down the cliff to the sea. So she collected the journal, a glass of iced tea, and made her way to the cove.

The path itself was steep, the footing uncertain enough to make her pause a couple of times, but when she reached the bottom, she caught her breath with pleasure.

An arc of white sand bordered an azure sea. Lustrous shells, as intricate and beautiful as tiny sculptures, were strewn across the sand; tall coconut palms swayed under the touch of a gentle breeze.

Kathryn sank down under one of the palm trees, leaned back against it and stared at the waves lapping the shore. It was so serene here; she almost dreaded opening the journal. Something—intuition, maybe—warned that what she was going to read was not going to be pleasant.

Hiram was at the house, installing new locks, fixing the shutters and looking for secret passageways but deep in her heart she knew the truth. Nothing he could do would change anything. The answers to what was happening at Charon's

Crossing lay inside this leather-bound book and it was time to find them.

Slowly, she opened the diary and began to read.

An hour slipped by, and then another. The sun moved higher into the sky but Kathryn was aware of nothing going on around her. She was caught up in a period that had existed almost two centuries before. It had been a dangerous time and an exciting one, and Matthew's brief entries made it clear that he had enjoyed every moment.

His ship was fast. His men were loyal. The Caribbean Sea offered prize after rich prize to *Atropos* and her dashing captain . . .

And Catherine Russell had stolen his heart.

An entry written on a day in March of the year 1812 was typical.

Today we have taken yet another French merchant ship. My men are jubilant, as am I. We are amassing riches beyond our wildest dreams and a reputation that precedes us on these blue waters. How I long to hold my sweet Catherine in my arms again and tell her of this victory.

Kathryn lingered over the last line, and over others like it in the entries that followed. There was no mistaking what had happened. Matthew McDowell, the man who had thought to conquer Catherine Russell, had been himself conquered. He was, at long last, in love . . . and it was tearing him apart.

His journal said it all.

I am torn with jealousy. Cat says we cannot yet let her father know that we have pledged our hearts to each other. I agree that she knows him best but I am beside myself with anguish when I see her laugh and flirt with the titled English

*bastards who flit in and out of Charon's Crossing. They all
speak as if the silver spoons they were born with are still stuck
in their mouths and look at me as if I were some exotic, dangerous specimen best viewed at a cautious distance.*

Cat laughs when I protest.

*"Why, Matthew," she says, slipping into my arms in the dark-
ness of the rose garden, "you are jealous!"*

*There is no sense in denying what is so painfully obvious.
Cat teases me gently, then assures me that I have no need for
jealousy. She says her actions are meant to keep her father
from realizing that she and I have fallen in love. He insists,
she says, that she should marry well. Cat, of course, sees that
a marriage to me would meet that condition. But her father
must be persuaded, and she is convinced he is not ready to
listen. She weeps sometimes, when she tells me of this, and it
breaks my heart to see her so distressed.*

*I have thought about the problem a great deal these past
weeks and I am convinced there is no longer a need for subterfuge. I am an American, yes, and I surely have no title, but
in all other ways, I am an appropriate suitor. I am captain of
the most successful privateer in these waters. I have amassed
more than enough money to provide well for a wife. Most im-
portantly, I adore Catherine. I will devote my life to making
her happy. What father would not be glad to give his daughter
in marriage under such circumstances?*

*Cat agrees but begs me to be patient, but I am running
short of that commodity. I also know what she does not, that
the international situation is fraught with danger.*

*The news from home makes it clear that President Madison
and his advisors have finally grown weary of dancing to the
English tune. Though I have profited by their dalliance, I am,
at heart, a patriot. I, too, have tired of the game. We fought
hard for our independence from British tyranny; that we succumb to it again makes my blood flow hot. In truth, I will not
be unhappy if War comes and I must go from capturing the*

French to ending the English stranglehold on ships that sail the high seas.

If that happens—nay, when it happens, for I know in my heart that it will—then Catherine must already be my wife. Otherwise, we will be trapped on opposite sides of a War, perhaps lost to each other forever.

Truly, this grows ever more complex. I have tried to make Cat see it but she is too unworldly to understand all the ramifications.

"We can always elope," she insists, and then she goes into my arms and kisses me and I am lost to logic.

How innocent she is, and how I love her!

Innocent?

Kathryn frowned and looked up from the journal.

It seemed almost painfully clear that the only innocent in this story was Matthew. Catherine Russell had been playing Matthew for a fool. Any woman would know that, today or back in 1812.

She had wanted to have her cake and to eat it, too. The miracle was that Matthew had not seen through her scheming ways but then, he was a man in love, though how he could have been in love with such a manipulative, spoiled brat . . .

Kathryn lifted her face to the sea breeze.

What was it to her? So he'd been a jerk. Lots of men were. Lots of women, too. People in love weren't always reasonable or sensible. They let passion rule their heads. Her parents had proved that until the day they'd finally ended their marriage.

And that was how Matthew had loved Catherine. You could sense it, in the words he'd written. You could feel it, in the way he'd touched her and kissed her and . . .

Kathryn blinked. What the hell was she thinking? She didn't know how he'd kissed Catherine. A dream, a hallucination, call it what you liked, wasn't reality. And even if you climbed out on the farthest limb of self-delusion and said it was, it wasn't she that Matthew had held in his arms, it was the woman he'd thought she was.

"Kathryn?"

A shadow loomed over her. She gave a start of surprise and her heart leaped but when she looked up, it was only Hiram.

"Hiram," she said, with a little laugh. "I didn't hear you."

"I wanted to tell you that I'm leavin' now, Kathryn. Shutters are fixed, locks are all changed." He jerked his chin up towards the house. "Everythin's locked up tight."

"Oh." Kathryn closed the journal and scrambled to her feet. "Sorry. I sort of lost track of the time."

"No problem." Hiram held out a ring of keys. "Figured you'd want these."

She nodded as she pocketed them. "Thanks."

"Figured you'd want to know, too, that I checked for hidden doors and such." The old man's eyes met hers. "Didn't find a thing."

Kathryn felt a light blush rise to her cheeks. "No. I didn't really think you would but I figured it couldn't hurt to check . . ." Her words trailed away. "Well," she said, and stuck out her hand, "thank you for coming by."

"My pleasure."

"Shall I write you a check now?"

"We'll add it on to the bill." Hiram smiled. "Eager to get back to your book, hmm?"

Kathryn looked down. She hadn't realized she was clutching Matthew's journal to her breast.

"Yes," she said with an answering smile, "I guess I am."

"Well, I'll see you next week." Hiram started up the cliff path. Halfway to the top, he stopped and looked back at her. "Just remember what I said," he called. "There's no disgrace in changin' your mind and takin' a place in town."

It was easier to nod than to argue. She was impatient for Hiram to be gone, impatient to get back into Matthew's world.

Moments later, she was.

June the twelfth, 1812
Sweet Jesus, I cannot believe what has happened! I am in possession of information that may well change the course of history.
Last night, I was at Charon's Crossing. Lord Russell was away, having gone to Jamaica on business for the Crown, and Cat and I were truly alone. We were almost carried away with passion in the darkness of the garden, but Cat regained her senses in time.
I know I should be grateful. God knows I would not wish to sully her innocence but I burn to make her mine, to strip away her gown and kiss her sweet flesh, to . . .

Color flew into Kathryn's cheeks. She turned the page quickly, unwilling to read such things. Matthew's longing for Catherine Russell was too intense. It was personal. And painful, though she knew it was crazy that the thought of a man she didn't know hungering for another woman should send such a sharp ache knifing through her heart.

The next page seemed safer. She took a breath and bent over the journal again.

. . . and, in my growing despair and frustration, foolishly blurted out what I have lately been thinking, that perhaps she finds more excitement in the secrecy of our meetings than joy in our relationship. Heaven forgive me, I said even worse things, accusing her of having no intention of letting me ask her father for her hand or, indeed, of ever becoming my wife.

"Finally," Kathryn said.
But the next sentence wiped the smile from her face.

I begged Catherine's forgiveness as soon as the foolish words had left my lips. I tried to explain that it had been desperation speaking, not me, but Cat was stunned, as well she might have been. She wrenched free of my arms and fled to the house, with me in pursuit.

And thus it was that I came upon an incredible scene . . .

They were in the drawing room, gathered around the fireplace, three men in huddled conversation.

Matthew only caught a glimpse of them before he fell back into the shadows as Cat slipped by, unseen. He recognized them all. One was Lord Waring, a despicable blowhard whom he'd seen slobbering over Catherine's hand far too often. Cat said he made her stomach turn but since he was head of the British garrison, she had no choice but to treat him politely.

The other was an influential Englishman, head of the most powerful bank on Elizabeth Island. The third man was the be-wigged Lord Russell himself, who had evidently returned early from his trip.

Matthew hesitated. Now what? The situation seemed to have been dropped into his lap by fate. He could storm inside and confront Russell, stand up and declare his intentions and to hell with Cat's pleas that he be patient.

But even in his present state of mind, he knew that it would be foolish to do such a thing. First he had to soothe Cat, for he had upset her terribly. Besides, there were others in the room with Russell. No, this was certainly not the time to ask for Cat's hand.

He took a couple of deep breaths. There was nothing for it but to slip out the way he'd come, through the garden, without being seen. Tomorrow, he'd get a note to Catherine, beg her forgiveness for the things he'd said.

The banker lit a cigar. Waring frowned, pulled a ruffled handkerchief from his sleeve and waved it ostentatiously before his nose. The banker paid no attention and Waring walked to the French doors. Matthew fell back further into the shadows as he cracked them open.

The men's voices drifted out into the night.

". . . great news, Killingworth," Russell said, "but can we trust this information?"

"Dammit, Russell, how many times must I tell you? Henry Clay and the Warhawks have won! On the first of June, President Madison sent the American Congress a secret message informing them that he intends to declare war on Great Britain on June the eighteenth."

Matthew stiffened. Christ, what was this?

"I'm simply trying to be certain we have our facts right," Catherine's father said in his upper-class English drawl. "If we make any precipitous moves . . ."

"Our spy in Washington has never been wrong, has he?"

Russell's appreciative chuckle drifted into the night.

"No. No, he has not. He's been worth every pound we've paid him."

"Then why should we doubt him now?" Waring asked. "The American government will make a formal declaration of war in six days."

"And no one in these waters will know it but us."

"Exactly."

There was a creak of wood, the sigh of upholstery. Russell's shadow drifted past the partly open doors.

"That's it, then, gentlemen. I shall move to seize all the American ships lying in the harbor on June the nineteenth, one day after war has been declared in Washington."

"Excellent," Waring said, chuckling. "By the time the Americans on Elizabeth Island find out they are at war with us, it will be all over."

"Remember," Russell said, "I'll want no ships destroyed. Make sure your troops understand that, Waring. Those ships will net the three of us a very tidy profit in a prize court. As for the Americans themselves . . . once we've pressed enough of them to give every British ship that sails these waters a full crew, the rest can rot in Dartmoor prison for all I give a damn." His voice roughened. "I have spent too much time pretending friendship for the roughnecks as it is. When I think how I've had to suffer their company in my home . . . the captain of the *Atropos*, especially. The man's a dirt-common bastard with pretensions of grandeur."

"His pretentions are all he'll have left, once his ship's been seized and he and his men are in chains," Waring said, and the three men laughed.

Matthew felt the blood drain from his face. He clenched his fists, felt his nails cut into his flesh. But he stood his ground, telling himself that there was more to avenge than his own honor.

When there was no more to learn, he slipped away into the night.

Luck, at least, was on his side.

Almost all the American ships that sailed the Caribbean under the protection of the British Crown were lying at anchor in the Hawkins Bay harbor.

The next day, working carefully and stealthily, Matthew sent word to their captains that there would be a meeting that evening on an isolated point of land on the far side of the island. By the time the meeting ended, Matthew and the others had hatched a plan.

They would strike first, at midnight on June the eighteenth, and seize Elizabeth Island from the unwary British.

The captains all agreed that an attack on Charon's Crossing and the capture of Governor Russell would force the garrison to capitulate and would avoid a difficult and possibly prolonged and bloody battle. They agreed, as well, that Matthew was the man to lead the attack since he was most familiar with the grounds of Charon's Crossing.

He was honored, and more than willing. But he had one demand.

Before he led the assault, he would go to Charon's Crossing and lead Catherine to safety.

The other captains looked at him as if he were daft.

"She is English," said the captain of the *Shenandoah*. "She cannot be trusted."

He found himself hauled to his toes, with Matthew's outthrust jaw inches from his own.

"She is my betrothed," Matthew snarled, lying only a little, for surely he and Catherine had pledged each other their hearts. "And I would trust her with my life."

"What nonsense is this?" the captain of the *Enchantress* said, glaring at the two men. "The English are the enemy! If we fight amongst ourselves, our cause is lost before it begins."

Matthew slowly let go of the other man's shirt.

"I tell you that I will not abandon the woman I love," he said.

"She will be safe," the captain of the *Decatur* insisted.

Matthew snorted with derision. "Safe? A woman, in the midst of what may well become a battle?"

"Yes," another captain called out, "she will be. We will tell our men to look out for her."

The others nodded their agreement, then turned their gaze on Matthew.

"Well?" the captain of *Shenandoah* asked. "Will that satisfy you? Or shall we forget this playing of soldiers and save our ships and ourselves, whilst we still have the chance?"

Matthew looked at the faces of his friends. They had agreed to risk their ships, their lives and the lives of their men for the honor of their country.

How could he argue for his own selfish ends?

He nodded and held out his hand.

"I am satisfied," he said.

The men shook hands, clapped him on the back and wished him well before rowing back to their ships.

That night, Matthew sat late in his cabin aboard the *Atropos*, finalizing a daring plan that no one else would know about.

He would slip ashore three hours before midnight on the night of the American assault.

I will spirit my Catherine to safety before the fighting begins, he wrote in his journal. *She will be safe and no one will be the wiser . . .*

It was the final entry he'd made.

Kathryn flipped through the remaining pages, but they were blank.

She shut the book and lay it aside. The hours had flown by while she sat reading. She was startled to see that the fiery sun was beginning to dip towards the sea.

A breeze sprang up, carrying with it a chill that made her shudder.

"Oh Matthew," Kathryn whispered, "what happened to you?"

"You know what happened to me, Catherine," a deep voice snarled.

She shot to her feet and spun around. Matthew was standing just behind her, legs slightly apart, hands fisted on his hips. His face looked as if it had been chiseled from stone. He looked enraged and intimidating, and Kathryn knew that it was time for her to stop denying the truth.

Matthew McDowell was not an intruder. He was a ghost.

For one racing beat of her heart, Kathryn almost laughed at the insanity of it. But then she looked into those cold green eyes and her throat choked with fear.

"You're wrong," she said. "I have no idea what happened to you."

He laughed, as if she'd made some terrible joke.

"Such sweet protestations of innocence, Cat. But then, I should have expected no less."

"Matthew, listen to me! I don't know what happened to you. I'm not your Catherine."

He started towards her, his eyes burning into hers.

"That, at least, is true. You never were my Catherine, though you swore that you were."

"No! I never was. I . . ."

God, oh God, he was going to kill her! She wanted to run but where was there to run to, with the sea at her back and the cliffs rising ahead?

He was on her before she could do anything, his hands clamping down hard on her shoulders as he dragged her to him. She had freed herself from his grip by kicking him the last time but there was no chance of that now. He had her tightly pinned against his hard, unyielding body.

His fingers wrapped around her throat.

"Bitch," he said, grinding the word out through his clenched teeth.

"No!" Kathryn forced her clasped hands up between his wrists. "Please," she gasped, "Matthew! You're making a terrible mistake!"

His thumbs pressed down into the hollow of her throat. She gasped for air, struggling fiercely against him, but he was far too strong.

The world started to grey before her eyes and a roaring began in her ears.

Was it the sound of the sea, or the sound of her approaching death?

"Matthew," she whispered, and then there was only darkness.

Eleven

It was one thing to kill a man in the heat of battle.

Matthew had done that before, with little compunction. With the stench of blood in your nostrils and the cries of the wounded ringing in your ears, you acted instinctively to survive.

But it was another thing entirely to take the life of someone who had no weapon, especially when that person was a woman.

He could feel the softness of Catherine's flesh as she struggled under the pressure of his hands and see the terror in her eyes as they grew cloudy. The frailty of her bones and sinew were no match for the strength of his. She was dying and that was what he'd wanted.

Wasn't it?

"Dammit to hell!"

Matthew's cry, as much of self-disgust as of anger, mingled with the roar of the sea as it beat against the shore. His grip on her throat loosened. Just as she began sinking to the sand, he slid one arm under her knees and hoisted her over his shoulder with no more ceremony than he'd have given a sack of flour about to be loaded aboard his ship.

It was hard going, making his way up the narrow path to the house, and he gave a grunt of relief when he was finally able to drop her onto the settee in the drawing room. She was no lightweight, that was for sure.

Not that she carried any excess fat on her body. Matthew's gaze swept over her as she lay sprawled before him. What she wore left little to the imagination. Her skimpy cotton chemise, if that was what it was, clung to her high, rounded breasts; her legs were bare under a pair of what he assumed were incredibly abbreviated men's trousers. They were shapely legs, long and elegant, and suddenly he imagined them locked around his waist, driving him ever deeper into her while her eyes, dark with desire, fixed on his.

"Hell," he said sharply.

He knelt down beside the settee, took her shoulders roughly in his hands and shook her.

"Open your eyes," he demanded. After a couple of seconds, she did.

He saw the flood of emotions play over her face. Confusion first, then slow comprehension, then fear as she suddenly remembered.

"You—you tried to kill me," she said in a shaky whisper.

Matthew let go of her and rose to his feet. That same sense of self-disgust and anger was washing through him again. He cloaked it with a cold glare and an even colder tone of voice.

"Unfortunately, I did not succeed."

Her hand went to her throat and his gaze followed. It was hard not to flinch at what he saw. The imprint of his thumbs on her pale golden skin was just now beginning to fade.

He swung away from her, walked to the French doors, and threw them open.

"Some air will do you good," he said brusquely.

She was standing when he turned around again. Her shoulders were back, her hands were on her hips and her feet were planted just slightly apart. It was a classic posture that spoke of defiance and he felt a grudging admiration for her ability to carry it off, though she could not control the faint but perceptible tremor of her mouth that told him she had not quite overcome the fear she was so determined to mask.

"Get out!"

Matthew's lips drew back from his teeth. "An excellent suggestion, madam. If only I could comply."

"I'll give you ten seconds. If you're not out the front door by then, I'll—"

"Please, spare us both the dramatic threats." His lips curved again in that smile that was not a smile, the one that sent a shudder along Kathryn's spine each time she saw it. "I cannot leave here, much as I wish it. As for your posturing . . . there is nothing you can do to enforce your demand. You know it as well as I."

He was right, but how could she admit that? She was trapped in the middle of nowhere with a lunatic ghost and . . .

A ghost. *A ghost?*

Kathryn clamped her teeth together to keep them from chattering.

He laughed, as if he could read her thoughts.

"You find it disconcerting, to learn you are hostess to me?" The smile fled his face. "Trust me when I tell you I find it more so to be your unwilling guest. How do you think it feels, to realize you are no longer flesh and blood but are, instead, a spirit?"

"I don't know. And I don't care. Either you get out or I'll— I'll call the police."

He laughed. "They would probably call you insane." He lifted one hand in a sweeping gesture that took in the entire room. "Besides, even if they believed you, they could not catch me. Shall I walk through a wall to make my point?"

"No," Kathryn said quickly. "Don't . . . don't do that." The last thing she needed was to see him slip through a wall. Or turn into a column of dazzling light. It was taking all her courage as it was, just to stand here and face him like this.

After a moment, she cleared her throat.

"What did you mean when you said you couldn't leave?"

"I meant exactly what I said. I am trapped here, held within the boundaries of Charon's Crossing as if by an invisible wall."

"But—"

"Do not 'but' me, Catherine." His voice was sharp, his eyes

4 BESTSELLING HISTORICAL ROMANCES BY YOUR FAVORITE AUTHORS CAN BE YOURS, FREE!

Kensington Choice, our newest book club now brings you historical romances by your favorite bestselling authors including Janelle Taylor, Shannon Drake, Rosanne Bittner, Jo Beverley, and Georgina Gentry, just to name a few! Each book is filled with passion, adventure and the excitement of bygone times!

To introduce you to this great new club which is part of Zebra Home Subscription Service, we'd like to send you your first 4 bestselling historical romances, absolutely free! And once you get these 4 free books to savor at home, we'll rush you the next 4 brand-new books at the lowest prices available, as soon as they are published.

The way the club works is that after your initial FREE shipment, you will get our 4 newest bestselling historical romances delivered to your doorstep each month at the preferred subscriber's rate of only $4.20 per book, a savings of up to $7.16 per month (since these titles sell in bookstores for $4.99-$5.99)! All books are sent on a 10-day free examination basis and there is no minimum number of books to buy. (A postage and handling charge of $1.50 is added to each shipment.) Plus as a regular subscriber, you'll receive our FREE monthly newsletter, *Zebra/Pinnacle Romance News*, which features author profiles, contests, subscriber benefits, book previews and more!

 So start today by returning the FREE BOOK CERTIFICATE provided. We'll send you 4 FREE BOOKS with no further obligation: A FREE gift offering you hours of reading pleasure with no obligation...how can you lose?

We have 4 FREE BOOKS for you as your introduction to KENSINGTON CHOICE! To get your FREE BOOKS, worth up to $23.96, mail the card below.

FREE BOOK CERTIFICATE

Yes! Please send me 4 Kensington Choice (the best of Zebra and Pinnacle Books) Historical Romances without cost or obligation (worth up to $23.96). As a Kensington Choice subscriber, I will then receive 4 brand-new romances to preview each month for 10 days FREE. I can return any books I decide not to keep and owe nothing. The publisher's prices for Kensington Choice romances range from $4.99-$5.99, but as a preferred subscriber I will get these books for only $4.20 per book or $16.80 for all four titles. There is no minimum number of books to buy and I may cancel my subscription at any time. A $1.50 postage and handling charge is added to each shipment. No matter what I decide to do, my first 4 books are mine to keep, absolutely FREE!

Name _____

Address _____ Apt. _____

City _____ State _____ Zip _____

Telephone ( ) _____

Signature _____

(If under 18, parent or guardian must sign)

Subscription subject to acceptance. Terms and prices subject to change.

KC0296

KENSINGTON CHOICE
Zebra Home Subscription Service, Inc.
120 Brighton Road
P.O.Box 5214
Clifton, NJ 07015-5214

dangerously bright. "I assure you, it is a fact, one that pleases me no more than it pleases you."

"What are you doing here? I mean, why are you—are you . . ."

"Haunting this house?" The taunting smile touched his lips again. "It isn't necessary to dance around the subject. I am a ghost. Ghosts haunt houses. There's little logic in pretending otherwise."

She nodded. He made it sound so matter-of-fact but there was nothing matter-of-fact about finding yourself standing around in broad daylight, having a polite little chat with a—a delusional blob of ectoplasm.

A strangled sound caught in Kathryn's throat. She turned away hurriedly and made her way out of the drawing room, through the foyer and into the kitchen. He was following after her. She could hear his footsteps.

How interesting, the still-rational part of her brain mused thoughtfully. *I never knew you could hear ghosts walk.*

His hand fell, hard, on her shoulder.

"What do you think you're doing?"

It was a good question and she searched for an equally good answer.

"I'm going to make some coffee," she finally said. "Any objections?"

"Coffee?"

His tone seemed almost wistful. She turned and looked up at him.

"Yes." She smiled politely. Maybe you were supposed to deal with a crazy ghost the same way you dealt with a crazy human being, by being calm and pleasant and by not doing what instinct was telling her to do, which was to throw up her arms and run screaming from the house. "Would you like a cup?"

Would he like a cup? Matthew almost sighed. That was like asking a drowning man if he'd like someone to toss him a line. Lord, he hadn't had a cup of coffee in . . . in . . .

His smile faded. It was such a simple question, yet he had

been doing his best to avoid it. Now, he knew he could avoid it no longer.

"What year is it?" he said.

"What do you mean, what year is it? Don't you—"

"Damn you!" She gasped as his hand bit into her flesh. "Answer the question, madam. What is the year?"

He didn't know the year? Kathryn took a breath. This was getting worse by the minute.

"It's—it's 1996."

What had she expected? That he would cry out? Fall to the floor in shock? He did neither of those things. He simply stood there, his eyes locked with hers, but she could see the swift flare of his nostrils and the sudden pallor of his skin.

"Nineteen ninety-six?" he repeated hoarsely.

She nodded. "Yes."

"Then, I have been de-... I have been here for 184 years?"

Kathryn nodded again.

"Sweet Jesus," he muttered. "One hundred and eighty-four years..." His hand fell from her shoulder. "It cannot be!"

"It is."

"Nay! So many years cannot have passed."

"I can't help it if you don't want to hear the truth. There's a calendar in my checkbook. Do you want to see it?"

"Your check...?" Matthew shook his head. It mattered not that she was speaking in riddles again. All that counted was the sudden realization burning inside his head. "But if I have been... if so many years have passed, then you cannot be... then you cannot be..."

"Your Catherine."

He nodded. "Yes."

Kathryn's eyebrows lifted. "I'm not. I tried to tell you that, remember? But you wouldn't listen."

"But you are her image," he whispered...

Except that she wasn't. She was not Catherine.

Oh God!

Matthew took a step back, his eyes riveted to her face. There was surely a resemblance. A striking one. But that was all it was. A resemblance, nothing more. And, in his heart, he had known it all along.

She was not Catherine.

For days, for eternity, he had planned an act of vengeance he had hoped would bring him release. Now he realized that his plans had been for naught. Vengeance was as useless as love in this godforsaken horror in which he was trapped.

He made a sound midway between a groan of despair and of fury. Questions whirled in his brain like whispers of madness. If she was not Catherine, if she was not here so he could bring their ugly little morality play full circle, why was this happening?

Why had he been called out of the blackness that had contained him?

Was it all some hideous game, played by a cosmic jokester? Had he been drawn out of the darkness so he could wander the halls of Charon's Crossing forever, a doomed prisoner of Catherine's perfidy and of the moment of his death?

He shook his head sharply, forced his gaze to focus on her. Her face was pale, her bottom lip was caught between her teeth.

"Why are you here, then, if you are not Catherine?"

"Because I inherited this miserable house!"

"Nay. It cannot be so simple." She flinched as he slammed his fist on the counter beside her. "I cannot have been called from the darkness for no purpose!"

"Listen, I don't know why you've been—"

"Who are you?" he said.

"My name is Kathryn Russell, but with a *K.* K-A-T-H-R-Y-N."

Kathryn. Not Catherine. Kathryn.

"You are her progeny."

"Her descendant. Yes." She tried to smile. "Several generations removed."

He remembered that last instant of his life, that second when he had felt his blood draining away. His own words, borne on his dying breath, echoed in his ears.

May you rot in hell, Catherine Russell, he had said, *may neither you nor your issue ever know love or peace . . .*

Was he supposed to take this woman's life in place of Catherine's?

He looked down into her eyes. Her head was tilted back; he could see the pulse racing in the shadowed hollow of her throat. She was frightened, even more than she had been on the beach. And well she might be. She was his to do with as he liked, to torment or to destroy . . .

His throat constricted. As a boy, his uncle had dumped him in an orphanage. It had been an ugly, brutal place and he had escaped it within a year, running off to Boston, talking his way into a berth as cabin boy and thus into a career at sea.

But first he'd had to endure those twelve months in the orphanage. It hadn't been easy. The place was run by the Reverend Silas Wickett, a narrow-lipped, bloodless man who raised his helpless young charges on a diet of unflinching piety, daily whippings and thin gruel. The bounty of the countryside—sweet apple cider, brown bread thick with honey, and mutton stewed until it fell from the bone—was reserved for the reverend's own table.

Matthew had quickly learned how to survive. He raided the pantry for raw potatoes and withered apples and dug for wild onions beside the creek in early spring. And he set snares for the cottontails that lived in the meadow behind the orphanage and learned how to roast them over a smokeless fire.

Then, one autumn evening, he'd come upon a snare which held not a dead rabbit but a live one. The tiny creature had been caught by the leg; it had stared at him through wide, liquid eyes, eyes filled with terror. And in that moment, he had hated himself and hated the rabbit, for he had known then that he would not be able to kill it . . .

Kathryn cried out as he grabbed her and shook her like a rag doll. Then he flung her from him.

"Damn you," he snarled.

She cried out as he began to shimmer. By the time he had become a column of spiraling silver light, her face was buried in her hands. She sensed to look at him now might be to court death.

Eventually, she peeped out between her fingers and mercifully found herself alone.

The morning sun was not just hot, it was hell. It beat down on Kathryn like the fist of a giant determined to bring her to her knees. Her shorts and shirt were soaked, most of her nails were broken, and she knew that by this evening her back would feel as if it were broken, too.

She sighed and wiped her forearm across her sweaty forehead.

All in all, she felt better than she had in days.

There was nothing like work to clear your mind of cobwebs. It had taken her most of a sleepless night to remember that, but once she had, she was home free.

First thing this morning, she'd crossed her fingers, opened up her computer and plugged it into an electric outlet. At first, nothing had happened. Then the hard drive had hummed, the screen had brightened, and she'd been in business.

For a couple of hours, anyway. Someplace around ten o'clock, the power had gone out and her computer screen had gone dark.

Well, that was life on Elizabeth Island. Not that it mattered. Work, any kind of work, was what was important. It was the great panacea.

Elvira, Hiram's wife, had turned up bright and early at the back door and immediately set out to wage what she insisted would be a one-woman war against dirt. So Kathryn had decided to direct her energies at the overgrown rose garden.

It had been an inspired decision, even better than the time she'd spent on the computer. She gritted her teeth as she clipped away at a rose branch with the rusty pruning shears she'd found inside the gardening shed. Ghosts? Columns of silver light? The odds were, she'd never see them again. Now that Matthew knew she wasn't his Catherine . . .

He was here.

So much for the odds being in her favor.

Kathryn froze, every sense on the alert. Matthew was definitely here, in the garden. She could sense his presence, just as she had in her dream.

She swung around, the clippers forgotten. Where was he? She couldn't see a sign of him anywhere.

"Matthew?"

There was no answer.

"Matthew?" Her voice rose in irritation. "Come on, you might as well show yourself. I know you're here, so what's the point in playing games?"

Matthew was there, all right. He'd been watching Kathryn work for the past few minutes, leaning back against the sturdy trunk of a tree and admiring the view. He supposed it wasn't very gentlemanly to watch a woman without her knowing it but then, he wasn't a gentleman anymore, was he?

He was a ghost, and it was reassuring to find that he could still react to the sight of a gently rounded bottom waggling in the air as its owner bent over to get a tool from the little stack of them at her feet.

But how in hell had Kathryn known he was here? She was looking straight at him now, as if she could see him. Had he forgotten and materialized without planning to do so? He wasn't expert at this stuff yet.

Last night, after he'd had time to calm down, he'd wanted to, well, to talk with her. Not to apologize. He had nothing to apologize for. He'd simply thought it might not hurt to tell her that his anger was nothing personal.

But she'd been locked in her bedroom by then—as if a lock

meant anything to him, he'd thought with a smile. But then he'd thought it over and decided that it might not hurt to be a gentleman about it. If she wanted to pretend she could escape him by locking her door, he'd go along with the game.

And a good thing he had, if just watching her work in the garden had his britches feeling snug. Heaven only knew what would have happened if he'd strolled through the door and into her room.

He watched as she tossed aside the shears and glared into the garden.

"I suppose that's one of the pleasures of being a ghost," she said coolly. "Voyeurism must be a blast."

He materialized instantly, just where she'd thought he'd be, leaning against a tree with an insolent half-smile on his handsome face, though it pleased her to see him flush.

"I have never had need to be a voyeur, Kathryn. And though I won't bother asking you what blasting and watching on the sly have to do with each other, I would dearly love to know if it is ever your habit to wear more than your smallclothes."

"Smallclothes?"

"Your undergarments." His eyes raked the length of her body, leaving her feeling as if she weren't wearing anything when, in fact, she had on an oversized T-shirt and a pair of denim shorts. "Do all women of your time garden in such outfits?"

It was her turn to blush. She felt the color rise from the tips of her sneakered toes straight up to her face but she didn't blink.

"Did all men of your time stand around watching instead of working?"

The gibe hit home. Matthew's jaw set. His eyes fixed on hers as he unbuttoned his shirt, shrugged it off, and tossed it across a bench.

"Move over," he snapped.

Kathryn grinned, sat down on her heels in the midst of an overgrown flower bed, and watched as he set to work.

* * *

He was a pleasure to watch, that was for certain.

She spent a few seconds wondering how she'd explain Matthew if Elvira happened to come out and caught sight of him. But the last she'd seen of Elvira, she'd been taking apart the library, book by book. It was doubtful she'd turn up for hours. Besides, Kathryn was too busy enjoying the view to worry about Elvira putting in an appearance.

Matthew was gorgeous. There just wasn't any other word that could describe him.

His skin was a pale gold, almost the color of the wildflower honey she sometimes spread on her breakfast toast. Beneath it, his well-toned muscles moved with a smooth assurance.

His shoulders were broad and powerful; in a few minutes, they glistened under a light sheen of sweat. His biceps were rounded and his forearms firm. He worked with an economy of motion that was at once elegant and beautiful to see.

Her gaze drifted down his body. Those trousers of his, black, tight and clinging, made the most of a trim bottom, powerful thighs, and long, great-looking legs.

A flush swept into her cheeks again. What sort of woman got turned on by watching a ghost?

Not that she was getting turned on. It was just that, well, she'd been raised by an artist. Admiring the human body had been as natural as . . .

Her breath caught as Matthew turned and began working on another tumble of rose branches. His front was even more impressive than his back. She had never liked men who had overdone pecs; guys with breasts bigger than hers were not guys she found attractive.

Matthew's chest was perfect. The muscles were long and pronounced, the skin overlaid with a light covering of chestnut curls that arrowed down an abdomen as ridged as a washboard to disappear beneath the waistband of those devastating trousers. For the first time, she noticed that they didn't have a fly. Didn't fly fronts exist in 1812? She couldn't remember, or maybe she'd never known. Either way, she approved of the looks of his tights, the way they buttoned down each hip so that the fabric was taut across his groin . . .

For God's sake, Kathryn!

She shot to her feet. "Aren't you finished yet?" she said sharply.

"Almost."

"I don't know what takes so long," she said, stalking towards him. She bent down, snatched up the couple of tools she'd been using, and stuffed them into her back pockets. "If you'd left me alone, I'd have been done by now."

Matthew cocked his head, took a last snip at a branch, then nodded.

"That should do it," he said, and looked at her. "I did leave you alone, Kathryn. I was content, watching you sweat and strain, remember?"

"Yes," she said irritably, "you certainly were."

He grinned, handed her the shears, and reached for his shirt.

"I can see that being out in the hot sun plays havoc with your temperament."

"There's nothing wrong with my temperament," she said, looking away as he tucked his shirttails in. "At least I don't go around, popping in and out of the woodwork, watching people when they don't know they're . . ." Her eyes shot to his face. "My God! Were you there each time I showered?"

"Showered?"

"Dammit, Matthew, don't play dumb! Showered. In the bathroom. Bathed. Oh, you know what I mean."

"Ah. The water machine." He chuckled softly, his eyes wicked and teasing. "I never tire of that view, madam." Her face turned crimson and he laughed. "The view of the water pouring down the wall, I mean. It is truly amazing."

Kathryn's eyes narrowed. "I know you find this very amusing," she said coldly.

"Well, considering that there has been little to amuse me the past couple of hundred years, you can hardly blame me."

"You might try seeing all this through my eyes, you know.

How would you feel, if you found yourself sharing a house with a ghost?"

"An excellent question, though I have a better one, Kathryn. How would you feel, if you found that you *were* a ghost?"

He was right, it was one hell of a question. But if he expected her to feel compassion for him after everything he'd done, he was wrong.

"I supposed I'd feel . . . confused."

"Confused?" Matthew smiled coolly. "Believe me, confusion is a mild description for what I feel."

Kathryn started towards the gardening shed.

"You're wasting your time if you expect me to feel sorry for you," she said over her shoulder.

"I don't expect you to feel anything. Hell, you're a Russell. Russells have no feelings for anyone but themselves."

"That's not fair. I'm generations removed from that woman."

"That means nothing. Her blood is in your veins."

Kathryn spun towards him. "Yes, and her house is in my name. I want to know why you're haunting it."

"It's none of your business."

"It damn well is my business!"

"Is this what the years have done for women?" Matthew slapped his hands on his hips and glared at her. "You dress like a trollop and talk like a shrew."

"And you," Kathryn said, slapping her hands on her hips and glaring right back at him, "dress like an extra from the New York City Ballet and talk like—like a leftover from last summer's Shakespeare in the Park!"

"What?"

"You heard me!"

"That's ridiculous. I know nothing of ballet. As for Shakespeare . . . I am an American and damned proud of it, madam! I was born not a hundred miles from Concord and I have lived my life sailing under the Stars and Stripes!"

"Except for the time you spent flying the Jolly Roger, you mean!"

"That's nonsense!"

"You were a pirate, bought and paid for by the King of England."

"I was a privateer, doing what I could to keep body and soul together while I waited for my president to take action against the English!"

They were nose to nose and toe to toe, inhaling each other's anger with every breath they took.

Hell's bells, Matthew thought, how could he ever have mistaken this woman for the Catherine he had known? She had none of Catherine's polish or delicacy . . . and a hundred times her fire and a thousand times her beauty, even with dirt on her face and rose leaves in her hair.

My God, Kathryn thought, how could this man have cut a swath through the boudoirs of the nineteenth century? He was imperious, arrogant and impossibly chauvinistic . . . and he was more masculine than any man she'd ever known and so handsome that just looking at him stole her breath away.

Matthew looked into Kathryn's eyes. They had blazed with anger a moment ago. Now, there was another sort of fire lighting their blue depths, one that made his muscles tense in anticipation.

"Kathryn," he said softly. He lifted his hand and touched it to her cheek.

"Matthew." Kathryn moistened her lips with the tip of her tongue. "Matthew, I don't think—"

"Miz Russell?"

Kathryn blinked.

"Miz Russell? Ma'am?"

Matthew's hand stilled. "Whose voice is that?"

"It's Elvira! Oh, you've got to hide!"

"Who?"

"The cleaning lady. Hiram Bonnyeman's wife. He's the local repair . . . Oh, never mind. Matthew, you've got to hide. She'll see—"

"Miz Russell?" Kathryn spun around. Elvira had come out

the rear door and across the terrace. "I thought I heard you talkin' to somebody out here."

Kathryn cleared her throat. "Yes. Well, I was. You see . . ."

"She can't," Matthew said softly, from just behind her.

"Can't what?" Kathryn hissed.

"Can't see me."

"Of course she can. You're not invisi—"

"I am."

"But—but you aren't. *I* can see you."

"No one else can. Your repairman didn't, nor did your attorney, nor did that woman you've engaged to sell Charon's Crossing."

"But how can that be? It's impossible."

Matthew laughed. "I have no idea. And it is surely no more impossible than the fact that I am a spirit."

"Miz Russell?" Elvira's voice rose. "Are you all right?"

"Yes," Kathryn said, her voice rising, "yes, I'm fine. I just . . ." Her words faded and died. Elvira Bonnyeman was staring at her but it was obvious that Matthew was right. She didn't see him. He might as well have been made of glass. "I, uh, I was talking to myself," Kathryn said with a quick smile. "It's an old habit of mine. I'm sorry if I startled you."

Elvira laughed with relief. "No, that's all right, I do it all the time. But I have to admit, you did have me goin' for a minute. Between what Hiram said and the stories . . ." Her hand flew to her lips. "Oh, I am sorry! I surely didn't mean—"

"There's no need to apologize." Kathryn smiled again, even more brightly than before. "Elvira, I was thinking . . ." *What? What lie can you offer to get her out of here? Come on, Kathryn, come up with something clever.* "I was thinking that—that you've done enough for one day."

"But I haven't. I just came out to see if you want me to take down the draperies at the library windows and hang 'em outside for a bit or if you'd rather I started on the dinin' room next."

"Yes," Kathryn said.

Matthew chuckled. " 'Yes' won't do it," he said softly.

"I mean . . . I mean, I'll have to think it over."

"Well, then, why don't I get started in the dinin' room? That chandelier surely needs washin', and—"

"Not today," Kathryn said quickly. She went up the steps, put her arm lightly around the older woman's shoulders and began walking her towards the house. "Thank you for all you've done today, Elvira. Now, you go on home and by the time you come back tomorrow, I'll have worked out a plan."

"If that's the way you want it, Miz Russell, but—"

"Call me Kathryn, please. And yes, yes, I think that's the best way to do this. I'll figure out in what order I want to get things done and . . ."

She kept talking as she led Elvira into the kitchen where she only gave her time to scoop up her purse. Then she hurried her through the foyer and out the front door to the car Elvira had left parked in the driveway. She kept talking, too, as she opened the car door and all but shoved the woman into the driver's seat. And she kept smiling, not just while she talked but while she waved a briskly cheerful good-bye.

When the car had rattled out of sight, the smile fell from Kathryn's lips. She took a deep breath, went back into the house—and walked smack into Matthew.

"Nice performance," he said with a lazy smile. "All that, just so we could be alone? I'm flattered."

"All that, so we could be alone," she said grimly. She put a hand out as he took a step towards her. "And so you could start talking, as fast and as hard as you can."

"Talk?" Matthew scowled and folded his arms over his chest. "You disappoint me, madam."

"Stuff it, Mr. McDowell."

"I beg your pardon?"

"This is my house you're haunting. And I want to know the reason."

Matthew stiffened. "It's none of your business."

"That's where you're wrong. It's very much my business. Cat Russell was my great-great . . . my ancestor, and you talk about her as if she were evil."

"An excellent choice of words, madam."

"Well, I want to know why."

A muscle knotted in his jaw. The last thing he wanted to do was bring Cat's perfidy to life again.

"It's a dull story, I'm afraid, one that would only bore you."

"Listen, Matthew, I'm not stupid. I've read your journal. I've spoken to people."

"And they remember me?" He grinned. "I'm flattered."

"What they remember," Kathryn said pointedly, "is that you were a pirate."

Matthew's mouth became a thin line.

"That is the second time you've accused me of piracy," he said tightly. "If you were a man—"

"But I'm not. I'm a woman, and you mistook me for someone who spurned you."

"Spurned? Spurned?" His hands knotted into fists and he took a step forward. Kathryn held her ground but it wasn't easy. Anger blazed in his eyes. "I was not spurned, I was betrayed."

"So you claim."

"It is the truth."

"The truth can sometimes be a matter of interpretation."

"Truth is truth, Kathryn. It needs no interpretation."

He didn't want to tell her anything. Kathryn could see that. But he owed her an explanation, dammit. When he'd thought she was Cat Russell, he'd cursed her. He'd even tried to kill her. Did he really think he could buy her off with a smug little lecture on truth?

Kathryn lifted her chin. "I believe in judging for myself," she said. "Or are you afraid that if you tell me the story, I'll punch it full of holes?"

Matthew glowered at this impossible woman. She was trying to embarrass him into telling her a tale that was none of her business. Well, she would not succeed. The tale was humiliating. It was bloody. And letting her hear it would change nothing.

On the other hand, perhaps it would. What if that was the

reason she'd been drawn here? What if it were the reason he'd been allowed to step out of the blackness?

Perhaps he was supposed to tell the story of Cat's perfidy to her namesake. It was not a pretty story; it would surely not be something one would wish to hear about one's forebear.

Maybe that was the whole purpose of what was happening. As acts of vengeance went, it wasn't much. But it was better than nothing. He would tell her the tale, she'd be pained by it. And then she would leave Charon's Crossing and he . . . he would find peace. Or perhaps he would fade back into the darkness.

A fist seemed to clamp around his heart. Either way, there would be no more sunshine on his face. No more scent of flowers to tease his nostrils, no taste of fine cognac slipping down his throat . . .

And no more Kathryn.

She would not be there to argue each and every damned point he raised. To look at him with defiance flashing in her magnificent blue eyes. To put her hands on her hips, lift her chin in that way that was enough to drive him into a rage and talk to him as if she were not a female but his equal.

He would have her for none of those things, nor would he have her to invade his dreams, to drive him senseless with desire and make him ache to be made of flesh and blood so he could take her in his arms, kiss her mouth and caress her breasts until she pleaded for him to strip away her clothing and sheathe himself in her heat.

He turned away abruptly. It was all foolishness. He could tell her what had happened or he could not. He knew, in his heart, that the telling would change nothing for him. But perhaps she was right. Let her judge for herself. Let her hear the truth.

No one had, in all these many years.

"Very well," he said. His voice was cold but so soft that Kathryn had to strain to hear it. "I'll do as you ask, Kathryn. I'll tell you why I haunt this place." He swung towards her and she saw that his face was as grim as his tone. "And once I have, you will wish you had never come here."

Twelve

The story Matthew had to tell her was not just inscribed in his head and heart but in every drop of blood that beat through his veins.

He had lived it once, relived it a thousand times since emerging from the black void in which he'd spent the past 184 years. There was nothing new in it, not for him, anyway.

Still, he dreaded the recitation. The telling of it would only make the pain of what had happened sharper. Poets wrote sweet words of torment when they spoke of those who had died for love but there was nothing sweet about the death of his men.

They had not died for love but for his own accursed stupidity.

He could not bear the thought of telling Kathryn the story within the confines of these walls. Even after so long a passage of time, there were moments he thought he could hear the echo of Lord Russell's laughter in this house. And then there was the Other, locked away in the blackness beyond the attic walls.

No. No, he could not speak of that terrible night on which he had lost everything—here, at Charon's Crossing.

He pulled open the French doors and motioned Kathryn outside. The sun was melting in the sky, tinting the terrace and the garden in shades of fuchsia.

Kathryn started down the steps but the pressure of Matthew's hand stopped her.

"Not there," he said quickly. "Let's walk down the path to the cove."

She hesitated and he knew she was remembering what had happened on that beach only a couple of hours before. Christ, what kind of man was he that a woman should be afraid of him?

"You needn't worry," he said. "I'm not about to confuse you with Cat again."

The air was chilly with the onset of evening; the sun was dipping towards the sea. The waves pounding against the shore seemed to echo the beat of his own heart.

It was the perfect setting for his story, and he began it quickly, without preliminaries.

He told Kathryn of his first meeting with Cat and of how he had been entranced by her, and of the subsequent, secret encounters that had seemed so romantic; of how Cat had refused to let him declare his intentions to her father.

"She told me that she had already tried to discuss modern ideas about love and marriage with him in the abstract," he said, his voice low, "and that he had chastised her, calling her thoughts stuff and nonsense bred by the revolution on the Continent. But she assured me that she'd gradually been winning him over and that she would tell me the instant she sensed his willingness to accept me as her suitor."

Matthew gave a short laugh, turned his back to the cliffs and stood staring out at the sea.

"I was such a fool. I believed her. Hell, why wouldn't I? I was besotted with love. I would have done anything for her." He took a deep breath. "And, eventually, I did.

"Perhaps Cat was bored with her life, perhaps she had done the same thing before. I only know that it was all a game. And it would have been a harmless one, with me the only loser . . . if something had not happened which would change the lives of everyone involved."

He began to walk along the shore, his steps long and steady. Kathryn kept pace with him. He glanced at her from time to time as he told her his story, watching the play of emotions on her face, the skepticism warring with pity and then both losing the battle and giving way to amazement that he could have been so foolish.

But he spared himself nothing. He knew now that he was telling the tale as much for himself as for her. It was time to say aloud the things he had been thinking for what might as well have been an eternity.

Confession was good for the soul, or so they said, which was almost as terrifying as it was amusing considering that he no longer knew whether a soul was something he possessed.

At last, he reached the point in his narrative that would be the most difficult. He paused and turned again to the sea.

"Sometimes," he said in a low voice, "sometimes, I almost wish I had never been at Charon's Crossing the night Lord Russell and his cohorts schemed to start the war before the Americans knew it had been declared. But I was, and I heard them plan to capture for the Crown all the American ships lying at anchor in the harbor."

Only the ugliest bit of the tale remained now. Matthew stared blindly across the sea to where the sun lay dying, bleeding crimson rays into the black water, and he shuddered.

"I know what you overheard," Kathryn said quietly, "and of your hope to rescue Catherine before the Americans made their move."

He nodded. "Yes. I know you read it."

"But I don't know what happened. The entries ended so abruptly . . ."

Matthew choked out a laugh. "As did all else on that night, Kathryn."

"That was . . . it was the night you—you—"

"Don't be shy, madam. Yes, it was the night I died, the night I lost everything, not just my life but . . ."

"But the woman you loved?" The simple words were hard to get out. Why should they have been? Why did they leave such a knot in her breast?

"Loved?" He laughed again, the sound bitter. "I never loved

Cat. I know that now. I was just too besotted to admit the truth. What I felt was lust, plain and simple." He bent, scooped up a handful of fine, white sand and let the breeze take it as it sifted slowly through his fingers. "It was the mystery I loved. The furtive meetings that held within them the tang of danger, the sly glances exchanged behind her father's back . . . Oh, Cat was good at what she did. She was as skilled at the art of deception as she was at the art of teasing a man until his body ruled his head, and I was fool enough to be taken in by it."

"What happened that night, Matthew? No one on the island says anything about you . . . about you dying in an American attack."

He laughed. "Nay, how could they? There was no attack."

Kathryn licked her lips. "What they say is . . . is that you were killed for piracy."

Anger flooded through him, rose like a foul medicine in his throat and flooded his mouth with the taste of bile. He swung towards her, the setting sun painting him in blood-red tongues of flame, and grabbed hold of her shoulders.

"Who says such a thing? Tell me, and I will stuff his lies down his throat until he chokes on them!"

"The islanders talk, Matthew. It's all old, meaningless gossip."

"Meaningless, to defame me?" His mouth twisted. "I have defamed myself enough without anyone adding to it. Russell must have concocted such a tale. It would have kept Catherine's skirts clean of scandal, but how could anyone have believed it? There were witnesses that night, people who must have seen, and heard, everything."

"What?" Kathryn whispered. Her eyes sought his in the thickening darkness. "What did they see? What could have been so awful that it turned you into . . . I don't know much about—about spirits, but surely, it isn't usual to—to end up trapped in the place where you . . ."

It was stupid, not being able to say the words. He was dead, he was a ghost, and he was haunting her house. But it didn't seem quite that simple, not when he was standing before her, more real than any man she'd ever seen, more embittered than any she'd ever known.

". . . Where I was killed," he said flatly. His hands tightened on her flesh until it was all she could do to keep from crying out. Then, slowly, his grip loosened. He took a deep breath and then he sat down on a driftwood log, turned his gaze inward and told her the rest.

"As you know from my journal, I gathered the other captains together. I told them everything, about Madison's plan to declare war on Great Britain and Russell's intention to seize our ships and our men."

"And you and your friends drew up a plan to strike first," Kathryn said softly as she sat down next to him.

He nodded. "They were as eager as I." He smiled at the long-ago memory. "Sturgess, of the *Dolphin*, clapped me on the back and said we would all go back to the States as heroes. Everyone laughed and we passed a bottle of rum, but the simple truth was that every man of us yearned to stand up for the Stars and Stripes and for our country in her hour of need."

His smile faded. "You know, too, that they balked when I insisted I must go ashore and rescue Catherine before any action began."

The night breeze stirred Kathryn's hair. It was warm and soft, yet for just a moment, she felt a chill.

"They told you not to do it," she whispered, "but you didn't listen."

"Of course I didn't." He looked up, his eyes flashing in the darkness. "Cat had promised to be my wife." He looked at Kathryn. "No decent man would abandon the woman to whom he had pledged his heart."

Kathryn nodded. "No," she said quietly, "no decent man would."

"And yet, I understood their concerns. Had our situations been reversed, I would have taken their position. But for myself . . . it was one thing to risk sacrificing my life for my flag. To risk Catherine's . . ."

He blew out his breath and got slowly to his feet. Kathryn did, too, and they stood side by side, looking out over the water.

"The night of our attack was moonless, perfect for what I intended. I took Hauser, my First Mate, into my confidence. I saw the doubt in his face but he was too good a man to question my commands. I told him my plan was foolproof— but that his obligation was to save both *Atropos* and my crew in the unlikely event something went awry in my scheme. Then I slipped from my ship and rowed a skiff around the island to where Charon's Crossing stood high above the sea.

"The moon was obliterated behind a heavy bank of clouds so that the sky was black as Hades, enclosing the island in velvet darkness . . ."

His voice faded to silence. The setting sun had finally been swallowed by the sea. Night had claimed the island, not the dark, inky night of long ago that he had just described but one lit by stars and a bright full moon, and yet Kathryn knew that he saw neither. His thoughts were in the past, as well as his heart.

The seconds passed and still he said nothing. His profile might have been cut from stone, it was so harsh and unyielding.

At last, she touched his arm.

"Matthew?" she said softly. "Aren't you going to tell me the rest?"

He sighed, such a deep sigh that she heard the pain of it whisper in the silence.

"Aye," he said. "Aye, I will tell you, Kathryn. And then you will leave this place, for whatever it was that brought you here has surely done it only to mock me."

A breeze swept in from the sea, ruffling his hair, but he paid no attention as he turned towards the cliff, raising his head as if he could see the mansion as it had been on that long-ago night.

"There was a ball at Charon's Crossing. The house was lit

like a beacon against the night." A half-smile touched his lips. "I had not been invited. Cat had said it would be torture for her, being forced to smile politely at other men and dance in their arms."

"Did you climb the cliff?"

He nodded. "It was not easy, in the pitch black night, and I knew that Catherine would be frightened when I brought her down, but she would be safe, for I was determined to let no harm come to her. When I reached the top. I skirted the front of the mansion, avoiding the carriages and drivers waiting outside, and made my way around back, to the terrace. I intended to peer into the ballroom, see Cat, and somehow catch her eye."

"And did you?"

Matthew's teeth flashed in a terrible smile.

"I found her, all right, but not inside the house. I had just started across the terrace when I heard voices in the garden. A man and a woman were whispering together and laughing softly in an intimate way that told me they were old lovers. I stepped back into the shadows when I realized they were coming towards me."

Kathryn's eyes fixed on his. "It was Cat, wasn't it?" she asked quietly.

"Yes." His voice roughened. "It was Cat and a pompous scoundrel, one of the bastards I'd overheard conspiring with Cat's father. He was an English lord named Waring."

"Maybe it wasn't what it seemed."

Matthew shot her a look that said she was crazy. And maybe it *was* crazy, wanting to shield him from his memories. He was nothing to her except an unwelcome, even dangerous, presence in Charon's Crossing. Besides, there was no changing whatever he was about to tell her. It had already happened, almost two centuries ago.

"Dammit, Kathryn!" His eyes glittered fiercely in the moonlight. "Why do you try and protect her? Is it because you share the same blood?"

"I'm not trying to protect her! I'm trying to . . ." She shook her head. "I'm just suggesting that you might have misinterpreted what you saw."

"I saw them," he said through his teeth. "Do you understand? They stood on the terrace not two feet from me and Waring took Cat in his arms. 'You have made me a happy man tonight,' he said, and then the son of a bitch bent her back over his arm and kissed her while his hand slipped down her neckline and cupped her breast. Christ, I went crazy! I flew at him like a madman, pulled him off her, and bashed him in the face with my fist."

Kathryn reached out her hand as Matthew swung away from her but something kept her from touching that proud, rigid back.

"Waring fell to his knees, his nose spouting blood, and I turned to Cat, convinced she'd been victimized by that horse-faced bastard." His face twisted with memory. "She looked at me as if I were a weevil she'd found in a piece of hardtack, rushed past me and dropped to her knees beside Waring, calling him 'beloved' and 'sweetheart,' cradling his head against her bosom. Then she glared at me with all the hatred of the world shining in her eyes and cursed me for having hurt the man to whom she had just become betrothed."

This time, Kathryn couldn't stop herself from touching her hand to Matthew's shoulder.

"Still, I could not accept the truth. I tried to take her in my arms. I reminded her of the vows we'd made and when she would not listen, I grew desperate. Time was racing by and I knew it. I tried to tell her that we could not waste our breath in argument." His head drooped forward and his voice fell to a whisper. "God help me, I told her everything. Of the Americans, waiting to take Elizabeth Island, of my plan to rescue her before the attack . . ."

"And Waring heard?"

Matthew lifted his head. "He heard," he said flatly. "He staggered to his feet, his face livid. Catherine threw herself into his arms, denying everything I'd said, but he thrust her aside and called her a whoring slut. I knew I had to stop him. I shouted his name and drew my sword. Waring drew his . . ."

Kathryn shuddered. She had only to close her eyes and she could envision what had happened next: the glint of sharp metal, the clang of steel upon steel, the looks of lethal fury, the thrust, the parry, the slash and riposte until, finally, there was a gush of scarlet blood.

"When it was over," Matthew said, his voice so low she had to strain to hear it, "we both lay at Cat's feet, mortally wounded and sinking into the dark river of death."

Kathryn's voice was choked with emotion. "Oh, Matthew! How horrible it must have been. To have been so deceived by the woman you loved . . ."

His hands shot out and clasped her forearms. "Dammit, Kathryn, I don't seek your pity. I was not the true victim of Cat's deception. It was my men."

Kathryn stared at him in bewilderment. "Your men?"

"My crew. They died that night, every last man of them, even my cabin boy, a foolish child barely old enough to have stopped whimpering for his mother each time he fell and skinned his knees." His voice broke and he turned away, but not before Kathryn had seen the bright glint of tears in his eyes. "It was my men who paid the price for my monumental stupidity, do you understand? They trusted me and I betrayed them, I sacrificed them for the deceit of love."

"Catherine told her father what you'd said about the planned American attack on Charon's Crossing," Kathryn said through stiff lips.

Matthew nodded. "Her shrieks brought Russell and his guests running. She told him a fanciful tale in which I was both pirate and rapist, unmasked by her pig of a fiancé, and Russell was only too happy to believe her. He had me bound, left me lying in a pool of my own blood, and led his troops to the harbor. The other ships were safe, for their captains had wasted no time in putting out to sea when I had been discovered missing . . . but the *Atropos* had disobeyed orders and waited for me."

Kathryn shut her eyes tight. "Oh God," she whispered.

"Nay," Matthew said hoarsely, "not even God could save my men that night."

"You can't be sure they all died," she said in a desperate attempt to ease his tortured conscience, "I mean, you weren't there . . ."

"I lived long enough for the battle to end, and for Catherine to stand over me and tell me that she wanted me to die knowing my ship was sunk and my men dead." He gave a bitter laugh. "I had ruined her life, you see, or so she said. Her father had an empty title. He had no money, no land and no influence back in England, either. Cat had schemed for power and position. I—I had just been a diversion."

"How you must have hated her!"

"Hate?" He laughed again, a terrible, cold sound that sent a tremor down Kathryn's spine. "That is too simple a word for what I felt. I gathered the last of my strength and cursed her with my dying breath. 'May neither you nor your issue ever know love or peace, Catherine Russell,' I said. What I did not realize was that I was dooming myself, for it would seem that to damn someone with what turns out to be your dying breath is to turn the curse back upon yourself."

Kathryn gave an uneasy little laugh. "But—but surely you don't believe in . . ."

The look he gave her made her swallow the rest of the sentence and the rush of hysterical laughter along with it. He was a ghost, a man trapped between the dead and the living, and she'd almost chided him for believing in curses and what happened to those who made them as they lay dying.

Of course, he believed. And so did she. He had doomed himself. Had he doomed her, too? She was Cat's descendant. Was Matthew's curse the reason she hadn't been able to return Jason's love?

"Have no fear," Matthew said softly, as if he had read her

thoughts. "The burden of my words plagues only the giver. I, and I alone, must bear their onus."

"I'm so sorry, Matthew. So very, very sorry."

Her face was turned up to his, her eyes wide and filled with compassion in the moonlight. His heart thudded and he thought how glad he was that his foolish words had not lived on through the years to hurt her. It was far, far better that he should suffer the consequences than she.

He longed to reach out and take her in his arms, tell her that he was sorry he had ever frightened her; to kiss her mouth until it parted beneath his, loosen her hair from its restraint and thrust his hands deep into the dark weight of it. He wanted to take her down onto the sand, strip away her clothing and tell her with his body and with his soul that she was the first bright and beautiful light to have penetrated the bleakness of his existence.

His mouth hardened into a tight line. Was he insane? No woman deserved such thoughts, especially not one who bore the blood of the woman who had betrayed him, no matter how many generations removed she might be.

He stepped back, his eyes like empty pools in his stony face.

"You are not welcome here, Kathryn."

"Don't be silly. This is my house."

"If you are wise, you will go back where you belong."

Kathryn's head lifted. "Don't threaten me, Matthew."

"I offer good advice. I urge you to take it."

What was the use in wasting sympathy on him? He was as arrogant, as impossible, as ever. Kathryn's eyes, so filled with compassion moments before, turned cool.

"I'll leave Charon's Crossing when I'm good and ready, and not a moment sooner."

Matthew glared at her and Kathryn glared back. She knew how he reacted when his authority was challenged.

A cloud, as dark and stormy as the look on his face, swept across the moon, plunging the sea and the land into darkness.

Kathryn held her ground.

Was he going to turn into a spinning whirlpool of silver

light and try to scare her silly again? Well, it wasn't going to work. She'd seen his gaudy Las Vegas act one time too many to be impressed.

But when the moon broke free of its clouded cage, Kathryn found herself alone on the beach.

Matthew was gone.

Thirteen

Matthew paced the length of the attic. Then he turned and paced the width.

He knew the damned room's dimensions by heart. It was still twenty feet wide by forty feet long . . . and he was still angry as hell.

Why didn't Kathryn leave Charon's Crossing?

He had told her to go and she should have done it by now.

She didn't belong here. The mansion was his by default . . . his, and the Dark Presence that was Waring were the only creatures suited to this purgatory.

Surely, she knew that.

"Damn," he said, slamming his fist against the wall without breaking stride.

Sweet Jesus, he hated this house, hated it almost as much as he hated himself.

What in hell was wrong with him? He hadn't been a man given to self-pity nor to regret and he'd be damned if he wanted to change that, now that he was a ghost, but self-pity and regret were what he seemed to be wallowing in lately.

And in weak-kneed, nonsensical shilly-shallying. Look at what he'd done last night, for God's sake.

First, he'd spilled his guts to Kathryn like some lily-livered jackass. Then he'd barked out a villainous warning to her about leaving Charon's Crossing and done one of the disappearing acts that surely would have raised the hair on the nape of his neck if he'd been the mortal and not the ghost.

And then he'd stood around on the beach in the dark, to make sure she got up that damned cliff in one piece. Not that she'd needed his help. She was as capable of handling herself as any man and besides, the moon had made things bright as day.

And why had he done it? What was Kathryn to him?

Nothing but a damned reminder of everything he had lost.

Before she had invaded this place, he had been alone in the darkness with only his bitterness and his pain as companions. There'd been no past, no present, no future, no hope.

Now, because of her unwanted intrusion, he'd begun to remember things, not just the treacherous perfidy of a woman he'd thought he'd loved, of innocent lives sacrificed for his own stinking ego, but things that brought just as much pain and even more anguish.

He remembered what life and the sound of laughter could be outside this place. He remembered the feel of a ship's deck creaking beneath his feet and the sweetness of the wind in his face as he looked out over a limitless sea from the masthead of a sailing ship. He remembered the crisp bite of snow and the uneasy stench of the Boston docks.

But God, most of all he remembered what it meant to want a woman with such fierce need that a fire seemed to burn in his belly each time he was near her.

No. Not just a woman. It was Kathryn he wanted, Kathryn he burned for.

"Damn," he snarled again, and he kicked out, hard, at the rocker.

Muttering under his breath, he slammed down the trunk lid and sat down on top of it, his hands fisted on his thighs, his mouth grim with self-contempt.

Of course, he wanted her, he thought cruelly. She had breasts and the proper equipment between her legs. What more did she need to satisfy him? He wasn't going to be particular, not after almost two centuries of celibacy.

The realization steadied his nerves, but not for long.

"Hell," he said, and shot to his feet.

Something was making an incredible racket outside. Glowering, he threw open the shutters and peered out.

Now what?

One of those ridiculous horseless carriages was coming up the drive, leaving noise and black smoke in its wake. The thing shuddered to a halt and the rear door swung open. A man stepped out, carrying a small valise. He was tall and dark-haired. Though he was lean, there was a look of softness about him.

Matthew's frown deepened.

Who was this?

The stranger handed some notes to the driver. The carriage pulled away and, as it did, the man turned and looked up at the house.

Matthew heard the front door slap open. Kathryn came flying down the steps. The man put down his valise, held out his arms, and she flung herself into them.

The muscle in Matthew's jaw contracted. First pirates, then this fop. Kathryn did not seem to be a woman of discriminating taste when it came to men.

The embrace seemed to go on for a long time. Kathryn did nothing to shorten it, nor to prevent the stranger's passionate kiss. God, but it was disgraceful to watch, especially since she was dressed in one of her usual immodest outfits. Surely, the man who held her would feel each soft, curving inch of her body.

At last, she placed her palms flat against the man's chest and leaned back in his arms, her lovely face bright with laughter as the man spoke to her.

She had never laughed that way for him, Matthew thought, his fists clenching.

Kathryn said something in return and the man grinned. He picked up his valise and she looped her arm through his and drew him up the steps and into the house.

Matthew turned his back to the window and folded his arms. From the looks of things, the visitor intended to stay for a while. Good. If Kathryn were kept busy, she'd have no time to get underfoot as she had done all this past week.

"Fine," Matthew said.

He upended the rocker and sat down.

He tapped his fingers against the rocker's arms.

He counted to ten.

Then he mouthed an oath that he'd given up using once he'd left the fo'c'sle and moved aft. He shot to his feet and marched to the attic door.

The slam of the attic door echoed like gunfire through the old house.

"What was that?" Jason said, as Kathryn tugged him into the foyer.

Kathryn smiled brightly. "You know how these old houses are," she said, mentally crossing her fingers. "Things slam and bump around all the time."

"Yeah," Jason said, looking doubtful.

Kathryn closed the front door behind them. "What a wonderful surprise," she said happily. Jason put down his overnight bag and she took both his hands in hers. "I didn't expect you until tomorrow."

He grinned. "I know."

"Why didn't you call? I'd have met you at the airport."

"It wouldn't have been a surprise then, would it?" His hands tightened on hers. "Are you really glad to see me?"

Was she glad to see him? Kathryn laughed. Was she glad to be reminded of reality and of a place where the most frightening thing you could bump into in your apartment was a cockroach searching for dinner in the kitchen?

She sighed and went into Jason's arms again. It seemed a million years and another lifetime since she'd talked with him on the phone and been less than pleased when he'd said he'd fly down for the weekend.

"You'll never know how glad," she said.

"That's great."

Jason shut his eyes with relief and hugged Kathryn to him. All the way to Elizabeth Island, he'd worried about the kind of greeting she'd give him. It had taken endless juggling to rearrange his schedule and change his ticket at the last minute, and the flight to the island itself had almost paralyzed him with terror, but now he knew it had been worth it.

Smiling, he clasped her shoulders, held her at arm's length and looked at her.

"What?" she said, with a little laugh.

"You're a sight for sore eyes, sweetheart."

That was an understatement. Her creamy skin had turned the color of the palest toast, her dark hair was loose the way he liked it but the way she hardly ever wore it, and her outfit—a pair of frayed denim shorts topped with a Museum of Modern Art T-shirt—made his body hunger for hers.

"Hell," he said gruffly, "I'd almost forgotten how beautiful you are."

She colored prettily. "I'm a mess. If I'd known you were coming . . ."

"Kathryn." Jason drew her into his arms again. "I missed you terribly."

"I missed you, too," she said automatically, ignoring the twinge of guilt she felt at the words. The truth was that she hadn't missed him at all. She'd hardly thought of him during the past few days.

But now that he was here, she was glad. Jason was steadfast and real. A couple of days with him would go a long way towards bringing her back to reality, despite the best efforts of a ghost with a surly attitude.

Should she tell Jason about Matthew? Heaven knew she wanted to. The question was how to do it without sounding like a candidate for the funny farm.

"Jason?"

"Mmm?" he said, nuzzling the place where her throat joined her shoulder.

"Jason, there's something you should know about Charon's Crossing."

"Tell me later," he murmured, gathering her closer.

Kathryn put her hands against his chest in gentle resistance.

"No," she said. "No, I really need to tell you now. You probably won't believe me at first, but—"

"You're right, Kathryn. He won't believe you, so why waste your breath?"

Kathryn almost jumped out of her skin. Matthew was standing less than ten feet behind Jason, leaning back against the banister of the staircase, arms folded and feet crossed casually at the ankles.

"Are you crazy?" she hissed. "Get out of here!"

Jason drew back in bewilderment. "But you just said you were glad to see me."

Kathryn's gaze shot to his. "I am," she said quickly. "Very glad."

"Then, why did you say—"

"I wasn't talking to you!"

"You weren't?"

"No. Of course not. I was talking to—"

"He can't see me, remember?" Matthew said lazily.

Kathryn ignored him. "I wanted to break the news slowly, Jason, so that it wouldn't come as a shock . . ."

"Are you going to tell him about me?"

". . . so that it wouldn't come as a shock," she said hurriedly, "but—"

"How generous," Matthew said pleasantly. He leaned away from the banister and strolled to where Kathryn and Jason stood, frowning as he peered into Jason's face. "Though I suppose it is wise to be solicitous of a man who looks like a lump of dough. You wouldn't want to put too much of a strain on his heart."

"Shut up," Kathryn said furiously.

Jason's eyebrows rose. "I didn't say anything."

"Oh, not you, Jason."

"But you said—"

"I know what I said, but I wasn't talking to you."

"Kathryn," Matthew said in the reasonable tone he might have used with a child or a puppy, "I think you really should reconsider. He's only going to think you're insane if you tell him about me. His sort will never understand things like me."

"You wish!"

"It's the simple truth."

"He will. You'll see! He loves me."

Matthew shook his head. "Female logic," he said with a condescending smirk. "It makes no more sense in this century than it did in the last."

"Kathryn?" Jason gave an uneasy laugh. "What's going on? Who are you talking to?"

Kathryn swept the tip of her tongue over her lips. "Look, Jason, I know this is going to come as a shock, but . . ." She gave a hopeless shrug. "Just turn around."

"Turn around?"

"Yes," she said impatiently. "Just turn around and . . . and look."

Jason turned. He looked. Then he smiled uncertainly.

"What am I supposed to be looking at?"

"What are you supposed to . . . Dammit, Jason!" Kathryn stabbed a finger in Matthew's direction. "At this piece of work, naturally! What else would I ask you to look at?"

"What piece of work? The wall?"

"No! Of course not. Look at this," she said, balling her hand into a fist and pummeling Matthew's shoulder. "This, Jason. This!"

"Ouch." Matthew frowned and rubbed the spot she'd punched. "Take it easy, will you? I may not be made of flesh and blood, but that hurts."

"Well?" Kathryn demanded. "What do you see, Jason?"

"A flight of steps? A banister? A newel post?" Jason cleared his throat. "What am I supposed to be looking at? Darling, are you all right?"

Matthew snickered. He strolled back to the steps, sat down on the bottom one, and stretched out his long legs.

"Darling," he said mockingly, "are you all right?"

Kathryn shot him a furious look before swinging towards Jason.

"Try," she insisted. "Just stare at those steps and—and concentrate."

Jason stared fixedly at the staircase. Matthew smiled, leaned back on his elbows, and waited.

"Uh, maybe you could give me a hint . . ."

Kathryn rolled her eyes to the ceiling. "Never mind."

"Kathryn, if you'd just tell me what you think I ought to be . . ."

"A mouse," she said wearily. "I mean, I thought I saw a mouse . . ." Her eyes flashed as Matthew chuckled. "Actually, what I saw was a rat. A big one, with a long tail and twitchy whiskers."

Jason repressed a shudder. "Rats? I hate the damned things."

"The feeling," Matthew said pleasantly, "is mutual."

"How could you do this?" Kathryn hissed.

"Make myself visible only to you?" Matthew shrugged. "I told you, sweetheart, I have no idea." He grinned. "A trick of the trade, I suppose."

"Darling?"

"Don't laugh at me," Kathryn said furiously. "And don't call me that!"

"I'm not laughing," Jason said carefully. "And I won't call you darling, if you don't like it."

Kathryn swung around. Jason was looking at her as if she'd grown two heads.

"No," she said quickly, "I didn't mean . . ."

"Kathryn, have you been ill? Too much sun, maybe? You're not used to it, you know."

"No, I haven't been ill."

"Are you sure? Your mother said . . ."

He broke off in midsentence, but it was too late.

"You spoke to Beverly?"

"Well, yes. I was concerned, darling, when I couldn't reach you and you hadn't phoned."

"So you called Beverly?"

"Is that so terrible? She was concerned, too. She said you hadn't called her, either."

"Of course I hadn't called her! Why would I? If we talk to each other once a month, it's a lot."

"Still, she was worried about you being all alone down here."

"Well, there was nothing to worry about." Kathryn glared at him as she tossed her hair back from her face. "As you can see, I'm fine."

"Very fine," Jason said softly. He reached out and cupped her face in his hands. "Deliciously fine."

Matthew groaned. "Spare me," he muttered. "Must I really listen to this?"

Kathryn stamped her foot. "Will you shut up?"

Jason's hands fell to his sides. "If that's how you feel," he said coldly, "I'll turn around and go back to New York."

"A fine idea," Matthew said, rising to his feet.

"A terrible idea," Kathryn said quickly. Slowly and deliberately, she put her arms around Jason's neck. "I'm not ill and I haven't had too much sun, but I have been without you for far too long. The last thing I'd want is for you to leave me now." She smiled, leaned forward, and pressed her mouth to his. "You see?"

Jason hesitated. Then he drew her tightly to him and kissed her back. She shut her eyes and did her best to let the moment carry her away, but it didn't work. Whatever she was supposed to feel—passion, excitement, arousal—just wasn't there.

But how could it be? She wasn't alone with Jason. They were embracing with an amused audience of one watching every move.

"Relax, darling," Matthew said softly. "You're like wood in his arms."

Kathryn's eyes closed more tightly.

"No little sighs, no sounds coming from the back of your throat as they do when I kiss you."

She linked her fingers tightly at the nape of Jason's neck.

Matthew's voice turned husky. "Did you know that your skin warms whenever we kiss, and that you rub ever so gently against me?"

A strangled sound rose in Kathryn's throat. She pushed free of Jason's embrace, her face flaming.

"You—you have to let me catch my breath," she said.

Jason, eyes still dark with passion, reached out for her.

"I like you better when you're breathless," he said with a little laugh.

"I know, but—but let's get your things upstairs. Elvira will be here before we know it."

"Who?"

"The woman who's helping me clean the place."

Jason sighed and picked up his overnight bag. "Well, I'm glad to hear you've got someone giving you a hand, Kathryn. This place is a mess."

"It was, but we've made lots of progress."

"No wonder you've got rats."

Kathryn's shoulders stiffened. "It's old, but—"

"Have you called in an exterminator?"

"An exterminator?"

"To kill the rats." He put his arm around her shoulders. "The last thing you want to do is share a house with vermin."

"I couldn't have put it better myself," Kathryn said, giving Matthew a cool look. "Come on, let me show you to your room."

Jason kissed her forehead. "Our room, you mean."

That wasn't what she'd meant at all, but she changed her mind when she caught the look of thunderous disapproval that had replaced Matthew's smirking grin.

"Of course, darling," she purred. "Where else would you sleep but in our room?"

Smiling sweetly, she led Jason up the stairs.

Darling?

Had Kathryn really called that man with the professional smile and the effeminate shudder, darling?

Was she really going to take him to her bedroom?

And was she going to walk straight through him to do it?

"Hey," Matthew said, jumping back just in time to keep the pallid popinjay from marching over his feet. "Dammit, Kathryn, what do you think you're doing?"

She looked back over her shoulder and gave him a smile that dripped acid. Then she looked up at the man beside her, her eyes as filled with adoration as a spaniel's as they climbed the rest of the steps and turned down the hall.

Matthew sat down on the bottom step, his expression grim.

Would she really let that man make love to her? It was clear that she'd felt nothing in his embrace. Any fool would know that. Any fool but the estimable Jason, apparently. Either he hadn't noticed that the woman in his arms had responded with all the ardor of a statue or he just hadn't cared.

Not that Matthew cared, either. Why should he? Kathryn could take whom she wished to her bed, she could make love to a hundred men if that was her desire . . .

Matthew shot to his feet.

"Bloody hell," he muttered, and strode up the stairs and into Kathryn's bedroom.

She must have expected him, for she didn't even blink when he came through the wall and straddled a chair with an air of nonchalance he only wished he felt.

"You can have the bottom drawer of the armoire," she said to Jason. "If you need to hang things up, just shove my—"

"I can't believe it!"

Jason was still standing in the doorway, staring around the room.

Kathryn smiled. She'd put in some time here in the last few

days. The windows, most of them still the originals, sparkled. The drapes had been taken down, brushed and re-hung. The armoire, polished to within an inch of its life, shone, and she'd hung some small paintings on the walls.

"I know," she said proudly. "Incredible, isn't it?"

"Is this really where you've been sleeping?"

"Well, except for a couple of nights at the begin—"

"This room is dilapidated!"

Kathryn blanched. "I know it looks a bit shabby."

"Shabby's hardly the right word."

It was true. Charon's Crossing needed a lot more than soap and water to make it presentable. So why did it irritate her to hear Jason say what she already knew?

"I admit, it's not the Plaza," she said with a tight smile, "but it's the best I can offer."

Matthew chuckled. "He's probably worried about the rats."

Kathryn gave him a murderous glare. "Don't be ridiculous."

"I don't think it's ridiculous at all," Jason said stiffly. "Maybe it sounds foolish to you, Kathryn, but—"

"No! I mean, I wasn't . . ." Kathryn chewed on her lip. This was impossible. "Look, why don't you put your stuff away while I go down and make us some lunch?"

The expression on Jason's face changed. "I have a better idea." He reached out and pulled her into his arms. "Why don't we say a proper hello and then I'll take you out for lunch?"

"It's a nice thought," she said, slipping out of his embrace, "but I'm not even sure there are any decent restaurants on the island."

"You could always take him down to the cove," Matthew said thoughtfully. "Pack a picnic lunch, sit in the sand. This hour of the day, there's bound to be a couple of dozen sand crabs scuttling about. A man who loves the sight of rats will probably love the sight of sand crabs."

Jason's hand stroked up and down her spine. "So we'll skip lunch," he murmured.

"But I already skipped breakfast," Kathryn said, lying

through her teeth. "Besides, don't you want to find out whether or not I can cook?"

"I'd rather find out other things."

"Jason." She put her hands lightly against his chest. "What's the rush? We have the whole weekend ahead of us."

Jason sighed and leaned his forehead against hers.

"You're right. I didn't mean to come on to you the minute I saw you, darling, it's just that you look so gorgeous and I've missed you so much . . ." He sighed again. "You go put up that coffee while I unpack, okay?"

Kathryn smiled. "Okay."

Jason let go of her and began unbuttoning his shirt. "I could use a shower, too, if that's all right."

"Sure. It's right down the hall, and you'll find clean towels in the linen closet next door."

"Terrific." He began shrugging off his shirt, revealing a hairless chest. It was a nice chest, as chests went, but compared to Matthew's . . .

Kathryn blushed, flashed Jason a quick smile, and fled.

She had driven into town early that morning, to lay in groceries for Jason's weekend visit. And it was a good thing she had. At least the refrigerator and pantry were stocked.

That was something to be grateful for.

She had the kitchen to herself, too. Matthew wasn't lurking in any of the corners.

That was another thing to be grateful for.

Kathryn raised her eyes to the ceiling. On the other hand, that only meant Matthew was probably still in the bedroom. What was he doing up there? Spying on Jason? Making the bed levitate?

The idea was preposterous. He'd never pulled any tricks like that on her. Still, she couldn't help smiling.

Poor Jason, she thought as she opened the refrigerator and took out a head of lettuce and some tomatoes. He was upset already, what with the condition of the house and her offhand remark about rats. Her smile broadened as she sliced the end off one of the tomatoes and popped it into her mouth.

If he looked up and saw what looked like a whirlwind of light making its way across the room, he'd probably leap out of his shoes.

She bit back a giggle. It was probably just as well Jason couldn't see Matthew. It would be bad enough if he ever found himself face to face with a guy who looked like he was on his way to a costume ball but if he found he could see through him . . .

"Who is he?"

This time, at least, she didn't scream, though she couldn't keep from giving a little jump and dropping the knife she'd been using onto the floor.

She bent down, picked it up and rinsed it at the sink. Then, as if she had all the time in the world, she turned and looked at Matthew, who was standing in the doorway.

"Walking into a room unannounced isn't very polite, you know." She opened the refrigerator again and took out a container of conch salad. "But I don't suppose you let things like that bother you much."

"I asked you a question, Kathryn. Who is that man?"

"I heard you. And it's none of your business."

"Are you his mistress?"

Carefully, she arranged lettuce leaves and tomato slices in a circle around a plate. Then she opened the container of salad and began spooning it into the center.

"Are you his lover?"

Kathryn looked up. "Is there a difference?" she asked politely.

"Forgive me. The questions were foolish. Obviously, you are neither."

"Isn't that nice?" she said, even more politely. "You're not only a ghost, you're also a clairvoyant."

Matthew looked grim. "If you were his mistress, you'd be in that bed with him now because he would want it."

"What an interesting perception."

"If you were his lover, you'd be there because you would want it."

Kathryn began to set the table. "A charming distinction," she said, "but wrong. I wouldn't be in that bed under any circumstances, not so long as you might be standing in the corner, watching."

"Your modesty is touching."

"Jason will be down soon, Matthew. I'd appreciate it if—"

"If you are not his mistress or his lover, what is he doing here?"

"I told you, it's none of your business."

"It is, so long as we share this house."

Kathryn's patience ran out. She swung around, eyes snapping.

"Sharing it certainly isn't my idea. If you don't like the arrangement, get out. I'm not stopping you."

For an instant, the arrogant look slipped from his face.

"No, you are not. But someone is. God. Or the Devil. I know not which."

What did he mean? And why did he look so upset? She almost asked him but then she remembered how he had treated her last night, the way he had told her to leave Charon's Crossing, and her resolve, as well as her spine, stiffened.

"I'm not going to get into a philosophical debate," she said coolly. "No matter what you say, this house belongs to me. And I'm not going to be questioned or ordered around while I'm in it."

The familiar, imperious look settled once again over Matthew's face.

"That is your right, madam. I ask only that you observe the rules of propriety so that neither of us is disgraced while we share the same domicile."

Kathryn laughed. "I don't believe it! You, talking about propriety? You appear like a rabbit popping out of a hat whenever you feel like it, you vanish in a puff of smoke when it suits you, you stand around kibitzing when I'm trying to have a serious conversation with someone—"

"Kibitzing? What does that mean?"

"It means making a pain in the ass of yourself."

His eyebrows rose. "My, my. Such inelegant language. I'm astonished."

Kathryn's smile was all teeth. "Stick around," she said. "You ain't heard nothin' yet!"

Matthew strolled past her to the stove. "The coffee's ready." He leaned forward and took a sniff of the steam rising from the pot. "Mmm. It smells wonderful."

"It *is* wonderful." She turned just as he took a mug from the cabinet. "I happen to make terrific coffee, but not for you," she said, snatching the mug from his hand, "for Jason."

"Jason." His voice was tinged with disdain. "The man who fears rats and a bit of dirt."

"Jason," Kathryn said coldly. "The man I'm engaged to marry."

Matthew's eyebrows shot skyward. He kicked a chair out from under the table, turned it around, straddled it and sat down.

"That explains it," he said.

"Explains what?"

"Why you were so unwilling to sleep with him. The rules of the game are unchanged, I see."

Kathryn's eyes narrowed. "What game?"

"The one in which a woman plays at remaining virtuous since she knows that a man will not marry her if he believes otherwise."

"Aha," she said.

She leaned back against the counter, her arms folded. God, Matthew thought, she was incredibly lovely. Anger had swept color into her cheeks and darkened her eyes to a stormy blue. Her breathing was quick, so that her high, rounded breasts rose and fell with a cadence that made his body tighten.

How easy it would be to kick aside the chair, go to her and

take her in his arms, kiss her until all that anger and heat turned to desire and passion.

Hell, he had to be going mad. How could he hate her one minute and want her the next? She was too stubborn by far, too cantankerous.

And then there was the little matter of Cat's blood, tainting her veins.

He had forgotten what in hell they'd been talking about.

"Aha, what?" he asked, frowning.

"Aha, you are such a dense male, Captain McDowell." Kathryn slammed a handful of silverware onto the table. "The times have changed, I'm happy to say. Women aren't judged by a double standard anymore."

"With regard to what?"

"With regard to sex. Today's women have the same freedom of choice men have always had."

He shrugged. "There have always been females willing to lift their skirts for the men who asked them."

"You're not listening. I'm telling you that women don't have to play games. If a woman wants to sleep with a man, she does."

"Just like that?"

"Just like that," she said, deliberately ignoring AIDS, Katie Rolphe, Gloria Steinem, and the ongoing debate on feminism.

"Really," Matthew said politely.

"Really."

"Let me be sure I have this right. What you are saying, then, is that you simply do not want to sleep with your Jason. Is that correct?"

Kathryn smothered a groan. It was check, but not mate.

"Not today, no."

"Because I'm here."

"Yes."

He smiled. "I cannot pass the boundaries of Charon's Crossing, but the estate covers lots of ground. Just say the word and you won't see me again for the rest of the weekend."

"What do you mean, you can't pass the boundaries of Charon's Crossing?"

"I mean exactly what I said, madam, and please don't change the subject. Do you wish me to make myself absent?"

Now, it was check and mate. She glared at him and then she pulled open a drawer and began taking out heavy damask napkins and silverware.

"Thank you for the offer, but my sex life is not dependent on your decisions."

Matthew let out his breath. And a damned good thing it wasn't, he thought fiercely, because he had no intention of leaving so she could fall into bed with that priapic fool upstairs.

Hell. Hell! Why were things getting so damned complicated?

"What is it dependent on, then?" he asked, pleased with the calmness of his voice. He reached out, took a slice of tomato from the platter, and put it in his mouth. The taste was ambrosial. "Poor Jason seemed quite filled with need."

Kathryn slapped his hand as he reached for another piece of tomato.

"Jason's needs, and mine, are none of your concern."

"I suppose not." He knew she was right, but that wouldn't stop him. He wanted to hear her admit that she'd melted like the molasses in a hot rum toddy in his arms and not in those of the man to whom she was betrothed.

Call it ego. Call it the frustration of a man who'd been celibate three times longer than most men lived. Call it the madness that had been driving him ever since he'd kissed her . . .

He wanted to hear her say it. Dammit, he wanted to have her show it, to go into his arms and lift that soft, sweet mouth to his, and to hell with whether it was logical or not.

He rose to his feet, kicked back the chair, and went to her. "Kathryn."

Kathryn's heart skipped a beat. Matthew was right behind her. She could feel the brush of his body against hers, the whisper of his breath stirring her hair. Nothing they'd said for the past half hour had been pleasant or even polite, and suddenly she knew why.

It had nothing to do with Jason.

What it had to do with was the river of flame running between them.

Matthew had not touched her in days but that didn't keep her from remembering the taste of his mouth or the heat of his body. She remembered what it was like to be in his arms, to feel his hand seeking the thrusting curve of her breast.

He whispered her name again and his arms went around her. Her eyes closed and her head fell back as he nuzzled her hair away from her throat and pressed his lips to her skin.

"No," she whispered, but she was already turning in his arms.

"Yes," he said, and then he was kissing her and there was no point in pretending it wasn't what she wanted, what she'd longed for since that first incredible dream. She breathed her surrender and he groaned and parted her lips with his in a deep, passionate kiss.

"Matthew," she whispered, and her arms wound around his neck.

"Kathryn?"

Her eyes flew open at the sound of Jason's voice.

He was standing in the doorway, staring at her. He'd changed into Bermuda shorts and a short-sleeved white shirt with the collar left unbuttoned, and his hair was still wet from the shower. Her brain registered all those details in a desperate attempt to avoid the only one that mattered, which was the look of complete bewilderment on his face.

"Kathryn? What the hell are you doing?"

Matthew let go of her and gave a throaty laugh. "Tell him, why don't you?"

"Go away!"

"Dammit, Kathryn," Jason said, "I am not going to go away!" He marched towards her, his face grim. "Not before you tell me what in blazes is going on around here!"

"I didn't mean you," she said hurriedly, "I meant . . ." Oh, it was useless! How could she possibly explain why she was standing here alone, her head tilted back, her arms lifted and curled around what must, to him, have looked like nothing but air?

"I—I was doing a—a Tai Chi exercise," she said in desperation.

"Tai Chi?"

"Yes. You know, the old Asian stuff where you do all these slow poses and stuff . . . I, ah, I didn't want you to see me doing them because—because . . ."

She gave a little cry as Matthew's lips brushed the back of her neck.

"You have an admirable imagination, Kathryn," he said, with laughter in his voice. "I'll leave you alone with it, and with your intended. Have a pleasant lunch."

She knew the second he vanished. The air behind her seemed cooler, and it became easier to think.

"Jason," she said, "don't look at me like that." She forced a smile to her lips. "I feel silly enough, getting caught in the middle of my exercises."

"That's not what it looked like. You seemed to be . . . you looked like you were . . ."

It wasn't easy, but Kathryn said nothing. After a moment, Jason shook his head and flashed a self-deprecating smile.

"Never mind. You'll think I'm nuts."

Kathryn scooted around the table and hurried into his arms.

"Oh, Jason. You don't know how glad I am that you're here!"

She closed her eyes tight and burrowed against him. He felt solid and familiar and comforting. After what seemed a long, long time, she drew back and smiled.

"Now," she said briskly, "let's have some lunch. And then I'll take you out and show you all the sights."

* * *

It was a pleasant day.

Kathryn relinquished the driver's seat of her ancient VW to Jason, who'd forgotten more about shifting gears and using a clutch than she had, so that they both ended up laughing each time the bright yellow Beetle lurched down a road.

They took a leisurely stroll along the narrow streets of Hawkins Bay. Jason bought them matching hats at the straw market and T-shirts that said Cool Caribbean Breezes on the front but "made in Hong Kong" inside the neck.

At sundown, they found a little café on the water that served garlic-drenched mussels and deep-fried grouper. They ate until they groaned, washing it all down with a pitcher of English lager. And they danced to old tunes blaring from a Wurlitzer so ancient it would have brought a bundle at any antiques market back in New York.

The moon was riding high in the black velvet sky when they returned to Charon's Crossing. The house was silent and dark, and Kathryn let Jason kiss her as they made their way up the stairs together.

But when they reached the bedroom and his kisses grew more intense, she turned her face away.

"Just relax, darling," he murmured. He took her face between his hands and brought her mouth to his. "It'll be good, I promise."

She wanted to believe him. She let him kiss her some more. She wanted to feel something; she wanted to feel what she'd felt in Matthew's arms. Why didn't she? Maybe Matthew was nearby. Maybe he was watching. Maybe that was why she couldn't react to Jason's increasingly passionate caresses.

But Matthew was nowhere nearby. She knew that she'd have sensed his presence.

Jason kept kissing her. His hand crept towards her breast. The feel of it made her skin crawl.

"Jason, wait."

He silenced her by trying to deepen the kiss. His tongue

slid into her mouth; she felt its warm slickness and almost gagged.

"Stop it," she said sharply, and when he didn't, she slapped his face.

Stunned, they stared at each other in the moonlight, each of them breathing hard but for very different reasons.

"Oh, Jason," Kathryn finally whispered. She reached out towards him but he stepped away and walked to the window.

"Listen," he said, "I think maybe I ought to fly back to New York in the morning."

Kathryn knew he wanted her to tell him not to go. She knew it was what a woman should say to the man she was going to marry.

"I don't think coming down here was such a hot idea, after all."

"Jason. Jason, I'm so sorry . . ."

"Don't be. You're upset, and I can understand the reason. Here you are, stuck with a house that looks like a strong wind might blow it down. The last thing you need is me, pressuring you."

Kathryn suspected she looked almost as miserable as he did.

"Yeah," she murmured, "I think you're right."

Jason nodded. Her easy acquiescence felt like a blow between the eyes, but what had he expected? That she'd beg him to stay? That the tropical sun would have burned off her inhibitions? Well, it hadn't. If anything, she seemed further away than ever. Each time today he'd tried to get close, she'd backed off.

Maybe it was the atmosphere of decadence and decay in this damned ruin of a mansion, or the miserable isolation of the place. Whatever it was, he was certain that hanging around would only make things worse.

It wasn't easy, but he managed to look at Kathryn and smile.

"How much more time do you figure you'll have to spend here?"

She'd expected the question. What she hadn't expected was her hesitation in answering. A few days ago, the thought of having to put in even an extra hour at Charon's Crossing would have seemed like a penance.

Now, though she didn't want to dwell on the reason, the thought of leaving put a hollow feeling into the pit of her stomach.

"Kathryn? What do you think?"

"Well," she said carefully, "I had thought a week would do it, but now I guess I really can't give you a definite answer. There are so many unknown factors, you know?" Her smile felt artificial. "I think they must have invented *mañana* on this island. I've got to work around the contractor's schedule, my lawyer's not even on the island, and the realtor . . ."

"How long?"

She shrugged and picked at a bit of nonexistent lint on her skirt.

"A couple of weeks, maybe."

Jason's face fell. "That long?"

"I'm just not sure, Jason. Actually—actually, I was thinking, it might be a good idea if I took some of my vacation time now, don't you think?"

What he thought was that something he couldn't understand was going on here. Kathryn, asking for more time away from the office? It was simpler to imagine the sun asking for a day off.

"Jason? Is that a problem?"

"No," he said quickly, "no problem at all. Maybe that's what you need, you know? Some time off."

She nodded. "You might be right."

"Remember that MicroTech Conference in Miami? The one we were going to pass on? Well, I've been thinking, you can never tell. They're running some seminars that might be interesting."

Kathryn couldn't remember what conference he was talking about. Come to think of it, she couldn't remember the last time she'd thought about business.

"So why don't we do this? You take your time here, get

things squared away with this house and all, and then fly to Miami and meet me at the conference. We'll sit in on a couple of seminars, maybe talk a little shop, and then we'll take a long weekend in the sun before you decide if you have to come back here—or if you're ready to fly home with me. How's that sound?"

He hadn't expected her to jump up and down with joy but he hadn't expected her to look blank and then bow her head and stare down at her feet, either. He held his breath and his patience while he waited for her answer. It was a long time in coming but finally, when he'd almost given up hope, she looked up.

"It sounds great," she said.

They smiled at each other politely. Then Jason collected his pajamas and his toothbrush. Kathryn showed him into the room across the hall and they spent the night alone, in separate rooms and separate beds.

Fourteen

Kathryn awoke early.

She dressed and opened her door quietly, breathing a sigh of relief when she saw that Jason's bedroom door was still tightly shut.

Quietly, she made her way down to the kitchen. As she put up the coffee, she thought about what she'd say to him this morning.

Jason was her fiancé. He had flown all the way down to Elizabeth Island for a romantic weekend, and when he got here, she'd treated him as if he carried the plague and she was a certified crazy.

Kathryn blew out a gusty breath as she took a bowl of fruit from the refrigerator.

And it was all Matthew's fault. If he hadn't treated the whole thing like a joke, popping in and out of the woodwork right under Jason's nose, deliberately drawing her into taunting conversation with Jason standing right in the same room, she'd never have gotten so edgy. Things would have gotten off to a better start and they'd have ended better, too, with her in Jason's arms exactly as she was supposed to have been.

As she had wanted to be, and never mind all that silliness last night when Jason's kisses had made her tighten like an overwound spring.

It was nerves, that was all. Between Matthew's performance that morning and the certainty that he'd been about to pop out of the walls last night, she'd been a wreck.

That he hadn't put in an appearance didn't change a thing. There was nothing like the anticipation of a visit from a ghostly jack-in-the-box for making you antsy.

Right now, for example, she kept expecting him to suddenly materialize in the middle of the room while she sliced oranges, bananas and casaba melon into an old, probably priceless, Waterford bowl.

Anything that would destroy her equilibrium would suit Matthew just fine.

Well, he was in for a surprise. Briskly, she wiped her hands on a kitchen towel, then set the bowl of fruit in the center of the table. Nothing was going to upset her this morning, she thought as she backhanded a couple of flyaway curls from her forehead, not even Harry Houdini! She was going to be calm and sensible, and when Jason came down the stairs and into the kitchen, she would greet him with a smile, a kiss, and, maybe the suggestion that he forget about cutting short his visit.

"Good morning, Kathryn."

She looked up. Jason was standing in the doorway. He was wearing a dark suit, white shirt, and maroon tie and she knew at once that she wasn't going to do anything of the sort.

"Good morning," she said.

"I phoned the airport," he said briskly. "There's a mail plane taking off for Grenada in a couple of hours. The pilot said he'd be glad to give me a lift."

Kathryn nodded. "That's good," she said brightly. "That the phone's working, for a change, and that you can get a ride."

He nodded, too. "Yes, it is."

There was a moment's silence and then she cleared her throat. "Well," she said, holding out a cup of coffee, "did you sleep well?"

"Eventually." She could see the conflicting emotions on his face, and then he sighed and accepted the cup as if it were an olive branch. "First I had to adjust to the silence. No police sirens, no fire trucks, no drunks yelling on the street corner . . . how can you bear it?"

Kathryn laughed and leaned back against the sink. "Awful, isn't it?"

"You've certainly settled into this mausoleum better than I would have."

"Well, it hasn't been that easy." She looked at him. "I suppose that's why my nerves are so on edge."

"I understand."

He didn't, not really, but how could he? She hadn't told him about Matthew.

All at once, she knew that was what she had to do, and never mind Matthew's smug insistence that Jason wouldn't believe her. Of course he would. He loved her. He trusted her. He knew she wasn't some sort of flighty dreamer with an overactive imagination.

Sharing this—this burden with him would be wonderful. He could advise her, help her deal with the insanity of being haunted, and taunted, by a ghost.

"Jason," she said quickly, before she could change her mind, "there's something I need to tell you."

A worried look crept over Jason's face.

"Ah, Kathryn, Kathryn." Matthew's whisper came from out of nowhere. "He thinks you're going to break your betrothal."

Kathryn stiffened. She turned, looked in every direction, but Matthew wasn't visible.

"Your precious Jason is so concerned about his own needs that it hasn't occurred to him that you might be about to seek solace."

"Jason," Kathryn said, "please, sit down."

"Kathryn," Matthew said, "if you tell him about me, he's not going to believe you."

Kathryn stamped her foot. "He will!"

"Will what?" Jason said, the worried look deepening.

"He's either going to think you've lost your senses or that you need reassuring, like a foolish twelve-year-old."

"Dammit," Kathryn said.

"Darling? What is it?"

"Sit down, Jason!" She pointed a trembling finger at the table. Jason sat.

"Isn't that nice?" Matthew drawled. "He's so well trained. I saw a hound like that once. It was truly amazing. The dog would do almost anything you asked of it."

Kathryn shut her eyes, counted to ten, then looked at Jason. "We need to talk," she said.

"Now, darling, I know you're still upset after last night. I don't think this is the best time to make any quick decisions."

Matthew chuckled softly. "You see? He's afraid you're going to tell him it's all over."

Kathryn sighed and pressed the heels of her hands against her eyes.

"It isn't a quick decision," she said. "I thought about it yesterday, and then most of last night." Her arms fell to her sides and she fixed Jason with a look. "And I know telling you this is the right thing to do."

"Please, Kathryn, don't say anymore. You aren't yourself, I know that. I understand, and——"

"You don't."

"I do. You think things aren't working between us, but——"

"This has nothing to do with us!"

Jason blinked. "It hasn't?" he said, and gave a long sigh. "Oh, wow. I thought——"

"Jason." Kathryn pulled out a chair and sat down opposite him. She folded her hands on the table. "I've got to tell you something. I know it's going to sound crazy, but . . . The thing is, Charon's Crossing is—is more than just a ruin."

Jason laughed and shook his head. "You're probably right, but if there's a stronger word to describe it, I can't think of it."

"I don't mean that. I mean, yes, the house is a mess, but . . . The thing is . . . the thing is, Jason, Charon's Crossing is haunted."

There. The words were out. Just saying them made her feel better—until Jason laughed.

"Haunted," he said.

Kathryn nodded. "Yes."

"Haunted," he repeated, chuckling. He shoved back his chair, got to his feet, and walked to the stove. "Haunted," he said, and poured himself more coffee.

Kathryn's eyes narrowed as she stood up. "That's what I said."

"Uh huh." He looked at her. "And just when did you find this out?"

"Almost as soon as I got here. It turned out that everybody knew about it. My attorney, the realtor, the guy who's going to fix the house up . . . Jason, dammit, will you stop laughing? This isn't funny!"

"No," he said, his lips twitching, "I don't suppose it is. It's going to be difficult enough to find a buyer for this wreck but if people think there's a resident spook . . ."

"Not everyone can see him."

"The spook?"

"The ghost," she said, folding her arms.

"No," Jason said with solemnity, "of course not." He leaned back against the counter and took a sip of his coffee. "What is he, anyway? Wait. Don't tell me. He's a pirate. They were big in these waters, weren't they?"

"He was a privateer."

Jason laughed. "Sorry. Fine distinctions are important in these things, I suppose."

"It isn't a fine distinction," Matthew said in clipped tones.

"It isn't a fine distinction," Kathryn said, and frowned. "I mean, a pirate was a pirate. But a privateer was legitimate."

Matthew chuckled. "Some were. Some were like me, who wouldn't have known their fathers if they'd tripped over them."

"This privateer," Kathryn said, ignoring him, "sailed for the British just before the War of 1812. He captured French merchant ships carrying contraband."

"Yes," Matthew said lazily. "And he was damned good at it, too."

He materialized suddenly, standing on the far side of the

room, leaning back against the wall in that nonchalant, arrogant posture that never failed to set Kathryn's teeth on edge, his arms folded, his feet crossed at the ankle. His hair was loose, hanging like thick, shining silk to his shoulders and his shirt was open halfway down his chest.

Had a man ever looked more dangerous, or more sexy?

Kathryn hated herself for the disloyal thought. She moved closer to Jason and deliberately took hold of his hand.

"The thing is, what am I going to do about it?"

Jason smiled and lifted her hand to his lips. "Nothing," he said, kissing her knuckles.

"Nothing? Don't be silly, Jason. I have to do something."

"For instance?"

"Well . . . well, for instance, how am I going to sell this place? You just said yourself, it was going to be hard enough but now, if people know there's a ghost . . ."

"Kathryn, darling, just listen to yourself." Jason smiled tenderly and enfolded her hand in both of his. "You almost sound as if you believe in this local nonsense."

Matthew laughed.

"It isn't nonsense," Kathryn said stiffly.

"What should we call it, then? Superstition?"

"It isn't superstition, either. This ghost is—"

"Be careful of what you say, madam. He's not going to believe you."

"This ghost is real," Kathryn blurted.

"To the locals, yes. But any intelligent person from outside will—"

"He's real, I tell you! I've—"

"Kathryn," Matthew warned, "tread carefully."

"You've what, darling?" Jason asked.

"I've . . . I've . . ."

Kathryn hesitated. Jason wasn't laughing anymore, or even smiling. He was looking at her with a cautionary gleam in his eye, and suddenly she thought of every movie she'd ever sat through where the unfortunate heroine tells the hero that she's seen something that clanks or rattles or goes "boo" in the dark.

"I've . . . I've spoken with several intelligent people about this ghost," she said. "And they believe in him, too."

Matthew gave a long, low whistle. "Good girl."

Jason laughed with relief. "Boy, for a minute there you really had me going. I was afraid you were going to insist you'd seen the spook yourself." He grinned. "I was already planning on the best way to whisk you off to the nearest shrink."

"Shrink?" Matthew said.

"Head doctor," Kathryn snapped. Damn, why did he have to be right?

"Yes," Jason said, patting her hand. "Could you have blamed me?"

"I suppose not," she said, withdrawing her hand from his and tucking it into her pocket.

"Poor darling," Jason said, "no wonder your nerves are shot." He looped his arm around her shoulders and hugged her. "What an awful thing to have had to deal with all on your own."

Matthew sighed, lifted his hand and carefully scrutinized his fingernails.

"Here comes the reassurance."

"Why didn't you tell me sooner?" Jason put his knuckle under her chin and lifted her head. "I'd have told you there's not a thing to worry about."

Kathryn disengaged herself from his encircling arm.

"There isn't?" she said stiffly.

"No, of course not. This place may be a wreck—"

"I wish you wouldn't keep saying that, Jason. I know it's a wreck but it's my wreck . . ." She frowned. "Never mind. What were you going to say?"

"Only that now that I've seen Charon's Crossing, I think you may not have as difficult a time selling it as we'd thought. The house needs work, yes, but it has great appeal. Just look at its location." He walked to the window and gestured out at the endless gardens stretching out behind the terrace. "All that land in the back, the sea practically at the front door . . . and every room is filled with antiques."

"So, what are you suggesting?

"I'm suggesting that you might want to get yourself a different realtor, darling, someone from the mainland with a wealthy, sophisticated clientele who can provide you with a buyer who'll be more than happy to pay for the special cachet of a haunted mansion on a tropical island." He smiled at her. "How's that sound?"

It sounded as if she might as well have saved her breath, Kathryn thought wearily. There was nothing wrong with Jason's suggestion on how she might sell the house. It was, in fact, damned clever.

But she hadn't wanted real estate ideas just now, she'd wanted Jason to listen to her. *Really* listen, instead of proving Matthew right.

"It sounds brilliant," she said, and shot a dramatic look at her watch. "Oh, just look at the time! When did you say your plane was leaving?"

Jason's smile wavered. "At eleven. But I thought . . . I mean, I'd hoped . . ."

She knew what he'd thought, that she'd changed her mind and would ask him to stay on for the rest of the weekend. It was what she'd thought, too, only a little while ago.

But it wasn't going to happen.

"I know," she said with a big smile, "you hoped we'd be able to have breakfast. But the time just got away from us, didn't it?"

She didn't give him a chance to answer; she snatched up the keys to the VW and her sunglasses and headed for the foyer. Matthew winked as she rushed past him but Kathryn never paused.

"You'd better not be around when I get back," she hissed.

"What did you say, darling?" Jason asked as he retrieved his overnight bag from where he'd left it in the foyer.

"Nothing," Kathryn said through her teeth. "Absolutely nothing."

* * *

They drove to the airport in her rented VW.

Jason kept up a line of pleasant, meaningless chatter. Kathryn didn't have to do anything except nod from time to time or say an occasional, "Really," which was a good thing because she couldn't get herself to concentrate on anything but what a total fiasco Matthew was making out of her life.

Jason was really a nice man. He was of her world and of her time, and he had never treated her with anything but kindness and affection. She knew what a stickler he was for routine, that he always planned his schedule well in advance so that there was no chance anything would remain undone, yet he'd flown down here on the spur of the moment, just to be with her.

And how had she thanked him?

Her hands tightened on the steering wheel.

By behaving like a jerk, that was how. By slugging him when he'd tried to show her some affection. By dismissing his perfectly logical ideas about how to sell Charon's Crossing. As for his reaction to what she'd said about ghosts . . .

Be honest, Kathryn, if somebody told you they'd been talking to a ghost, what would you do?

She'd do exactly what Jason had done, of course, take it all as a joke or else wonder if the person were going around the bend . . .

Unless someone as helpful as Matthew were standing by, all too ready to try and confuse you more than you already were.

She glanced at Jason, who was in the middle of a complicated joke about a pair of computers, a cable, and a malfunctioning fax modem.

Why was she taking him to the airport?

Why was she letting him leave?

Only because Matthew had taunted her into it, that was why.

"Jason," she said, interrupting him in the middle of the not very funny punchline, and then she frowned.

No. It was better to let him fly back to New York. That

would leave the field clear for her to go back to Charon's Crossing and tell Captain Matthew McDowell just what she thought of him.

Then she'd phone Olive, tell her what she should have told her right away, that when Amos decided to come wandering back to Elizabeth Island he could damn well phone her for authorization on each and every thing Hiram thought needed fixing. Then she'd pack, get on a plane even if she had to charter one, and put this whole disaster of a week behind her.

"Yes, Kathryn?"

She shook her head, smiled with all her teeth, and stomped down on the gas.

"Nothing," she said. "Absolutely nothing."

By the time they reached the airport, the VW was almost flying.

Kathryn stood on the brakes and tried not to wince as the little car bucked and stalled because she hadn't remembered to disengage the clutch and take it out of gear.

"Here we are," she said.

Jason heaved a sigh of relief. "Right. And in one piece." A small, propeller-driven aircraft was standing on the runway. He looked at it and laughed. "That must be my flight. I hope the rubber band is big enough."

Kathryn laughed, too. "Yeah, but you're lucky. You get to fly with a load of mail. I flew in with pigs and chickens for company."

He took his valise out of the back seat and they made their way through the knee-high grass. Butterflies and tiny birds fluttered up ahead of them. When they were a few yards from the plane, Jason put down his bag.

"I'm sorry this visit didn't work out," he said softly.

Kathryn sighed. "Me, too."

"Kathryn?" Dark tendrils of hair had come loose around

her face. He reached out and took one between his fingers. "Are you sure you don't want me to stay?"

She smiled and clasped his hand in hers. "You were right," she said. "My nerves are as tight as guitar strings. I'm better off just being by myself down here. That way, I can roll up my sleeves and finish what needs finishing."

"Cleaning Charon's Crossing?"

"Among other things."

He smiled, brought her hand to his mouth, and kissed the wrist.

"Don't work too hard, okay?"

"I won't."

"You'll remember about Miami?"

For a second, she looked at him blankly. Then she caught her lip between her teeth.

"The conference, you mean."

"Right. You're going to meet me, remember?"

"Uh huh."

"Promise?"

She smiled and held up her right hand in a three-finger salute.

"Scout's oath," she said. "I'll be there, I swear."

Jason's smile slipped from his face. He clasped her shoulders and looked deep into her eyes.

"Are you sure you're okay?" His fingers massaged her shoulders. "I've had this feeling, ever since yesterday, that there's something you're not telling me."

She stiffened a little and almost said, well, I tried to tell you . . .

But she didn't.

"Only about the house being haunted," she said briskly.

He grinned and tipped her chin up with one finger.

"Yeah."

A sudden gust of wind swept over the airstrip. Kathryn put her hand to her hair to keep it from whipping loose from its knot.

"Have a safe flight, Jason."

He nodded. Then he bent and kissed her gently on the mouth. "I'll see you in two weeks."

She smiled and laid her hand against his cheek. "You bet you will."

The sudden sputter of the plane's engine roared into the silence. A man in a leather bomber jacket scooted around its tail. He pointed at Jason, then at the plane. Jason nodded and picked up his overnight case. He kissed Kathryn again, turned and trotted towards the plane. Halfway there, he stopped, waved, and said something.

Kathryn shook her head. "I can't hear you."

Jason repeated the words, mouthing them with slow exaggeration.

She shook her head again, smiled, and flung her arms into the air.

"I still can't hear you," she shouted.

He grinned, shrugged, and climbed into the plane. The door shut, and the little craft began taxiing down the runway.

Kathryn sighed. She walked back to the VW, got inside, and slouched down in her seat.

She knew what Jason had been saying.

"I love you, Kathryn."

So, why hadn't she been able to say it in return?

Because her unwanted and unwelcome ghost had screwed up her head, that was why.

She turned the ignition key, shot the car into a tottering U-turn, and headed back to Charon's Crossing and a final showdown.

By the time she reached the house, her anger had turned to sizzling rage.

She parked, slammed her way out of the car, and marched into the foyer.

"Matthew?" she yelled. Her keys clinked as she tossed them onto a table. "Matthew, where are you?"

She stalked into the drawing room, then into the library. Both rooms were empty.

"Dammit, Matthew, show yourself!"

Were they going to play games? Jaw set, Kathryn marched into the kitchen. There was a shortwave-band radio over the stove. She had no idea if it worked but now she switched it on, hoping against hope it would play and fill the mocking silence.

Static hissed from the speaker. She fooled with the dial, sweeping past a station playing reggae and another playing tangos until she picked up some station in the midst of a commercial.

". . . from sunny St. George on Grenada," a booming voice said, "your favorite station playing nothing but the best of the oldies."

The best of the oldies. That, plus an afternoon of keeping busy until the estimable captain decided to show himself, should do the trick. Kathryn filled the sink with hot, sudsy water. Then she took the coffee pot from the stove, tossed the grounds into the garbage can, and dumped the pot into the sink.

The fruit salad she'd prepared had begun to wilt in its bowl and it went into the trash, too. It was a waste of perfectly good food, yet another reminder of what a mess the weekend had turned out to be, courtesy of Captain Matthew McDowell. The pantry and refrigerator were full of still more stuff, butter and eggs and all kinds of goodies, stuff she'd never use with Jason gone.

Well, at least one thing had come out of his visit. He was right about not trying to cover up the fact that the house was haunted. The right buyer would probably lap up the tale of a man who'd been so in love he'd given up his life for a woman.

A woman who had not deserved him.

Kathryn made a face.

"Oh, stop it," she muttered. She snatched up the coffee mug she'd been drinking from hours before and lifted it to her lips. The coffee was cold and bitter, and she shuddered as she swallowed it.

It was all nonsense. There was nothing romantic in any of this. She'd let her emotions get out of hand, that was all, and it was Matthew's fault.

"Oh, hell!" she said fiercely, and flung the mug at the wall.

The mug and the wall never connected. Matthew appeared before she could blink and plucked the mug out of the air.

"A temper is not becoming in a woman," he said primly.

Kathryn's heart did an untidy little two-step at the sight of him, which only sharpened her anger.

"Where have you been?" she demanded.

He grinned at her. "Ah," he said, "I am touched. I didn't think you cared."

"I know you think nothing of materializing at will, but I find it infuriating!"

"That's unkind, madam." His tone was still proper and formal but she could see that his green eyes glinted with laughter. "It is not my idea to make such dramatic entrances but being a ghost leaves me with little choice in the matter."

Kathryn glared at him. "Give me that," she said, snatching the mug from his hand and dropping it into the sink. Then she wiped her hands on her bottom, turned and glared at him again. "It's time we had a talk, Captain McDowell."

"Such formality, and after all we've shared together."

"We've shared nothing," she said, her eyes snapping.

"You call sharing living quarters 'nothing'?" He frowned at the radio. Elton John was complaining about candles in the wind. "What is that noisy thing?"

"A radio."

"Another peculiar invention of your time?"

"Does it bother you?" Kathryn said sweetly. "Because if it does, I can always make it louder."

Matthew's brows arched. "I see you are not in a good mood today, Kathryn."

"My goodness, but you are perceptive!"

He moved past her, his arm just brushing hers. It sent an unnerving tremor up her spine.

"What are you doing?" she asked irritably.

"Looking for something to eat," he said, peering into the refrigerator.

She reached out and slammed the door shut. "You see? That's exactly what I mean about unbecoming behavior."

"If you're referring to the fact that you don't think ghosts are supposed to have appetites—"

"I'm referring to the way you think nothing of popping into rooms and doing whatever comes into your head without so much as a by-your-leave." Elton John had given up and Bruce Springsteen had taken over. Somehow, she wasn't in the mood for "Born in the USA." She shut the radio off and turned back to Matthew. "I called you when I came in a little while ago," she said crossly. "Didn't you hear me?"

"I assure you, Kathryn, if I really popped into rooms, as you call it, and did whatever comes into my head, last evening would have ended far differently than it did."

Kathryn went very still. "What's that supposed to mean?"

"Only that a woman who expects to share her bed with a man shouldn't end up sleeping alone."

Crimson streaks swept into her face.

"You were spying on us!"

"I was not."

"You were sneaking around in my bedroom, waiting to see if—if . . ."

"I was not in the house at all," he said, his tone filled with indignation. "I spent the night at the foot of the cliff, beside the sea. When I returned this morning, you were in one bedroom and your betrothed was in another."

Kathryn frowned. "Why did you spend the night on the beach?"

A tiny muscle leaped in Matthew's jaw. Until now, it had been easy to keep a bantering tone.

"I thought I owed you privacy," he said stiffly.

Kathryn folded her arms. "How gallant."

Matthew didn't answer. There was no reason to tell her that

gallantry had had nothing to do with his decision to spend the night out of the house, that what he'd really figured was that she had the right to a fiancé who was all in one piece, which would surely not have been the case if he'd caught the son of a bitch in bed with her.

"How noble." Her tone was frigid. "How out of character."

He couldn't keep from grinning. "Yes, it was. And unnecessary, as it turned out. Not that I was surprised. I could tell from the way things had gone between you yesterday that you were not about to succumb to your Jason's manly charms."

Color blazed in Kathryn's face again. She turned her back and began scrubbing out the coffee pot.

"I should have known better than to think you could be polite."

Matthew hitched one hip on the table and folded his arms over his chest.

"Where did your Jason take you last night?"

"Don't call him that!"

"Isn't he yours? You said he was."

"I said we were engaged to be married. As for where we went . . . it's none of your business."

"Nowhere special, I suppose."

"Well, you suppose wrong. We went out to dinner."

"Dinner, then home? Nothing more imaginative?"

"What would you suggest? This is Elizabeth Island, in case you'd forgotten. There are no concert halls or museums or movies."

"Movies?"

"Yes. Movies." She puffed out her breath, refilled the coffee pot, and set it on the burner. "Take my word for it, okay? There aren't any."

"It sounds like a very exciting evening," Matthew said politely.

"It was a very pleasant evening."

"And then you came back to Charon's Crossing and sent Jason to bed alone."

Kathryn flushed. "I am not going to discuss my private life with you," she said coldly. "In fact, I'm not going to discuss anything with you, anymore. From now on, you are to keep out of my way."

Matthew clapped his hand to his heart. "For shame, Kathryn. You cut me to the quick."

"I don't want you talking to me when other people are around, or turning on and off like snow on a TV set."

"Like snow on a what?"

"And you're to stop making everything into a bad joke," she said, ignoring the question. "It's bad enough you haunt my house, but to pretend it's funny is unconscionable!"

"Gallows humor, madam. It helps me deal with my reality but if it offends you, I will do what I can to restrain myself. Is there anything else?"

"Yes." Kathryn moistened her lips. "I wish you'd leave Charon's Crossing."

"My wish precisely, madam. Unfortunately, it is not possible."

"Then at least tell me why you haunt it," she said, turning towards him.

"I already have. Surely, you do not wish me to repeat the tale."

"No," she said quickly, "no, I understand about Catherine and Waring and that night. What I don't understand is why you're here instead of wherever it is people go after—after . . ."

"After they die?" he said with a twisted smile. "I've no idea where they go, Kathryn, but I do know why I have not gone there. It is because of what I have already told you, that it is against the laws of the cosmos to utter a curse with your dying breath. Fate turned my ill-chosen blasphemy back upon me. I became the accursed, doomed to spend eternity here, knowing neither love nor peace."

All Kathryn's anger seemed to drain away. "How horrible!"

"An eye for an eye and a tooth for a tooth, the Bible says. And, it would seem, a curse for a curse."

"Oh, Matthew, I'm so sorry . . ."

"Waste no sympathy on me," he said coldly. "It is a punishment that fits my own stupidity for having believed in love."

"You were stupid to have believed in Cat. There's a difference."

"I watched you with Jason," Matthew said bluntly. "You are no one to offer a defense of love, Kathryn."

She blushed but didn't deny it. "I don't feel any great passion for Jason, that's true, but—"

"Love is a lie that can cloud a man's mind more than the strongest measure of laudanum. I, of all men, should have known that. I never knew my father, and my mother beat me until the day she died of consumption, when I was nine. I rejoiced in what I thought was my salvation, but when none of her relatives would have me, I was given over to the tender mercies of an orphanage run by a man who called himself a servant of God." He smiled tightly. "After a year of being whipped and starved for the love of the Lord and the instruction of my immortal soul, I ran off to sea, where the cat with nine tails gave instruction to my mortal flesh and the captain was the only God I had to love. I tell you this not to elicit sympathy," he said coldly, when Kathryn started to speak, "but to make certain you understand that I am fully enlightened with regard to the meaning of 'love.' "

His tone twisted the word into an obscenity. Kathryn wanted to move towards him, take him in her arms, tell him that— that . . .

She swallowed hard, then cleared her throat.

"And what about that—that thing in the attic? What is it? And why is it here?"

Matthew frowned. "I told you, that was a dream."

"Now, who's handing out reassurances fit for a twelve-year-old? Come on, Matthew. I know it wasn't a dream. This is my house and that—whatever it was—came after me. I've a right to know what it is."

He sighed and got to his feet. She was right, and he knew it.

"It is Waring," he said in a low voice. "The man I found with Catherine, who killed me even as I killed him."

Kathryn felt her blood turn to ice. "You mean, he's a ghost, too?"

"Nay. Not a ghost. A thing, just as you called him, existing in a place different than this, as I once did."

She sank down in a chair. "I feel as if I've stumbled into a time warp," she said, with a nervous laugh. "I don't understand any of this."

Matthew leaned towards her over the wide oak table, his hands planted firmly on the scarred wood.

"I will tell you what I have surmised," he said. "Waring was an aristocrat, a son of a bitch who despised anyone not of his class. Can you imagine what it must have done to him, to have died on the sword of such as me and for a woman who was little better than a whore?"

"So he's here because he hates you?"

"He is here to avenge himself, if he can break through from where he exists to this place."

The day was hot, the sun bright. Kathryn could hear birds singing outside in the garden. But in here, in the kitchen, the air had taken on a chill as cold as the grave.

"You mean . . . You mean, he's tried to hurt you?"

Matthew showed his teeth in a chill smile. "To kill me. Yes."

"But how can he do that if you're already—if you're already—"

She couldn't say the word, but Matthew could, and without any sign of emotion.

"If I am already dead?" His shoulders lifted and fell in an eloquent shrug. "I don't know. I can no more explain the laws of the universe now than I could when I was mortal." His eyes darkened. "The only thing I'm certain of is that Waring has grown stronger in the past days."

"Since I came here, you mean."

He hesitated. "Yes."

"Why?"

The word was a whisper on the silence. Matthew shook his head.

"I don't know." He saw the look on her face, the sudden terror in her eyes, and he mentally cursed the table that separated them and kept him from pulling her into his arms. He reached out and took her hand. "Don't be afraid, Kathryn. He will not hurt you. I swear, I will not let it happen."

"I'm not afraid for myself," she said in a tremulous voice. "But if he were to—to . . ."

She caught her breath. An electric tingle seemed to flash from his fingers to hers.

"Kathryn . . ."

An acrid stench erupted in the kitchen. Matthew's gaze shot past her, to the stove.

"Hell," he said, and vaulted the table.

Kathryn spun around. The coffee she'd put up was boiling madly and spilling out of the spout. For some insane reason, the sight immobilized her. Matthew grabbed for the pot.

"How do you stop this damned thing?" he said.

"That knob . . ."

He nodded, shut off the stove, and put the coffee pot on a back burner.

"No damage done," he said, "just a bit of a mess . . . Kathryn? What is it?"

She shook her head fiercely. Then, with no warning, she gave a hiccuping sob and tears began coursing down her cheeks.

"Sweetheart, don't cry. It's only coffee."

"I know," she said, her voice wobbling, and cried even harder.

Matthew pulled her into his arms and silently called himself every kind of fool. Why had he told her about Waring? It had been stupid of him, and thoughtless. Gently, he held her at arm's length and smiled down into her tear-stained face.

"If you knew how often in my life I've drunk burned coffee, you wouldn't be so upset."

Kathryn wiped the back of her hand across her nose. "Don't try and make me feel better, Matthew. God, that stuff smells like burning rubber!"

"Like burning what?"

Despite herself, and despite the tears that were still escaping down her cheeks, she laughed.

"We're going to have to do something about introducing you to the new world."

"Here." Matthew reached past her and tore a paper towel off the roll hanging over the sink. "This should do," he said, holding it to her nose. "Blow."

She did, noisily. "Thank you."

He smiled, his fingers moving lightly across her cheeks, tracing the elegant arch of bone that lay beneath her silken skin.

"You're welcome. And I meant what I said about the coffee. I'm sure it's drinkable."

"Oh sure."

"You forget how long it is since I have had coffee to drink, Kathryn."

He sounded so serious. But when she looked into his eyes, she could see that they were filled with teasing laughter. A giggle broke from her throat, and then another, until she was laughing and crying all at once.

"Oh, Matthew," she said, "I was so furious at you when I drove back here from the airport."

"From what?"

"Never mind that. What I'm trying to tell you is that I'm not angry anymore."

"You're not?"

"No. I just wish I could say something that would make everything better. This must be so awful for you, being trapped inside this miserable house because of something that happened so long ago."

"Are your tears for me, then, you foolish woman?"

"Of course not," she said fiercely. "Why would I cry for a ghost?"

Matthew looked at her face. Her eyes were puffy and the tip of her nose was red. Her hair, which she'd been wearing in a ladylike knot, was coming undone and curling from the heat. There was a dark coffee stain on her white cotton shirt. She looked disheveled and unglamorous, and infinitely more beautiful than he'd ever imagined a woman could look . . . and he wanted her. He knew it was wrong, straight down into the marrow of his bones. He knew, too, that he could no more keep from wanting her than he could keep from drawing breath.

"There is no need to weep," he said softly. He took her face between his hands and tilted it up to his. "I regret nothing, sweetheart, for whatever has happened, it has brought you to me."

His words brought another glitter of dampness to her eyes. He smiled, looked deep into their shining depths for a long moment, and then, slowly, he lowered his head to hers and kissed her.

Kathryn sighed into his mouth as his lips touched hers. She rose on her toes, her hands clasping his wrists. He had never kissed her this way before, not just with fire and passion but with an almost indescribable tenderness, and she gave herself up to the magic of it.

It was Matthew who broke the kiss. He drew her head to his chest and struggled for self-control.

"And I don't regret coming here," Kathryn whispered, "because if I hadn't come . . . if I hadn't . . ."

He stopped her words with another kiss and, as he kissed her, he knew that he should tell her she was wrong, that coming to this damned place had been the worst mistake of her life.

But she was warm and sweet in his arms. A sudden fierce sensation swept through him. For a moment, he didn't know what it was.

And then he did.

What he felt was joy.

Fifteen

Joy? He felt joy?

What the hell kind of an emotion was that, for a man like him to feel?

He had no right to any emotions, dammit, except perhaps the rage that had drawn him out of the darkness in the first place.

And he had no right whatsoever to hold this flesh and blood woman in his arms, as he was doing now. Or to want her. Or to exult in the knowledge that she wanted him. Hell, there was no sense being modest about it, she did want him, with the same driving need as his own.

Well, what was wrong with that?

Dead though he might be, he had all the bodily urges of a mortal. As for Kathryn . . . hadn't she told him herself that women of her time weren't troubled by issues of feminine chastity and virtue?

Dammit, it was so simple. All he had to do was kiss her again, lift her into his arms and carry her up the stairs to the bedroom.

It didn't matter that he had no right to her, that she was human and he was whatever in hell he was; that she was betrothed to another man. Nothing mattered, but this driving need to have her.

And, after he'd had her, then what? She would leave the island and he would be alone again, and the loneliness would be more desperate than ever. Images of Kathryn, of a woman and a life he could never have, would torment his mind and heart for the rest of eternity.

Never mind all that, you scurvy bastard. What of her? Doesn't she deserve more than being bedded by the likes of you?

Kathryn stirred in his arms. "Matthew?" she whispered.

He looked into her eyes and he knew, with absolute certainty, what he must do next.

He bent his head, crushed her mouth under his.

"Good-bye, Kathryn," he said.

And he was gone.

Matthew was gone.

One minute, he'd been holding her in his arms and the next, Kathryn was swaying on her feet, all alone.

At first, she thought it was some kind of joke. A ghostly version of hide-and-seek. But if it was, he'd picked a strange moment for playing the game.

"Matthew?" she said.

There was no answer.

"Matthew, where are you?"

She went from room to room, calling his name.

"This is silly," she said. "I know you're here someplace. Come on out and show yourself."

He didn't.

"Okay," she said, "okay, that's fine."

And it was. She'd asked him to get out, hadn't she?

Yes. But that was before . . .

Before what? He'd kissed her, but he'd kissed her many times. There'd been nothing different about that kiss except that she'd let her imagination run away with her, let herself think that . . . that . . .

Kathryn stood still. There was nothing to think. Not really. She'd gotten carried away, and so had he. It was just a good thing one of them had come to their senses in time, and embarrassing that it had been Matthew and not her.

Maybe it was a good thing he didn't want to show himself.

Maybe it was a very good thing.

Good-bye, Kathryn, indeed.

"Good-bye, Matthew," she said to the silent house, "and good riddance."

Damn, but she was such a charming, and gracious, female. Matthew gritted his teeth as he paced the hot, still attic.

Good-bye, and good riddance?

"What a wonderful sentiment, Kathryn," he growled.

He had turned his back on what could have been a night in her bed and this was his thanks? He had given up the chance to undo almost two centuries of celibacy for this?

No good had ever come of pretending to be a gentleman, not in the real world and not in this one.

Kathryn hadn't recognized an act of decency when she'd been confronted with it. She hadn't even maintained an ongoing interest in finding out what had become of him. She'd spent, what, twenty minutes searching for him? Then she'd written him off the way a banker might write off a bad loan.

"Hell," Matthew growled, "bloody hell."

If that was what a man got for doing the right thing, he was just as glad he hadn't wasted his energies doing the right thing too many times during his life.

By the time Elvira arrived Monday morning, Kathryn was up to her elbows in Lysol and hot water, scrubbing down the old bricks on the terrace with a vengeance.

Elvira raised her eyebrows. "Hot day for that kind of thing, don't you think?"

Kathryn sat back on her heels. Her shirt and shorts were

already stuck to her skin, her hair was damp and sweat was streaming into her eyes.

"Is it?" She shrugged her shoulders. "I hadn't noticed."

Elvira's brows lifted another millimeter. Oh my. Kathryn Russell was angry as a hornet. Not that Elvira was particularly surprised. Everybody from one end of the island to the other knew that Kathryn's young man had flown in Friday night and flown out again not twelve hours later, jammed into the mail plane like a sack of parcels.

Sam Patterson, who ran the airstrip, had joked about it.

"Might call it a case of returned male," he'd said.

Nobody knew exactly what had happened but here was Kathryn, on a morning where the temperature was already up to ninety and still climbing, scrubbing down the terrace with a look on her face that said, go on, just try knocking this chip off my shoulder and see what happens.

Elvira bit her lip to keep from smiling. Even after forty-something years of marriage, there were still times Hiram got her dander up so far that only cleaning her already clean house from top to bottom would get it down again.

She took the hatpin from her straw boater, lifted the hat from her head, and stabbed the pin through the crown.

"Just let me change into my housedress," she said calmly, "and I'll join you."

By midafternoon, the old bricks were as clean as they were ever going to get.

And a good thing, too. Kathryn dumped her scrub brush into her bucket and wiped the back of her hand across her sweaty forehead.

The sun had long since passed its zenith but it was still hot and airless. Not a breath stirred the palm trees.

"I'm finished," she called to Elvira, who'd been working on the opposite side of the terrace.

Elvira sat back on her heels.

"So am I." A smile split her dark face. "Hope I don't look as bad as you do, Kathryn."

Kathryn laughed. "I hope you don't feel as bad, either." She groaned, put her hands in the small of her back, and staggered to her feet. "I have aches where I never knew I had muscles! How about you?"

Elvira grinned and rose as lithely as a dancer. "Raise enough children, you find out about all your muscles early on. I'll clean up. You go on, take yourself a nice bath, then sit down with a cup of tea and you'll feel lots better."

"No, that's okay. I'll clean up with you and then head for the tub—assuming the water heater cooperates, that is."

Both women sighed with pleasure as they stepped into the comparative coolness of the house.

"Heater givin' you trouble?" Elvira asked.

"All the time. It's probably going to be number one on Hiram's fix-it list."

"Well, a cool shower would do the trick, too, on a day like this." Elvira emptied her bucket, then Kathryn's, and put them away under the sink. "Though the temperature'll be droppin' off, soon enough."

Kathryn smiled. She took a pitcher of iced tea from the refrigerator, filled two glasses and handed one to Elvira.

"You know something the weatherman doesn't? According to him, this heat wave's going to last through the weekend."

"Weatherman's wrong." The older woman took a long sip of tea as she peered out the window at the sky. "A storm's comin' in, goin' to blow the heat clear back to Grenada."

Kathryn looked out the window, too. She saw a blazing sun, a placid sky, and one puffy, Norman Rockwell cloud.

"Wishful thinking."

"You'll see. Storm'll be here by tonight."

"Well, I'd like to think you're right, but this morning's forecast was for at least another day of the same misery."

"Sure. But I've been livin' on this island all my life, listenin' to what it wants to tell me. And it tells me that if you're wise, you'll close this house up good and tight before you go to bed." Elvira finished the last of her tea and put the glass in the sink. "You might even want to come into town for the night."

"My money's on the weatherman. Besides, even if he's wrong, I'm not afraid of a little rain." A slight flush rose on Kathryn's cheeks. "I admit, it upset me last time, but I wasn't used to this house then."

"I wasn't thinkin' of that, Kathryn, I was thinkin' that this storm's goin' to be a lot more than rain."

Kathryn patted the older woman's arm. "I'll be fine," she said. "Really, don't worry about me."

By early evening, it was obvious she'd put her money on the wrong forecaster.

Elvira was right. A storm was brewing. The signs were right out there, easy to read even if you were a city person who never noticed much beyond whether or not it was raining.

Kathryn had managed enough hot water for a shower, not a bath, and then she'd made herself a light early supper of fruit, cheese and coffee and taken it out to the terrace.

By the time she'd finished eating, the weather was beginning to change.

The sky had turned a metallic shade of blue that exaggerated the bright glare of a sun so orange it was harsh enough to hurt the eyes. When she walked around to the front of the house and looked down at the sea, she noticed that it had taken on a glassy sheen. Light swells moved with lazy ease towards the beach while grey clouds clustered like a dirty ruff on the distant horizon.

The melancholy cry of a sea gull pierced the silence. Kathryn lifted her head and followed the bird's flight. It was heading inland, and for an uneasy couple of seconds she thought about Elvira's suggestion that she do the same.

But why? She'd already survived a storm at Charon's Crossing, and this one would be easier to endure. Hiram had secured the shutters so she wouldn't have to jump at the sound of them banging, should the wind pick up. And she wasn't about to get hysterical if the lights went out this time, now that she knew that her "intruder" was a ghost who'd decided to make himself scarce.

Where was he? Not that she really cared. It was just natural curiosity, that was all. As far as she was concerned, if she never saw Matthew McDowell again, it would be too soon!

A gust of hot, humid wind slapped at Kathryn's cheeks. It had an unpleasant, clammy feel to it. She made a face, went back to the house, and switched on the shortwave radio while she poured herself more coffee.

". . . latest update. Moderate winds and seas are expected and a small crafts advisory has been issued. Persons living in low-lying shore areas might want to take precautions but there is no cause for alarm."

The wind chose that moment to rattle the house like a giant castanet.

Kathryn laughed. "Of course not," she said.

Well, it wouldn't hurt to be prepared. She dug out the candles and matches, checked to be sure the flashlight still worked, and made a circuit of the house to be certain the shutters were all secured.

Just before dusk, she turned the radio on again. It seemed to her that the wind had grown a lot stronger but with the shutters closed, she couldn't see the sky or the sea.

". . . upgraded to severe," the impersonal voice on the radio said. "Persons in low-lying locations are advised to move to higher ground and . . ."

Kathryn licked her lips. Was there anything to worry about? No. She was already on higher ground, up here on the cliff. Besides, how bad could a storm be? Hurricane season was over.

She hesitated, and then she picked up the flashlight and went to the front door. She could hear the wind just beyond it and the door was hard to open, as if something were trying to shoulder it closed . . .

Dear God!

It was like walking into another world.

The sky was the color of charcoal, the clouds so thick and low Kathryn had the uneasy feeling she could almost reach up and touch them. The wind whistled through the trees and whipped at her hair.

She had never seen a storm like this, never imagined it was possible for nature to be so raw and powerful.

What would the sea look like, under this dark and primitive sky? How tall were the wind-driven waves that must be crashing wildly against the beach?

The logical thing to do was go back to the shelter of the house . . . But the sea would be a magnificent sight, something she'd never forget. Kathryn took a breath, ducked her head and fought her way to the edge of the cliff for one quick, quick look . . .

Nothing could have prepared her for what she saw.

The placid blue Caribbean she knew, the one that had sighed gently against a crescent of white, glistening sand, was gone. The sea was black as ink, tipped with sharp white claws that had already surged over the beach and were tearing at the cliff she stood on. The pound of the waves was like the beat of a heart and now she could hear something else, too, as if a freight train were fast approaching . . .

It was the wind, tearing across the water like a howling beast determined to drive everything out of its path.

Run, Kathryn. Turn for the house and run!

Sobbing, terrified, she obeyed the voice in her head but it was impossible to outrun the wind. It hit her like a fist, first driving the breath from her lungs, then curled around her like the unseen hand of some ancient behemoth determined to snatch her up and hurl her down into the raging torrent below.

A scream broke from her throat.

"Matthew," she cried, "Matthew, help me!"

Strong arms closed around her and lifted her off her feet.

"Hang on to me, Kathryn," Matthew shouted.

Sobbing, she wound her arms around his neck. He raced for the house while the wind screamed and howled and clawed, fought the door open and half-carried, half-dragged Kathryn inside. She clung to him as he kicked the door shut, slid home the bolt and the lock.

"Oh God," she sobbed, "Matthew . . ."

Gently, he lowered her to her feet, wrapped his arms around her and held her tight.

"Shh," he murmured, "it's all right now."

They stood that way while the rain pelted the roof and the wind shrieked at the siding, taking comfort in the heat of each other's bodies and the beat of each other's hearts. Then Matthew grabbed Kathryn by the shoulders and shoved her to arm's length.

"You damned little fool," he snarled, "what in bloody hell were you trying to do? You almost got yourself killed." He snapped his hands from her shoulders and raked his fingers through his hair. "Lord, woman, don't you ever stop to think?"

"Now, just a minute—"

"You were almost swept off that bloody cliff!"

"Dammit, Matthew, it wasn't as if I—"

"As if you what? Took two minutes to think?" He thrust his face towards hers, his eyes flashing with anger. "Nay, Kathryn, why would you do something so foolish as give a moment's thought to anything?"

Kathryn lifted her chin and glared at him in defiance.

"Listen here, Captain McDowell, I'm grateful for your assistance, but—"

"My assistance?" Matthew threw his hands on his hips, tossed back his head, and laughed. "You mean, you're grateful I was there to save your damned fool neck!"

"You did not save my neck. And I'd appreciate it if you wouldn't punctuate every other word with an obscenity."

"Your thinking processes are the obscenity," he snarled, this time punctuating each word by jabbing his forefinger into her chest. Kathryn staggered back and he stalked after her until her shoulders hit the wall. "What in hell were you doing? Playing some kind of bloody game? That's a hurricane out there, madam, or hadn't you noticed?"

His words sent a chill racing up her spine but it was too late now to give an inch.

"That storm?" Kathryn tossed her head. "Hah! Don't make me laugh. It's a bad storm, but a hurricane? It's nothing of the sort."

"Are you now an expert on weather?"

"I don't have to be an expert to know that hurricane season is over!"

Matthew's lips drew back from his teeth. "Be certain to so inform any crew that's sailed these waters in midwinter."

"Very well." Kathryn's voice was cold. "I'll bow to your expertise in these matters, Captain. But I don't have to take your insults."

"You still haven't answered my question, dammit. What were you doing out there?"

"I haven't answered it because it's stupid! What do you think I was doing? Looking out at the sea."

" 'Looking out at the sea,' " Matthew said in cruel parody. "What's the matter, madam? Didn't you have anything better to do to occupy your time?"

Kathryn glared at him. "I've had enough," she snapped, and pushed past him towards the stairs.

"Kathryn!" His voice roared after her. "Where in hell do you think you're going?"

"It's none of your business."

"Damn you, don't turn your back on me!"

She stopped on the second step and spun towards him in a rage.

"What's the problem, Captain? Did I drag you out of some nice, cozy corner where you've been curled up like the egotistical bully you are, getting your kicks by wondering if I'd miss you? Well, I didn't. Not one damned bit."

Matthew thought of the damnable attic, of how he despised its dark corners and walls that imprisoned him as if it were a dungeon, of how he'd been pacing it like a trapped beast until something had drawn him to the window and to that sight he'd never forget, Kathryn fighting for her life against that wicked predator of a sea.

Bloody hell! How could one woman be so infuriating? It was all he could do to keep from turning her over his knee and whaling the daylights out of her.

"I am relieved to hear that you did not miss me," he said coldly, "for I did not miss you, either . . . which is surely a good thing since you spent all of five minutes searching for me in this misery of a house!"

He hadn't meant to say that. What did he care, how long she'd bothered to look for him? Unfortunately, it was too late to call back the ill-chosen words, especially since Kathryn's temper was already rising to the challenge.

"Five minutes?" she said. Her eyes turned flinty. "What do you mean, five minutes?" She came down a step and slammed her fist on the banister. "I spent hours looking for you, you stupid fool!"

Matthew's face whitened. "Be careful with what you call me, madam."

"Don't tell me what I can and can't call you, dammit! Not that I really gave a damn if I found you or not! Not that I cared a fig for where you'd gone or what you were doing. It's just that I was furious that you'd run out on me before I could tell you that I—that I . . ."

"That you what?" Matthew said in a tightly controlled voice.

She stared at him, at that stern, handsome face, at the angry green eyes and the unforgiving mouth.

"I wanted to tell you that—that I hate you, Matthew, that I . . ."

The rushed words ended on a broken sob. Kathryn swung

away, but not in time. Matthew had already glimpsed the tell-tale shimmer of tears in her eyes.

All his anger and rage drained away. What was the sense in pretending? His blind fury had nothing to do with Kathryn and everything to do with the knowledge that he had almost lost her.

He choked out her name and she turned towards him, her eyes dark and enormous in her beautiful face. He said something, though he would never know what, but it must have been the right thing because the next instant, she was in his arms.

"Where were you?" she said, between kisses. "Why did you leave me?"

"I was right here all the time, sweetheart, playing at being noble."

"Noble?" She drew back in his arms. "I don't understand."

"I wanted so badly to make love to you yesterday, Kathryn, but I knew it was wrong. That was why I left you."

There were tears on her lashes, but she was smiling.

"How could what we both wanted be wrong?" she asked softly.

Matthew shook his head. "I should never have let you become so important to me. Don't you see, this can only end badly?"

"It can end here," Kathryn whispered, "where we want to be, in each other's arms."

She caught his hair in her hands, dragged his mouth to hers and silenced any protest he might have made with a kiss. For a long moment, he didn't respond. Then he groaned, swung her into his arms and carried her up the stairs and to her bedroom.

He kicked the door shut behind him. The howling of the wind, and the grey shadows of the room, closed around them.

Slowly, so slowly, Matthew lowered Kathryn to her feet. A moan broke from her throat as her body traveled the length of his. Was that his heart racing, or was it hers? The hardness and heat of him burned through the layers of fabric that separated them, scalding her with desire.

She felt the hard press of his erection against her belly. The sheathed power of his flesh made her heartbeat quicken, but not with fear. She moved against him, slowly and deliberately, pressing her softness against his male rigidity, shuddering with delight when he groaned again before crushing her mouth under his. His hands cupped her bottom, seeking the shape of her through her wet clothing, and then he drew back, his eyes hot on hers.

"I want to see you," he whispered.

His eyes held hers while he undid the buttons down the front of her shirt and eased it back from her shoulders. He waited, prolonging the moment like a man with a special gift on Christmas morning. Then he looked down to feast his eyes on what he had unwrapped.

Her skin was the same pale gold as the rest of her, though it seemed dark against the whiteness of her chemise. The chemise itself was like none he had ever seen, feminine and lacy but covering only her breasts. He feasted his eyes on the proud, lush rise of them. Then, slowly, he lifted his hands and cupped their weight.

Kathryn made a soft, breathless sound of pleasure that shot straight into his loins.

"Ah, sweetheart," he murmured, "how beautiful you are."

He bent his head, gently kissed the curve of each breast, closed his mouth around the lace-enclosed flesh until she was moaning with pleasure, until it was no longer enough to imagine the sweetness of her naked flesh against his tongue. But the front closure of the chemise almost defeated him.

She gave a soft, very feminine laugh.

"Wait," she whispered.

Her hands joined his, the lace parted, and her breasts tumbled into his hands. He caressed them, paid them homage with his lips and teeth, and all the while Kathryn was sighing his name in a husky, sweet voice that made the blood pound in his loins.

Go slowly, he told himself, slowly, man. You have waited so long for her . . . don't spoil it now.

His hands dropped to the abbreviated pantaloons she favored. Like the chemise, they gave him a bit of trouble until he figured out how to undo the row of tiny metal teeth that served as a closure.

But the delay was good. It was what he needed, if he were to retain any sort of control over himself. He wanted to spin these moments out until they were as fine and slender as silk thread, to watch Kathryn's lovely face as he slowly divested her of her clothing, for he knew even as this began that it must end.

This night, and the storm raging between them, were what he would carry with him through all eternity.

At last, she stood before him naked.

And oh, she was so beautiful.

If only he knew the words to tell her exactly how beautiful she was, but he was not a man of poetry, he was a man who had lived his life on the seas. Would she understand if he said that her skin was as silken as the moon reflected on a still ocean? That her hair fell over her shoulders like the waving grasses in the southern seas? That her eyes were stars in a midnight sky and her face and body surely those of the Sirens that had lured the ancient mariners?

In the end, all he could do was whisper her name.

"Kathryn," he said thickly, "my Kathryn . . ."

He reached out, watching her face as he stroked his fingers lightly, lightly over her nipples, then over her belly to her thighs. When he saw what his touch did to her, it was almost his undoing. He could feel his control slipping, feel the urgency to possess her sweeping through his muscles.

Quickly, he pulled his linen shirt over his head, kicked off his boots and stepped out of his trousers. He saw her eyes widen at the sight of him, hard and swollen and aroused.

He took her hand, brought it to his throbbing flesh, shuddered at her touch.

"Kiss me," she whispered, and he did, lifting her off the ground, his lips parting hers until he could taste her heat. She made those little sounds in the back of her throat, the ones that were driving him crazy, and laced her fingers into his hair.

God, he was drowning in pleasure.

He had wanted her for so long. Not just since he had stumbled into her dreams but since the moment the world had begun, since the planet and the heavens were nothing but whirling bits of matter.

He'd told himself it was not so, that his hunger for her had been fired by his years of celibacy. He'd told himself that what beat in his veins was simply the need of the flesh, that his cock, like any man's, was a divining rod blindly seeking entry wherever it might find it.

He had told himself all that and more but all of it had been lies. He knew it now, as he pressed kisses to Kathryn's face and throat, as he inhaled the scent of her, rain and flowers and all life's treasures. He knew that what he felt for her he had never felt for any woman and would never feel again.

He clasped her face between his hands and kissed her, his tongue slipping between her lips and moving against hers. His need was fierce but he fought to be tender. He was a mass of contradictions altogether. He wanted to ravish Kathryn and to gentle her; to have her vulnerable beneath him and to hold her close in his arms; to ride her until she was sobbing and wild, then soothe her with kisses.

He sat down on the edge of the bed and stood her between his legs. He bent his head to her breast and drew the sweet, beaded tip into his mouth.

"Matthew," she whispered. Her voice was high and breathy and filled with desire. He had never heard a sound so sweet.

He drew his hand down along her hip, over her gently rounded belly. His fingers danced along her thigh, brushed the curls at the juncture of her thighs.

"Matthew," she said again, on a harsh, indrawn breath.

He cupped her hips in his hands and kissed his way down to her belly. The scent of her arousal rose to his nostrils and he groaned, for no perfume had ever smelled as exquisite. He palmed her buttocks; he drew her closer and his mouth began to trail lower on her flesh.

She gave a little whimper of distress and jerked back.

"Matthew, don't."

He looked up. Was she going to ask him to stop?

No. The flush in her cheeks, the rapid rise and fall of her breasts, were more eloquent than words. Her desire for him was as deep as his was for her.

She tried to smile. "I'm not . . . I just can't . . ."

Sweet heaven. She was embarrassed!

The realization made his throat tighten. He was no stranger to displays of modesty in the boudoir. There were some women who thought a bit of maidenly coyness heightened a man's pleasure and perhaps it did for some, but he had never been much affected by pretense.

But this was no pretense.

Kathryn was blushing from head to toe, as if no man had ever looked his fill before. As if no man had ever . . . had ever . . .

Nay, it was impossible. She had told him that the women of her time were not shy about taking pleasure. She would surely have been with other men . . .

The thought of her with anyone else was like a knife, driving into his gut.

But it didn't matter. Tonight, he would erase the memories of any other man. He would burn himself not just into her flesh but into her heart and soul. After tonight, she would never look at another man, never want another man . . .

His blood turned cold.

Dear God, what a son of a bitch he was!

He had no right to take Kathryn for his own. He was not a man, he was a . . . a thing. He was a creature without life or substance, existing on the icy fringes of a dark and ugly world that she could never comprehend.

It took all his strength to do what had to be done, but he did it, pushed her from him and rose to his feet.

"Get your clothes on," he said in a gruff whisper.

"What?"

"I said—"

"I heard what you said, Matthew. But . . . but why?"

Her voice was tremulous. He looked at her, seeing the mingled confusion and hurt in her eyes. Pain shot through his heart and he turned away.

"Just do it, Kathryn!"

"Matthew." The light touch of her hand on his shoulder was like flame. "I—I didn't mean . . . I wasn't asking you to—to stop, I was just—it embarrassed me to have you lo- . . ."

He swung around and caught her by the shoulders.

"Don't you understand? We can't do this."

She was looking at him as if he'd lost his mind and maybe he had, for a little while anyway, but he'd regained it now and nothing she said or did would change it.

"This is wrong, Kathryn."

"Who says so?"

"I do," he growled. He bent down, grabbed for his discarded clothing. "Dammit," he said, as he straightened up, "I should never have—"

"Shut up, Matthew."

His eyes widened. "What did you say?"

"I said, shut up and . . . oh, never mind."

She rose on her toes and kissed him. Her mouth was warm and sweet and moved gently against his. For one whispered heartbeat, his lips softened under hers. Then he blinked and pulled away.

"Don't," he said sharply.

She smiled. Her hands lifted to his chest. Slowly, slowly, she began to move them down his torso.

"Kathryn." He caught hold of her hands. "Kathryn . . ."

His breath caught as her fingers trailed over his belly and down into the thick curls that surrounded his sex. "Sweetheart, don't . . ."

"This is what I want, Matthew, what I've always wanted, ever since you first came to me in my dreams."

"Dammit, woman, you don't know what you're . . ."

"I'm not a fool. You think we mustn't make love because— because of our situation."

He jerked back and glared at her. "Don't speak in platitudes, dammit. What I think—what I know—is that you're alive and I am not. If that's not the best reason in the world for stopping this before it begins—"

Had she touched him, had she moved against him, he could have resisted her. Instead, she did the one thing he was powerless to fight.

She smiled into his eyes and said, "I love you."

"Nay," he said, "you cannot . . ."

He groaned, caught her to him, and carried her down to the bed. How could he fight destiny? This moment, wrenched out of the fabric of time, was theirs. To have denied it would have been to deny whatever warped laws of the universe had brought them together.

He kissed her over and over, with a hunger that was insatiable. Right and wrong no longer had any meaning. He only knew that he would never be the same after this night.

She would never be the same after this night.

Never, Kathryn thought in wonder, not if she lived for another thousand years.

Matthew was everything she had imagined, and more. He was beautiful, the purest form of masculine grace, all hard planes and long muscle. Looking at him was intoxicating. Touching him was driving her to the edge of sanity.

His skin was hot under her hands and carried the scent of

his passion. His flesh was hard and exciting, and his kisses were all the nourishment her heart would ever need.

How could she have ever imagined making love would be like this?

She was a rainbow of brilliance, a symphony of dazzling, dizzying sensations. Her body was electric and alive with response, and now all of it was centering in one place, that hidden, secret part of her.

Matthew's thigh, hard and powerful, lay locked between hers. He was moving his leg against her, up and down, back and forth . . .

Ah. *Ah!* She was moving, too, sliding against his flesh, lifting herself to him and pressing against him while she made breathy little sounds of pleasure.

She was soaked, so wet and hot . . . She felt like a flower, opening to the burning heat of a hot summer sun. All these years, all her life, she'd thought this was nothing, really, that to lie with a man could not be any great miracle or mystery. Sex was nothing she'd wanted and it had been easy to avoid, in this era of caution.

And then she'd dreamed of Matthew.

She moaned as he kissed the hollow of her throat, then trailed open-mouthed kisses to her breast. His hand cupped the soft weight and she caught her breath and watched as he bent his head to her, his hair falling like sun-kissed silk over her flesh.

The sight of him taking her nipple into his mouth was so erotic that she sobbed his name.

"Matthew," she said brokenly, "Matthew . . ."

Her cries as he suckled her, coupled with the taste of her on his tongue, were sweet torture. Her hips lifted and surged towards his and for one terrible instant, he was afraid he was going to unman himself.

He told himself to think about something else. A diversion.

Count from one to one hundred, he'd once heard a man say, it always works.

Nothing would work now. Hell, he couldn't have counted from one to five without getting lost after three. He was feverish with desire, desperate to thrust into Kathryn's heat and end this torment for them both.

Ah, but it was such exquisite torment. He could not get enough of kissing her mouth or of sucking on her nipples. She tasted of milk and of honey; she smelled like the Gardens of Babylon and the mystery of Venus.

He eased his hand down her belly, lightly stroked the damp curls that awaited him. She shuddered against him and he hushed her, whispering words without knowing what he said, knowing only that he was beyond thought and reason.

His hand slipped between her legs and parted her. He touched her, his fingers sliding against that hidden rosebud he had sought, and she cried out in ecstasy.

"Matthew," she sobbed. Her hips lifted to him, drowning his stroking fingers in her sweet juices.

His head was spinning. There was so much more he wanted to do. To her. With her. He wanted to bury his face in her neck and savor the scent of her, to put his mouth where his hand was and taste her. He wanted to start from the beginning and do everything again.

But it was time. It was past time. He was going to explode if he didn't take her now. He drew back, gently drew her thighs apart, and knelt between them. He looked at her, touched her, and her eyes flew open.

"Matthew," she whispered.

"I won't hurt you, love. I promise."

Carefully, so carefully, he eased himself forward, letting just the head of his blood-engorged penis touch her damp heat.

Her eyes shut and her head thrashed back against the pillow.

"Kathryn," he said in a choked whisper.

Her eyes flew open. He saw himself reflected in her pupils.

"Watch me," he whispered. "Watch me make you mine."

He moved forward again and rubbed himself lightly over that delicate pink bud. Once. Twice. His teeth clenched together; sweat glistened on his skin. Wait, he told himself, Lord, wait until you're deep inside her . . .

Kathryn cried out and arched off the bed. Matthew groaned, slipped his hands under her bottom, and gave up the battle.

"Yes," he said, and thrust home.

Sixteen

By morning, the storm had blown over.

Matthew sat straddling a chair in the kitchen, his chin resting on his folded arms while he indulged in the nicest sort of philosophical speculation.

Which was the more perfect sight? The blue sky and golden sunlight visible through the open door that led to the terrace—or Kathryn, bustling about the room as she made breakfast?

He smiled. It was no contest. Kathryn was far more wonderful than the warm, shining day, more wonderful than any miracle of Nature or of man. He had never known a woman like her, nor even imagined one. She was the embodiment of a man's dreams, sweet one moment and sassy the next, as fiercely independent as any man yet feminine and soft when such things mattered, and so bright and quick of mind that sometimes, when they were talking, he almost forgot she was female, though he wasn't fool enough to tell her that. She bristled at the slightest suggestion of differences between the sexes.

His smile tilted.

Nay. He could never forget she was female. How could he, when she was so incredibly lovely, so sensually feminine?

An answering throb in his loins told him his body agreed with his brain's assessment, a minor miracle if ever there were one because only a little while ago he'd felt so sated that even the thought of rising from the bed had seemed a physical impossibility.

He had awakened first this morning, with Kathryn in his arms. Just the pleasure of watching her as she slept, her head on his shoulder, her dark hair spilled like the finest China silk over his skin, had made him turn hard as granite.

He'd promised himself he wouldn't wake her. He'd begun stroking her skin with the gentlest of caresses. Her cheek, and her mouth. Her throat, and her shoulder. And then her breast. Just a grazing brush of his fingertips, that was all, and when she'd sighed in her sleep and the faintest smile had curved over her lips, he'd bent his head and kissed her, first her mouth, his lips just skimming the soft fullness of hers, and then her throat, where he'd left a trail of tiny kisses which had inevitably led to his burying his face between her breasts.

The intoxication of her scent, the warmth of her skin, the steady beat of her heart beneath his ear had all conspired against him until the pledge he'd made himself was as worthless as a farm boy in the foretop with a squall on the horizon.

His tenderness had changed to passion, his gentle kisses deepened with need, his touch burned with desire and then Kathryn had been awake and aroused and hot as flame in his arms.

When, a long time later, she'd sighed and said she'd thought it might be a good idea if they had something to eat, he'd groaned, fallen back on the pillows, and said, hell, yes, a meal was an excellent idea if she didn't want to see his bones melt into a puddle before her very eyes.

She'd started to dress, but he'd stopped her.

"Here," he'd said, tossing her her shirt, and when she'd protested that she could hardly go downstairs wearing so little, his response had been one of perfect logic.

"Don't be silly, Kathryn. The shirt covers more of you than the smallclothes you generally wear."

A wicked smile danced in his eyes because watching her now, he knew just how much he had lied, and how clever he'd been to have done so.

It wasn't that what he'd said hadn't been true. The shirt was loose and long and covered her from her throat to mid-thigh. It was what her glorious body did for the shirt that was driving him crazy. The rise of her breasts, pushing gently against the soft linen, was an instant reminder of the silken weight of them in his hands. The dark outline of her nipples brought back the taste and feel of that honeyed flesh when his lips and tongue adored her, and the sweet, exciting sounds that purred in the back of her throat.

And as she moved, doing all the mundane things one did in the preparation of a meal, the shirt was accomplishing things that were eons from being mundane. The hem fluttered against her slender, golden thighs, tantalizing him. The open neckline shifted, never enough so he could see her breasts but teasing him with hints of their lushness. And when she bent down or rose on her toes to reach for something, her softly rounded bottom peeped at him from beneath the tailpiece.

Matthew smothered a groan. A gentleman would surely have offered to do the stretching and bending for her but he was no gentleman, especially not at this moment. What he was, was a man in danger of being castrated by his own trousers, if he didn't do something to stop the pictures crowding his fevered brain.

Kathryn opened the refrigerator door, bent down and peered inside. This time, his groan was audible.

"What?" she said, bumping the door shut with a provocative tilt of one hip.

He shrugged his shoulders and worked at looking casual as he rose carefully to his feet.

"Nothing," he said blandly.

"Are you sure? You have the strangest look on your face."

"Do I?" He smiled, or hoped he did. "Well, that's probably because I'm close to starvation."

She laughed as she set a bowl of fruit on the table. "We can't have that, Captain. Why don't you tell me what you'd like for your breakfast?"

That was easy. What he'd like was Kathryn, right there on

the table, with that smoky look in her eyes and her knees up and him hard and driving between her thighs . . .

Another thought like that and he was liable to embarrass them both. He frowned and turned to glare at the coffee pot while he tugged surreptitiously at his trousers.

"Coffee, for starters. How long does that thing take until it's ready?"

"Another minute and it should be done." Kathryn's brows rose in a delicate arch. "Are you one of those people who's a grouch before you have your first cup of coffee in the morning?"

"I am never a grouch," Matthew said grouchily. Kathryn snorted, and he turned and tried to glare at her but it didn't work, and they both began to laugh. "All right, perhaps I am. Take pity, woman. I am a man in desperate need of sustenance."

"Sustenance, hmm?"

"Aye. A dozen eggs, a couple of rashers of bacon, oatmeal, potatoes and some buckwheat cakes with maple syrup would go down right."

She looked at him. "Tell me you're joking. Please."

"Well," he said, poker-faced, "it is only what I will need to restore the energy you have drained from me."

"The energy *I* drained from *you?*"

"Aye. Everyone knows women do not need to do anything in the boudoir save lie back and think pure thoughts."

He laughed, ducked as Kathryn pretended to aim a sugar bowl at him, and he caught her in his arms. She laughed softly, put down the bowl, and curled her arms around his neck.

"My thoughts are anything but pure this morning."

"Is that so?" he said, smiling.

Her cheeks pinkened. "Well, to tell the truth, this is the first time I ever made breakfast for a man who's wearing nothing but his pants."

Matthew grinned. "Am I a distraction?"

She laughed. "You know you are."

His smile faded as he raised her face to his. "This has been a night of firsts for you, sweetheart, has it not?"

Kathryn's color deepened. She nodded. "I suppose I should have told you, but—"

He stopped her words with a kiss. When it ended, he drew her head to his chest.

"It has been a night of firsts for me, as well," he said softly, "for I have never been so happy or . . ."

"Or what?" she asked, smiling.

The smile died on her lips when she looked up and saw his face. "Matthew? What's wrong?"

Everything, he thought, dear God in heaven, everything was wrong! He let go of her, walked blindly out onto the terrace, to the railing, and wrapped his hands around it until the bones of his knuckles showed white beneath his skin.

Or so much in love.

That was what he'd almost said, but it was impossible. How could he be happy? Or in love? The curse would not permit it. That was what he had wished on Cat Russell, all those years ago; it was what had gone full circle and been visited upon him as he lay dying.

A hand seemed to reach inside his chest and squeeze his heart.

All along, ever since he'd understood that he had damned himself with his own words, he had thought he understood his fate. He would be alone, through eternity. Last night, in a moment of treacly, self-indulgent nonsense, he'd built upon that conviction, imagining himself carrying the image of this idyll with Kathryn on his lonely journey.

Now, with a clarity that made him want to pound his fist through the wall, he understood.

What he would carry with him was the pain of a heart torn and bleeding. He had found joy with Kathryn, yes, and passion, but he had found much, much more. He had found love— love so powerful it filled his heart with each beat it took.

That he, of all men, could love so deeply—and be loved as deeply in return—was beyond imagining.

And that was to be his torment.

The darkness that had once surrounded him would be blessed release, compared to what lay ahead. He was doomed to forever remember and mourn that which he could not have. Kathryn, whom he loved. Kathryn, who loved him . . .

"Matthew?"

Her hand fell lightly on his shoulder but it made him flinch.

"Please," she whispered, "what is it?"

He shook his head, laid his hand over hers. He knew what he should do. What was it the surgeon who had tended *Atropos*'s casualties had said, just before he'd applied a red-hot blade to a sailor's wound that would not stop bleeding?

"Don't flinch," he'd muttered. "The best way to deal with pain is to accept it." Then, whether or not the rum or the laudanum had taken effect, he'd jammed the hot blade against the man's flesh and let him scream.

That was the way to handle this. A man of honor would not flinch. He'd send Kathryn back to her world, before she became any more deeply involved in his. He'd lie and say, Kathryn, this was pleasant but now it is over.

He took a deep breath. His hand tightened on hers. With the words on his lips, he turned and faced her.

The morning sunlight was caught in her hair, surrounding her beautiful face with a soft, golden glow. She was smiling, though it was a worried smile, and her eyes, those deep blue pools, were filled with concern as they focused on his.

"Kathryn," he said. "Kathryn, sweetheart . . ."

He tried to tell himself it was she who moved first, that he would have done what he'd intended otherwise, but in his heart he knew that they moved as one so that suddenly she was in his arms. He kissed her and tasted tears on her lips, either his or hers, and what was the difference?

He would take what a malevolent, laughing Fate had sent him and cherish it, one day, one night, at a time.

He rocked her gently in his arms, his lips against her hair, his hand stroking the length of her back.

"I know what you're thinking," she whispered.

His arms tightened around her. "Do you?"

"You're thinking that there's no future in this for us."

Matthew sighed and did what he could to lighten the moment.

"Women have grown too clever by far," he said.

She made a sound that was half sob and half laugh.

"Women have always been clever. Men just never noticed."

"You're right." He smiled. "Things have not changed that much, then?"

"No."

"Good." He gave her a quick kiss. "In that case, I expect you to march back into that kitchen and make me a huge breakfast."

She laughed and swiped her hands over her wet eyes. She had asked him to tell her what had put that stricken expression on his face and he hadn't, but she knew. She knew.

Now, he was deliberately trying to lighten the moment. He was right to do it. There were only so many days and nights left. Why waste them in tears? Not that she was ready to admit defeat. There had to be a way for them to be together. They had bridged their two worlds now, hadn't they? There had to be an answer.

"Well? Do I get a meal, or do I just keep listening to my stomach telling me it's empty?"

"Tell your stomach help is on the way," Kathryn said briskly. "I'll do the bacon and eggs, you do the toast."

"Do the toast?"

"Yes."

Matthew's expression suggested she had just asked him to fly to the moon.

"You want *me* to make toast?"

"Right. I want you to take the bread and butter from the

fridge, pop the bread into the toaster, push down that lever right there . . . see? It's not very complicated."

"Well, I'm sure it isn't. But I don't cook."

Kathryn smiled sweetly. "You do, if you want to eat."

She was arranging strips of bacon in a pan, humming softly to herself and paying him no attention. With a shrug, he took the bread and butter from the contraption she called a refrigerator, then gave the metal box that toasted the bread the benefit of his full attention.

It worked with amazing speed and so did he, consuming one slice for every two he toasted and buttered. By the time he had six slices piled on a plate, Kathryn was cracking eggs into a bowl.

"How do you like your eggs?"

"Whatever way you make them is fine, just as long as the bacon's crisp."

"Speaking of the bacon . . . see if it needs turning, would you?"

Matthew peered into the pan of sizzling bacon. "Nay, it's fine."

"Good. Just keep an eye on it, please. So you can turn it when it's ready."

"Me?" he said in horror.

"Yes."

"Kathryn, I am not a cook."

"No?"

He drew himself up in as dignified a fashion as a man could when he was chewing a mouthful of toast.

"No," he said. "I am a sea captain."

"Ah," she said with a sweetness that he knew boded ill, "of course. How silly of me. I suppose you had a seafaring Julia Child to prepare your meals."

"A what?"

"A chef. You know, white toque, white apron, *haute cuisine.*"

Matthew thought of every ship's cook he'd known. They'd all been grizzled old sailors with missing teeth, blackened fingernails, and a nasty propensity for not always picking the weevils out of the biscuits before they served them.

"I would not call a ship's cook a chef, Kathryn."

"Perhaps not, but you'll agree they're all men?"

He laughed even harder, imagining a woman in the galley of a ship.

"Indeed. But on shore—"

"Don't tell me," Kathryn said with wide-eyed innocence. "On shore, cooks are always female."

"Certainly."

She laughed. "Well, we've done away with all those separate gender distinctions."

"Separate gender . . . ? What sort of humbug is that?"

"It's not humbug at all," Kathryn said, bristling. "There's no such thing as men's work and women's work anymore." She watched him as he buttered another piece of toast. There was something incongruous and wonderfully sexy about the sight of all that bare male skin and muscle. Her mouth softened. "Of course," she said demurely, "not all men could possibly look as handsome doing kitchen duty as you."

Two streaks of crimson swept across his high cheekbones.

"Why, Matthew," she said in delight, "you're blushing!"

"Don't be silly. Men don't blush."

"Oh, but they do." Her smile took on a wicked edge. "They've learned to get in touch with their feminine side."

Matthew's eyebrows shot towards his hairline. "What feminine side? Men don't have—"

"Of course they do." She turned her back to him and chewed on her lip to keep from laughing. "Oh, it's wonderful, how men today let their feelings out. You know, share their emotions. It's all part of learning to nurture one's inner child."

"Whose child?" Matthew demanded. "I have no—"

"Everybody has an inner child, unless they're mired in self-denial."

"What in heaven's name are you talking about?"

Laughter burst from her throat. "Basically," she said, "I

guess I'm talking about you taking this fork and dealing with the bacon."

He looked at her, smiled, and took the fork. "Why do I get the feeling I'm being mocked, madam?"

She watched as he began turning the strips of bacon with an expertise that suggested he'd been teasing her almost as much as she'd been teasing him. Emotion welled up within her, constricting her throat with its impact, and she turned all her concentration on the eggs, beating them with much more force than they deserved.

"Actually," she said, pouring the beaten eggs into the skillet, "you're lucky there's bacon to cook."

"I would have thought your cold chest would keep it well."

"Oh, it does." She reached for the salt and pepper and shook some of each over the frothy eggs. "But, like most people, I hardly ever keep the stuff in the house, except for special occ-
. . ."

She bit her lip, but it was too late. Matthew smiled.

"Meaning, you purchased it for Jason." He reached out and touched his hand gently to her cheek. "It doesn't bother me to hear his name, sweetheart, not when I can remember how quickly you sent him away."

"I didn't." Their eyes met and Kathryn sighed. "All right, I suppose I did."

"You did," he said smugly, "and it was because of me." He shook his head dramatically as he lifted the strips of bacon from the pan and placed them on the paper towels Kathryn had laid on the sink. "Where is Elvira, by the way? Doesn't she usually come to help you try and tame this monster of a house?"

Kathryn blushed. "I phoned and told her not to bother coming."

Matthew grinned. "Got rid of her, too, did you?"

"Get that self-satisfied look off your face, Captain! I just figured it would be easier than having you whisk around under our feet while we worked."

"And why would you think I'd do such a thing, madam?"

"Well . . . well, considering . . ." She swallowed. "I mean, I just thought . . ."

"You mean," Matthew said, whirling her into his arms and laughing, "that you didn't want to miss an opportunity to make wild, passionate love with me."

She shot him an indignant glare. "What an ego you have! Do you really think I'd . . ."

"Yes." His laughter faded. "Yes, sweetheart, and I wouldn't want it any other way."

They smiled at each other, kissed gently, and then Kathryn sighed and eased out of his arms.

"We wouldn't want the eggs to burn."

Matthew smiled. "No. We wouldn't. You go and sit down, then, and I'll serve."

In the end, they worked together, then sat opposite each other over a breakfast so enormous Kathryn was sure she'd have to toss most of it out, but Matthew was as good as his word, eating every bit she put on his plate.

"You're a fine cook, Kathryn," he said, after he'd devoured another slice of buttered toast thickly spread with marmalade.

She smiled, pushed aside her plate, propped her elbows on the table and leaned her chin on her hands.

"Well, I can do a pretty mean lamb stew. And people have been known to swoon over my chocolate souffle. Not that I have much time to cook, though."

"Why?"

"Why, what?"

"Why don't you have time? Here, aren't you going to finish those eggs?"

She laughed. "Don't tell me you want them!"

Matthew took her plate, tipped her eggs onto his, and smiled at her. "So tell me," he said, "why haven't you time to do much cooking?"

"Well, my job keeps me busy."

"Ah. Another sign of gender equality, hmm?"

"Uh huh. Most women work today."

"At what?"

"At everything. Some are waitresses, some work in offices. There are women lawyers and doctors . . ."

"Doctors? Female doctors? Do they have men as patients?" When Kathryn nodded, Matthew grimaced and pushed his empty plate aside. "I don't know if I approve of such a thing."

She laughed. "I'm sure my internist—my doctor—will be heartbroken to hear that."

"Is that what you are?" he asked warily. "A physician?"

"Would it upset you if I were?"

Matthew sighed. He rose from the table, got the coffee pot and filled their cups.

"Aye," he admitted, "I suppose it would. The thought of you touching another man . . ." He sighed again. "But, I suppose, if that is the way of your time . . ."

Kathryn reached across the table and linked her fingers through his. All her feminist leanings told her that his jealousy was wrong, but her heart enjoyed everything about it.

"I would never touch another man as I've touched you," she said softly.

Her words were like fire in his blood. The promise was all he could ever wish for, but he could not accept it from her. There would be someone else for her, there would have to be, for she could not be his and both of them knew it.

"Nay," he said, forcing a smile to his lips, "I would surely not permit you to saw off a limb of mine or dose me with salts."

Kathryn laughed. "You'll be happy to know the practice of medicine's changed quite a lot, over the centuries—and even happier to know I'm not a physician. I'm in computers."

"In what?"

"Comp . . ." She took a breath, then blew it out. "Computers are machines. People use them to do all kinds of stuff."

"What kinds of 'stuff'?"

"Writing letters and books. Working out mathematical problems. Drawing up plans for buildings. And for ships, I suppose. Anything you can think of, really. What I do is create programs for stock brokerage firms and . . ." She looked at his puzzled face. "Are you sure you want to listen to all this? It's going to take a long time to explain."

He smiled, but his eyes were narrowed above the smile. "I am capable of comprehending whatever you tell me."

"Oh, Matthew, I didn't mean—"

"Nay," he said, leaning forward and clasping her hand, "nor did I. Forgive me, sweetheart, I don't mean to be sharp-tongued. It's just, well, I see that the world has changed more than I'd realized." His hand tightened on hers. "Kathryn? We did win the war, did we not?"

He'd asked the question in an almost casual way, but the look in his eyes guaranteed that that wasn't how he felt. Her heart went out to him. How awful it had to be, to wake up in a world you didn't know.

"Nobody won it, really. I suppose you could say it ended with honor on both sides."

"Did we regain freedom of the seas?"

She nodded. "Yes."

A faint smile curled across his lips. "Are the United States and Great Britain still enemies, or have we patched up our differences and become allies as English-speaking nations should?"

"Allies, ever since."

"That's good news." Matthew hesitated. "Have there been other wars?"

Kathryn sighed and rose from the table. "Far too many," she said, as she began clearing their dishes.

His chair scraped as he pushed it back. He went to the sink, turned on the water and began scrubbing the pans they'd used.

"And were we victorious?"

She thought of conquest of the Native American tribes and of the agony of Vietnam, and she came up behind him and slipped her arms around his waist.

"Not entirely. But we're still a proud and great nation."

"There is so much I don't know. I suspect I might not recognize the world as it is today."

"It doesn't matter," she murmured, kissing the hard, bony ridge of his spine.

"Aye," he said, "you are right, it does not, for I shall never be a part of it."

She felt the sudden tension in his muscles, heard it in his voice, and cursed herself for having been so thoughtless.

"This world, the one at Charon's Crossing, is the only world that counts," she said fervently, "because it's ours."

Matthew turned off the water and dried his hands.

"Aye," he whispered, "for a little while, at least, it is."

He turned and took her in his arms. He kissed her, gently at first, and then with a desperate hunger Kathryn met and quickly matched.

Between them, they forced reality to slip away.

At noon, they packed a picnic lunch and carried it down to the beach.

The storm had left gifts of the sea on the shore. Exotic shells, driftwood, kelp, and coconuts littered the white sand. The Caribbean itself had recovered its shades of azure and sapphire. Only gentle swells, rolling in over the sea, were left as reminders of last night's powerful display.

Kathryn looked up at the cliffs as she and Matthew strolled slowly down the beach, their bare feet splashing in the warm, frothy surf.

"I'm amazed the cliffs are still standing. I thought the waves were going to topple them for sure."

"Aye, I can understand how you might think that. Wind and rain have been trying to reclaim these islands for centuries."

"Matthew?" Her hand clasped his more tightly. "What happens if a storm like that catches a ship at sea?"

He sighed. "Then the lives of the ship and the men who

sail her are in God's hands. It is far simpler for nature to claim a ship than an island."

Kathryn shivered. "I've always thought that men who went out in sailing ships were incredibly brave."

"A ship is always at the mercy of the sea, sweetheart. Sailors are not brave, they are merely pragmatic and make the best of things."

"I read once that sailors often didn't know how to swim. Is that true?"

He nodded. "Aye."

"But why? I mean, when I think of those little ships and the vastness of the sea . . ."

"Exactly. There are those who see it as futile to hope to survive a ship's sinking. Not all, of course. Some of us swim like fishes."

She looked at him and smiled. "You?"

"Aye, me."

"Did you learn when you were a boy?"

"In New England?" He laughed. "Nay, sweetheart, such frivolity was out of the question. I did my learning in a warm South Pacific cove, with the trade winds sighing through the palms."

"Taught by a golden-skinned native girl in a grass skirt?"

He chuckled, wrapped his arm around her waist, and tugged her towards him.

"Jealous?"

She was, that was the damnedest part of it, though she knew it was ridiculous to be jealous of something that had happened almost two centuries ago.

"Of course not," she said primly. "I'm just curious."

"Let me see . . . ah yes, I remember it well. My teacher was an incredible sight."

"Was she?" Kathryn mustered up a smile.

"Oh, indeed. Brown hair, slender, five foot nine or ten with a shiny bald head—"

She swung towards him. "What?"

Matthew grinned. "I got my swimming lesson from a mean-tempered captain, who decided the stench of his cabin boy was bad enough to offend even his nostrils."

"Ah, I see."

"A golden-skinned girl would have been much more to my liking, especially since I damn near drowned. But after I'd swallowed half the sea, I surfaced and found, to my amazement, that I could keep my head above water. What about you? Do you swim?"

She nodded. "I can't remember when I learned, it was so long ago. I just know we lived in this wonderful old house on Cape Cod, I think, and . . ."

"What's the matter, sweetheart?"

"Nothing. Well, it's just that I always thought of that house as miserable but now, for some reason, I thought of how much I really liked it. And how my father used to put me on his shoulders on summer mornings, and carry me down to the water where we'd wade and search for shells."

"You loved your father a great deal, did you?"

"No," she said, frowning. "Why would I? He left us, my mother and me, and forgot all about us."

"I don't think so, love, not if he left you this—God almighty, what is that?"

Matthew's voice had turned sharp with fear. He knocked Kathryn to the sand and fell on top of her, protecting her with his body as two dark shadows swooped over the island and roared out across the sea. When they were nothing but black dots on the far horizon, he rose slowly to his knees.

"What in hell were those things?"

Kathryn sat up. "Airplanes," she said gently. "Ships that fly."

"Ships that fly?" he whispered. "Like what Montgolfier flew in Paris back in '83? No. They were more like the drawings by what's his name, the Italian . . . Leonardo da Vinci?"

She smiled. "Very much like his drawings."

Matthew shook his head, rolled onto his back, and threw his arm across his eyes.

"Your world is like a magic box," he said quietly. "The more I look, the more there is to see."

"A lot has happened since . . . in the past couple of centuries, I guess."

"What powers these ships of the air? Not sails, surely."

"They have engines."

"Steam engines?"

"No. No, not steam." Kathryn lay down on her stomach, her elbows propped in the sand and her chin in her hands. "I don't know much about this, Matthew. Some—the older ones—run on gasoline. Oil, I guess you'd call it. Others—the ones that just swooped over us—have jet engines. And before you ask, I haven't the foggiest idea how jet engines work."

"And what is their burthen?"

"Their what?"

"How much can they carry?"

"Well, some are really big. The one I took from New York to Grenada, for instance—"

His eyes popped open.

"You have flown in these things?" She nodded. "What is it like? Can you see the entire world from up so high?"

"It feels that way, sometimes, especially when you fly above the clouds, but—"

"Above the clouds," he said in a reverential whisper. "God, I cannot imagine such a thing."

She thought of what he would say if she tried to explain rockets, and space stations, and flights to the moon.

"There's so much I should tell you," she said, "but I can't. I'm already in over my head. I live in a high-tech world . . . a complex one, I mean. And I work in a complex field, but I never realized how many things I've just accepted on faith without really understanding them."

"Like me," Matthew said softly. He put his arm around her

shoulder and drew her close to his side. They lay quietly, not talking, just luxuriating in the simple joy of being together.

"I feel like a man just awakened from a long sleep," he murmured after a while. "My head spins with questions."

"Well, ask them. I'll do my best to answer."

"I should like to know more about the war. My war. It ended honorably, you said."

"Absolutely."

"How long did it last? What were the decisive battles? Did the Prince of Wales remain Regent or did the English finally find the balls to rid themselves of their corrupt aristocracy? And what of Madison? Did he—"

"Stop!" Kathryn flung out her arms and groaned in mock dismay. "I give up."

Matthew grinned, rolled onto his belly, and traced the outline of her lips with the tip of his finger.

"Too many questions at once?"

"Too many questions I can't answer. I can see now that I should have paid more attention to my history textbooks."

"I find it difficult to believe you weren't a good student."

"Oh, I was." She smiled. "But not of history."

He bent his head and kissed her gently. "I wish I had had more formal schooling. At least, I learned to master my letters."

"How?"

"The mate of my first ship had a theory about idle hands and idle minds. He taught me to read and figure." He grinned. "I admit, other than the Song of Solomon, I didn't get much out of the Good Book, but I did come to enjoy reading Tacitus, years later, and a bit of Virgil and Caesar, without the mate's cane to goad me." He bent his head and kissed her, slowly and deeply, until she sighed with pleasure. "What were you like, when you were a little girl?"

Kathryn linked her hands behind his neck.

"Let's see . . . well, I suppose I was obedient. And quiet."

"Mmm. That's certainly difficult to picture."

She laughed. "You seem to have brought out another side of me, Captain."

Matthew smiled. "And you didn't like history."

"No." She tugged his hair, pulled his face to hers and kissed his mouth. "But that was before I met a bit of history, in the flesh."

"Aye," he said. He moved over her, so that his warm, bare chest brushed against her. "Very much in the flesh, if you'd like some proof."

Kathryn's breath caught. "You're trying to change the subject."

"Nay, why would I? The subject interests me greatly. Tell me more."

Smiling, she stroked his hair back from his face. "You tell me. What do you think I was like, when I was little?"

"Well, I can't envision you locked away in a schoolroom with that pretty nose tucked inside a book."

"What do you see me doing, then?"

"Picking flowers in a meadow, perhaps. Gazing at the stars. Reading poetry. Listening to old tales." He smiled. "And dreaming about princes and princesses, and dragons and knights and damsels in distress."

Kathryn blinked. For the second time in one afternoon, forgotten memories were surfacing. It was like looking into a kaleidoscope and seeing old, familiar shapes become brand new.

"You know, you're right," she said, her voice soft with surprise. "I loved stories like that, until my father went away."

"And then?"

"And then, I decided that I'd be better off trusting math and science texts instead of . . ." She fell silent and turned her face away, but not quickly enough to keep Matthew from seeing the glint of tears that suddenly appeared on her lashes.

"Sweetheart?"

"It's nothing," she choked, "just that—that all of a sudden,

I find myself wanting to believe in princes and princesses and forever after all over again."

Gently, he turned her face to his and looked down at her. He knew that it made no sense to let her hope—but to know something with your intellect, and to believe it with your heart, were not the same. He whispered her name and gathered her into his arms. He kissed her, again and again, until her lips were soft and clinging to his and their heartbeats mingled.

"Love," he said softly, "you must know that you were right to give up believing in children's tales."

"No." She caught her hands in his hair and drew his face down to hers. "Don't say that, please."

"The time of princesses and princes, of dragons vanquished, is long gone, sweetheart. There are no 'happily ever afters,' not in your world or in mine."

Her smile was sweet and tremulous, and it shot straight as an arrow into his heart.

"My dream was a fairy tale," she said, "that you were my lover, that we were together, like this, here at Charon's Crossing."

"Aye. And we will live that dream, for a while."

"No. Not just for a while, Matthew. I lo- . . ."

His fingers fell across her lips. "You don't," he said roughly, and rose to his feet. He stood staring out to sea, ramrod straight, eyes dark. "It is a happy infatuation, nothing more."

Kathryn stood up and laid her hand lightly on his arm.

"Is that what you feel for me?" she asked. "Infatuation?"

"Yes," he said quickly.

Too quickly. The truth was there, in his voice. She could hear it.

She stepped out in front of him. "I don't believe you," she said.

"What must I do to convince you?"

She smiled. "Kiss me," she said softly. "And then say, 'Kathryn, this is nothing but infatuation.' "

"Very well." He put his hands on her shoulders. "Kathryn, this is nothing but—"

"You have to kiss me, first."

"Nay. Nay, I cannot." His eyes swept her face and then he groaned and pulled her into his arms. "God forgive me, but I cannot lie. I love you, Kathryn. I've loved you from the instant I first crossed from my world and saw you. I wish I had the courage to pretend that you haven't stolen my heart and made it your own, but I do not."

Her smile was like the glow of a beacon on a dark night, leading a ship to home and safety, and he knew he would remember this moment, that it would add to the pain throughout the dark, emptiness of the eternity that awaited him . . . and yet, he would not have given it up for anything.

"I love you with all my heart," she whispered.

"As I love you, sweet Kathryn. I adore you, with all that I am or ever was."

She took his hand, carried it to her lips and pressed a kiss into his hard, work-roughened palm. Then she laid her head against his chest.

"We'll find a way," she said. "I know we will."

Matthew shut his eyes and pressed his lips to her shining, sweet-scented hair. His arms tightened around her and they stood locked together, as alone as if they had been the last man and woman on the face of the earth.

Seventeen

Early Thursday morning, Kathryn was at the wheel of the old VW, rattling along the road to town. The windows were down, the radio was on, and she was warbling along with Linda Ronstadt at the top of her lungs.

She grinned, swooped her hair back behind her ear as the warm breeze tried to tug it free, and wondered what Linda would say if she knew what a talented soprano was singing harmony.

Kathryn laughed. "Forget it, Linda," she said. "You've got nothing to worry about."

The truth was, she'd never been able to sing anything on key.

"Kathryn," her sixth grade music teacher had said kindly, "we need someone to keep the scores organized. Would you be willing to give up being in the chorus in order to help me with something so important?"

It had been a relief to say yes and she'd never willingly opened her mouth to sing a note since, except—on very, very rare occasions—in the shower, when the sudden sound of her own awful voice would make her wince.

But this morning was different. This morning, by God, it wasn't enough to listen to the birds belting their little hearts out. She needed to do the same thing, to sing at the top of her lungs because there was no other way to let some of the happiness out and if she didn't . . .

If she didn't, she felt as if she might burst.

Linda gave way to a lush orchestration of "Stardust."

Kathryn sighed, hummed along softly, and tried to imagine what Matthew was doing just about now.

Had he awakened yet? She smiled as she remembered what she'd asked him late last night, as she lay in his arms.

"Matthew?" she'd whispered drowsily. "Do ghosts really need to sleep?"

He'd laughed softly and drawn her closer against his heart.

"I don't know," he'd whispered back. "I just know that I need to sleep with you."

This morning, she'd lain alongside him, watching him as he slept. The hard angles and planes of his face seemed softened in sleep. His hair, tousled on his forehead, gave him a look of vulnerability that tugged at her heart.

"I love you," she'd whispered softly, and then she'd kissed him, not enough to waken him but just enough to bring a soft curve to his mouth. Then, moving quietly and carefully, she'd risen from the bed, gathered her clothes and slipped from the room.

Once downstairs, she had dressed quickly, set up the coffee pot and left a note on the kitchen table, telling Matthew she'd had to run into town for groceries. It was true, in a way; they'd run out of everything over the last couple of days and both the pantry and the refrigerator needed replenishing. But there were other things she wanted to pick up in Hawkins Bay, gifts for Matthew that would surely please him.

Kathryn smiled and tapped her fingers on the steering wheel. The Beatles were giving their all to "Hey, Jude" and they needed all the help they could get.

". . . take an old song, and make it be-heh-heh-terrr," she sang, and she stepped harder on the gas pedal because the sooner she got to town, the sooner she could get home again, to Matthew.

The storm had done more damage in town than it had at Charon's Crossing.

A small sailboat with a gaping hole near the bow was beached near the quay. Two or three others were heeled over and listing alarmingly at their moorings. Several palm trees had lost their leafy heads and stood like blinded sentinels just where the road turned into Front Street.

Nothing else seemed to have been damaged. The narrow sidewalks and the street itself were crowded with cars, mini-vans and pedestrians. The shops were open and doing their usual brisk business.

Kathryn made a slow circuit of both main streets. Finally, she gave up. The only clothing store in town, unless she'd missed something, was the one right next to Amos Carter's law office.

Not that it mattered where she made her purchases. It was nobody's affair what she did. With a shrug of her shoulders, she headed for Front Street again, drove slowly up and down its length twice, and got lucky. A red minivan left the curb just as she came by the third time. She pulled into the space, got out of the VW and made her way past Amos's darkened office to Ada's Ladies and Gents Fine Apparel shop.

A bell jangled above the door as Kathryn opened it. The shop was long, narrow, and jammed with racks and shelves of clothing. A young salesclerk was unpacking some boxes and she looked up and smiled, but before either she or Kathryn could say anything, Ada yoo-hooed from behind the counter where she was waiting on a couple of teenaged boys.

"Kathryn! How nice to see you again. Remember me? We met your first time in town."

"Of course." Kathryn smiled. "How are you?"

"Fine, thank you. Are you in a hurry?"

"Well . . ."

"Good, good." Ada beamed. "You just look around, then, while I finish up here and then I'll wait on you myself."

Kathryn sighed as Ada turned her attention to the boys. Given a choice, she'd have preferred to deal with the young clerk who was doing all that unpacking.

"Don't rush on my account," she called. Maybe, if she were lucky, she could select the things she wanted before Ada finished with the boys.

The shop was cool after the midday heat of the street, and pleasant. The ceiling was old-fashioned, made of stamped tin, and the floors were wide-planked and dark with age, but the clothing jammed on the racks nearest the door was up-to-date and trendy. Bikinis fought for space with cropped tops and hot pants; wildly patterned men's shorts competed with Spandex swimsuits in shades of neon pink, hot orange and a chartreuse bright enough to make you blink.

Kathryn paused and fingered a bikini that was little more than three triangles of black and white leaves. It was beautiful and sexy—and she'd never worn anything like it in her life.

"See the matchin' sarong?"

She jumped. Ada had come up just behind her and was leaning over her shoulder.

"Right there, you see? You can wear it as a skirt or tied over one shoulder like those old-timey Roman ladies used to do. Pretty outfit, isn't it?"

Kathryn tucked the bikini back into the rack. "Very. But I don't need a swim suit today."

"No woman ever needs a suit like that, unless she's determined to make a man find her sweeter than a stalk of sugar cane." Ada chuckled. "It's good to see you, Kathryn. How did you weather the storm?"

"Oh, no problems. It looks as if the town bore the brunt of it."

"Yes. It wasn't bad at all, though, considerin' how these things sometimes go. Can I offer you some tea?"

Kathryn shook her head. "No thanks."

"Coffee? A soft drink, maybe?"

"No, really. I just need to pick up some things."

"Well, we have whatever you might need, everythin' from undies to dresses and shoes."

Kathryn cleared her throat. "Well, actually . . ."

"What size would you be? Ten? Eight?" Ada eyed Kathryn's

cut-down denims. "If you're lookin' for some nice shorts, we just got some in I think you'd like."

"Actually, I'm, ah, I'm looking for men's clothes."

Ada's eyebrows soared. "Men's clothes?"

"Yes."

In New York, that one word, "yes," delivered with such determination, would have been enough to squelch any further questions. But this wasn't New York, and Ada Truman's curiosity wasn't easily squelched.

"What on earth for?"

Kathryn ran the tip of her tongue over her lips. Go ahead, she told herself, come up with an answer for that.

"Well," she said, "well . . ."

"Surely you're not like me," Ada said, "preferrin' men's clothes to work around in!"

Just in the nick of time, Kathryn thought giddily, and smiled.

"That's exactly right. I mean, men's stuff is so much more—"

"Comfortable."

"Right."

"It's cut looser. Gives a person more room to move."

Kathryn offered up her best and brightest smile. "Uh huh."

"Couldn't agree more," Ada said, "though I figured that was my personal preference." She chuckled. "Because there's so much of me, you see."

"Oh, I'm sure there are lots of women who feel the same way."

"Well, you just tell me what you need and I'll get it for you."

"Jeans," Kathryn said, following on Ada's heels as the shopowner wove her way between the crowded racks towards the rear of the store. "And shorts. Cut-offs, if you have them."

"Certainly."

"Shirts, too. And shoes."

Ada paused alongside a display of Levi jeans. "Here are the men's jeans and such, but shoes . . . well, of course, you wouldn't want men's sizes there, would you? But I only carry men's shoes, you see, sneakers and sandals mostly. You'll find fine shoes for ladies up the street, at Allenby's."

Kathryn stared at Ada. Now what? she thought helplessly.

"Well . . . well, actually . . . the thing is . . ."

"Miss Ada?"

Ada made a face and looked towards the front of the shop. "Yes?"

The young salesclerk was hidden by the racks but there was no mistaking the nervous apology in her voice.

"I don't know where you want these things."

"Lord have mercy," Ada muttered. "Figure it out, Mary," she shouted. "It's not very difficult."

"Well, it is. These shirts marked 'unisex.' Where do I put them? And there's stuff missin', I think. Accordin' to the invoice, we were supposed to get a dozen of these red scarves but I only see eight."

Ada sighed dramatically. "Kathryn, you're going to have to excuse me for a few minutes."

It was difficult not to sigh with relief.

"That's okay."

"I'll be back soon as I can. Honestly, the help you get these days . . ."

"You just take your time, Ada . . ."

. . . enough time so she could find what she needed without the shopkeeper watching. Ada headed for the other end of the store and Kathryn whirled into action.

"Levi's," she muttered, "Levi's . . ."

What size would Matthew wear? That narrow waist. The trim hips. The neat little backside and those long, oh so masculine legs . . .

Heat rose in her belly. She made a face, told herself to stop being silly, leafed through the rack and picked out a pair of jeans that looked just about right.

Denim cut-offs were easier. They were displayed on a nearby table and she didn't have to try and figure out what length the legs ought to be.

T-shirts took a moment's consideration. Medium? Large? Matthew was lean but he was muscular, not in the silly-looking way of men who looked like walking advertisements for trendy gyms and even trendier drugs but in the way of a man who'd earned his muscles the hard way, through work and sweat.

Large, definitely. And in half a dozen colors, ranging from navy to butter yellow to pink, although she could just imagine his reaction to pink.

Ada was still giving her clerk a firm but gentle tongue-lashing. Kathryn offered a silent apology to the gods for hoping the poor girl would have to endure just another few minutes worth of whatever lecture it was. She moved on towards a display of shoes, snatching up white crew socks and a woven leather belt on the way.

Shoes were going to be tough. Kathryn poked her tongue out between her teeth. What size would he wear? She didn't have a clue. Who ever paid attention to feet? Shoulders, yes. Waists and hips, sure. Height and weight and whether legs were long or short, okay. But feet?

". . . take these things into the storeroom while you finish up here, Mary. Try not to mess up anythin' for the two minutes I'm gone, would you please?"

Kathryn chewed on her lip. Ada would be gone for two minutes?

Oh, what the hell!

She snatched up a pair of Adidas in a size that didn't look as if they'd fit either a midget or a giant, plucked a pair of all-terrain sandals from the next table, and headed for the counter.

Mary, who was still kneeling amidst the boxes, looked up. She wasn't smiling anymore.

"Miss Ada will be right out," she said.

Kathryn flicked the tip of her tongue over her lips.

"Yes, but I'm afraid I'm in an awful hurry."

The girl shot a glance towards the back of the store. "I suppose I could go and get her, if you insist."

"Oh, there's no reason to bother her," Kathryn said quickly. "Why don't you just ring this stuff up yourself?"

"I don't think Miss Ada would—"

"Miss Ada will probably praise you for keeping a customer happy."

Mary hesitated.

"Well, if you don't want to wait on me, I can always leave these things and maybe come back later." The girl didn't move. "Then again, maybe not," Kathryn said, crossing her fingers and telling her conscience to stop its muttering.

Mary sighed. "Well," she said slowly, "in that case, I suppose . . ."

"Terrific." Kathryn gave her a big smile, reached out and snagged the black and white bikini and its matching sarong from the rack. "You're doing the right thing, Mary, you'll see."

Minutes later, she dashed out of the shop carrying an armload of parcels. Just a few more stops before she headed home.

Home, to Matthew.

The VW was just pulling away as Ada came hurrying out of the storeroom.

"Well now, Kathryn . . ." Her beaming smile faded. "Where's Miss Russell?"

Mary cleared her throat. "Gone."

"Gone?" Ada plumped her hands on her ample hips and fixed the hapless girl with a stony glare. "What did you do to offend her, you useless child?"

"Nothin'," Mary said quickly. "Oh, nothin' at all, ma'am. She said that if I didn't ring up her order right away, she'd leave. It was a big order, Miss Ada, I didn't think you'd want to lose it, all that clothin' and shoes and things."

Ada cocked her head. "Shoes? Men's shoes?"

"Yes ma'am. It was all men's things, Men's jeans and shorts, shirts and socks and a belt, too."

"Everythin' bought for a man? Are you sure?"

Mary thought for a minute. "Well, not everythin'. The lady bought that bikini, too, the one with the skirt? The really expensive one?" She drew a breath. "Did I do the right thing?"

Ada waved her hand. "Yes," she said absently, "you did the right thing." A minute passed. Then she picked up the telephone and dialed a number. "Elvira? Elvira, the strangest thing just happened . . ."

Kathryn gunned the VW up the drive at Charon's Crossing and brought it to a bone-jolting stop.

She'd spent most of the trip home thinking about Matthew's reaction to all the wonderful things she'd bought. Clothes. Magazines. A couple of terrific books that showed how planes flew and computers worked. And the best thing of all, the Sony TV set, sitting safely boxed on the rear seat.

She only wished she'd thought of it days ago, of how simple it was going to be to share her world with Matthew. He was fascinated by everything she took for granted, from something as simple as the shower to something as complex as her portable computer which she'd plugged in and showed him last night. And his mind was so quick . . . he absorbed whatever she told him, then tossed out endless, complex questions in his quest for more information.

But she'd grown up a child of the millennium, accepting miracles like nuclear energy and space travel as everyday reality. The answers she gave him were often superficial. Not that Matthew ever complained. Still, it was easy to see that he yearned for more information about this strange, new world.

Kathryn gathered up an armful of packages, grabbed a couple of magazines from the top of the stack—*Discovery,* with a wonderful cover shot of the latest spacewalk—and *PC World,* with the new IBM portable computer splashed across its face—and hurried up the steps. She juggled the stuff in her arms, struggling to work a hand free so she could open the door.

"Matthew?" she called as it swung open. "I'm home."

The magazines slid to the floor as she dumped her parcels on the hall table.

"Matthew?"

The rooms that opened off the foyer were all empty. In the kitchen, the note she'd left him hours ago still lay on the table, one end waving lazily in the breeze coming through the open window, the other neatly pinned by the sugar bowl.

Kathryn went to the steps.

"Matthew? Are you upstairs?" Smiling happily, she trotted up the staircase, automatically detouring around the cold spot, and headed for the bedroom. "You lazy thing," she said, laughing, "are you still . . . ?"

No. He wasn't. The bed was neatly made, looking as if no one had slept in it. The room itself was empty.

"Matthew?" she said uneasily.

Where was he?

Somewhere nearby, she told herself, somewhere safe.

Her heart clenched.

Why would she even think such a thing? Of course he was near, and safe.

She turned and retraced her steps, pausing at the top of the stairs.

"Matthew," she said sternly, "answer me! Where are you?"

The answering voice, sly and soft as a cat's whisker, breathed into the heavy silence.

He's in the attic, Catherine, it whispered, *why don't you come and find him?*

Terror flooded through her like a wave of nausea. She spun around and stared down the hallway. A cold, milky vapor was oozing down the attic steps.

Come along, Catherine. He's waiting.

Kathryn made a soft, whimpering sound. Slowly, as if in a dream, she walked to the steps. At the bottom she stopped and looked up.

The door to the attic, though still bolted shut, quivered with a grotesque light that shone eerily through the white mist. The door was pulsing, swelling on its hinges, straining like the fevered heartbeat of some great beast.

Kathryn wanted to scream, but no sound would come from her throat. She moistened her lips, parted them and croaked out Matthew's name.

Catherine, sweet Catherine. It is he who you want now, is it? Well, then, mount the steps and come to me, here in the attic, and you will be with him, I promise you.

Her hand trembled, but she reached out and clasped the banister. It was frigid beneath the brush of her fingers.

One step.

Two.

Another . . .

"Kathryn!"

This time, she did scream. But it was Matthew's arms that had closed tightly around her, Matthew who drew her roughly from the stairs and down to the landing.

"Matthew," she sobbed, "oh, Matthew, thank God!"

He held her, his heart pounding wildly against hers.

"Are you all right?"

She nodded and sniffed damply against his chest. Dimly, her mind registered that he wasn't wearing a shirt, that his skin smelled of sun and roses and sweat.

"I thought," she whispered, "oh, I thought . . ."

"Kathryn." He put her from him, holding her at arm's length, and his tone became commanding. "You are to leave Charon's Crossing."

"No! Not without you."

"Do you hear me? Run until you're outside the gate and it is shut behind you."

"I won't do it! Not without—"

"Dammit to hell, don't argue!" He spun her around, put his hand in the small of her back and pushed her. "Get out of this abomination of a house, off the land that surrounds it, and do it now. Damn your eyes, woman! This isn't subject to discussion. You are to get out of here and not turn back, no matter what happens, no matter what you hear or think you hear. Is that clear?"

"Matthew, what are you going to do?"

Soft laughter oozed from above them.

Yes, Matthew. What are you going to do? Are you going to face me, or are you too cowardly to confront someone again who is so obviously, in all respects, your better?

Matthew smiled grimly and looked up at the swollen door, pulsing with evil like an obscene, blood-engorged leech.

"It will be a pleasure to kill you again, Waring!"

"No!" Kathryn's voice was shrill with terror. "Matthew, please, I beg you . . ."

He caught her and kissed her hard on her parted lips.

"Go," he said, and he slipped from her hands, a sudden whirl of silver, streaking up towards the loathsome, swelling door. Kathryn cried out as a lipless mouth opened in the pulsing mass, stretching wider and wider.

"Matthew," she screamed . . .

The gaping mouth clamped shut.

And then there was only silence.

Matthew had ordered her to leave, but where would she go if he couldn't be there, too?

Kathryn stumbled back, her breathing ragged. Her legs wouldn't support her. She reached back, groping for the wall. Her hands found its cold, clammy surface and slowly, leaning against it, she sank down to the floor.

She waited. She had no idea how much time passed. All her senses were focused on the door while her imagination focused on what might be happening behind it.

She heard things, or thought she did. Distant sounds. The ring of steel. A man's voice, strident with the challenge of rage.

Then, when her fear had driven her almost to the edge of sanity, the door began to change. The grotesque light brightened, then flickered, then began to dim. The sickening pulsing motion lessened, then stopped.

At last, the door was just a door and when it was, the mist lifted, dissipating like fog over the sea. Sweet, clean air swept over the landing. Kathryn dragged it deep into her lungs. Then she rose to her feet, legs trembling, eyes still locked on the attic.

"Matthew," she whispered, "oh my love, please, please . . ."

A sob burst from her throat as he materialized before her. There was a cut high on his cheek, another on his bare shoulder, but he was whole and real and she flew towards him and hurled herself into his waiting arms. He held her tight, kissing her hair, her cheeks, her trembling mouth while he thought of what might have happened to her, and the more he thought, the more his rage grew until he suddenly thrust her from him and glared into her flushed face while his fingers bit deep into her shoulders.

"What in hell are you doing here?" he growled. "I told you to leave this place."

Kathryn smiled through her tears. "I know."

"You know. But you chose to disobey."

"Matthew . . ."

"Perhaps you'd like to tell me what you were doing on the attic stairs in the first place."

"I was looking for you." She reached out, her hand seeking his face, but he jerked his head back.

"You know the attic is a place of evil, dammit!"

"Yes, but Waring said—"

"Dammit, Kathryn, where is your head?"

Kathryn's chin lifted. "Stop shouting at me, Matthew. I know you're upset."

Upset? Hell, no. He wasn't upset. He was close to crazy, thinking of what could have happened to her if he hadn't sensed Waring's evil presence, if he hadn't gotten here in time.

Christ, he couldn't dwell on that, not if he wanted to keep from punching his fist through the wall.

It was simpler to let his anger out where it belonged, on Kathryn. She was impossible, a headstrong, disobedient female, and if she was an example of what women were like today, by God, it was just as well he wasn't a twentieth-century man!

"Matthew, if you'd just listen—"

"I? Listen?" His mouth tightened, his eyes went from green to a dark and dangerous ebony. "Why should I do what you will not, madam?"

"Don't madam me, Matthew. I'm trying to explain. I was worried about you. I didn't know where you'd gone."

"Where in hell *could* I have gone? Answer me that."

"I don't know. That's just the point, isn't it? So I went upstairs and you weren't there and—"

"Of course I wasn't! I was out back," he said tightly, letting her go and stabbing a forefinger into the center of her chest for punctuation. "I was in the fucking garden, fixing the fucking rose trellis because the fucking storm had almost—"

"Don't you yell at me!" Kathryn slapped the offending finger aside. Her cheeks glowed with angry color. "And don't use that language. I don't like it."

"She doesn't like it." Matthew threw out his arms. "She doesn't bloody like my bloody lang—"

"You bastard!" she hissed, banging her fist against his chest. "You heartless, thoughtless, self-centered, arrogant bastard! Don't you hear what I'm telling you? I heard that—that thing, that godawful whisper saying you were in the attic and . . . and . . ."

Her voice wobbled and broke. She made a strangled sound and started to turn away but Matthew caught her, dragged her into his arms, and kissed her. She fought against him, trying to tear her mouth from his, to slap his face, but he was relentless, his hands sweeping over her, his teeth nipping, hard, at her mouth until she groaned, fisted her hands in his hair, and kissed him with all the love and despair in her heart.

"I thought I'd lost you," she sobbed against his mouth.

"Never," he said thickly, knowing even in his blind passion, in his need for her, that "never" was not a word meant for them.

"If you hadn't come in time . . ." She shuddered. "How did you know?"

"I don't know. Maybe I sensed Waring's presence. I only knew that you needed me, that I had to come to you."

"He said you were in the attic, Matthew. I thought he'd hurt you, or—or—" She shuddered again, closed her eyes tight, and buried her face against his throat. "What happened up there?"

Matthew made a sound that was not quite a laugh.

"I wish to God I knew."

"Is he . . . is he . . . ?"

"It was like a stage set, Kathryn. Waring, or whatever remained of him, was standing in the middle of the attic, holding a sword."

"A sword?" she said in disbelief.

"Aye."

"What did he look like? That time I saw him he was so—so horrible . . ."

"He looked like Waring," Matthew lied. What was the point in telling her that the Thing he'd fought had to have been even more hideous than her memory of it? Or that it had whispered of what it would do to her once it had dealt with him?

"He wounded you." She touched her fingers gently to the cut on his face and then on his shoulder.

"The wounds are nothing, sweetheart. I've given myself worse nicks while shaving." He drew her close and pressed his lips to her hair. "I was the one who delivered the telling blows."

"But you had no weapon."

"I had these." He held his hands up between them. "A sword can't hurt you once you get past its point and inside its arc. It's just a matter of being quick enough. A man can kill with his hands, Kathryn, if he knows how."

Kathryn's eyes widened. "You killed him?"

"I destroyed him, aye. He went down hard, turned transparent as glass, and disappeared."

She gave a long, shuddering sigh and went back into his arms.

"We're free of him, then," she whispered.

Were they? Matthew wasn't so sure. It didn't seem reasonable that you could kill a man twice, especially if he wasn't a man at all but a specter when you killed him the second time.

But he wasn't about to say any of that to Kathryn. Why frighten her when there was no need? He was certain—as certain as he could be, at any rate—that even if Waring were going to return, it would take time for him to gather enough strength to make it happen. By then, Kathryn would be safely back in New York. She would be gone from Charon's Crossing, gone from being a part of this twisted, unholy world of his.

He thought of everything that had happened, not just now but in the past, the mistakes he would pay for through the eternity that stretched ahead of him, that Kathryn would pay for, as well, despite her innocence in this nightmare. Pain, despair, anguish . . . a hundred different emotions closed around his heart and he knew that there was only one thing that could drive them all away.

"Kathryn," he said in a rasping whisper.

She fell back against the wall under his weight, her hands already tearing at his trousers as his tore at her clothing. He knew he was being rough, that he might be hurting her, but he couldn't have stopped what he was doing if the sun had taken that moment to fall from the sky.

And she wouldn't have let him. She was as wild as he, sobbing his name, fisting her hands in his hair, sinking her sharp white teeth into the soft flesh of his lip.

"Now," she said, "now . . ."

He lifted her and drove into her hard and fast, impaling her on his swollen sex. She was hot and wet and she cried out and convulsed around him almost immediately.

"Kathryn," he said brokenly, "Kathryn, my love . . ."

She kissed him, her black hair hanging like a silken curtain about both their faces, her legs wrapped tight around his hips, and Matthew clenched his teeth, threw back his head and exploded like white-hot lightning into the sweet, satin warmth of the woman he loved.

Eighteen

Kathryn sat cross-legged in the center of the four-poster bed, watching Matthew as he tried on the clothing she'd bought him.

She'd guessed right about the sizes. The shorts and jeans fit him perfectly, as did the T-shirts. Right now, he was wearing only a pair of sandals and the Levi's, and doing things for them she was certain no other man could. They rode low on his hips, showing off his flat, hard-muscled belly, hinting at the power of his sex that lay cupped within the soft denim.

"The jeans look great," she said happily. "Here. Try on this last shirt."

She snatched up the shirt she'd been saving and tossed it to him. He caught it, held it out, and looked at her as if she'd gone crazy.

"Good God," he breathed, "what were you thinking?"

She looked at the shirt, then at him. "Don't you like it?"

"Like it?" he said. "Like it? Kathryn, love, a gift's a lovely thing, but this must have cost you a fortune!"

Kathryn gave a little laugh, uncrossed her legs and scooted to the edge of the bed. "Actually, it was the least expensive of the lot. Come on, let me see you in it."

Matthew held the shirt at arm's length. "You expect me to wear a work of art?"

Was he joking? She looked at the shirt. She'd bought it on impulse at the open market where she'd stopped to buy fruit and vegetables on her way out of town. The shirt had been hanging in one of the stalls and she'd thought of Matthew the instant she saw it because of the sailing ship splashed across the chest.

Now, she looked at it through his eyes. She had no idea if the ship was drawn accurately but it certainly looked pretty good, all silver and black and heeled over hard on a sea of bright blue waves, white sails flying in what she supposed was a stiff breeze.

To her, it was a mass-produced, silk-screened Fruit of the Loom T-shirt. To him, it was priceless. How could she not have realized that something so commonplace would seem a miracle to him?

"I cannot possibly accept this, Kathryn."

"Believe me, you can."

"Nay, I cannot. The cost—"

"I paid less than ten dollars for it, Matthew."

"Ten Continentals or an Eagle?" he said, his face a study in amazement.

"Ten dollars, American. I'm sure ten dollars means a lot less now than it did in your day."

"Things have changed, aye, but surely ten dollars is still—"

"It wouldn't have paid for the groceries I bought in town this morning." She looked at him, her expression one of complete innocence. "And all I bought was some bread, some cheese, some fresh fish, fruits and vegetables . . . and oh yes. Some ale."

Matthew sighed and carefully pulled the shirt on over his head.

"Everyone in your world must be as rich as Midas, or . . ." His head popped through the neck of the shirt. "Did you say you'd bought ale?"

"Uh huh. I thought . . . well, what little I know of your time . . . I mean . . ."

She laughed as Matthew plucked her from the bed and whirled her around in a circle.

"Stop trying to be diplomatic, woman. Aye, we drank ale. And aye, I have longed for the taste of it, cool and sharp, slipping down my throat." He kissed her, deposited her on the floor, and gave her a light pat on the bottom. "Lead me to it, then, and I will tell you what a nineteenth-century man thinks of twentieth-century lager."

He smiled and Kathryn smiled in return, even though there was a sudden tightness in her throat.

Nineteenth-century he might be, but he looked every bit a man of the 1990s. It was easy to picture him holding her hand as they strolled along the streets of Greenwich Village on a cold winter evening, their breath streaming out in white plumes as they headed home for cups of rich hot chocolate and a sinful assortment of those wonderful cookies you could get at the little Italian bakery just off Fourth; so easy to imagine him at her side on a drowsy June Sunday in Central Park, sprawled in the sun on the Great Lawn while they ate lemon ices and tried to decide what movie to go to see in the evening and, in the end, deciding they'd be happier going home and making slow, tender love in their own bed.

It was all so easy . . . and all impossible.

None of it could ever happen, not without a miracle. Her century had produced everything from heart transplants to men on the moon, but it was woefully short of the kind of miracle she needed.

"Kathryn?"

She blinked to keep back the tears that threatened and looked towards the bedroom door where Matthew stood, holding out his hand.

"Come with me," he said, and it took all her self-control to keep from saying that she would go with him anywhere, even into that dark world of his, if she could only be certain it meant they could be together always.

The ale, he said, was excellent. Perhaps not quite as good as what was served in a little pub down by the wharfs in New York, but excellent nevertheless.

But it was the books and the magazines that made his eyes go wide.

"Is this true?" he said, as he turned the pages. "And this? By God, are such things possible?"

Kathryn smiled as she watched him, his fair head bent over an illustration of how jet engines worked. They hadn't even gotten to the television set, which still squatted in its box in the foyer.

An hour or so later, Matthew looked up at her, his eyes shining, and held out his arms. She went to him and he sighed as he drew her down on his lap.

"Thank you, sweetheart, for all these wonderful gifts."

"I hoped they'd please you. I know how eager you are to learn all you can about what's happened in the world since . . . I'm just happy you like the books."

"The books, the clothing . . ." He kissed her. "I love it all. But didn't you buy anything for yourself?"

She thought of the black and white bikini, lying unwrapped in the bedroom. Who had she bought it for, Matthew or herself? Not that it mattered. It seemed silly now, even embarrassing.

"You did get yourself something," he said, "I can see it in your eyes."

Kathryn laughed and shook her head. "No. I mean, I did, but—"

"What?"

"Matthew, really, it's silly."

"And it's making you blush!"

"It isn't." Kathryn shot to her feet. "Come on outside. There's one last thing in the car, and I can't wait for you to see it. It's called a television set, and—what? Why are you shaking your head?"

"I'm not moving an inch until the mystery is solved."

"What mystery? Honestly, Matthew . . ."

"You bought yourself something that makes you turn pink even to think about, and now you won't tell me what it is."

"This is ridiculous!"

"Aye, we are in agreement on that. To pique a man's curiosity and then refuse to satisfy it is, indeed, ridiculous."

Kathryn put her hands on her hips and tapped her foot against the floor.

"Look, I bought a swim suit, all right? And—and now I've changed my mind about liking it. Okay? Are you satisfied?"

"Nay, I am the more confused. What is a swim suit?"

"It's a . . . a suit you wear to go swimming."

"A garment, you mean?"

"Yes," she said with relief. "That's right. Now, come help me get the TV out of—"

"What sort of garment?" He frowned. "I should think it would be cumbersome, even dangerous, to swim in a dress."

"No, no, it isn't a dress. It's just . . ." She waved her hands in front of her. "It's got two parts to it, a top and a bottom."

Matthew's gaze followed the movement of her hands. "A very small top and bottom, I take it," he said with interest.

"Look, I bought the damned thing by mistake, okay?"

"Temper, temper, Kathryn."

"I am not angry," she said through her teeth. "I'm just irritated that you won't leave this alone."

"Why did you purchase this garment if not to wear it?"

Kathryn threw out her arms and rolled her eyes to the ceiling.

"I don't believe this! A cross-examination, and all because—"

"It is a reasonable question, sweetheart."

"I told you, I bought it in error."

"I assumed you bought it to swim in."

"I did. I thought, it's such a nice day . . . we could pack lunch and go down to the beach."

He smiled. "An excellent idea."

"You can wear a pair of those new denim shorts."

His smile tilted. "If you insist. I have always thought swimming naked was far more pleasurable. The silken slip of the water against your skin, the heat of the sun . . ."

"And I," she said, refusing to be sidetracked, "can wear the suit I brought with me, from New York."

"Ah. You won't object to me seeing you in it?"

"Of course not."

The words were hardly out of her mouth when she realized her mistake.

"The mystery deepens, enough to compel me to restate my earlier conviction." Matthew sat back on the settee, arms folded behind his head, legs outstretched and crossed at the ankle. "I am not rising from this settee until I've seen you in this swim suit that makes you blush."

"You're impossible!!"

"I am cut to the quick, madam. A few moments ago, you were praising me for having such fine intellectual curiosity."

He didn't look cut to the quick. He looked smug and supremely masculine, and it was hard to know which she wanted to do more, slap that little smile from his handsome face or kiss it away.

"All right," she said through her teeth, "have it your way."

She turned and stormed from the room.

Honestly! Such a fuss, over a bathing suit.

Matthew was acting like a jerk.

And, to be painfully honest about it, maybe she was, too.

It was just a bikini, for heaven's sake. Women wore them all the time . . .

But not me. Lord, no, never me!

So, why had she bought it?

Because it was pretty. And it would let me get more of a tan. And . . .

Because she'd imagined Matthew seeing her wearing it, the look in his eyes when he saw her in those seductive scraps of black and white.

Oh, give us a break, Kathryn! He's seen you naked.

Naked was different. Naked didn't toss its head and roll its hips and say, hey, sailor, look at me . . .

Kathryn laughed. Quickly, before she lost courage, she stripped off her clothes and put on the bikini. Then she looked into the mirror.

"Wow," she whispered.

She turned in a little circle, peering at her reflection all the time. Then she reached for the sarong, wrapped it around herself, tied it at one shoulder.

She didn't look Roman. She looked like a refugee from Animal House.

The sarong looked much better tied at the hip. Much, much better.

Kathryn shot one last look into the mirror. "Ready or not," she said softly. She fluffed her fingers through her hair and sauntered out the door.

But when she reached the sitting room, her courage failed her.

What was she doing? She was no *femme fatale.*

True to his word, Matthew was still sitting on the settee, the same as when she'd left him, head back and resting against his linked hands, legs outstretched. He was whistling softly and pleasantly through his teeth.

Her throat tightened. He was so beautiful. The T-shirt stretched like a second skin over his back and his shoulders, defining every muscle. His hair was loose, a spill of chestnut silk shot with a dozen different shades of gold.

Oh, how she loved him! How could she ever leave him?

She couldn't. She wouldn't! Not ever. Not—

"Kathryn?"

She blinked her eyes, which had suddenly blurred with tears, and realized that Matthew had turned and seen her. Now, he was rising slowly to his feet.

"Great God," he whispered. He was very still, nothing moving but his eyes, which had turned into dark pools of desire as his gaze swept over her. "This is a swim suit?"

She nodded and felt herself coloring.

"I have never seen anything like it."

She laughed nervously. "No, well, actually, neither have I. I tried to tell you how silly it was. I bought it on the spur of the moment, but—"

"Kathryn, you are so incredibly beautiful."

She couldn't help but smile. "I was just thinking the same thing about you."

He smiled, too. "A man cannot be beautiful."

"You are," she said softly.

Their eyes met, and what he saw in the blue depths of hers put a lump into his throat. He was wrong. She was not beautiful, his Kathryn; she was exquisite. She was all he had ever wanted in a woman and never hoped to find, a rare combination of sweetness and spirit, innocence and sensuality.

Looking at her as she stood before him, with her dark hair a loose cloud about her face and shoulders, the rich curves of her body an almost painful contrast to the shy flush of color in her lovely face, he wished with all his heart that he could drop to his knees and offer her what men had offered the women they loved from the time the world had begun.

But he could not. He could offer her only that which was his to give, his adoration and his love for whatever little time they had together.

He took a step towards her and held out his hands.

"Kathryn," he whispered, "come to me."

His voice was soft and husky, so filled with tension that the simple words sent an arrow of heat racing from her breasts to her belly. She ran the tip of her tongue over her lips and his gaze followed the gesture with an almost palpable hunger.

"Please," he said. "Come to me, sweetheart."

She went to him slowly, the coolness of the marble against the soles of her feet a shocking contrast to the heat of his eyes on her flesh.

"Do you like the suit?" she whispered, when she reached him.

"Aye," he said. A muscle knotted in his cheek.

He undid the knot of the sarong. It slipped to the ground, puddling at her feet. He caught his breath as he looked at her, and then he slid his hands over her, slowly and gently, his fingers stroking and teasing.

She made a soft little sound in her throat and he smiled.

"My Kitten," he whispered. "Do you like that?"

"Yes. Oh yes. Oh . . ."

She rose on her toes and kissed him, her mouth open and soft against his, and then she kissed his throat. Her hands slid under his shirt and she heard the sharp hiss of his breath when she touched his hot skin.

"And you?" she whispered. Her fingers slipped down his chest, over the waistband of the Levi's, and stroked the taut fabric that strained over his erection. "Do you like that?"

He caught her wrist, and his whispered reply sent the blood racing in her veins, and then he stripped the black and white leaves away with such slow, exciting care that by the time he pulled off his own clothes, carried her down with him onto the settee and slipped inside her, she was half-delirious with need.

"Tell me you love me," he whispered.

"I love you," she said, moving blindly beneath him, "I love you . . ."

He drove deep into her, and the world shattered.

In late afternoon, she put the suit on again. Matthew donned a pair of the new denim cut-offs and they made their way down to the cove.

The water was warm, the surf gentle. They swam and played and, eventually, Matthew challenged Kathryn to a race for shore. She charged out of the water first and he shouted that she'd cheated and he tackled her and they fell to the sand together in a heap, laughing.

"For shame, madam." He was gasping for breath but that didn't keep him from straddling her to hold her down. Water streamed from his face and hair. "You won but only because you resorted to subterfuge."

"I won fair and square," Kathryn panted. "You just don't want to admit you've been bested by a woman!"

"You pinched me, just as we reached shore."

"Me? Me, pinched you? Nay, Captain. You met up with a sand crab."

He grinned. "A sand crab, hey?"

"That's right. And if you don't let me up . . ."

"What?" His smile tilted, and suddenly they were both aware of the hot sun and the warm sand and the way she lay beneath him. "What will you do, if I don't let you up?" he said huskily, and he bent slowly toward her.

Kathryn's lashes fluttered to her cheeks. Her lips parted in anticipation . . .

"Kathryn?"

Her eyes flew open at the sound of the intrusive voice.

"Kathryn? Up here, on the cliff."

Matthew let go of her and she rolled onto her belly and looked up. It was hard to see, in the glare of the sun; she shielded her eyes with her hands.

"It's your attorney," Matthew said. "And that handyman."

"Amos? And Hiram? But that's impossible. Amos isn't even on the island, and Hiram would have phoned . . ."

"Impossible it may be, but they are here, nonetheless."

Matthew stood up. He knew he sounded curt and cold— knew, too, that it was wrong. This was Kathryn's house; these people were of her world. They had every right to be here. It was only that the day had been so perfect. It had been so easy to forget the truth.

Kathryn scrambled to her feet. "I didn't expect them. Honestly, I didn't even know——"

"Kathryn?"

She turned towards the cliff and looked up again. Amos was looking down at her, his hands cupped around his lips.

"Will you come up? Or shall we come down?"

Go away, she wanted to say, just go away and don't ever come back.

"Do you hear me, Kathryn? It's Amos."

Matthew spoke from just behind her. "Go on," he said. "Go up and talk to the old man."

She swung around. "But where will you be?" she started to ask, but the answer was self-evident.

He wouldn't be anywhere, for he was already gone.

She had left the sarong in the house, but at least she and Matthew had brought a bath towel down to the cove with them. She draped it around her shoulders, tugged the ends together, and made her way up the path to where the men waited.

Amos greeted her with an outstretched hand.

"Kathryn. It's good to see you again."

"Yes," she said, smiling politely as they shook hands, "it's good to see you, too."

"I'm truly sorry I had to be gone so long, but—"

"A family emergency. I heard."

"My aunt took seriously ill. She's all that remains of the Carters, you see, and—"

"Amos. I'm pleased you're back but as you can tell, I wasn't expecting company. So—"

"Are you alone, then?"

"Of course."

The two elderly men exchanged quick glances. Hiram cleared his throat.

"We thought you were talkin' with somebody, down on the beach."

Kathryn's smile stiffened. "You thought wrong."

"Rollin' around in the sand," Hiram said, his words resonating with disapproval, "as if you were—"

"What Hiram means," Amos said quickly, "is that you didn't seem to be alone."

Kathryn knew she was coloring, but she wasn't about to

give an inch of ground. "Is that what you came here for? To stand up here and watch me?"

"You shouldn't be out here, all by yourself," Hiram said brusquely. "I said that from the beginnin'. All the stories about his house . . ."

"Why, Hiram," she said sweetly, "what's the matter? Are you suggesting I might have been cavorting on the beach with a ghost?"

Hiram started to answer but Amos put his hand on his arm.

"Your young man hasn't come back to stay with you, has he, Kathryn?"

"My young . . . ?" Kathryn laughed sharply. "I don't believe this. What do you people do, keep a list of what I do and who I do it with? No, Amos, you needn't call out the morals squad. My 'young man' is safely back in the States."

"But you'll be joining him in Miami, as he told Ted Nash?"

"This is incredible! Who's Ted Nash?"

"The pilot who flew him out."

Kathryn smiled grimly and started for the house.

"Well, you can give Mr. Nash a gold medal, Amos. He's got his facts straight. Would you like the name of Jason's hotel, just so your records are complete?"

The two men fell in on either side of her.

"Kathryn," Amos said, "please understand. We're not trying to interfere in your life."

"You could have fooled me."

"We're simply concerned for your welfare. Elvira said . . ."

Kathryn came to a dead stop and swung towards him. "Don't stop now, not when this is just getting interesting. What did Elvira say?"

The lawyer cleared his throat. "Well, she happened to talk to Ada Truman, and Ada mentioned—"

"Ada said you'd bought a mighty strange bathin' costume and a bunch of men's clothin' and so far as anybody can tell, there's no man out here with you to sashay in front of in that costume or to dress up in any of that clothin'," Hiram said in one long, triumphant breath.

Kathryn looked from one man to the other, her face pale except for two crimson splashes high across her cheeks.

"That's one of the things I really love about this island," she said coldly. "There's such marvelous privacy."

"Ada's only lookin' out for you, Kathryn. It's what we all do for each other."

"Well, I don't need looking after. Please tell that to your wife, and to Ada, and to anybody else who decides I need to be spied on."

Hiram bristled with indignation. "It isn't spyin'!"

"No? What would you call it, then? I make some purchases and the next thing I know, I'm a topic of discussion."

"You listen here, Miz Russell. Just 'cause my Elvira has your well-bein' at heart—"

"I didn't ask her to have anything of mine at heart!"

"Now, now," Amos said hastily. "Hiram, Kathryn . . . there's no reason to quarrel." The attorney slid one arm around Kathryn's stiff shoulders and the other around Hiram's. "We didn't come out here to argue, did we, Hiram?"

The old man didn't answer. Then, slowly, he nodded his grizzled head.

"I s'pose not."

Kathryn pulled free of Amos's arm. "Why did you come here, then?"

"We came in a professional capacity, Kathryn. I wanted you to know that I had returned to the island. And Hiram, here, thought he'd best make arrangements to begin work on your house."

"To begin . . . ?" She stared at Amos blankly, and then she remembered. He was talking about the repairs that had brought her to the Caribbean in the first place. The rotting moldings, the creaky outside steps, the walls, the antiquated heating and plumbing, everything that had once seemed so urgent. "Oh," she said, "of course. The repairs." She forced a smile to her lips. "Well, in that case, why don't we go into the house? You gentlemen can have some iced tea while I change out of this wet bathing suit."

"Heard you might have some ale on hand," Hiram said.

Kathryn looked up in time to see Amos elbow Hiram in the ribs.

"You heard right," she said coldly. "Would you like some?"

The old man met her gaze unflinchingly. "Ale doesn't strike me as a woman's drink."

"All right, what is this?" Kathryn glared from one elderly face to the other. "I want to know what's going on."

"I'll tell you what's goin' on," Hiram said. "It isn't healthy, young woman like you out here all this time by yourself, buyin' things that don't make sense, talkin' to somebody nobody else can see."

"Hiram," Amos said sharply, putting his hand on the other man's arm, but Hiram shook it off.

"I'm only speakin' the truth and she knows it. Elvira said—"

"Elvira's been busy as a bee, hasn't she?" Kathryn snapped furiously.

"Calm down, Kathryn."

"I *am* calm. And you have ten seconds to tell me why you're here before I throw the both of you off my property!"

Amos shot Hiram a warning look.

"I told you already. Hiram's here to check things over. I'm here to let you know that I'm back and ready to help you sell Charon's Crossing. Surely, that meets with your approval?"

"Why ask me? You seem to know all the answers already." Kathryn marched through the front door and headed straight for the stairs. "I'm sure both you gentlemen know where everything is in this house. Make yourselves comfortable and if you run out of small talk, you might want to inventory the fridge or the pantry. I'll be down in five minutes."

Back straight, she trotted up the steps, strode down the hall to the bedroom and slammed it after her with enough force so that a small, badly faded oil portrait of some long-ago Russell flew off the wall.

She scooped it up, slung it into a chair, then shrugged off the towel and hurled it across the room.

"Nosy old bastards," she muttered,

"Now, Kathryn, be polite."

She whirled towards the sound of Matthew's voice. Dressed in the jeans and T-shirt, his hair still wet from the sea, he was leaning back against the door, arms folded and feet crossed.

"Why should I?" She wrenched open the armoire, pulled out a cotton dress, and tossed it on the bed. "They weren't very polite to me! You should have heard the things they said, especially Hiram."

"I did hear," Matthew said calmly. "I was there, right beside you, all the time."

Just for an instant, her face softened. "Were you?"

He nodded. "They're concerned for your welfare, sweetheart."

Kathryn's chin tilted. "Oh, come on! They're just a pair of old gossips. You'd think the people on this island would have something better to do than waste time talking about what I bought."

"Sweetheart." Matthew walked towards her and clasped her shoulders. "Try and see it from their point of view. You're living all alone in the middle of nowhere, and all of a sudden you go into town and buy a load of men's clothing."

"So?" Her eyes flashed with defiance. "Is that a crime?"

"Elvira's probably not forgotten the day she found us talking together."

"She didn't see you, remember?"

"She saw you behaving oddly, and now Amos and Hiram come along and see what appears to be some even stranger behavior, down on the beach."

Kathryn didn't flinch. "What they see or don't see, and what I buy or don't buy, is no one's business but my own."

"You're right. But there's no need to be angry. They mean well."

Kathryn glared a couple of seconds longer. Then she sighed and slumped against him.

"I know. It's just that it's so hard, pretending you don't exist."

"I don't," Matthew said softly.

"Don't say that!" She pulled back, her mouth trembling. "You *do* exist. Why, you're as real as they are!"

"To you."

"Matthew, stop it. If you're trying to upset me—"

"You must face facts. As far as the rest of the world is concerned, I have no substance."

"You do!" Kathryn threw her arms around his neck. "And I won't listen to this. I don't give a damn about the rest of the world. I'm going to send Hiram and Amos away and—"

"You will not!" Matthew held her out at arm's length. "What of the repairs you'd planned?"

"I don't want Hiram or anybody else underfoot."

"But you must fix this house, in order to sell it."

"I've changed my mind. I'm not going to sell."

"What?"

"How could I sell Charon's Crossing? What would become of you?"

It was an excellent question, one he had spent time pondering himself, but he was not going to tell her that.

"I'll endure." He forced a smile to his lips. "I can always learn to rattle chains for the amusement of the next owner."

"And how will we spend time together, if the house isn't mine?" Kathryn pulled out of his hands and folded her arms. "Well? Any clever answers?"

"Kathryn. Darling, be reasonable."

"No. No, *you* be reasonable. How will I see you, if I sell this place?"

Matthew took a deep breath. "You won't," he said softly. "Once you go back to New York, this will all be over."

"No!"

"Yes." He caught her as she started to turn away. "Dammit, Kathryn . . ."

"Is that what you want?" She swung towards him, her eyes like tear-stained flowers. "For this to be over? For us never to be together again?"

He knew what he should say, and what he should do. But he couldn't, and his arms closed tightly around her.

"Nay," he whispered, "nay, my love. I would give anything to be with you but it is impossible."

"Nothing is impossible," she said fiercely. She kissed him, then stepped out of his arms. "Turn your back, please."

He wanted to laugh, as much at her silly, sweet modesty as at her defiance, but he could not. The modesty was amusing. The defiance was not. It worried him.

"Kathryn," he began, "listen to me."

"Are you going to shut up and turn around? Or am I going to go into another room?"

He sighed, decided there was no way to win this battle at the moment, and vanished.

An hour later, Kathryn, Amos and Hiram had completed a circuit of the house and were standing in the kitchen.

"Well?" Kathryn said. "What do you think?"

Hiram scratched his head. "Kathryn, I keep tellin' you, this isn't what we'd agreed to do. I was supposed to come out here, see what needed repairin' and give you an idea of the cost so you could decide whether or not you wanted to go ahead with the work."

"I know all that, Hiram, but I've changed my plans. I don't want a lot of work done on the house. I'm willing to do whatever will keep it from falling down around my ears, but that's about all."

Hiram sighed. "Well, in that case, the one thing you've got to deal with is that hot water heater."

"I couldn't agree more. I'm getting tired of trying to shower in a thimbleful of lukewarm water."

"No, it's more serious than that. My guess is that heater is fixin' on quittin' any day now. It works on propane, you know." Hiram jerked his thumb over his shoulder. "Tank's right out back, in case you hadn't noticed."

"Is the tank empty?"

"No. And that's not the problem. Have you ever noticed a funny smell comin' from that cellar? Down where the heater is?"

"Nothing but the damp and the mold."

"Propane gas has no smell of its own. Gas company adds hydrogen sulfide to make it stink like rotten eggs as a warnin'."

"A warning of what?" Kathryn sighed. "Hiram, I'm trying to follow you but I'm not getting anywhere."

"What I'm sayin' is that that heater looks to be on its last legs. Get yourself a gas leak, get enough gas built up, add the teensiest spark or flame and boom, this place goes up like a bomb."

Kathryn shuddered. "Can you fix it?"

"Sure. But I'll need to order some parts, arrange for a new heater . . ." He scratched his head. "Probably can do it next week sometime. If you can't stay around that long, just give me an okay now and—"

"I'll be here."

Amos's brows lifted. "There's no need to stay on, Kathryn. I can take care of this for you."

"Thanks, but I'll deal with it."

"Won't be comfortable here," Hiram said pointedly. "For safety's sake, I'm goin' to have to shut off the electricity to the heater right now." He looked straight at Kathryn. "You won't have any hot water except what you boil on the stove. Might be better if you moved into town."

"I'll manage."

"Kathryn." Amos gave her a pleasant smile. "Have you

thought of the ramifications? You'll have to heat water to bathe, to wash dishes . . .

"Will it be safe?" Kathryn asked. She cleared her throat. "Until you can fix it, I mean. I, ah, I wouldn't want anything to happen to this house."

"Oh, it'll be safe enough. I'll shut off the gas to the heater. Just so long as you don't smell nothin' and nobody opens that valve and strikes a match, you'll be fine."

"Still," Amos said officiously, "as your attorney, I would advise you to vacate Charon's Crossing at once."

Kathryn's smile was cool. "It's a little late to start offering me advice, isn't it? Go ahead, Hiram. Do whatever you have to do."

Amos steered his car slowly down the driveway. He was silent, as was Hiram.

They were almost at the gate before Amos stirred.

"Well, what do you think?"

Hiram snorted. "Since when do you care what me or anybody else thinks, Mr. Attorney?"

Amos stopped the car and looked at the handyman.

"I am asking your opinion. Do you wish to give it?"

Hiram Bonnyeman sighed and leaned back in the seat.

"I think Elvira and Ada were right. That girl's actin' strange."

Amos sighed, too, and flexed his hands on the steering wheel.

"I agree. I don't quite understand it, but . . . Perhaps she's become ill. Perhaps she has a history of illness."

"Don't you know?" Hiram said sternly. "Goodness sakes, man, you're her lawyer!"

"I was her father's lawyer. There's a difference. He didn't tell me anything about the girl, except that he thought she, of all the people he knew, would benefit the most from inheriting that bloody pile of stone."

Hiram snorted. "Man must have been crazy. Elvira's great-grandma was alive when we got married. Old lady spooked the life out of everybody on this island, talkin' of things she'd seen out at Charon's Crossin'."

"Oh, don't let's get back to that," Amos said impatiently. "Whatever that girl's difficulty is, it has nothing to do with ghosts."

"What, then? Why would she buy all that stuff, make out as if she was laughin' and talkin' with somebody, if she hadn't seen somethin' nobody else could see?"

"How would I know?" Amos said with sharp impatience and started the car again. "I'm an attorney, not a psychiatrist."

"You think that's what she needs? A head doctor?"

"I think she needs to get off the island and back into her own life. And she will do exactly that next week, when she flies to Florida to meet her young man and they return to New York together."

"I agree," Hiram said with an emphatic nod of his head.

Amos nodded, too, and let out the clutch. "Just another week," he said, "and then Miss Kathryn Russell will be gone."

He stepped hard on the gas, and the car shot out the open gates that marked the boundaries of Charon's Crossing.

Long after the dust of the car's passing had cleared, Matthew was still standing inside the gates, his hands wrapped tightly around the bars, his eyes fixed sightlessly on the distant horizon.

Nineteen

"Those interfering old men!" Kathryn, standing at the kitchen sink, up to her elbows in hot, soapy water, glared at Matthew while a kettle boiled on the stove. "Get down the rest of those glasses, will you please?"

Matthew eyed the shiny array of glassware, dishes, pots and pans and assorted odds and ends that lined virtually every surface in the kitchen. Kathryn had been scrubbing and polishing since dawn and from what he could tell, she showed no signs of stopping.

"Kathryn," he said gently, "this is foolish. There isn't any reason to be so angry."

"Angry? Do I look angry?" She plucked a wine goblet from his hand, glowered at it as if it were the enemy, then plunged it into the water, "I am not angry. I don't know where you got that idea."

"They meant well. Surely, you know that."

"Ha!"

"It is true. The both of them are worried about you."

Kathryn jerked another glass from his hand and submerged it in the water.

"Amos was so worried that he took off without so much as a by-your-leave within days of my arriving on this island." The water roiled as she swished the glass through it. "And Hiram was so worried that he put me dead last on his list of people who had jobs that needed doing."

"Kathryn, sweetheart—"

"Jason's another one," she said furiously. "You should have heard him this afternoon!"

"This afternoon? You spoke with him today?"

"I called him while you were reading." Kathryn plucked a goblet from the soapy water, rinsed it off, and set it into the dish drainer. " 'Jason,' I said, 'I'm really sorry to tell you this over the telephone but there's no other way.' " She looked at Matthew, her eyes snapping. "I'd expected him to be upset, I guess, even angry, although he must have suspected I was going to break things off after the way things went when he was here, but—"

"You ended your engagement?"

"Of course."

Matthew knew it wasn't right to feel so pleased. There was no sense in pretending Kathryn would not marry eventually, and even to hope such a thing was selfish and cruel. He loved her; he wanted her to find happiness.

But not with that fop, Jason. Not with any man he knew, for that matter. It was one thing to think in broad, philosophical terms, to tell himself that she deserved a rich and full life once she left Elizabeth Island . . .

And another entirely to have to envision her in any arms but his.

The goblet he'd been holding shattered in his knotted fist. He blinked and looked down dumbly as shards of glass bit into his flesh and rained to the floor.

"Matthew?" Kathryn swung towards him, her eyes wide. "Oh, what happened? Are you cut?" She grabbed his hand and a thin line of blood oozed up across the palm.

"I'm all right."

"You're not. You're bleeding."

"I'm fine, for God's sake." Matthew snatched back his hand, wiped it on the seat of his jeans, and glowered at her. "Perhaps it would have been kinder to have given the man such news when you see him next week in Florida."

"Let me see that hand, please."

"Kathryn, dammit—"

"Do you have any idea how often you say that?" Kathryn took his hand, tugged him onto the terrace and into the sun, and peered intently at the cut. "Kathryndammit? As if it were all one word."

His throat constricted as he looked at her bent head. Sunlight had put glints of flame into the dark silk which had parted to fall forward over her shoulders, exposing the delicate curve of her neck. God, how he loved her!

"If I say it as one word, and say it often," he said gruffly, "it is because you specialize in irritating me."

She lifted his hand, pressed a kiss to the tiny cut, then looked up at him and laughed.

"What you're trying to say, Captain, is that I piss you off. It's inelegant, but if you're going to be a twentieth-century male, you'll have to learn the lingo."

Matthew smiled. It was impossible to do anything less, with those blue eyes of hers teasing his but then his smile faded, his frown returned, and he pulled his hand from hers.

"I am not a twentieth-century male, Kathryn. That is what you refuse to accept."

"Don't be so stubborn." She put her hands flat against his chest, reveling in the steady drum of his heart. "This is 1996 and here you are. What else would you call yourself?"

"A freak of nature," he said coldly, "or of darkness. I am not certain which."

"Honestly, Matthew, in some ways you're as impossible as Jason. When I told him I wasn't going to meet him in Florida, that I'd decided to stay here, at Charon's Crossing—"

"You told him what?"

Damn, Kathryn thought, oh damn! She hadn't meant to break the news this way. Matthew was going to try and talk her out of it, she was certain of it. Well, she was just as certain that she wanted a life with him and not with Jason. She'd made a decision. Sooner or later, he had to be told of it and now was as good a time as any.

"I'm not going back," she said softly. Her eyes met Matthew's. "I told that to Jason when I telephoned him."

A muscle knotted in Matthew's jaw.

"What do you mean, you're not going back?"

"How much more clearly can I put it, Matthew? I love you. You love me. And we want to be together. Isn't that right?"

"Kathryn." He shook his head, knowing the rest even before she said it. "Listen to me, Kathryn . . ."

"No. You listen to me, for a change." Her words were rushed, with an almost desperate intensity. "I'm going to live here, with you, at Charon's Crossing."

"Dammit, Kathryn!"

She laughed and looped her arms around his neck. "You see? You're doing it again."

"Kathryn, this is no time to be clever." Matthew put his hands on her waist to keep her from settling against his chest. "There is nothing for you here. This house is little better than a ruin!"

"We'll fix it up together. You can figure out what we need in the way of lumber and paint and all the rest, and I'll go into town and buy it."

"Don't be crazy!" He reached one hand behind his neck, clasped her wrists, and drew her arms down between them. "What sort of life would you have here, madam? In a house in the middle of nowhere, with a man who is not a man."

"You're all the man I'll ever want," she whispered.

She lifted herself towards him, eyes languorous and lips half-parted, and he breathed an oath and pushed her back.

"I am not a man at all," he said coldly. "Shall I walk through a wall by way of reminder?"

She stared at him and then her mouth began to tremble. "All right," she said. "Okay. You come up with a better plan, then." She crossed the terrace with quick steps, turned and glowered at him. "If I could travel back in time to be with you, I would do it. But I can't. This isn't like some—some old 'Star Trek' episode, where characters can float back and forth through a hole in the space-time continuum."

" 'Star Trek'? What is—"

"Dammit, Matthew!" Kathryn stamped her foot. "Do not do that! I'm not going to let myself be sidetracked. You know what I mean. We aren't caught in—in some kind of time warp!" She took a deep breath, then blew it out. "You can't enter my world."

"The woman speaks the truth at last!"

"So I—I thought about the possibility of entering yours."

Matthew frowned. "I don't under . . ." His face whitened and he strode to where she stood and caught hold of her. "Do you mean, you thought of dying?"

"Matthew! You're hurting me!"

"Are you insane?" he demanded in fury. "There is nothing romantic about death, and nothing predictable, either. I know only what happened to me, not what happens to anyone else. Do you have an answer to the question people have been asking since time began? Nay, Kathryn, I think not!"

"I think not, too. I mean, I don't know what happens. That's why I gave up the idea. Why are you getting so angry? And would you please let go? You're going to leave fingerprints on my arms!"

"I ought to leave handprints on your bottom!" A muscle knotted and unknotted in his jaw. "Just because I ended up here is no guarantee that you—"

"I keep telling you, I realized that! That's one of the reasons I've come up with this plan!"

Matthew's eyes narrowed. "What plan?"

"The one I was explaining before you flew off the handle!" Her expression softened. "I'm going to stay here, with you."

"For how long? You cannot expect to shut out reality forever."

Kathryn smiled. "That's exactly what I do expect. I'm never going back, Matthew. Don't you understand? I'm going to stay with you forever."

He could not help himself. Her soft words sent his heart racing before he realized how futile they were.

"Nay. You cannot."

Kathryn laughed softly and moved into his arms.

"Have you forgotten everything I told you? The world has changed, my love. Women don't let men tell them what to do anymore."

"Kathryn, listen to me. You might as well sentence yourself to life imprisonment."

"Imprisonment? To live the rest of my life with the man I love in a tropical paradise?" She laughed again and put her arms around his neck. "Nay, Captain, I think not."

"Think, Kathryn. You would lack all the wonderful things in your books."

"Indeed. Air pollution, noise, traffic jams . . ." Her sigh was long and dramatic. "What a tragedy."

"You would have no one to talk with but me."

"Ah. Yet another tragedy."

"You have a life in the world, Kathryn, a career you've said you enjoy."

"The wonder of computers. Wait until I show you what happens with a phone jack, a modem, and an adaptor."

"And what of Waring?"

"What of him? He's dead."

"I don't know that. He may come back, and if he does—"

"Are you afraid of him?"

"Aye. Not for myself, but for you."

"I'm more afraid of the emptiness of a life without you."

"Kathryn," Matthew said tightly, "I will not let you do this."

"I am a free and independent woman. I can do anything I want, and what I want is to be with you." Gently, she pulled his head down to hers and kissed his mouth. "I love you, Matthew."

He tried not to close his arms around her, but it was like trying to keep from breathing.

"Kathryn," he whispered in despair.

"Shh," she said, and kissed him again.

After a while, there was no more to say that could not be better said with mouths and hands and hearts.

Kathryn would not be moved.

"Stubborn woman," Matthew said grimly, and she smiled and said that "stubborn" was simply another word for "determined."

He gave up arguing. There was no point to it. She had an answer for everything, no matter what he asked or how brutally he phrased it. Even when he reminded her that she would age and grow old while he remained young, she only blanched for a second and then she said that if she could love a 184-year-old man, he could love a 60-year-old woman.

"Especially if she takes a week or two off for plastic surgery," she said, and set him first to grimacing with an explanation of what such surgery entailed and then to laughing with an exaggerated mimicry of what the results might be.

But, in his heart, he didn't laugh. He thought, instead, of what it would be like for him to watch her grow old. Not that he would care about the wrinkles she would collect, nor the sags. He knew, with the clear instinct of a man deeply in love, that his Kathryn would be forever beautiful in his eyes.

What he imagined instead was what agony it would be to see the years race away as she gave up her youth, her very life, for him.

She deserved better. He had to find a way to ensure that she got it, that she had a future instead of a present that was forever mired in the past.

But she was beyond convincing.

And then, quite by accident, Olive Potter paid an unannounced visit and showed him the way.

* * *

"Kathryn," Olive said brightly, when Kathryn opened the front door. "How good to see you again."

"Hello, Olive. Won't you come in?"

Olive stepped inside the house, the smile still affixed to her lips. "My, you have accomplished wonders, haven't you? The place is so polished and bright lookin'!"

"You can't really be surprised." Kathryn's smile was pleasant but her tone was cool. "Surely, you've had a full report from Elvira."

"Sorry?"

"Or from Hiram. Or Amos."

"I'm sorry, Kathryn. I don't know what you mean."

Kathryn sighed. "It doesn't matter. Actually, I'm glad you came by. I wanted to speak to you about selling Charon's Crossing."

"Yes? Well, that is why I'm here this mornin', to tell you—"

"I've decided not to sell."

"Kathryn," Matthew said sharply, "don't tell her that."

Kathryn glared past Olive's shoulder to where Matthew stood in the door to the sitting room.

"Mind your business," she said.

Olive's eyes widened. "I beg your pardon?"

Kathryn smiled at the realtor. "I wasn't talking to you, Olive. Look, I changed my mind about getting rid of the house. I meant to tell you sooner, but—"

"Dammit, Kathryn!"

"Dammit, Matthew!"

Olive screwed her head around and glanced nervously over her shoulder. "Who are you talkin' to, Kathryn?"

"Olive, I want you to take this place off the market."

"Off the . . . ? But I don't understand."

"Nor do I," Matthew said grimly. "Nor will anyone with half a brain."

"It's my decision to make, not yours."

"Well, of course it is," Olive said, "but why have you changed your mind?"

"What a good question." Matthew smiled coolly and folded his arms. "Go on, try explaining yourself to her. Tell her you've decided to give up your life for a ghost and see what she says."

"I don't have to explain anything!"

"No," Olive said, "of course you don't. It's only that you've taken me by surprise, especially since I've brought the most wonderful news."

"What news?"

"I've found a buyer!" Olive said triumphantly. "An excellent buyer, I must say. This gentleman owns half a dozen exclusive health and beauty spas in the States and he's been thinkin' of expandin' and, well, he thinks Charon's Crossin' will be just perfect!"

"Sorry. You'll have to explain that it's not for sale."

"Oh, but he's made a fine offer." Olive leaned forward, her eyes bright. "Of course, he wants to see it himself but I've shown him photos, told him it needs lots of work—"

"Well, untell him. Charon's Crossing isn't for sale."

"But why?"

"I'm going to live here, that's why." Kathryn swung the front door open.

"Live here?" Olive looked around her in disbelief. "Surely you are jokin'. Short of rebuildin' this place from top to bottom, the only thing Charon's Crossin' is good for is a bonfire for toastin' marshmallows!"

"Good-bye, Olive," Kathryn said firmly.

As soon as she shut the door she turned around, prepared for another verbal battle with Matthew. But he was standing as he had been, with such a strange emptiness in his eyes that her heart dropped.

"Matthew?" she said. "Are you angry with me?"

He blinked, as if she'd called him back from some dark place, and opened his arms to her.

"No, sweetheart," he said, as she went into them, "I'm not angry. How could I be, when I love you with all my heart?"

* * *

He had the plan now, thanks to Olive.

He stood below the cliff, staring out over the ocean, and wondered why it had taken him so long to see it.

If Kathryn would not leave him, he would leave her.

It was as simple, as perfect, as that.

He could not change what he was, nor the restrictions of his existence. That he was doomed to haunt Charon's Crossing forever was irrefutable.

But what if there were no Charon's Crossing for him to haunt?

With its demise would surely come his. He didn't know what would become of him. He might cease to exist. He might return to that terrible blackness in which he had awakened.

It didn't matter. This had to be done.

The thought that he would never again see a sunrise, or hear the cry of a gull on the wind or taste the salt spray of the sea, made him smile with bitter irony.

What did any of that matter?

Only weeks ago, he had told Kathryn what a fool he'd been to sacrifice himself for love, that love was an illusion. Now, he knew he had been wrong.

Love, true love, was no illusion. It was life's greatest gift, as he had finally learned, and he could rejoice that it had been his, if only for a short time.

It wasn't his sacrifice that had been foolish, it was the cause. Cat had been worth nothing. But Kathryn . . . she was worth the world.

The faulty hot water heater would make it simple. The old man, Hiram, had explained everything. The valve that must not be opened, the evil-smelling gas that would fill the room, the spark or flame that would so easily ignite it. All that remained was to find the right moment, and quickly, before he lost courage. He could face whatever unknown lay ahead for himself but as time went by, would he be strong enough to take the steps that meant he would lose Kathryn at the same instant he liberated her?

Matthew bowed his head to whatever power might still exist in the cold and desolate world that was his.

He had the plan, and the resolve. All he needed now was the opportunity.

"Help me," he whispered.

And that came, too, with the sunset. Kathryn was dressing for dinner and he was out on the terrace, waiting for the charcoal in the grill to reach the right color before putting on their steaks, when he heard a knock at the front door.

He went inside the house just in time to see an envelope come sliding under the door. He bent down, picked it up, and peeped out the window. A boy was racing down the driveway on a strange, two-wheeled vehicle.

Matthew looked casually at the envelope. It was addressed to Kathryn from something called Western Union. He shrugged, started to toss it on the table . . . and hesitated.

Open it, a voice inside him seemed to whisper.

He frowned. He had never opened nor read correspondence not addressed to him in his life and this letter was surely not for him.

Open it!

He cast a quick glance up the steps. He could hear the shower running. Quickly, he ripped open the envelope, unfolded the note inside, and read it.

It began with today's date and was from Kathryn's mother. She had had a call from Amos Carter and another from Jason. "Both of them are worried, and now so am I," the note said.

She was in Miami and would be flying into Hawkins Bay late tonight by charter. Kathryn was to meet her at the airfield promptly at ten.

Matthew read the note again. Above, on the second floor, the sound of the shower stopped.

"Forgive me, Kathryn," he whispered. He crumpled the note

and the envelope in his fist, went quickly out to the terrace, tossed both onto the fire and watched them burn.

"Ah," Kathryn sighed, stretching luxuriously, "that was wonderful."

Matthew smiled. He reached across the table, took her hand and kissed the fingertips. She looked especially lovely to him tonight, in a pale blue halter dress and with her hair tumbling over her shoulders.

"It was nothing, madam," he said. "A candlelit table on the terrace, a bouquet of roses . . ."

"Pink roses. My very favorite kind."

Matthew grinned. "Excellent news, since those are the only ones that grow at Charon's Crossing."

"The wine was lovely, too."

"A vintage bottle, unearthed from the wine cellar to accompany a pair of steaks grilled to absolute perfection. 'Twas nothing but a modest repast."

Kathryn smiled. "You were teasing me the other day, when you said you didn't know how to cook."

"Every man knows how to char a side of beef."

"Starting with the first caveman. What is it with guys and open fires?"

"Something deep and primitive, perhaps." Matthew's eyes glittered. "Akin to what seems to be our native dexterity with television remotes."

Kathryn laughed. He was right. For a man who'd never seen a television set until a few days ago, Matthew had shown a remarkable and, she suspected, completely male affinity for channel surfing.

"I can't deny that you took to the tube like a veteran."

"Well, the TV is a remarkable invention. But I think, in the final analysis, I prefer the radio."

"Really? Why?"

Matthew smiled and got to his feet. "Stay right where you

are and I'll show you." Moments later, soft, romantic music drifted out into the flower-scented night. When he came back to the table, he held out his hand. "Because of that. The music." His smile was bittersweet. "It takes me back to a time when both I, and Charon's Crossing, were real."

"Don't say that! You're as real to me as anyone could ever be."

"Close your eyes," he whispered, slipping his arm around her waist, "and picture this place with candles blazing in every room."

Kathryn laid her head on his shoulder.

"It must have been beautiful."

"Oh, aye, it was. The lights, the music, the food and drink . . ."

She smiled. "Impressive, hmm?"

"Very." He turned her towards him and smiled in return. "And, though you have not deigned to ask me, madam, I can assure you that I, too, was an impressive sight."

Kathryn laughed softly. "No pink T-shirt and faded Levi's, hmm?"

"Please, m'lady. My buttons and buckles were so highly polished they could have served as signal lamps. I was a wonder to behold."

She smiled but for all his joking words, it was easy to imagine him in his nineteenth-century finery. He would have been the most handsome man at the party, and the most sought after.

"Catherine must have been a wonderful sight, too," she said softly, stroking her palms over his shoulders.

Matthew grimaced. "Do you mean Cat? To tell you the truth, sweetheart, I cannot even remember her face."

"You don't have to say that."

"I say it because it is true." He put his hand under her chin and lifted it gently. "She was a cat with sharp claws and a cold heart. You, sweetheart, are a kitten, sweet and soft and always warm in my arms." He bent his head and brushed his mouth over hers. "I love you, Kathryn. You will always be with me."

"Always," she sighed.

Matthew's arms closed around her. He drew her close and, as he did, he looked past her, into the kitchen.

The clock on the wall read eight-fifteen.

God, he thought, God, let me be strong enough to see this to the end.

"Was there dancing, at the parties here?" Kathryn asked.

"Dancing?" he repeated, and cleared his throat. "Well, reels and such. Four steps forward, four back, turn to your partner, bow and curtsy." He smiled. "Nothing like what we saw in that television drama the other evening. What did you call that style of dance?"

"It was slow dancing."

"It looked immoral." He grinned. "And wonderful. Do you think you could teach me how it's done?"

Kathryn laughed and looped her arms around his neck. "Trust me, Captain You'll be an expert in no time."

They began to move slowly to the soft music, their bodies so close together that they might have been one.

"You see? You're a natural."

"With you in my arms, I am."

His arms tightened around her. The pain of knowing what came next, that he was going to break Kathryn's heart, was almost unbearable and yet, it was the only way he knew to send her back to the world in which she belonged.

As for himself . . . what would become of him after tonight? Would he be able to take these memories into whatever dark place lay ahead? He closed his eyes and concentrated on the feel of Kathryn in his arms, on the silky brush of her hair against his cheek.

Remember this, he told himself fiercely, remember the taste of her skin as you press your mouth to her throat, the way she sighs with love and desire, the swift race of her heart as you cup her breast . . .

"Matthew," she whispered.

Her face lifted blindly to his. He kissed her, more and more deeply, until she was trembling. Then he swung her into his arms and carried her through the dark house and up the stairs to the bedroom.

Moonlight kissed her skin with silver as he undressed her.

He told himself to savor each moment, to feast his eyes on her body and fill his heart with all this woman meant to him.

He caressed her breasts and kissed them; he tasted the nectar hidden between her thighs. He whispered to her of how he loved her, and of how beautiful she was. He knew that the sand was running faster and faster through the hourglass. His anguish grew, as did his passion. It surged through his blood with each beat of his heart. so that when the moment came at last, he entered her not slowly, as he had intended, but with driving, almost feverish, haste.

She cried out, the sound so wild and primitive that it stopped him.

"Kathryn, my love, I've hurt you," he said hoarsely.

She shook her head, wrapped her legs around his waist, and rose to meet his thrust.

"No," she whispered, "no, don't stop, don't stop, don't ever stop . . ."

When it was over, he collapsed on top of her, both their bodies spent and gleaming with sweat.

"I love you," Kathryn said softly.

He kissed her, then rolled onto his side and held her close. "Promise me something."

He felt her smile against his throat. "Anything."

"Promise me you'll always be happy."

She laughed softly. "I'll do my part, if you'll do yours."

"I'm serious, Kathryn." He rose up on his elbow and looked down at her. "Even if there comes a time happiness seems an impossible goal, I want you to strive to find it, to remind yourself that it is what I wish for you, with all my heart."

"Matthew," she said with an uneasy laugh, "you're frightening me."

"Nay, love, I've no wish to do that. It's only that I love you." He kissed her gently. "Will you remember that?"

What was he trying to tell her? She could feel a cold knot forming in her belly and she tried to ease the tension with a joke.

"You'll remind me, in case I forget, Matthew. We both know how modest and humble you are."

But he didn't smile. Instead, he kissed her again. "You are the miracle of my life, Kathryn Russell," he whispered. "You are everything I dreamed of and more than I ever hoped."

"Matthew, what is all this? Is something . . ."

The phone rang.

It was twenty minutes past ten.

Kathryn sat up, frowning. "Who could be calling at this hour?"

Matthew rolled from the bed, got her robe and slipped it around her shoulders.

"There's only one way to find out, sweetheart. You'll have to go downstairs and answer it."

He paused just long enough to pull on his jeans. When he reached the library, Kathryn was standing with the telephone to her ear and an incredulous expression on her face.

"I wish you hadn't done this without consulting me, Beverly," she was saying. She put her hand over the mouthpiece. "It's my mother," she whispered. "You won't believe this, Matthew. She's on the island!"

Matthew's brows lifted. "Really."

"Yes. Dammit to hell, I wish . . . Yes, Beverly," she said into the telephone, "I'm listening. Your plane landed twenty minutes ago and you're tired of standing out in the middle of nowhere and why aren't I there to meet you. I told you why. Because I had no idea you were coming, and if I had known, I'd have told you to stay home!"

Matthew put his arm lightly around Kathryn's shoulders.

"You can argue with her after you've gone and fetched her," he said softly.

Kathryn rolled her eyes and slapped her hand over the phone again.

"I don't *want* to go and fetch her," she hissed.

He smiled and kissed her forehead. "Is there a choice?"

Kathryn sighed. She reached up, touched her fingers to his lips.

"All right, Beverly. I'll be there as soon as I can. Yes, just wait. I know it's dark, dammit! This is Elizabeth Island, not the Riviera!"

She slammed down the phone, turned into Matthew's arms, and shook her head.

"She says she sent a telegram."

"Perhaps she did."

"Not that it matters. What on earth's gotten into her? We see each other twice a year at best, talk on the phone a few times more than that, and now, all of a sudden, here she is, where I least want her."

Matthew smiled. "Surely, you can endure her company for just a little while."

"A little while? Who knows how long she plans on staying?" Kathryn said darkly. "And what are we supposed to do while she's here? Pretend you don't exist?"

He wanted to remind her that he didn't, not in any way her mother or anyone else would understand, but the time for such reminders was long past. Instead, he kissed her and did what he could to pretend this was just another evening and Beverly's visit just another interruption.

"For tonight, anyway," he said, "that's probably precisely what we should do. You go and pick her up and when you get back, I'll stay out of sight. It will be easier for you that way, love. You can talk with her without being interrupted by my presence."

He was right. She went upstairs and slipped into a pair of shorts and a cotton shirt. It was impossible to imagine what misguided maternalism had brought her mother to the island but she had the feeling she'd need to muster all her concentration to deal with it.

Moments later, she stood with Matthew at the front door.

"Okay, I guess I've got no choice but to go get her."

"Neither of us has a choice tonight," he said softly. "Each of us must do what we must."

She knew what he meant, that he would have to keep out of sight, at least for tonight, and that she would have to deal with her mother. Still, that same sense of unease she'd felt earlier swept over her.

"Matthew? If something were wrong, you'd tell me, wouldn't you?"

He smiled, took her hands in his, and kissed them.

"I love you," he said. He drew her close to him. "Now, go on. Go get your mother."

"I'll miss you tonight."

"Aye. As I will miss you."

She smiled, reached up, and brushed her mouth to his.

" 'Til tomorrow, my love," she whispered.

" 'Til tomorrow," he said softly, and then, very gently, he sent her out into the night.

He watched from the doorway until the lights of her vehicle had faded. He listened as the sound of its engine grew faint. When he could hear it no longer, he shut the door. He had planned carefully; it was just a matter of pausing to pick up a wrench and light a candle.

Then he went to the cellar.

It smelled of damp and of mice. The odor was not pleasant but he did not mind for it was of life. Moonlight fell across the earth floor and across the propane heater, standing silent in the corner.

It was important to move quickly now, so that it would all be done well before Kathryn's return. He had paid careful attention to Hiram's warnings about the faulty heater; he knew which was the supply valve, which the pipe that connected to the tank outside.

He put the candle high on a nearby shelf. By its flickering yellow light, he carefully loosened the connection between the heater and the supply tank. Then he opened the valve.

There was a hissing sound and the air around him began to fill with the stench of rotten eggs. The gas was heavier than air; it would fill the room eventually but, at first, it would stay close to the floor.

"I love you, Kathryn," he whispered.

The stink grew more powerful.

"I love you, and I will be in your heart forever, as you will be in mine."

The air was thick with the smell of the gas now. Soon, it would reach the candle flame.

Matthew felt his eyes blur with sudden dampness.

"Good-bye, Kathryn," he said softly, "good-bye, my love."

Kathryn was halfway to the airport when she heard Matthew's voice.

"Good-bye, Kathryn. Good-bye, my love."

Her skin turned icy with fear. "No," she whispered, and then she screamed. "Matthew, no!"

She jammed on the brakes and the car skidded wildly across the road but even before its engine sputtered and died, the sky behind her exploded into a million shooting stars.

Twenty

After her divorce, years before, Beverly Russell had been left penniless and with a teenaged daughter to rear.

"So, what else is new?" she'd said with a wry smile, to anyone who cluck-clucked over what her friends delicately called her "situation."

Trevor Russell had never made enough money to matter nor held on to what little he'd had. And, towards the end of the marriage, he'd spent more time tromping the mountains, veldt, tundra and beaches of the world's more exotic places than he had staying at home.

Beverly had tried her hand at selling cosmetics, used cars and encyclopedias—"Not all at the same time," she'd say with a smile when she talked about that period in her life—but nothing had clicked. Then, at a friend's urging, she'd decided to try turning what had always been a hobby into an occupation.

Beverly called it creating jewelry out of found objects.

Kathryn called it making necklaces, bracelets and earrings out of junk.

To the surprise of them both, more people saw it Beverly's way than Kathryn's, including the owners of a world-renowned shop with branches in Manhattan, Paris, London, Madrid and Palm Beach. Just about the time Kathryn had finished college, Beverly was transformed from flea-market craftsperson to sought-after designer.

Ever since then, as she often said with a cat-ate-the-canary smile, life had been very, very pleasant.

She lived on Central Park in a vast, high-ceilinged apartment with a breathtaking view. Kathryn had never much liked the place. Despite its size, the apartment seemed cramped, thanks to Beverly's propensity for ballooning velvet drapes, silk shawls, eclectic furnishings, and table-top collections of whatever struck her fancy, from French snuffboxes to Chinese jade. The building itself was one of those New York landmarks, all turrets and stone gargoyles. Kathryn's tastes ran more to the spare elegance of the newer glass skyscrapers that loomed in the Fifties.

At least, it had.

Strange, how her tastes had changed.

Sitting in the living room of Beverly's apartment on a late spring afternoon, she found herself admiring what she'd once thought of as clutter. Not very long ago, she'd have found the antique silk shawl flung across the baby grand in the corner pretentious, the Duncan Phyfe occasional table crowded with tiny porcelain dogs unattractive, the Empire sofa facing the pair of Mies van der Rohe chairs just plain out of place.

She didn't, not anymore. Instead, she took pleasure in the richly furnished rooms, even in the turrets and the gargoyles of the building itself. She saw now that these things had their own beauty and were soothing not just to the eye but to the soul.

Kathryn sighed, put down the copy of *Vanity Fair* she'd been pretending to read, and walked out onto the little balcony that overlooked the park. It was probably all those weeks of living in the ruined splendor that was Charon's Crossing that had changed her attitude towards what she'd once thought of as out-of-date clutter.

Not that she thought about Charon's Crossing very much anymore.

She had, at first. For weeks after the explosion and fire that had reduced the mansion to rubble, she really hadn't been able to think about much of anything else. It was as if the explosion, and the subsequent fire, had burned themselves into her brain.

She saw the flames shooting into the black sky over and over again, heard herself screaming Matthew's name.

The nights had been the worst. Asleep, she'd had no control over the images; they'd swooped down on her like visions out of Hell. It was always the same. She saw the house, and her car driving away from it. She saw Matthew, going to the cellar.

Don't, she'd say in the dream, *oh God, please, please, don't!*

Hush, sweetheart, he'd whisper, and then Charon's Crossing would explode in terrible, agonizing slow motion and she'd shoot upright in bed, screaming and screaming, until Beverly came rushing in from her bedroom across the hall, switched on the lights and took her in her arms.

"It's all right, darling," her mother would croon, rocking her as if she were a child instead of a grown woman. "Don't think about it anymore."

She hadn't, after a while. Weeks of therapy had done the job. She knew now that what she'd remembered about Charon's Crossing wasn't true. The house had been real, and the fire.

But not Matthew. He had never existed. He had been a creation of her own imagination.

"Stress," Dr. Whalen had told her, "stress, Kathryn. It can do amazing things to the human psyche."

"You don't understand," Kathryn had insisted, at the beginning. "Matthew was real!"

"His journal was real," the psychiatrist had said gently. "I've no doubt you found it, read it, and absorbed it. Your mind did the rest."

Gradually, she had come to realize that the doctor, and Beverly, were right. There were no such things as ghosts. How could she have ever thought there were? She'd regained her appetite. She'd begun to sleep through the night even though she knew she sometimes still dreamed without ever remembering the dreams. Why else would she so often awaken with tears in her eyes and a lump in her throat?

Kathryn looked down at her hands, wrapped around the balcony railing. The knuckles were white and sharp. She forced herself to take a deep breath and deliberately loosened her grip on the railing.

She was having a bad time today. She kept thinking about Charon's Crossing. About Matthew. No, no, that wasn't right. How could you think about a man you'd never known? Dr. Whalen would say she was obsessing on a dream image she'd created.

Of course she was. But it was an image so exciting and wonderful that no real man would ever be able to take its place . . .

Kathryn shut her eyes tight. "Stop it," she whispered.

What was the matter with her today?

Just last week, Dr. Whalen had given her a clean bill of health. Sessions on the couch, three times a week, coupled with medication, had done the job.

"It's graduation day," the doctor had said, and smiled. "We're going to reduce our sessions together to once a week and lower your dosage of medication. You're going to be fine," she'd said, patting Kathryn's hand, "absolutely as good as new."

And I am, Kathryn thought firmly, as good as new and maybe better.

For the first time in years, she and Beverly had a positive relationship. Beverly had been her rock since the night of the explosion, the only one who'd been able to get through to her as the pillar of fire touched the sky.

Kathryn had no recollection of what had happened. She knew only that she'd raced back towards the flames through the night, that sirens had wailed, that people had surrounded her and held her down as she clawed and fought to go to Matthew.

"He's burning," she'd screamed, "Matthew, Matthew, my love . . ."

She remembered a sea of faces—Amos and Hiram and endless others, and then one face, Dr. Simpson's, and the sharp, cold prick of a needle.

"No," she'd said, "no, please . . ."

Beverly's arms had closed around her.

"It's all right, Kathryn," she'd said, and Kathryn had tried to tell her that it wasn't, that Matthew was trapped somewhere inside that hellish inferno . . .

And then she'd tumbled into a bottomless well.

The days had passed in a blur of light and dark. She knew now that she'd been heavily sedated. Still, she remembered asking Beverly the same question each time she'd surfaced.

"Is he dead?" she'd whisper, and her mother would kiss her forehead and tell her that everything was going to be fine.

Eventually, she'd stopped asking. The periods of light had increased until they'd outweighed the dark. Beverly had taken her back to New York via charter flight.

There'd been no real question of Kathryn going back to her own apartment. She'd been too ill. Once she'd started to get better, she'd known she could never walk into those dreary rooms where she'd first dreamed of Matthew. And it took no great genius to figure out that one gurgle from the ancient hot water pipes in the Greenwich Village walk-up would have sent her screaming into the street.

It was the hot water heater that had caused the explosion that had destroyed Charon's Crossing. Not the heater, exactly; the propane tank. The safety valve had failed, somehow; the gas had ignited . . .

"A terrible, terrible accident," she'd heard Beverly whisper over the phone to a friend.

But it hadn't been an accident! Kathryn knew what had happened, that Matthew had caused the explosion, that he'd planned it and found a way to get her out of the house, that he'd sacrificed his own existence for hers.

What had become of him? Was he gone forever? Was he trapped in that awful darkness he'd described? Was he wandering some worse hell, with Waring breathing his foul stink upon him?

"Kathryn?"

Matthew. Oh Matthew, why did you do it? I loved you. I'll always love you. I would have stayed with you forever . . .

"Kathryn? Darling, what are you doing out here all by yourself?"

Kathryn swung around. Her mother was standing in the doorway. She was smiling but it was a tense, worried smile.

"It's chilly out here, Kathryn. You ought to be wearing a shawl."

Kathryn swallowed hard.

"Hi," she said brightly. "Did you just get in?"

Beverly nodded. "My meeting ran a bit long. Darling, are you all right?"

"I'm fine."

"You don't look fine." She frowned, came closer, and put her hand to Kathryn's forehead.

Kathryn jerked back. "Really, I'm fine."

"I just wanted to see if you have a fever. Your eyes are so bright . . ."

"So," Kathryn said briskly, "how did your meeting go?"

Beverly smiled. "The way I'd expected. They want me to try working in platinum. I said I'd give it a try."

Kathryn laughed. "No sacrifice too great, huh?"

"Of course, I told them we'd need a new contract, one for lots more money." She leaned her arms on the balcony railing and gazed out over the park. "I wish you'd let me send you on a little vacation, Kathryn. It would do you good."

Kathryn sighed. "We've been all through this, Mother. What I need is to get back to work, find a place of my own . . . get my life started. Which reminds me, I've got a terrific interview lined up for tomorrow morning, did I tell you?"

Beverly turned and leaned back against the railing. A breeze ruffled her hair, still as dark and lustrous as Kathryn's.

"You're quite sure you don't want to go back to your old job, darling? Jason keeps pleading for you to return."

"I know. It's kind of him, considering how I treated him, but it wouldn't work out. He's a dear, sweet man and I hope we'll always be friends . . ."

"But you don't love him."

"No. Not the way I loved . . . not the way a woman should love a man."

Something in her daughter's voice alerted Beverly. She reached out and took her hand.

"Are you having a bad day?" she asked gently.

Kathryn hesitated. "Yes," she said. "I keep thinking about . . . about . . ."

"Did you call the doctor?"

"Not yet."

"Well, I think you should. Perhaps you need to go on some other kind of medication."

Kathryn shook her head. "I'm sick of taking pills, Mother. I feel like a walking pharmacy as it is."

"When's your next appointment with Dr. Whalen?"

"Monday."

"Don't wait that long, please. Call her, tell her you need to see her. Talking with her might make you feel better."

"I'll call her, tomorrow, if I don't stop . . . if I don't feel better."

"Promise?"

Kathryn smiled and squeezed her mother's hand. "Promise."

"That's my girl."

The women were silent for a couple of minutes and then Kathryn cleared her throat.

"I know I'm not supposed to talk about—about him."

"There was no 'him,' " Beverly said sharply. "You know that, Kathryn."

"Oh, sure. I know that. It's just a figure of speech, Mother." Kathryn licked her lips. "It's just that—that . . . The thing is, what happened all seemed so—so real."

"Of course it did." Beverly smiled. "What's the point in having a hallucinatory experience if you don't give it everything you've got?"

Kathryn laughed. She felt her tension easing away.

"Your father would say the same thing. I remember one time, he went off to an ashram in the Himalayas. He was determined to experience what some much-lauded swami was calling a 'mystery journey of inner discovery.' " Beverly chuckled. "Trevor came back and said no journey of discovery was worth giving up red meat, alcohol and sex, especially if you had to chant RamiDamiDoo or something like that while you worked yourself into a trance."

"You didn't go with him?"

"I was four months pregnant with you, darling. The only mystery that interested me was what was going to happen in the labor room!"

"But Father left you anyway."

"Of course. That's just the way he was, Kathryn. He didn't mean to be selfish or unkind."

"And you took him back."

Beverly sighed. "I always did, until I finally decided I just couldn't live that way anymore. No real home, no money in the bank, no future . . ."

Kathryn's mouth thinned. "What a relief it must have been, to have it over with."

"Not really," her mother said softly. "I still loved him. I suppose I never quite stopped loving him."

"It's too bad he didn't feel the same way."

Beverly's brows arched. "But he did, Kathryn. He loved the both of us until the day he died."

"Yeah. He loved me so much that he forgot I existed."

"He never forgot you."

"Come on, Mother. What else do you call it when a man never sends his daughter a letter or even a birthday card?"

"Actually . . ." Beverly cleared her throat. "Actually, he did."

"All right, maybe I'm overstating it. He sent a couple of postcards, I remember, but—"

"He sent you many letters. And gifts."

Kathryn's eyes grew wide. "What?"

"I kept them from you," her mother said in a hushed voice. "I still have them all, if you want to see them."

For a moment, Kathryn was too stunned to speak. "But—but why would you do such a thing?" she finally asked.

"I told myself it was because I wanted to keep him from being a bad influence on you." Beverly gave a deep sigh. "I've thought about it a lot lately, ever since you were ill and I—I almost lost you, and I've decided that the truth was far less noble. I think I hid Trevor's letters to punish him for having left us."

"But you said it was your decision, that you wouldn't take him back when he wanted to come back—"

"I know. But that's how I thought of it, you see, that he'd left us by choosing to search for something that was missing inside him, to live a life he knew I despised." She looked at Kathryn and smiled faintly. "I know it's crazy, but that's how I loved your father, so deeply that for a long time, my emotions ruled me instead of my head. Does that make any sense?"

It made all kinds of sense to Kathryn, though it wouldn't have just a few months ago. But her time at Charon's Crossing had taught her a great deal about love so intense and deep that it could change the way you viewed life . . . even if that love hadn't been real.

"Kathryn?" Beverly's voice trembled. "Please, don't hate me. If you only knew how often I've regretted the lie . . ."

Kathryn clasped her mother's hands. "I don't hate you." Tears stung behind her eyelids. "I just wish I'd known . . . I mean, he must have died, thinking I'd never answered his letters because I didn't love him."

"No. No, I told him the truth, just before he had the accident. He called me, God only knows why, and he asked how you were and before I knew it, I told you you were fine, no thanks to him or to his letters and all the presents he'd sent over the years because I'd never let you know about them." She gave a strangled laugh. "Lord, he was so angry! We screamed at each other over that phone, just the way we had in the old days, and then he stopped yelling and said he missed me something awful and he was going to come and see us both."

"But he never had the chance."

"No, he never did." Beverly sighed. "So you see, darling, it wasn't so strange that Trevor left you Charon's Crossing. He probably thought that old house was wonderfully romantic, the perfect final gift to leave the daughter he loved."

Kathryn nodded. She knew better than to try and speak. Her throat was so tightly constricted that it hurt.

"Of course," Beverly said with a little smile, "he was as wrong about that as he'd been about most other things in his life. The house wasn't romantic at all, it was a miserable ruin."

"Maybe," Kathryn said in a choked whisper, "but I was happy there."

"Nonsense," Beverly said quickly. "You *thought* you were happy there."

"That's what I meant. Mother, stop worrying. I'm just a little edgy today, that's all. I guess it's the prospect of that interview tomorrow morning."

"I know the perfect stress-reducer." Beverly grinned and looped her arm around her daughter's waist. "How's about we go someplace down and dirty for supper? That diner, down near the river, maybe. How's that sound?"

"It sounds terrific," Kathryn said, hoping she sounded more eager than she felt.

"And first thing tomorrow, you'll phone Dr. Whalen, yes? Just to touch bases, darling, that's all."

Kathryn nodded. "Of course."

But she didn't call the psychiatrist, not the next day or any of the days that followed.

How could she, without admitting that she was obviously slipping backwards after so many weeks of progress?

Matthew was constantly in her thoughts. She had begun dreaming of him again, too. She'd hear him whispering her name, feel the sweet brush of his lips against hers, and then she'd wake up, weeping quietly in the night, reaching out for him even though she knew it was impossible for him to be there.

Tell stuff like that to Dr. Whalen and she was liable to find herself in a genteel rubber room.

On her own, she raised the level of her medication to what it had been when she'd first entered therapy. The pills made her groggy but they helped. She stopped dreaming, started sleeping through the night.

"I am fine," she told herself.

And she was. She started her new job—the interview she'd told Beverly about had gone well—and, a month later, she moved into a wonderful apartment in Soho. It wasn't the glass-walled, ultramodern sort of place that had once seemed so desirable. She'd looked at half a dozen of those, found them chillingly impersonal, and opted instead for an old, handsome duplex with a working fireplace, a brick-walled kitchen and wide-planked floors.

"A gem of the early 1800s," the realtor called it.

It wasn't a gem, not quite. The windows leaked, the floors sagged . . . but it reminded her of Charon's Crossing, and that was all that mattered.

The new job, the new apartment—both were great. Things went really well for a couple of weeks. And then, one afternoon, during a presentation meeting for a new client, she heard someone speak her name.

Kathryn?

She came sharply upright in her chair.

Kathryn, sweetheart. Where are you?

Kathryn's pen fell from her hand and clattered on the floor. The man next to her looked at her. Then he picked up the pen and nudged her in the ribs. She blinked and looked at him.

"You okay?" he whispered.

She nodded, took the pen from him, and forced her attention back onto the meeting.

I can't find you, love. I search and search, but I can't find you.

Kathryn's chair squealed as she shoved it back and shot to her feet. Eight pairs of eyes fixed on her wild-eyed, pale face.

"Miss Russell?"

She looked around the room. The CEO of the company they were trying to impress looked irritated. Her own boss was smiling but it was the sort of smile you saw on the face of a shark.

"I—I'm sorry," she said, "I thought I heard—"

Kathryn, my love. Where are you?

She flew from the room like a rocket, her assistant on her heels as she made for the elevator.

"Kathryn? Are you sick? Kathryn, what am I going to tell them?"

"Tell them anything you want," Kathryn said, as the elevator doors closed.

Dr. Whalen agreed to see her at once.

She listened. And listened. Then, finally, she spoke.

"What you're describing isn't uncommon, Kathryn," she said in her most soothing tone of voice. "We might describe these episodes as 'flashbacks.' "

"Flashbacks? I thought those had to do with real experiences."

Dr. Whalen looked momentarily flustered. "Not necessarily. I suspect this is your subconscious mind's attempt to come to grips with what happened to you."

"I don't understand, Doctor. Wasn't it my subconscious that created my hallucinations to begin with?"

The doctor cleared her throat. "It's complicated, Kathryn, too complicated for a layman. Here." She scribbled something on a prescription pad, tore off the sheet and handed it over. "Have that filled and take one tablet three times a day."

"I don't want to take any more pills. They make me dopey. Isn't there something else I can do to stop these hallucinations?"

"Well," Dr. Whalen said thoughtfully, "I suspect you need to find closure for what happened."

"Yes, all right, but how?"

"You still own that property on Elizabeth Island, do you not?"

"The land, yes. The house . . ." Kathryn swallowed hard, trying not to remember the flames. "The house is nothing but a pile of rubble."

"I would advise you to sell the property."

"Sell Charon's Crossing?"

"Yes. Get it out of your life, once and for all. Sign it away, physically, and there's an excellent chance you'll sign it away emotionally, too."

"But—"

The psychiatrist looked at her watch. "I'm sorry, Kathryn, I do have another patient scheduled." She stood up, smiled pleasantly, and held out her hand. "Sever your ties with that house, and you'll have both feet firmly planted on the road to complete recovery."

Amos was delighted to hear from her.

Everyone missed her, he said, and hoped she was feeling well.

Kathryn smiled at his delicacy, lied and said she was fine, and then got down to business.

"Amos," she said, "I very much want to sell Charon's Crossing."

"Really," he said, and chuckled. "That is wonderful news, Kathryn, truly wonderful. Olive's had an offer, you see, but we didn't know whether or not to contact you about it."

Kathryn sank down on the sofa in her old-fashioned living room. What had only been an idea had suddenly turned into a reality. She tried to feel happy about it but she could feel a knot of tension forming in her stomach.

"An offer?"

"From a hotel chain. They want to raze the ruins and put up

a luxury retreat. I must say, they've made a most generous offer."

It was more than generous. It was extraordinary.

"Kathryn? Shall I fax you the necessary papers?"

Kathryn took a deep breath.

"No."

"No?"

She could hear the confusion in Amos's voice and she almost told him he was no more puzzled by her sudden change of heart than she was, but she didn't.

"I—I'll have to think about it," she said, and hung up the phone before the attorney could say anything more.

An hour later, she called him back.

"Sell it," she said quietly.

Amos hesitated. "Are you sure it's what you want, Kathryn?"

She nodded. "Yes. Send me whatever documents need to be signed and let's get it over with."

Amos kept her informed, every step of the way. She signed endless documents, faxed paper after paper to his Elizabeth Island office. It was almost anticlimactic when ownership of Charon's Crossing finally passed from her to the hotel chain that had bought it.

Beverly insisted on their having dinner together. "The past is over," she said, clinking her glass of white wine against Kathryn's.

Kathryn smiled. It wasn't. Not yet, though she didn't tell that to Beverly. The door to the past would not be firmly shut until the end of the next day, for that was when the equipment would be rolling in to tear down what remained of the mansion.

Beverly suggested they have coffee and dessert at her place but Kathryn begged off. She was tired, she said, and she had a long day ahead of her at the office. She didn't add that people had been looking at her as if she'd lost her marbles after the day she'd bolted from the meeting. She'd explained her actions by saying she'd had a terrifying ulcer attack and even though everybody had said, oh, of course, they understood, the truth was that people still gave her odd looks.

"They should only see me now," Kathryn muttered as she paced her living room.

What in hell was the matter with her? Charon's Crossing was sold. It was out of her life forever.

She went to bed early, with the latest best seller and a cup of cocoa. She drank half the cocoa, read the same paragraph three times, gave up, and turned off the light.

A long time later, she fell asleep.

"Kathryn."

She knows exactly where she is, when she hears his voice. She is right here, in her own bed, and she can hear him as clearly as if he were right beside her. But he isn't.

"Kathryn, my love."

"Matthew?"

A hand brushes lightly over her cheek.

"Never forget me, sweetheart."

"Matthew!" Tears stream down her cheeks. "Matthew, where are you? Please, please, come to me. I love you. I need you . . ."

"Good-bye, my love. Good-bye."

Kathryn's eyes flew open. She sat up. It was a dream. It was nothing but a dream. Matthew had never been real . . .

There, lying on the pillow next to hers, was a single pink rose, the kind that grew in such profusion over the arched trellis at Charon's Crossing.

Matthew was real.

He was real!

How could she have convinced herself of anything else?

She was shaking as she threw on her clothes. She had to stop them from razing the ruins of the mansion. If it was gone . . . if it was gone, Matthew would be gone forever.

Just before she left the house, she tried calling Amos, then Olive, then Hiram and anyone else she could think of on Elizabeth Island but she got only squawks and buzzes.

"Dammit," she said, slamming down the phone.

It was business as usual on the island . . . except that after today, Matthew would . . . he would . . .

No. She couldn't let herself think that way. She wouldn't let herself think that way and she didn't, not through the endless ride to the airport or the charter flight to the island.

"Hurry," she whispered as the plane wobbled to a touchdown. "Hurry," she demanded as the surprised gentleman who was on duty in the tin hangar handed over the keys to his Jeep after she'd shoved a one-hundred-dollar bill under his nose. "Hurry," she pleaded, as she jammed her foot to the floor and urged the Jeep to speeds undreamed of by its maker.

But it had all been for nothing.

She knew it as soon as she barreled through the gates and whipped the Jeep up the drive towards the house. She had arrived too late. She knew it with a sense of dread as cold and heavy as the fog that was rolling in from the sea.

A pair of huge bulldozers stood where there had once been a garden. And all that remained of Charon's Crossing was a heap of dusty stone.

Kathryn stopped the Jeep and lifted her hand to her mouth. Her eyes filled with tears as she climbed from the Jeep and walked slowly towards the chalky rubble. There were men working nearby. They looked up as she approached, their faces curious.

"Lady?" one called. "Lady, hey, watch your step, okay?"

Kathryn didn't hear him. She couldn't see anything but the terrible ruin of what had once been a proud house where love had flourished.

"Matthew," she whispered, "my love, how could I have doubted? How could I have abandoned . . ."

Her breath caught in her throat.

A man emerged from the fog. He was tall and broad-shouldered, and the sea breeze blew his shoulder-length fair hair back from his sculpted face. He was wearing . . . "Oh God!". . . he was wearing a T-shirt with a sailboat emblazoned across the chest, faded Levi's and, incongruously enough, a pair of knee-high black leather boots.

"Matthew?" Kathryn's sobs turned to laughter. "Matthew?"

He smiled and opened his arms, and she cried out his name again and flew to him.

He held her for long, long moments, his heart thudding against hers, his tears mingling with her tears, and then he kissed her.

"Kathryn," he whispered, "Kathryn, my beloved."

She drew back in his embrace, clasped his face in her hands and searched his eyes with hers.

"Are you really here?"

He laughed. "Aye, sweetheart. I am really here, and so are you."

"But I thought . . . the house burned . . ."

He nodded. "It did, yes."

"Then, how did you escape?"

"It is beyond me to explain. I know only that I awakened in a cold, dark place, more alone than I had ever been, and longing for your arms. And then, one day or perhaps one night, for there was no meaning to time, I heard your sweet voice calling to me."

He drew her close and kissed her again. When the kiss ended, he cupped her face in his hands.

"You must know that I caused the explosion, Kathryn."

"I know." She shuddered. "You should never have done it. We might have lost each other forever."

"Aye." He put his arm around her waist and they began

walking away from the ruins of the mansion. "But it was the only way I knew to set you free."

Kathryn leaned her head against his shoulder. "You stubborn man," she said gently, "didn't I tell you that men couldn't make decisions for women anymore?"

He smiled and kissed the top of her head. "I suspect it will take you years to change me, sweetheart."

Suddenly, she stopped and turned towards him.

"I just realized . . . if Charon's Crossing is gone and you're here, what does it—?"

The blast of a horn drowned out her words. A pickup truck filled with construction workers was trying to edge past the Jeep Kathryn had abandoned in the driveway. The driver leaned out his window and pointed at Matthew.

"Hey, mister," he yelled, "you want to move this thing?"

Kathryn looked at Matthew. "Did you hear what he said?" she whispered.

"Come on, pal. Do us a favor, okay?"

"Hey," Kathryn yelled, "can you really see this man?"

The men in the truck grinned slyly at each other. "Why?" said the driver. "Is he supposed to be a ghost?"

Kathryn laughed. "Is he supposed to be a ghost . . ." She laughed harder, and Matthew began laughing, too. "Is he supposed . . ." Tears rose in her eyes. "Matthew, did you hear what he said?"

"Aye, love. I did."

It was difficult for him to speak. Kathryn was weeping as well as laughing but she wasn't the only one. Matthew's eyes were wet, too, and the lump in his throat felt large enough to choke him. Tenderly, he gathered her into his arms and stroked her hair.

"I was afraid to believe it," he murmured, "but now I know it is true. I cannot walk through walls, Kathryn, though I have tried. And now this man sees me." He laughed and whirled her in a circle. "Sweetheart, I am real!"

"He's real," Kathryn sang, "he can't walk through walls and

he's real." She threw back her head as they came to a dizzying stop. "Oh, isn't that wonderful news, world?"

The truck driver looked at the man seated beside him and tapped his forehead with his forefinger.

"Nuts," he mouthed, "the broad and the guy, too."

"Matthew? I almost forgot . . . What about Waring?"

"Gone, and without a trace."

"You're sure?"

"I would sense his presence, sweetheart, if he had survived."

Kathryn sighed and laid her palms flat against Matthew's chest. The beat of his heart was as solid and real as the rest of him.

"I have to admit, I don't understand any of this," she said softly.

"Nor do I, except to know that it was your love that freed me."

"No. No, it wasn't me. You freed yourself, Matthew. By believing in love, by giving your life for mine, you removed the curse."

"You gave me a love worth believing in, Kathryn."

He kissed her again and they clung to each other until another horn blast brought them back to reality.

"Listen, buddy," the truck driver said, "we just love seeing you havin' all this fun, you know what I mean? But maybe you and the lady could save the rest until you get that Jeep out of the way."

Kathryn laughed, dried her eyes, and clasped Matthew's hand in hers.

"How would you like to take your very first driving lesson, Captain? And then, maybe, how'd you like to take a ride in an airplane?"

Matthew laughed, too, but then his laughter faded and he looked deep into her eyes.

"I will love you forever, Kathryn," he said.

She rose on her toes and kissed him.

"Forever," she said softly.

Somebody in the pickup truck applauded. Kathryn grinned, waved her hand, and led Matthew to the Jeep.

He got behind the wheel and she scooted in beside him. She leaned towards him, her dark head nestled against his fair one. The men in the truck rolled their eyes as she pointed to the dashboard, then to the gear shift, then down towards his feet.

"This guy's somethin' else," one of the men said. "Doesn't he know how to drive a stick shift?" His voice rose. "Hey, lady, where's your boyfriend been all his life?"

Kathryn laughed, but her answer was for Matthew alone.

"He's been right here," she said softly, "right here, waiting for me."

Matthew caught a handful of her hair in his hand, drew her close and kissed her soundly. Then, to a chorus of cheers, applause and whistles, he turned on the engine and coaxed the Jeep into a wobbling U-turn.

"Ready?" he said to Kathryn.

"Ready," she said.

The Jeep lurched down the drive. Then Matthew stepped hard on the gas and it shot out the gates of Charon's Crossing, carrying Kathryn and Matthew into a bright, new world.

Dear Reader:

Now that you've come to the end of *'Til Tomorrow,* do you feel as I did, when I finished writing this book?

It was so hard for me to let go of Kathryn and Matthew. I'm sure you know that leaving characters behind is always difficult for an author but in this case, it was especially painful.

I spent months with Kathryn and Matthew. They were as real to me as if they were flesh and blood.

The characters I create usually come to life slowly inside my head. Not this time. Matthew was there the instant I saw the house that became Charon's Crossing in my story. I could feel his anger and pain. Kathryn appeared just as quickly. She was so real that I could almost reach out and touch her.

As for Charon's Crossing . . . the abandoned mansion that inspired me was only a shell of its former self. Interior walls were missing and there was no furniture. Even the grounds were shapeless and completely overgrown.

But I could see the setting for *'Til Tomorrow* as clearly as if it really existed. The peeling walls. The tumble of pink roses. The rusted gate. And the attic, where immortal evil waited in foul darkness to separate Matthew from the only woman he would ever love, the only woman who could save him . . .

For a long time, I wanted to call this book *Charon's Crossing.* My editor, Denise Little, felt the same way. Then, at the last minute, both of us had the same eerie sensation. As important as the ruined mansion is to the story of Matthew and Kathryn, there is one thing that is far more important and that is their belief in each other.

The prophetic words they share just before Matthew's terrible sacrifice best sum up the heart of the story.

For those who truly love, there will always be a tomorrow.

With all my very warmest wishes,

Sandra Marton